... writing name for Cyrus Mewawalla, a leading
... r twenty years' experience in the City, Cyrus left
... ng to set up independently. In 2006 Bloomberg
... e No. 1 telecom analyst in the UK. He lives in
... his wife and two children.

City of Thieves

CYRUS MOORE

sphere

First published in Great Britain in 2009 by Sphere
This paperback edition published in 2010 by Sphere

Copyright © Cyrus Mewawalla 2009

The moral right of the author has been asserted.

*This is a work of fiction. Whilst the book aims to capture the culture
of the City the events described and characters and institutions portrayed are
entirely made up with the exception of those clearly in the public domain.*

A CIP catalogue record for this book
is available from the British Library.

ISBN 978-0-7515-4256-1

Little, Brown Book Group
100 Victoria Embankment
London EC4Y 0DY

An Hachette UK Company
www.hachette.co.uk

www.littlebrown.co.uk

For Behroz

PROLOGUE

16 November 2007

'What does your gut tell you?'

'My gut tells me I'm right. The problem is I don't have Larry's support.'

'Larry doesn't know what he's talking about.'

'Maybe. But he's my boss.'

Charlie took a sip of wine and placed his glass down firmly on the table. 'Hold your ground and Larry will respect you. You won't last a minute without his respect.'

'I'm just scared that if I go out on a limb with this one, then I'm fucked.'

'You're fucked anyway, kiddo. Look, anyone who tries to predict the future is going to screw up at some point. But right or wrong is not what's important in this business. If you want to be a winner in this game, you need to follow my three little rules.'

A waitress glided over to take their order. Charlie dismissed her with a wave of his hand. 'Rule number one: stand up for what you believe in – your reputation is all you've got,' he declared. 'Rule number two: don't follow the crowd – if you can't think of anything original to say, keep your mouth shut. And rule number three . . .' He looked furtively right and left, leaned forward and eyed Niccolo with steely precision. '. . . never trust anyone in this business. They're all a bunch of dirty, lying motherfuckers.'

CHAPTER 1

2 March 2006

Niccolo forced himself to let the phone ring once. Then twice. Only on the fourth ring did he pick up the receiver.

'Niccolo Lamparelli? This is Larry Sikorski.' The voice was heavy, the tone blunt. 'We really liked that feature article you wrote on Ultrafone. Your analysis was truly thought-provoking. And your BBC interview last week – that was pretty impressive too.'

'Thank you . . .'

'We'd like to offer you a job at Saracen Laing.'

Saracen Laing! Niccolo forced himself to breathe deeply, to sound calm, when in fact he was light-headed with euphoria. 'What sort of job, Mr Sikorski?' he asked.

'Analysis, the kind of thing you've been doing for the *Financial Telegraph*. Only you'd be doing it for us.'

'And . . .'

'How much are we offering? Well, I'm afraid I have no scope to be flexible on your base salary – we have a hundred-thousand-pound ceiling. It's the suits in New York; they want to keep our fixed costs as low as possible.'

'I see.' Niccolo forced himself to count to ten – slowly.

But before he finished, Sikorski continued, 'However, I can guarantee your bonus at the end of your first year with us.'

'How much were you thinking of?' asked Niccolo cautiously.

'One hundred per cent.' The reply was curt, with a ring of finality.

The money was obscene – two hundred grand a year – but Niccolo sensed he could get more. 'If you guarantee me a one hundred per cent bonus for the first two years, you've got a deal.'

'A hundred per cent in year one. Fifty per cent in year two.'

'Hmmn,' said Niccolo, feigning indifference.

'I'm afraid I must press you for an answer today. I have other candidates who would jump at this offer.'

'I'd still like a few more days to think about it.' *Christ, Lamparelli, what are you saying?*

'Bear in mind that's the minimum you will make,' Larry Sikorski responded quickly. 'There's a discretionary bonus on top of the guarantee. Play your cards right, and this time next year you can expect to take home a million. After that, there's no limit on what you could earn. I can make you obscenely rich, young man. Take your time. Think about it. But call me back by the end of the day.'

'I'll take the offer,' replied Niccolo, smiling coolly.

'Great. I'll send you the papers tonight. As soon as I receive a signed contract, we can set your starting date. I want you on board fast. There are some big deals coming up.'

'I look forward to working with you, Larry.'

'Welcome to Saracen Laing.' And Larry Sikorski hung up.

Niccolo put down the receiver and yelled, '*Yes*!' to the empty room. Larry Sikorski was no ordinary investment banker. He had been in the business for thirty years. His work was highly regarded by the banking industry and his name was associated with the biggest and most prestigious deals. He was the very best in his field. Niccolo could not believe his luck . . .

Along a narrow alleyway just behind the Bank of England, a winding cobbled path leads up to an old inn. Since 1847, the Moneypincher's Inn has been the pub most favoured by the Bank's officials. In those days, the corner table at the Moneypincher's was reserved for special guests. The Governor of the Bank himself would often be seen dining there, brandishing his cigar, his cognac and his rolling dice. A century and a half later, many things have changed at the Governor's favourite haunt. Where once there was a magnificent log fire, there is now a lone candle. Slim, sophisticated waitresses, mostly with foreign accents, have replaced the busty English barmaids of the nineteenth century. Pricey French wines have edged out London's ales. But the corner table is still reserved for special guests.

A black cab crawled towards the inn, the driver carefully manoeuvring his vehicle within the strict confines of the narrow lane until he stopped safely outside the tall oak doors. A suit emerged from the taxi and entered the Moneypincher's Inn, slipped off an overcoat and handed it to a smartly dressed receptionist.

'It's a pleasure to see you again, sir,' said the maître d', and led him quietly to the corner table. 'The Doctor is expecting you. I shall let him know you are here.'

'Thank you, Pierre. But bring me a Bloody Mary first, would you? Make it spicy.'

'Of course, sir.'

A minute later the Bloody Mary arrived. The suit took a sip and glanced at his watch. It was ten minutes to midday. He felt a hand on his shoulder, and turned his head. A bearded gentleman with a wrinkled forehead and thick eyebrows peered down at him through fine-rimmed spectacles. The suit stood up and offered his hand. 'Dr Picton?' he enquired.

'Indeed,' said Picton. 'Thank you for coming down here in person. I prefer to conduct my business face to face. I'm sure you understand.'

The suit nodded. 'Fewer misunderstandings that way.' He offered Picton a seat.

Picton signalled the maître d'. Moments later, a waiter discreetly placed a set of leather-bound menus on the table and disappeared.

'My client is investing a lot of money in your project,' began Picton. 'We're relying on you to have the right people in place to make the right decisions – people who will not buckle under pressure.'

'Of course.'

Picton moved the menus to one side and placed his arms on the table. 'My contacts are interested in your proposals. We're talking one billion dollars – all at your disposal.'

The suit checked over his shoulder. As yet they were the only customers; the staff were still scuttling to and fro in preparation for the first sitting.

'That's far more than I was led to believe, Dr Picton.'

'If you can't handle it, I understand.'

'I didn't say I couldn't handle it,' snapped the suit. 'I said it was more than I expected.'

'Very well,' continued Picton. 'Assuming we agree to your proposal, how soon can my people expect to see a return on their investment?'

'This is a complex operation. No one's going to get rich overnight. If you're in, then you're in for the long term – be prepared to have your money tied up for a couple of years.'

'Very well, let's say we're in for the long term. What can we expect from you?'

'I'll triple your money in two years – three at most. More importantly, it will be clean and above board.'

6

Picton smiled. 'How can I be sure your team will deliver the goods should things get rough?'

'Dr Picton, I know my clients, I know my people and I know my business. You can depend on me to deliver.'

'With the amount of cash I'm placing under your supervision – and the commission you're charging – you'll forgive me if I do more than merely *depend* on you.'

The suit clasped his hands. 'Name your terms.'

'My employers are happy to agree to your rates. But, in return, they will expect you to deliver on your promises.'

The suit from Saracen Laing eyed his host. 'I always deliver on my promises, Dr Picton.'

'Good. We understand each other.' Picton unfolded his napkin and placed it squarely on his lap. 'Now, let's have some lunch.'

After his father had died, Niccolo had turned to Jack Ford for everything. And over the years Jack had shepherded Niccolo through life's twists and turns like a big brother. Even when Donna had sashayed into Jack's world, Jack still took care of Niccolo.

As a stock analyst at Saracen Laing, with a competent team of junior analysts beneath him and a flamboyant boss above, Jack was paid exceptionally well. Donna had married him imagining that she would permanently occupy the top slot in his list of priorities. But he was a workaholic, and rarely saw her. So in fact she never reached the top slot, and three years after tying the knot, resentment was beginning to set in.

They lived in a detached house in Hampstead, dined at upmarket London restaurants, had weekends away at spas and spent a fortune on fine wines, and Donna had grown accustomed to the fringe benefits of having a husband who demanded little but provided much. As a sports injury physiotherapist at the local hospital, she earned very little, and they both knew their lifestyle depended on Jack's bonuses. Instead of loving her husband, Donna had come to love the lifestyle he could provide – Gucci handbags, Prada shoes, luxury holidays – and it didn't come cheap.

Even so, to Donna, her husband was a failure – he was always one step behind, never the man he could have been. She would urge him to do more with his life. 'Look at all the chances you've missed,' she would rail at him. 'Think of the opportunities you've wasted!' She saw ambition and enterprise, like grains of sand, slipping slowly from his grasp. But what Donna wanted, Jack could not give, for fate had placed upon his shoulders a burden of responsibility from which he refused to walk away.

'You must promise never to let any harm come to Nicco-san,' the old fisherman had told him. And from that day on, Jack had appointed himself Niccolo's big brother and guardian angel. Even now Niccolo was thirty, Jack remained conscious of his promise. This was intolerable for Donna. *Put yourself first, damn it*, she would constantly demand. *Nicco can take care of himself!* But Jack knew better. Niccolo had the looks, the brains and the drive to go all the way to the top. Yet there were times when he was all too ready to throw it away. He needed someone to watch over him, to guide him. Since the day Jack had given his word to Mizuno-san, he had honoured it in every sense. No matter what it cost him, Jack had always been there for Niccolo. And despite his wife's taunts, he had never once looked back with regret at the way he had lived his life.

When Jack got home that night, dinner had already been served and dessert was on the table. Niccolo was sitting opposite Donna with a smile etched across his face and a glass of wine in his hand. 'I got the job, Jack,' he announced excitedly. 'Telecom analyst at Saracen!'

Jack threw his briefcase in the corner and came over to hug his friend delightedly. 'When do you start?' he wanted to know.

'In two weeks. Just given my notice to the *FT*.'

'Great,' said Donna glibly. 'Now you two can see each other all day at work as well.'

Jack and Niccolo exchanged glances and grinned. 'Any wine left?' asked Jack. Donna shrugged as Niccolo checked the bottle. It was empty.

'I'll get a fresh one,' said Jack. 'We're going to celebrate, Nicco.' He discarded his jacket and tie and darted down a tiny stairway into the cellar. The wine was stacked according to age, whites on the right, reds on the left. Jack had a system – the higher up the shelf, the better the vintage. He reached up towards the top left, fumbling for a while, until he found the 1967 Pétrus.

Halfway up the stairs, he paused to peer into a tiny alcove in the wall. In a sort of shrine stood a wooden picture frame, gently balanced on the uneven masonry, containing an old black-and-white photograph that was fading around the edges. On a sunny beach, a middle-aged Japanese fisherman sat cross-legged in the sand, in front of a badly weathered fishing boat, surrounded by three young boys. Twenty years on, Niccolo's features had not changed much. He was tall, with a sinewy frame, and an eternally wayward look about him. Jack was the shortest boy in the photograph, despite being the eldest by three years. He had kept his stocky build, but lost much of his puppy fat, and with it had gone his impudence. The third boy was a younger carbon copy of the fisherman. Like his grandfather, he looked uncomfortable in front of the camera.

Jack undid a shirt button and felt the silver chain that hung round his neck. He gripped the shark's tooth dangling from it and kissed it gently. There were two other people who deserved to be present tonight to celebrate Niccolo's good fortune.

*

'Good morning, sir. My name is Domingo. I've been expecting you.' The newly appointed Head of Security, who hailed from the Dominican Republic, was a graceful man quite at ease with his exceptional height. 'I have your security pass ready, sir. Welcome to Saracen Laing.'

'Thank you,' said Niccolo, smiling as he accepted an envelope.

'Please take the elevator straight up to the mezzanine floor. Mr Sikorski's personal assistant is expecting you.' Niccolo ignored Domingo's advice and took the stairs. It was a few minutes past seven and he was early.

The building was impressive. Built in an age when beauty of form took precedence over cost or practicality, it was one of those buildings where each room told a story. It had probably taken a few hits during the war, but was tough enough to shrug them off.

The trading floor was already alive and kicking. Whilst the London exchanges did not open until eight o'clock, some traders were already making markets on the European bourses. Others were on the phone to Tokyo and Hong Kong and Singapore. Everybody was busy.

Anne-Marie Smith did not say much. She showed Niccolo his desk as if it were a task unworthy of her status. As PA to the Head of Research, she was efficient, courteous and – in her own way – hard-working. Her duties included screening Larry's telephone calls, deleting his emails, collecting his laundry, arranging his weekend parties and typing his letters. But her ability to delegate everything to the typing pool freed her up to perform a host of other activities. She excelled at running up colossal telephone bills at the bank's expense, surfing the internet for exciting holiday deals and taking most afternoons off to work out in the gym.

Anne-Marie was the gateway into Larry's world. Bypassing her was difficult but not impossible. Only a handful of the bank's most valued clients had direct telephone access to Larry's office line.

Niccolo spotted Jack a few rows down, raised a hand, and received a nod and a wink in return.

A few minutes later, Larry Sikorski emerged from a glass-fronted office on the edge of the trading floor, accompanied by Rupert Southgate, Saracen Laing's Head of Telecoms. Even though too many late nights and too many bottles of wine had begun to take their toll, Larry was still a good-looking man. Dark circles had become a permanent fixture beneath his eyes, and a second chin was starting to cohabit comfortably with the first, but his mature features were tempered by an even tan, and he was impeccably dressed in a matt-black single-breasted suit. He radiated style, panache and confidence.

'Good morning, Larry,' said a few anonymous voices.

'Hi, everyone,' Larry replied. 'Hey, Ru, did you see that shit on Ultrafone in the papers? See if JC is all over it, will you?' Then he turned to his new stock analyst. 'How are you, Niccolo?' he asked. 'Welcome to the trading floor.'

'Very well, thank you. And yourself?'

'Ready for action – just returned from my yacht in the Canaries. I left my two daughters to enjoy the rest of the winter on the boat. I get custody whenever I go on holiday. The bitch doesn't think I can handle the kids any other time!'

There was a round of forced laughter.

'Now this guy you already know,' Larry said, turning to the Head of Telecoms. 'Rupert will be your day-to-day boss, as we discussed before. But I want you to know that my door's always open. Tell me if he treats you like his bitch and I'll straighten him out!' Niccolo chuckled in unison with the others because he thought he had to.

Rupert was in his early forties, with thinning blond hair and grey eyes. 'Great to have you on board,' he said, loosening his collar. 'You've done some really interesting work in the past.' His public-school accent revealed a privileged upbringing, though his tired, nervous demeanour made him seem older than he probably was. He and Niccolo shook hands.

'OK, so I have eight telecoms analysts who report directly to me,' Rupert said. 'This guy is my number two analyst.'

A young man glanced up. Though tall and athletic, he looked as if he carried the weight of the world on his shoulders. 'James Heath. Hi. I'm in the middle of something. I'm sure we'll talk later,' he said. He spoke abruptly, in short, sharp bursts. Niccolo preferred the directness of James to the unfounded flattery of Rupert.

Larry continued, 'Now I want you to meet a very special person. She is your lifeline to the outside world. She has the top institutional funds eating out of her hand. It's her job to market your work. But first she has to like you. Piss her off and you won't last a minute.'

Niccolo glanced at his lifeline, and tried not to let his jaw drop. Odile Théveneau was a stunner; petite and curvaceous, she was simply but elegantly dressed and her skin glowed with a luminous intensity. Odile escorted Niccolo around the trading floor. It was a vast open tract, buzzing with maybe four or five hundred traders and analysts and secretaries, but made up largely of white males. Everyone seemed to be multitasking: some waved to colleagues using a kind of sign language, whilst holding two telephone receivers and still managing to write things down; others stared apparently mindlessly at the arrays of computer displays, alternating between them, unfazed by the mayhem. On two cinema-size screens at either end of the trading floor, prices for at least a hundred stocks, bonds, indices and exchange rates were flickering up and down, causing heads to turn randomly, swear words to fly and phones to slam down in fits of rage.

'The traders are busy today,' observed Niccolo.

'They're busy every day,' replied Odile, flashing a perfect set of teeth. 'They make virtually all the bank's profits. It gives them very big heads. They think they're God, but in fact they rely on you guys, the analysts, to tell them which way the markets are going to move. And when you get it wrong, all hell breaks loose.' Niccolo looked around. The traders might think they were God, but the trading floor looked more like hell than heaven.

'What about Larry?' he enquired.

'Larry's not so bad once you get to know him.'

They talked some more, discovering that they had much in common. Odile was French by birth, but her father's diplomatic status meant that her childhood had been spent on the move, much as Niccolo's own had been because of his father's naval career. Niccolo suspected that he would get on very well with Odile. At his new desk, he assessed the tools at his disposal. Facing him were four flat-screen monitors, one linked to Reuters, another to Kloomberg, and two to use as he wished. The Reuters and Kloomberg screens contained a mass of information: arrows flashed up and then down; news alerts popped in and out; money moved back and forth. The information was live and profits were instantaneous. Prices for the most actively traded stocks were changing direction in the blink of an eye.

From the quiet, well-positioned seventh-floor office of an imposing glass-fronted tower block overlooking the river, Amanda Sanderson, Chief Enforcement Officer at the Financial Services Authority – known as the FSA – leaned back and admired the view. Piled on her desk were management reports telling her precisely how badly her department had been performing for the last two quarters.

On a coffee table in the corner lay copies of the *Financial Times*, the *Economist* and the *Wall Street Journal*. Piles of confidential dossiers were spread all over the floor, and strewn the length of an ancient battered Chesterfield sofa were an open copy of *The British Journal of Criminology*, extracts from the Proceeds of Crime Act, and crumpled transcripts of previous cases unsuccessfully prosecuted by the FSA. They all confirmed her worst nightmare. Her caseload was full of long shots, unworthy of even the most speculative wager. Things were made far worse by a zealous, headline-grabbing counterpart in New York; the New York Attorney General had turned his hobby of trashing American investment banks into a full-time job. He made Amanda Sanderson look like an amateur.

The FSA's hit squads went off on far too many wild goose chases that stood little chance of yielding results in England's impossibly lenient justice system, Sanderson was left with the onerous task of explaining the department's dismal statistics to the Chancellor of the Exchequer twice a year, and teams of fraudsters continued to operate with impunity inside the Square Mile. The newspapers reported more frauds than the FSA did.

Morale amongst the agency's enforcement officers had hit an all-time low, and Sanderson's own job was probably up for grabs. The only cause for celebration was that nobody in their right mind would want to step into her shoes in the current climate. Yet that could not prevent whispering campaigns in the corridors of power. She needed to win a high-profile case. She needed the scalp of a big name – a City high-flyer – to hold up in Westminster. Just one.

Odile treated Niccolo to lunch in the office canteen. They cornered a table at the back of the television lounge just before the twelve-thirty rush. Odile opted for a salad, whilst Niccolo helped himself to three courses, a can of Coke and a Mars bar.

'Hey,' he said, pointing to the screen. 'Who's that guy on TNBC?'

'That's Charlie Doyle, known to his friends as Popeye,' Odile replied, toying with some lettuce leaves. 'He sits just behind you. He's a lovely guy. I must introduce you.'

'Jack's told me a lot about him. He loves working for him – says he's the best boss he's had in a while.'

Odile edged closer. 'I hear you and Jack go back a long way.'

'That's right. We grew up together – school, summer holidays, university and all that. Does Charlie appear often on TV?'

'Yes, he's Head of Technology Research. He knows his stuff and he never pulls his punches.'

Charlie, rotund and jowly, wore thick spectacles, and looked scruffy even though his clothes were expensive. He seemed totally at ease with the cameras. Niccolo and Odile were unable to hear everything he was saying as the chatter of lunchtime arrivals smothered much of his performance.

'Everyone likes Charlie,' continued Odile. 'He's fun. If he weren't a technology analyst he'd make a great comedian. Clients like him because he's amusing. Best of all, he can laugh at himself. And that's a rare commodity in our world. You should see some of the shit I have to put up with from the other analysts. They're a bunch of misfits with fragile egos and excess testosterone. But Charlie doesn't need to prove anything – he's done it all. In the late nineties he was rated the number one technology analyst for five years running. He made money – big money – during the dot-com boom. And he has a reputation for being able to predict the next big thing in technology well before anyone else. He's American, but he's lived over here for twenty years, ever since Saracen granted his request for a transfer from Wall Street to London.'

'Working with him sounds great.'

'I warn you, though – he's going through a mid-life crisis. His wives and kids are embarrassed to be seen with him ever since he bought the Ducati.'

15

'I like him already! But . . . *wives*?'

'Several. All ex. Or should I say expensive?'

Team 19 at the FSA's Enforcement Division had been assembled for an important meeting. Team 19 knew all about Dr Picton. They knew what he did for a living. They knew of his reputation for ruthlessness. They knew he had laundered money in several jurisdictions across Europe and the Middle East. They suspected he had pocketed a small fortune by profiting from the financial market crash in the aftermath of the 9/11 terrorist attacks in New York, though it was impossible to say for sure that he had had prior knowledge of them. And they were 99 per cent certain he was up to his old tricks again.

There was only one problem.

They had nothing on him.

Dr Picton covered his tracks. His name had been linked to four homicides in ten years, yet not a single arrest warrant had been issued. He had contacts at the highest levels within the British government and was not afraid to use them. He was fiercely loyal to his paymasters and bitterly intolerant of those who crossed him.

Team 19 was led by Arnaud Veyrieras, who had been head-hunted from Interpol in Paris for his expertise in organised crime. Like others in his position at the Enforcement Division, he had been allocated an impossible caseload. Arnaud did not like being given advice, and after thirty years in the job, he figured he did not need any. But that did not stop Sanderson from dropping the odd hint now and again. Cracking the older fraud cases, she had told him, had a lot to do with meticulous investigation and an obsessive attention to detail. Discovering a new fraud, by contrast, had more to do with luck. Veyrieras made his own luck. As soon as he arrived in London, he had hand-picked

Team 19 and devoted the best part of a year to training them up. If the Doctor had anything to hide, Arnaud wanted to be the one to expose it.

Once all seven members of the team were present and accounted for, Arnaud dimmed the lights and switched on the projector.

'We're going to see some action, people,' he began. 'And we're going to see it soon. I want you lot to get your arses into gear. Sanderson is under pressure to deliver results. You guys work for Sanderson. Ergo, *you* are under pressure to yield results.'

The team had got used to his accent over the months, but had grown weary of his perennial bursts of machismo. Two men at the back of the room muttered, *Bloody Frog*! Arnaud's eyes scanned the room, but it was too dark to locate the culprits. 'We're dealing with a syndicate of big investors,' he continued. 'This syndicate is led by a young Usmani prince called Mubarak bin Majid Al Shahaan. His friends simply call him Prince. His father is the Sultan of Usman, who owns UsmanOil. Mubarak heads a group of young Arab men playing with their daddies' money, oil money from the Gulf mostly. They're well educated, these guys – most have MBAs from the top business schools, and many have worked for Tier 1 investment banks. And they have connections – *serious* connections. But they're still just a bunch of rich kids with no real idea of how the world works. Even so, they've managed to make huge profits in Western stock markets. In the last seven years, the earnings they've generated have been too good to be true and too consistent to be ignored. Which leads us to believe that Dr Picton has been steering the syndicate all this time. There's no way these boys could have done it without him.'

Arnaud flicked a switch on the projector for the first slide, a photograph of a middle-aged bearded Caucasian man dressed in a dark suit, entering a restaurant.

'As most of you will know, this is Dr Picton. The name is fake – he has several aliases. The doctorate, however, may be real; something fancy in the field of particle physics, we believe. Picton's brain works faster than an Intel Centrino, and he covers his tracks with the utmost care. He seems to spend a lot of time at this place, the Moneypincher's Inn on St Swithins Lane. He lunches there most days and his offices are upstairs. He also sleeps there some nights. We want this man to lead us into the lion's den.'

Arnaud casually flicked a button on the projector to view the next slide. A dark-skinned young man with short-cropped hair, dressed inconspicuously in a casual white collarless shirt and blue jeans, was shaking hands with Picton in an empty restaurant. 'This is the Prince. Like his syndicate friends, he graduated from MIT and has a Harvard MBA. But he's not all that bright. So he uses Picton as a fixer. Picton prefers to describe himself as a strategist.'

Arnaud turned his back on the screen to face his audience. 'What I am about to tell you next is just my own hunch. But if I'm right, this could turn out to be a much bigger catch than any of us have ever seen.'

CHAPTER 2

Rupert's team were not a friendly crowd. They owned their turf and marked it out with their own distinctive scent. Welcoming a newcomer was so far down their list of priorities that it made more sense to wait until the probationary period was over.

New blood could bring in new business. Equally it could rock the boat. The rules of survival were simple: Rupert made them, and everyone else followed them. Not all teams operated like Rupert's, but things were heading that way, because Rupert's team, under Larry Sikorski's tenure, always managed to secure the biggest share of the bonus pool.

Equity research was not a profitable business unit in itself. Nonetheless, a strong research division was the silent engine of the bank, for it opened doors for other business units that *were* profitable. Research provided the bank with its intellectual podium, on permanent display to the rest of the world. As the public face of an investment bank, it enabled its rainmakers to claim expertise in a wide range of fields, allowing them to win bigger mandates with fatter fees. Naturally, the research analysts – who embodied that expertise – carried a lot of clout.

As the new boy, Niccolo was made to cut his teeth on some of the smaller stocks – Wire & Satellite, Telecom10 and Maiden Media. He wanted the big one – Ultrafone – but he would have to wait for such a prize until he was higher up the pecking order. The days passed and he struggled to keep up with his workload. He needed to understand his stocks, speak to company management, keep up to date on corporate news, read widely on the telecoms sector and write his quota of research notes. Neither Rupert nor James volunteered any help. The other analysts took their lead from their boss, and Niccolo's requests for assistance were deferred, declined or ignored. Most of the analysts seemed to operate exclusively from within their own silos, rarely sharing resources or knowledge. Niccolo was surprised; in the Information Age, this was an extremely wasteful way to work.

James filled the role of Rupert's deputy with relish. He would review the team's output prior to publication, referring any contentious issues upwards. He operated a command-and-control mentality that tended to stunt creativity. Niccolo did not appreciate his ideas being stifled at birth. But after a week, he had run out of ideas anyway. His work did not meet James' standards, so it was edited, rewritten, re-edited and rewritten again. And so it continued for days. James' reviews became more and more abrasive, whilst Niccolo felt more and more frustrated.

The Head of Telecoms watched from a distance, making no attempt to intervene.

The security officer took a bunch of keys from his pocket and searched for the one he wanted. The labels were illegible, so he fiddled about until he found the most likely match. The fourth key he tried clicked and the lock opened. He entered a dark, windowless room, two storeys beneath the underground car park, and patted the wall in search of the light switch. When he turned it on, two fluorescent lights flickered for a while before settling down. There was dust everywhere and the air smelt stale. The room was long and narrow, the walls lined with an array of computer servers. The constant flicker of the neon tubes irritated him.

He surveyed the room. The layout was exactly as he had expected. He sat down in a dust-covered chair at the main work-station and tapped the keyboard. The screen lit up. In a flash, he pulled out a memory stick from his shirt pocket and plugged it in.

Run? asked the machine.

The security officer clicked to confirm, then watched as the program installed itself on to the main server. The servers housed back-up files containing digital voice recordings of all front-office telephone conversations made by Saracen Laing employees, as required by their dealing licence. The voice-recognition software was programmed to search for two words in sequence – 'Doctor' and 'Picton'. The software then transmitted the files that matched the sequence through the Ethernet, busting through the corporate firewalls on to the internet towards its final-destination server.

Dr Picton arrived at Toni's Café at twenty minutes past ten, but failed to apologise for being late. 'How is the new boy doing?'

The man from Saracen Laing looked confused. 'How do you know we hired a new boy?'

'I'm keeping a close eye on you all.'

'Dr Picton,' replied his guest, suppressing his displeasure, 'I don't think we've got off to a very good start. Let me tell you how this is going to be. You line up the money and I line up the deals.'

'I'm not sure about this Lamparelli.'

'Niccolo Lamparelli is the right man for the job.'

'He might prove a problem for us,' said the Doctor. 'My people have already checked him out. He's young, and may be hard to control.'

'Nonsense. He's thirty years old. He spent his first few years after leaving college bumming around the world with a rucksack.

Later, he developed a decent reputation as a journalist. He also has a reputation as a ladies' man. Look, we're paying the guy very handsomely; the last thing he's going to do is jeopardise that. Anyway, Rupert Southgate is keeping a close watch over him, and Rupert runs a tight ship. There will be no trouble, I assure you . . . Another thing, Niccolo's a close friend of Jack Ford, one of our tech analysts. Jack's a hard-working company man with an expensive wife to support, maybe a family down the line, never rocks the boat, does as he's told. What's more, Niccolo looks up to him. So if he steps out of line, I can get Jack to straighten him out. Two sets of muppet strings are better than one.'

'This guy might be smarter than you think – he went to Cambridge, didn't he?'

'He scraped through with a third. Spent all his time chasing girls and practising judo.'

'Karate.'

'Sorry?'

'Karate. Not judo.'

'Sure, sure. Anyway, Niccolo Lamparelli is the least of our problems, trust me.'

'My friend, I don't trust anybody.' The voice was as smooth as silk. 'That is precisely why my clients hire me.'

CHAPTER 3

'So how are you settling in, Nicco?' asked Larry, positioning himself at an adjacent urinal.

'Just fine, Larry,' said Niccolo, zipping up and stepping back.

'Now, listen. My door's always open. I want you to feel free to come to me if you ever have any problems, understand?'

'Thanks, Larry. I appreciate it.'

'Good.'

Larry zipped up and left the men's room without washing his hands.

Niccolo returned to his desk and began to tidy up the mountain of unread reports, business journals and paperwork that had piled up with remarkable speed in recent days. But the clamour from behind him soon became too loud to ignore.

'There they are!'

'Who?

'The Kloomberg girls!'

Niccolo turned around to see what all the commotion was about. Charlie Doyle had climbed up on to his desk for a better view of something at the other end of the trading floor. Jack stood next to him on a chair, similarly mesmerised.

Three Kloomberg girls were working their way around the trading floor – two blondes and a redhead, dressed like American cheerleaders – distributing play-size footballs with the Kloomberg logo. Their tanned legs and short skirts assured them the undivided attention of every trader, analyst and IT person on the floor.

'What are they doing?' asked Niccolo.

'Who cares? Just look at them!'

Jack had a point. The girls were hot. To the majority of traders and analysts on the floor, these girls were made to order – the ultimate fashion accessory. They all wanted one.

'God, *she's* fit,' drooled Jack.

'Which one?' asked Niccolo, climbing clumsily on to a desk beside him.

'The one with the big jugs.' Jack pointed to the prettier of the two blondes. 'Juicy Lucy.'

At that moment, Juicy Lucy smiled devastatingly up at the three watching men, and waved. And each of them was convinced she was waving only to him.

Charlie and Jack made a formidable team. As head of the tech team, Charlie hogged most of the limelight whilst Jack did most of the detailed work. It suited their individual characters and it made them inseparable. But twice a week they would work out together at the gym, and in a room full of iron dumb-bells, their roles reversed.

Charlie was the older by fifteen years, and had trouble keeping up with Jack's pace. Often they would end their gym session with ten minutes in the sauna. It allowed them to relax, absorb the heat and bask in the joys of seeing half-naked women seated beside them. Soon after Niccolo joined the bank, the twosome evolved into a threesome.

'So how are things with Rachel and Sarah?' asked Jack, pouring some water on the stove, producing a large cloud of steam.

24

'Rachel *and* Sarah?' Charlie enquired, brightening. 'Young Lamparelli, are you something of a stud?'

'Am I allowed to tell Charlie?' Jack asked Niccolo.

Niccolo sighed resigned consent.

'Well, Sarah is – or was – Nicco's ex-girlfriend,' Jack began. 'And Rachel is – or was – his current girlfriend.'

'Is or was?' Charlie hooted. 'This is starting to sound good.'

Niccolo took over. 'Sarah rang me; she was upset because she'd just broken up with her man. So I asked her round for a drink. And, well . . .'

'One thing led to another, eh?'

'Something like that. And Rachel walked in and found us.'

Charlie roared with laughter. 'Oh, this is just priceless!'

'Not really,' said Niccolo glumly. 'They both stormed off in different directions, and I haven't heard from either of them since.'

'Kanto sanchi,' said Jack quietly.

'What?' asked Charlie.

'It's a story we were once told by an old man in Japan.' Jack took a deep breath and began. 'Once upon a time there was a monk . . .'

Niccolo closed his eyes. Instead of Jack's voice, he could hear the old fisherman recounting the tale. Every night Mizuno-san would tell the boys a story about a Buddhist monk. And every morning he would ask them to decipher its meaning.

'. . . who spent most of his youth in a Buddhist temple in Okinawa, where the older monks taught him as much as they could about life. When he became a man, he was told to leave the temple and to seek adventure, to experience freedom and to learn from his mistakes. After ten years he was to return to the temple to pass on what he had learned. That way the junior monks would be prepared for life outside, just as he had been made ready by those before him.'

The acoustics in the sauna transformed Jack's voice into that of a great storyteller. He poured some more water on the stove. Sweat poured from their bodies, and as the steam rose, he continued the tale.

'One day the monk was crossing Kanto sanchi, a mountainous region north-east of Kyoto, well known for its dangerous and rugged terrain. A hungry tiger suddenly leapt out from behind a bush. The monk fled for his life.

'But he ran out of luck. The ground beneath him fell away and he slid off a precipice. He grabbed at whatever he could, and eventually managed to cling to a piece of rock. When he had caught his breath he assessed his position. Below him lay a two-hundred-foot drop on to a bed of solid rock. Above him sat the tiger, waiting, and hungry.'

Jack stopped talking, and for a few moments there was complete silence in the sauna except for the slight hiss of steam.

'So what happened?' Charlie asked eventually.

'That's it,' answered Jack. 'That's the end.'

Puzzled, Charlie turned to Niccolo. 'I don't get it.'

'The monk got himself into a situation where he loses no matter what he does,' explained Niccolo. 'Either way he's a dead man.'

'Is there a moral in there somewhere?'

'The moral of the story,' concluded Jack, 'is that sometimes – no matter what you do, no matter how hard you try – you're completely fucked.'

'Or, in Niccolo's case,' said Charlie, 'not fucked at all.'

A software engineer with a bad cold and three days' stubble swiped his security pass to get into the sound room, sat down at the main terminal, put on a set of Bose headphones and quickly located the heavily encrypted files he was looking for. It took a handful of mouse clicks to unlock them. The results that appeared on screen showed that the voice-recognition software planted in Saracen's servers had found two recordings that matched the programmed sequence. The engineer opened the files and played around with the graphic equaliser to eliminate the background noise. Then he clicked the play button, and a slow smile spread across his face. The system was set up. The software worked. From this point forward, it was just a waiting game.

CHAPTER 4

Every year, during the first week of May, Larry hosted a birthday party at his country home just outside Godalming, in Surrey. In the past, invitations had been limited to Saracen employees, but this year he would turn fifty, so the guest list was opened up to spouses and partners as well. The dress code was 'James Bond', and the costs would, of course, be charged to the company.

Niccolo hitched a lift with Jack and Donna. He and Jack came as 007, and Donna, in a jet-black cocktail dress, was a slinky Bond girl. Donna's ravishing looks and long blond hair made Jack wary of parading his wife in public at the best of times, but today he was on high alert. The cocktail dress revealed a damn sight more cleavage than he felt comfortable with.

'I'm really looking forward to this,' Donna sighed rapturously, once they were clear of London.

'We're not going just to party,' Jack reminded her. 'For me, this is work.'

'You work. I'll play,' she giggled.

'OK, but it would help if you could play the corporate wife – you know, hobnob and schmooze, and charm the pants off the right people.'

'Not if they're going to be boring,' Donna pouted. 'I want to have some fun.' And she turned to look out of the window and sulked for the next half-hour. Niccolo, in the back seat, thanked the Lord he was single.

Saracen Laing's Head of Research lived in a beautiful old manor house that had been converted two generations earlier into a sprawling family residence comprising eighteen rooms, a stable, two guest houses, a tennis court and a swimming pool. A river ran through part of the garden.

When they arrived, waitresses dressed in Playboy bunny outfits were serving drinks and canapés, and an elderly gentleman in a tuxedo was entertaining a group of excited young ladies at a black-jack table. The glamorously dressed guests were mingling and the champagne was flowing. Their host, who had chosen to be Goldfinger, was circulating, playing his part to the full. Jack, apprehensive at first, jettisoned his worries about Donna within minutes. She played the charming corporate wife from the word go. 'This place is fabulous,' she enthused. 'I'm soooo impressed . . .'

'Then I insist on giving you a guided tour,' Larry said, and without a word to Jack he whisked Donna away.

The two British agents looked at each other and shrugged. 'Oh well,' Jack sighed, draining his glass, 'let's go and see if we can find Charlie.'

Amanda Sanderson worked evenings and weekends. Even at her Hampshire cottage, with her undemanding husband, Tatiana the cat and the latest John Grisham saga to keep her company, she still managed to keep up a barrage of short emails from her BlackBerry. Moreover, she expected her staff to follow a similar work ethic.

So it came as no surprise to Arnaud Veyrieras when he received her call early on a Sunday afternoon.

'I want you in my office within the hour,' she snapped. Arnaud had a damn good hunch what she wanted. And that was what worried him. At that moment he did not have the answers she needed. He knew he would get them eventually – he just needed time. The question was: how much time would Sanderson give him?

On the orders of His Majesty Sultan Majid bin Mohammad Al Shahaan, Usman's international airport was undergoing a facelift. Tourists were experiencing delays, air-traffic control was overwhelmed and flight crews were confused. But the incoming Airbus 318 had been given priority clearance to land and was carefully guided off the runway by an army of flag-waving ground crew.

A turbaned man was standing by to greet the aircraft's sole passenger. 'Good morning, Dr Picton. My name is Singh. I have a car waiting for you, sir.'

Dr Picton grabbed a leather satchel and followed his escort across the scorching tarmac to a nearby limousine. He accustomed himself to the air-conditioned cabin and poured himself a chilled beer.

A convoy of three black Range Rovers guided the limousine through a set of heavily armed gates and on to the Sultan Majid highway. The driver radioed ahead to signal the guest's arrival. A little while later, the limousine turned in through a set of solid iron gates and drew to a gentle halt outside the principal residence of Prince Mubarak bin Majid Al Shahaan, a palace designed to replicate the Blue Mosque in Istanbul.

Picton was led up a flight of granite steps, through the front courtyard, past a fountain, under the main dome and into the tea room in the North Tower. The room was empty but for a table and two chairs. A bearded man in a white gown and red chequered keffiyeh poured him some tea, then went to stand guard in the doorway. The Prince had already been informed of his arrival, Picton was told.

Donna felt she had been transported to another world. Each room was alive with a character of its own, and a sense of history dating back centuries. She imagined what it would be like to be an aristocrat, to live by right amidst such ancient glory.

They entered Larry's bedroom. On the far wall hung a portrait of a beautiful young woman in an ivory silk dress.

'What a lovely painting,' Donna said admiringly, knowing what was expected. But her attention was really drawn by the twenty-one-stone diamond necklace around the young woman's neck.

'Her name was Augusta de Mournay,' explained Larry. 'She was said to be the illegitimate daughter of King George II and his mistress, the Countess of Yarmouth.' He edged a little closer to Donna. 'In 1760, when George II died, the throne passed to his grandson, George III. Six thousand pounds in banknotes was found in the dead King's desk, with a request that the money was to go to Lady Yarmouth. George III not only honoured his grandfather's wish but added a further two thousand guineas to the bequest. So Augusta was brought up by Lady Yarmouth in great style. Some say that George III himself had an affair with her and that the necklace – originally intended for his own wife, Queen Charlotte – somehow found its way to Augusta without knowledge of its existence ever reaching the Queen.'

'She's beautiful,' Donna breathed.

Larry caressed the back of Donna's neck and whispered softly, 'I have a surprise for you.' He located a switch behind the painting. A tiny motor hummed into action, moving the painting sideways, revealing a metal safe. Larry punched in the combination and the door popped open.

'Larry, what are you—?'

Larry turned around, holding a diamond necklace that closely resembled the one in the painting. He placed it gently around Donna's neck. 'When I bought this place, the painting came with it. Legend has it that King George III made love to Augusta in this very room, and that he commissioned her portrait as a gift. It's said that anyone who takes it down will face ten years of bad luck. None of the owners of this castle have dared break the spell.'

Donna caressed the diamonds longingly. 'These are gorgeous.' She stepped over to the mirror, and the sun refracted rays of rainbow-hued light spectacularly on to the walls.

'So that meant I inherited the painting,' continued Larry. 'And I asked Hugh – my art-dealer friend – to find the original necklace. It took him four years, but he finally tracked it down somewhere in France.' With a provocative sparkle in his eye, he added, 'It looks fabulous on you, Donna.'

Donna blushed. 'I've never worn anything so beautiful in all my life.'

'You are a beautiful young woman, my dear. You deserve beautiful things.' Standing behind Donna, Larry carefully undid the clasp. The warmth of his hands on her neck sent a shiver down her spine. He returned the diamonds to the safe and repositioned the painting.

'Well,' he said briskly, 'I suppose I had better get you back to your husband.'

Even when he was so drunk that Jack and Niccolo had to prop him up against the bar, Charlie was a crowd-puller. A dozen or so Saracen employees with their spouses were gathered round, drawn as if by magnets. Amongst them, Rupert Southgate, with his wife Daisy, stood next to Jean-Claude Bouvier – one of Saracen's corporate financiers – and his wife Geneviève. Hovering in the background was 'Cuddly' Dudley Rabinowitz, the bank's Chief Compliance Officer.

'Why don't you lot just bugger off,' Charlie slurred, 'and leave me to get another – *herk!* – drink?'

'So what do you do at Saracen?' Daisy Southgate enquired brightly, as if she had just read a manual of social etiquette.

'My dear,' replied Charlie with a leer, 'I do the same thing your husband does. Only I do it better.'

Daisy's smile froze, Rupert twitched uncomfortably, and Niccolo and Jack retreated to a safe distance. Geneviève Bouvier stepped in as if to back Daisy up. 'So what do you do *exactly* – for the bank, I mean?' she asked.

'I'm a tech analyst, darling. I tell people which tech stocks to buy and sell. Take Microsoft . . .' Charlie hiccupped. 'They've just launched the latest version of the Xbox. Kids love it, and parents love it even more. I call it the SEXbox . . . You should get your husband to give you one . . .'

Jean-Claude suddenly woke up to the way the conversation was going, but Rupert stepped in for him. 'You've had a bit too much to drink, Charlie. Perhaps you should—'

Charlie lurched forward, an unpleasant look on his face. 'You know something, Rupert?' he sniped. 'You really are an excuse for a wet fart.'

Rupert went pale. 'Daisy, why don't we go and find something to eat?' he said, and without waiting for her agreement he turned and walked away, his wife following in his wake. Charlie broadcast a victorious smile, which made the others distinctly uneasy.

Just in time, a pair of welcome intruders arrived, armed with champagne flutes. 'You have a beautiful wife, Jack,' remarked Larry, kissing Donna's hand before delivering it dutifully into Jack's.

'Thank you,' replied Jack politely. 'I think so too.'

'Larry took me on a tour of the house,' explained Donna, her cheeks flushed with alcohol. She tossed her hair back and giggled, splashing champagne on to Larry's trousers in the process. He pulled out a handkerchief and dealt with it effortlessly.

'Now then, ladies and gentlemen, I must ask you to make your way into the house for the speeches,' said the host, leading the way.

As they walked back, Jack put his arm firmly around Donna's waist, whilst Niccolo provided sufficient support to help Charlie walk in a straight line. But before they reached the main residence, Charlie and Niccolo split off from the rest, deciding to give the speeches a miss. A wooden seat with a view of the stream looked far more appealing.

'What does Jean-Claude do?' asked Niccolo.

Charlie slumped on the seat and took a deep breath. 'Sod all,' he declared.

Niccolo frowned. 'I thought he worked in M&A.'

'So does he.'

They sat contemplating the river for a few minutes, until a loud snore told Niccolo that Charlie was sound asleep. He stood up and looked back at the little groups of guests who had not gone indoors for the speeches. Suddenly a lively giggle and a flash of blond hair caught his attention – it was the Kloomberg girl! Juicy Lucy. He ran a hand nervously through his hair and set off towards her.

Arnaud had expected a heated exchange with Amanda Sanderson. What he didn't expect was a foregone conclusion.

'You're off the Picton case,' she said in a matter-of-fact tone the moment he entered her office.

'But I have Team 19 working full time on this case. I believe we can—'

'You've spent months investigating Dr Picton. You've had a

significant amount of resources at your disposal – including some of my best investigators – and you've come up with nothing. I gave you a deadline, Arnaud. It passed one month ago. Close the file.'

'But ma'am, I believe he's about to start something big and we can—'

'I said close the file, damn it! Team 19 is to be reassigned.'

Arnaud Veyrieras and the head of the FSA's Enforcement Division glared at each other for several seconds. Then, in total silence, Arnaud turned and walked out, shutting the door firmly behind him.

'Did you have a pleasant flight?' asked the Prince. He spoke with an Eton accent.

'It was perfect, Your Highness, thank you,' replied Picton.

'Excellent. I have arranged for you to stay in my personal quarters.'

'I am honoured.'

'Tonight there is a dinner I would like you to attend. It's just a small gathering of my father's friends – perhaps fifty or sixty people. It would not be appropriate, of course, to discuss business at dinner, so let's get it out of the way now, shall we?' The Prince nodded to the doorman. Tea was served and a hookah pipe set down on the table between them. The Prince took a puff, stared at the ceiling for a few moments and finally exhaled a cloud of smoke. 'Tell me your plan,' he said, offering Picton the pipe.

'Well, Your Highness, my people are now in place. The systems are up and running. I expect a number of large deals to come our way very soon – most likely in the telecoms space. All I'm waiting for is the all-clear from you and we're in business.'

'You're waiting for my money as well, eh, Doctor?'

Picton inhaled the smoke through the bubbling water. 'Yes,' he agreed.

'How much?'

'The more you invest, the more you stand to make.'

'How much do you want from me?'

'One billion dollars.'

'I can put up one hundred million myself. The rest will come from our syndicate friends. It might take a month or two.'

'That's fine.'

'How long will our money be tied up?'

'Two years, but I expect to triple it in that time.'

'And what will be your cut?'

'Five per cent straight up, and fifteen per cent of any profits I make.'

'What if you make a loss, my friend?'

'That is not possible.'

'Anything is possible.'

'Let's just say that the odds are stacked heavily in my favour.'

'Listen, Picton, we've worked together for a long time, so cut the crap. Why should I trust you with so much money? If I invest this much, I want a cast-iron guarantee.'

'A cast-iron guarantee is exactly what you will get.'

'My friend, how the hell can anyone guarantee a two hundred per cent return in two years?'

Picton took another puff and exhaled slowly. 'If they know in advance which way a stock will move,' he said.

To Jack and Donna's surprise, Niccolo politely refused their offer of a lift home.

'I bet he's pulled that blonde,' Donna observed as they headed back up the A3 to London.

'Which blonde?' Jack said, only half paying attention.

'Very short dress? Giggled a lot?'

'Christ, Juicy Lucy!' He was paying attention now. 'The

Kloomberg girl. Nicco, you jammy bugger!' Then he reached for Donna's hand. 'Thanks for making such an effort with Larry, darling. I know these events bore the shit out of you.'

'Don't be silly. I had a great time. Your boss is so charming. He has impeccable style. And he isn't at all bad-looking for a fifty-year-old. I hope you look that good when you're his age, Jack.'

That night Jack and Donna made love on autopilot. Jack was exhausted and Donna's mind was elsewhere.

Afterwards, just as they were drifting off to sleep, she asked, 'Do you think we'll ever get to live in a house like that, Jack?'

'What's wrong with this place?' he mumbled.

'Come on, Jack. I'd be embarrassed to ask your banker friends over for dinner to *this* place. There isn't even enough space for a decent dining room. And we're about five bedrooms short . . .'

Jack mulled over her words. Five more bedrooms? In Hampstead? He was certainly well paid, but he didn't earn *that* much! 'Relax, honey. I'll give you everything you ever dreamed of.' He kissed her and rolled over. 'I love you,' he said.

Her usual echo of confirmation remained unspoken, but Jack was too tired to think beyond the silence.

Within moments he was fast asleep.

Jack could not move. Everything was very quiet. There was cold murky water all around. And blood. The shark glided past the small boat. Then it turned, and in slow motion, almost aimlessly, came back again. Its cat-like eyes were blankly expressionless and its open mouth was full of fearsome jagged teeth. Jack tried to scream, but he had no voice. He thought of thrashing the water to frighten off the predatory monster, but his limbs were numb and helpless. The creature's hideous head broke the surface of the water again, and it seemed to grin at him, like the Cheshire Cat, as it swam lazily past, as though it knew it could take him at any time . . .

He woke up with a start, sweating and nauseous, his heart pounding painfully.

He did what he always did, and forced himself to breathe slowly and regularly until his heartbeat calmed. He tried to relax. Would this nightmare continue to haunt him for ever?

On Monday morning, Team 19 of the FSA's Enforcement Division was disbanded. It had been assembled for one case alone. That case was now dead in the water. Arnaud was given a week's leave of absence on full pay, and the remaining team members were reassigned. A memo was sent by secure mail to the Chancellor of the Exchequer confirming the sequence of events that had led to the closure of the Picton file, and the file itself was sent to storage.

When the memo reached the desk of the Chancellor of the Exchequer, it was read in private. Then it was sealed in an envelope and sent by special courier to another government department.

CHAPTER 5

In the weeks that followed, Niccolo spent many nights in the office. By now he had moved out of Jack's house and was renting a pied-à-terre of his own a mile down the road in Hampstead – same postcode, but a cheaper area. On weekends he locked himself in his flat with a pile of broker reports to keep him company. He learned fast. And though there were many questions he needed to ask, he never asked them; he knew he would never receive the answers.

Odile had warned him he would be on his own. 'The City has bred a highly competitive culture amongst stock analysts. It discourages individuals from sharing information,' she said calmly one day as she took a puff of her cigarette at the back entrance of the building.

'You sound like a management consultant,' Niccolo said.

'I was once, but that's not the point.' She exhaled coldly. 'Nobody wants to work in a team.'

'That doesn't make sense.'

'Well, the theory behind it is this.' She paused to light up another Marlboro. 'If you give any more than the minimum necessary help to a fellow analyst – even one in your own team – then you're helping a potential rival reach star analyst status. Star analysts get bigger bonuses. But bonus pools are finite. So by helping a colleague you potentially reduce your own bonus.'

'But that makes the team totally dysfunctional.'

She flicked her cigarette butt on to the street and glanced casually at the diamond-encrusted Jaeger-LeCoultre on her wrist. 'Most analyst teams in the City are,' she snapped.

Investment banking was an altogether different game from journalism, and there were times when Niccolo wondered if he really wanted to play. After all, few had made the move. But Charlie seemed pleased to have a fellow ex-journo around the office.

'We're two of a kind, you and I,' he would say expansively. 'We should stick together.'

One day he suggested lunch. 'Time we had a proper talk,' he said, as he walked with Niccolo in the direction of the Thai Garden. 'The food's OK,' he said as they entered the restaurant. 'The wine's pretty good too. But the waitresses – hell, now we're talking!'

A slim, long-haired girl in a long silk dress with slits all over the place seized their coats. Another showed them to a table, whilst a third took their order. Charlie didn't have to open the menu. Names of exotic dishes flowed effortlessly from his mouth.

'So where were you before you came here?' he asked Niccolo.

'*Financial Telegraph*,' replied Niccolo. 'Business section. And you?'

'Oh, it was a long time ago. Journalism was a respected profession then.'

'So was banking.'

'Can't argue with that, kiddo.' The wine arrived. Charlie tasted it and accepted the bottle. 'I started out with the *Washington Post*. It was just after Nixon was booted out of the White House. There were no PCs back then and I could hardly use a typewriter in those days, but I could read the future like the back of my hand. I could spot the trends in the technology market. I could see the big picture. When Saracen offered me a job as a Wall Street analyst, I jumped at it. Never looked back.'

'Was it easy to make the transition?'

'The thing is, Niccolo, there *is* no transition. A journalist and an analyst – they essentially have the same skill. Both tell a story. Both use the story to sell a product: with journalists it's newspapers; with bankers it's stock. You've got to be able to tell the story with total conviction. If you can do that, you'll go all the way to the top. The trick is finding the right story.'

Niccolo realised that he had much to learn from the older analyst, and judging by the fervent look in Charlie's eyes, it was there for the asking. 'Larry showed me some of your articles,' continued Charlie. 'You write well. And that's why they hired you. It's a rare skill, Niccolo.'

'Thanks. I thought they hired me because I specialise in telecoms.'

'Anyone can write about the telecoms market. They hired you because you write from the heart. When people read your work they believe in it, because they know *you* believe in it. When people read your work they question their own judgement, because they know *you're* questioning yours. You have a talent, my friend. Banks need that talent. Look, in our business we have to make markets. That means telling our clients to buy when we want them to buy and sell when we want them to sell. And no client will place an order for ten million Ultrafone shares unless you give them a damn good story to persuade them.'

A waitress appeared, filled their glasses with iced water, then disappeared. Charlie leaned forward. 'You've got to look at these companies differently from the way everyone else looks at them.

Find a fresh angle. When you look at a company, what do you see?'

'Well, I . . . er . . .'

'When I look at a company, I see a woman. Doesn't matter whether she's sexy or a real dog, my job is to find out what's under her clothes. Am I making sense?'

Niccolo chuckled. This he could understand.

'One more thing, kiddo. A big bank means big politics. I take it you've figured out by now who you need to keep happy?'

Niccolo hesitated. 'I think so,' he replied, unconvincingly.

'OK. First there's Odile.' Charlie paused just long enough to whet Niccolo's appetite. 'You like Odile?'

Niccolo smiled.

'I'm not surprised. Just about everyone does. She's got more curves than the Monte Carlo rally and she knows how to use them. And you fancy her, right?'

'Right.'

'Wrong, motherfucker! And wipe that little smirk off your face. Fancy anyone else, but don't fancy your saleswoman. When you come to work in the morning, you need to make sure the right bit of you is doing the talking and everything else is zipped up. Pocket Venus she may be, but Odile doesn't want your dick – she wants your wallet. And you can't afford her, so clear any dirty muck out of your head. You need to keep her happy – but only at a work level.'

'But she's just a saleswoman.' Niccolo leaned forward. 'All she does is dial and smile. What do I—?'

Charlie cut Niccolo off. 'Jesus, motherfucker, do I have to start from the beginning?' He pulled his chair forward and placed his hands on the tablecloth. 'She's not just any saleswoman. She's the best fucking saleswoman in town. She's the flavour of the month, the floozy with the Uzi, the bunny with the honey. Get the picture?'

42

'She looks more like the bunny with the money to me.'

'She makes more money for the bank than you or I will ever make. She can sell anything. She will make you or break you. Do you understand?'

Niccolo nodded.

'Now let's talk about you. Have you come up with any bright investment ideas lately, or have you just been lounging about doing fuck-all like that deadbeat excuse for a boss you allegedly work for?'

'Rupert?'

'You can call him Rupert. I prefer to call him deeplyunimpressive.com,' sneered Charlie. 'That loser has about as much talent as the Spice Girls. He lives in some godforsaken village in the middle of Surrey, for Christ's sake, full of inbred halfwits. Life down there is a hot tub of sexual frustration and missed opportunities.' Charlie paused to reflect. 'However, he's close to Larry. They travel in on the same train. They get on like a house on fire – invite each other round at Christmas, schmooze at the same tennis club, share babysitters, swap wives – you know, the whole country thing. So you need to handle him with care.'

After a few minutes the conversation moved on to Larry. 'Well, Larry Sikorski's a law unto himself,' offered Charlie. 'You've got to admire him. I mean, he's got a brain the size of a planet, he's worth millions, he drives a Porsche, he's hung like a sperm whale and he's better looking than De Niro.'

'So you're jealous?'

'I'm always jealous!'

'And what's he like to work for?'

'Oh, he's a prick . . .' Charlie leaned back and tucked his napkin into his shirt. '. . . but he's smart. His mind's got more moving parts than a Patek Philippe. You can learn from him, son.'

Niccolo shifted forward. 'I hope you don't mind if I use you as a sounding board from time to time, Charlie. Sometimes Rupert's team can be awfully cold.'

Charlie flashed a smile. It was a genuine smile – warm, wholesome, trustworthy. 'That's what I'm here for, my friend. I've got loads to teach you, kid.' At that moment the food arrived. 'But right now, I'm hungry.' They toasted to good health and grabbed their chopsticks.

Gradually, by piecing together snippets of information, Niccolo was able to build up a picture of Charlie's life. From a humble beginning, he had climbed the corporate ladder and reached its upper echelons with nothing to help him but sheer hard work and raw determination. His Irish-American father had left school at sixteen to work in Pittsburgh's steel industry. In time, Danny Doyle climbed the ranks to become chief welder, only to be thrown out some months later for thuggery, thievery and drunkenness. Despite this, every afternoon he would join his former co-workers for a beer after their shift had ended. It never occurred to him to leave the town in search of work. Worse, he had a weakness for the horses, and squandered what little money there was on 'sure things' that somehow never won. So he resorted to petty burglary to pay for his drinking and horse-racing, and sent his wife out to make enough money to feed their son.

Charlie's mother brought him up with strong principles. The Catholic Church played a large part in her life and she spent every minute of every day drumming a traditional set of values into her son. Charlie never forgot what she taught him. He knew right from wrong because wrong smelt of whisky and wrong hit him until he cried and wrong ended up in jail. His mother was happiest when wrong was not in the house. But, strangely, Charlie loved his father dearly, and always longed for his attention. By the time his mother had died of lung cancer and teams of lawyers and accountants had eventually sealed the fate of the steel mill, Charlie's father was a lonely, broken man. By then Charlie had long since left home to start work as the lowest form of human life – a journalist at the *Washington Post*. After a couple of big scoops, he had made a name for himself in the business pages. It was not long before he was poached by Saracen Laing. As a young stock analyst on Wall Street, his cunning and intelligence soon won him a series of promotions. 'Hey, those investment banker guys, they're nothing but thieves,' Danny Doyle would sneer with contempt, blind to the irony of what he – a convicted felon – was saying. 'What they do is, they use fancy jargon and broken promises to make their ill-gotten profits look good. And what does the government do? Turns a blind eye!'

For years, Charlie scarcely saw his father, though he dutifully remitted a decent allowance to the old man every month. The sort of wealth that could take generations to accumulate, Charlie had acquired in a matter of years. Yet it was as though the old man disdained his son's financial success. And the more money Charlie made, the more viciously his father spurned him, and the deeper the void in Charlie's heart became. When the opportunity came for him to move to London, he didn't hesitate.

Yet even when he was labouring under the financial strain of three failed marriages and two lots of children, Charlie still sent a generous monthly remittance to Pittsburgh. And still he never heard a word of thanks.

Often Charlie would cast his mind back to his days as a journalist, the days when he searched for truth, for knowledge, for a sense of right and wrong, for the things his mother had taught him to value as a child. Yet truth alone did not pay four lots of private-school fees, and right and wrong no longer existed in the world in which he worked. Over the years the void at his heart was partially filled by his voracious appetite for knowledge. His public image –

of a highly successful and outspoken analyst – was merely a façade behind which lay his greatest gift: his ability to pass on his knowledge in the most tactful and unobtrusive fashion to others who had a similar thirst for it.

When Jack arrived home it was late and he was exhausted. Donna was listening to the radio, sipping a half-finished glass of red wine in front of a warm fire. 'Your dinner's in the oven. I've eaten,' she said bluntly.

Jack emptied the dried-out pasta on to a plate, scraping out every last morsel, and poured a glass of wine. He sat down on the sofa at a safe distance from Donna and wrestled a forkful of pasta from the caked mess. 'This is fantastic, honey,' he grovelled.

Donna remained silent for a few moments. When she finally spoke, she asked, 'Are they treating you OK at work?'

Jack seldom told his wife what went on at work and she seldom asked. 'I'm sick of the place,' he shot back. 'I'm constantly having to watch my back. And now I'll have to watch Nicco's as well. They're all a bunch of arrogant motherfuckers!'

'But so are you, sweetheart,' whispered Donna teasingly. She stretched her legs. 'What's the difference between you and them?'

'I'm confident,' he said firmly. 'They're arrogant. Those guys would sell their mother at the right price. Me, I've got my principles, and I'll stand by them.'

She laughed. 'Will your principles buy us a bigger house? I'd rather you just sold your mother.'

He tossed a half-eaten plate onto the coffee table. 'Donna, I don't know how long I can stand it,' he said, burying his head in his arms. 'I don't know who to trust.'

Donna had become accustomed to Jack's complaints and knew exactly what to do. She caressed his soft wavy hair, then led him to bed and put him down to sleep like a little child.

CHAPTER 6

Niccolo arrived late for work. A few analysts lifted their heads from their paperwork and glanced at their watches disapprovingly. It was four minutes past seven. Rupert failed to acknowledge his junior analyst's arrival. His eyes were firmly glued to his Reuters screen. News stories about Telecom10 were pouring on to the screens faster than the human eye could read them.

'You're late,' snapped the Head of Telecoms. 'T10's just reported its first quarter profit figures. James has put a copy on your desk. I want you to go through them and comment at this morning's meeting. Run it by me first.' Rupert turned to James and said, 'OK, now he's here, you don't need to speak on T10 this morning.'

James scowled irritably and shot Niccolo a filthy look.

Niccolo checked his watch. The morning meeting was in twenty minutes' time. Before then he had to read the forty-five-page earnings release from Telecom10, summarise the main points in a morning meeting note, update his model, review his Sell recommendation and get everything approved by Rupert.

He loosened his tie and unbuttoned his collar. Odile had already got him a latte. She often arrived before the telecoms team because she drove into the City from Notting Hill in her Aston

Martin DB9. Traffic was far lighter at 5.30 than at 6.30. She was addicted to coffee and had got into the habit of getting one for Niccolo in the mornings. He raised his hand to thank her before sipping it. It tasted especially good that morning.

The earnings release contained a lot of crap. Niccolo scanned it for relevant crap and made some notes. At 7.18 he passed a draft to Rupert, who took a few minutes to run his eye over it. 'Are you changing your stock recommendation?' he asked.

'No, sticking to Sell.'

'Fine,' said Rupert, busily drafting a note of his own.

'It's already seven twenty-two, Ru,' cried James. 'We're late.'

'Let's go!'

Morning meetings in the Oval Room usually lasted around fifteen minutes. Their purpose was to generate investment ideas for the bank's clients. Larry sat at the head of the table. At the other end, Odile was playing noughts and crosses with Patrick O'Shea, the Head of European Equity Sales & Trading. The tall Irishman had his notebook open, an oversized Montblanc poised for action. Huddled around the table were many of the bank's research analysts, traders and equity sales people, the late arrivals having to prop themselves up against the wall.

The equity sales people were, in many ways, the front-line soldiers – the face of Saracen Laing to the outside world. Analysts often generated the investment recommendations, but the sales force had to sell those ideas to clients. And clients had to be persuaded to trade on them. So to sell the ideas, the soldiers needed to understand them. And the morning meeting was their opportunity to hear them first hand from the analysts themselves.

Dudley Rabinowitz, the Chief Compliance Officer, normally opened the meeting and chaired it. Dudley's job was to monitor what was said and to ensure it was fit for client consumption. The meeting was recorded and broadcast live on the bank's website so that traders and salesmen in the bank's overseas offices could listen in too.

Dudley Rabinowitz liked his puddings, and his tailor liked his ever-expanding waistline. The girls in the typing pool found him cute, cuddly and lovable. Affectionately known as 'Dud' or 'Cuddles' on the trading floor, he was a father figure to most of the younger traders and an object of ridicule for the older ones. Receiving a nickname from the traders was a badge of honour, and Cuddly Dudley wore his with pride.

Once Saracen's Chief Economist had finished his rundown of world affairs, Dudley stepped up to the microphone. 'Today we've got three analysts speaking – Charlie on Celltalk, Rupert on Ultrafone and Niccolo on Telecom10.'

Each analyst had a slot of three minutes. One by one they stood up proudly in front of the microphone and did their business. When Niccolo's turn came, he got a wink and a pat on the shoulder from Rupert, who handed over the hot spot to him. He cleared his throat and grasped the microphone firmly.

'Good morning. This is Nicco Lamparelli on Telecom10. The company released its first quarter numbers this morning. The top line was far better than the market expected, but their losses have widened. Telecom10's debt is ultra-high risk, one notch away from junk. I believe S&P or Fitch might downgrade it today. I reiterate my Sell rating.'

'Right, folks,' said Dudley. 'Meeting over. Get back to work!'

An ordinary black London cab pulled up outside the entrance to the Moneypincher's Inn. A suit climbed out and walked briskly up the steps. The maître d' opened a leather-bound reservations book. 'I believe your guest is waiting at your table, sir. Follow me, please.'

The suit from Saracen followed the maître d' into a private dining room. The wall panels were mahogany and the cutlery nineteenth-century silver. An old, dusty chandelier hung from the ceiling and the oak floors creaked.

'Good to see you, Ken,' said the suit from Saracen.

'Likewise,' replied the second suit. 'Glad you found the time to see me. I know you have a busy schedule.' They shook hands and sat down. 'The telecoms market is too volatile right now. We may have to wait a long time before we pull this deal off.'

'That's not a problem. No one's in a hurry.'

'Stay tuned. As soon as market conditions are right, we will need to act fast – bloody fast. There will be no room for fuck-ups. Your boys will have to play ball – almost on cue. That could be tricky for you if there are any troublemakers on your team.'

'There are no troublemakers on my team.'

'How can you be sure?'

'I run the department. Nothing leaves the building unless it has my stamp on it.'

'What if some holier-than-thou hotshot analyst with his principles up his ass and more integrity than he knows what to do with insists on doing things his own way?'

'People like that are figments of our imagination. They don't exist. You see them only in the movies. In real life, things are simpler. There is far too much at stake. I can ruin a man's career with a single phone call. I hire hungry analysts. I hire guys with families to support, expensive wives to maintain, kids at private school and shit like that. If they're single, I make sure they're poor and ambitious. Then I give them a taste of the good life. Once they're on board, they won't rock the boat – too much to lose. I've never had a problem with loose cannons – not on my watch.'

'So long as you're sure there won't be a problem on your side.'

'I'm sure.'

'I guess we can do business, then.'

'Excellent. Shall we order?' The suit from Saracen opened an à la carte menu and scanned the entrées. 'You should try the Dover sole here. It's the best.'

Between 2002 and the summer of 2006, the oil price had risen almost in a straight line from twenty dollars per barrel to seventy-five. The impact on the balance of the world's wealth was just as mind-boggling. Truckloads of US dollars, euros, yen, rupees and yuan entered the world's oil-producing nations, transformed overnight into petrodollars. The rising oil price turned rich Arabs into filthy-rich Arabs, many of whom had more money than they knew what to do with. The growth in petrodollars led to a surge in hot money entering the City. Anti-American sentiment worked in London's favour. Someone somewhere was certain to profit by finding a home for this money.

Prince Mubarak bin Majid Al Shahaan was not entirely stupid. He saw the opportunity, had the connections and – having been educated at Eton – spoke the right languages. By early 2003, the Prince had formed a syndicate of investors, many of whom were the sons of rich oil sheikhs. Whilst their fathers were busy winding up their empires, they were just getting started with theirs. The Prince quickly convinced a number of them to pool their wealth, invest it in the world's capital markets under his direction, then lie back and watch their net worth multiply.

On the day of the 9/11 terrorist attacks on New York, the Prince was heavily short of the Dow Jones Industrial 30, a stock market index that tracked the share prices of the thirty largest companies in the United States. Sure enough, in the week that followed the attack, the Dow fell off a cliff. The Prince was rumoured to have made almost half a billion dollars in a single week. His family and friends were dazzled by his financial brilliance, and were now

51

falling over themselves to secure a place in his new investment syndicate.

Yet what some saw as wisdom, others from further away saw as inside information. And they were particularly interested in the point at which inside information crossed with terrorist activity. Though the Prince's finances were kept deliberately opaque, the British and American authorities communicated their suspicions to their political masters, and rumours spread freely beyond that. Yet apart from a small group of political sabre-rattlers, the world's great and good turned a blind eye. Nothing was done for lack of credible evidence. The Prince kept a low profile for a few years after the attacks, confining himself to Gulf countries and even forgoing his annual summer visit to Harrods for fear of a diplomatic reprisal.

As time went by, international law-enforcement agencies, keenly aware of a distinct lack of political will on both sides of the Atlantic to see the matter through to its logical conclusion, gradually gave up all hope of any kind of successful prosecution. A diligent Interpol agent by the name of Arnaud Veyrieras, however, had other plans. Arnaud Veyrieras was certain that Dr Picton was involved.

CHAPTER 7

He caught a glimpse of her from the corner of his eye, but carried on working. Kloomberg, of course, had several saleswomen working on the Saracen account, but Lucy Grey was *the* saleswoman. And she was headed straight for Niccolo's desk with a determined look in her eye.

Most of the City's investment banks had begun to cut their expenditure on non-essential services. But Kloomberg's contract to provide Saracen with market data 24/7 was worth seventeen million dollars. When sales were down or a contract was up for renewal, Kloomberg sent in their top troubleshooter. Lucy always delivered the goods. She was every man's dream, and she used the oldest trick in the book – her body. The trading floor was ninety per cent male, with a generous dose of testosterone, and Lucy's sexy ripeness simply made most men want to triple their IT budgets overnight.

Someone once ascribed her success to her approach being 'bottom-up rather than top-down', to which Charlie inevitably rejoined, 'Well, she can approach me with her bottom up and her top down any time she likes!' In practice it meant that, rather than discussing the contract with Antonio Sanchez, the bank's Head of

IT, she would work the trading floor, persuading each analyst and trader individually that their Kloomberg terminal was indispensable. Front-office staff generated revenues, so if push came to shove, their views carried more weight with management. And her charms had no effect anyway on Antonio, who was gay.

As she approached Niccolo's desk, his pulse cranked up a few notches.

'Sir, you didn't return my call,' she said in a theatrically husky voice, which made Niccolo blush.

'Er . . . hi, Lucy,' he stumbled. 'I've been pretty busy.'

'I get upset when my clients don't return my calls.'

Niccolo crossed his legs underneath his desk. 'You're absolutely right, Lucy. I won't do it again.'

'Good,' she whispered. 'Because I may have to give you a spanking if you're naughty again . . . sir.'

A few heads jerked up. Rupert tuned in. Lucy leaned forward. 'Mr Lamparelli, your manager tells me you need some training in how to use our service.'

'Lucy,' pleaded Niccolo. 'Can we talk later? I'm pretty busy.'

She blinked in slow motion. 'But at Kloomberg we work 24/7. I could conduct a training session with you tonight, perhaps over dinner?'

'Tonight's going to be tough. Are you free tomorrow?'

'Let me check my diary . . . sir.' She reached down for her handbag, allowing Niccolo to catch a glimpse of her breasts. She pulled out a little red book and turned the pages. 'Tomorrow is great.'

She blew him a kiss and departed from the trading floor with the swagger of a model on a catwalk. Once she was out of sight, a crowd of analysts hurriedly gathered around Niccolo's desk.

'Hey, Nicco, I can't believe she asked you out for dinner!' Jack marvelled.

'And you said no! Silly fucker!' was Charlie's contribution.

'Fuck off, guys.'

'She never offers *me* personal training sessions,' one of the other traders complained. 'Why's that?'

'Well,' said Charlie pensively, gearing up for a withering put-down, 'you've got no money, no talent – and you look like a horse's ass.' He turned to Niccolo. 'And you – you'd better be careful, young man. That woman is hotandhorny.com and she's coming straight for you. So you just make damned sure that you've got an exit route – you might need it.'

Later that week, Rupert decided it was time to get Niccolo involved in his first deal. 'I've got a meeting with the Mergers and Acquisitions boys. Want to come, Nicco?'

'Sure.'

'It's going to be you, me, Mortimer and JC.'

'Fine.'

Mortimer Steel was the notional Head of Mergers & Acquisitions – sometimes referred to as the Corporate Finance Unit – part of Saracen's Investment Banking Division. The son of a high-profile British property magnate, he could count the Prince of Wales, President Bush, Richard Branson and Madonna among his close friends. Mortimer went to Harrow, achieved a degree in Land Economy at Cambridge, and married the daughter of Jim Kuzinsky, President of Saracen Laing Bank, which gave him one of the best CVs in the business. Unfortunately for the M&A Unit, his thoroughbred education – whilst undoubtedly impressive on paper – bore little resemblance to reality. Mortimer was as thick as two short planks. What he lacked in brains, however, he made up for in friends. They tended to be his father's friends, but the bank was not fussed. Big friends meant big business.

In the seven years that Mortimer had worked for Saracen, Jean-Claude Bouvier had taught him everything he knew about investment banking, but it did the Frenchman little good. Come promotion time, he discovered that he had the wrong nationality to take on the top position in the M&A Unit. He was sidelined and soon found himself working for the well-connected Brit who had once been his trainee.

In normal circumstances Jean-Claude would have walked out in the face of such a blatant insult. He had been a legendary rainmaker in his day, and legends did not come cheap. But these were not normal times, and jobs were hard to come by in the City. JC took the insult on the chin and remained as official number two to Mortimer, though he negotiated himself a pay rise with Mortimer's boss and father-in-law in New York on the grounds that the department would fall apart without him. The high regard in which Head Office held him was amply reflected by the fact that Jean-Claude was given everything he asked for. To the outside world, Jean-Claude Bouvier remained the effective Head of M&A for Saracen Laing.

'The M&A boys like to run every meeting they attend,' sniped Rupert on the way up, 'regardless of whether they've any idea what they're talking about. They see themselves as the elite team.'

'Why?' asked Niccolo. 'Did they pull in an obscene amount in advisory fees last year?'

'No, they made a loss of nine million. They're just damn good at taking the credit for other people's work.'

The meeting had been called to discuss the bank's strategy for winning business from Globecom, a relatively young telecoms company. Its founder and CEO, Kenneth Oakes, had started the company in 1988. Under his leadership it had grown, mainly by acquisition, to become the second largest British telecommunications company after Ultrafone.

Globecom built optical fibre networks all around the world and specialised in being a 'carrier's carrier', which meant that it sold wholesale telecoms services – mainly space on its 'pipes' – to other telecoms operators, who preferred to lease capacity rather than build more pipes themselves. Globecom's strategy was simple – as more and more people and businesses used the internet, the pipes would fill up with voice and data traffic and they would make lots of money. Globecom shares were trading at £4.56 a piece, so the company was already worth £129 billion. That made it one of the biggest stocks in European telecoms.

For Rupert, that meant that he needed to cover the stock himself. He rarely gave the high-profile stocks to anyone else. Jean-Claude had tried for several years to bring in the Globecom account; for him, Globecom was a 'must have' client. As part of his efforts he submitted embarrassingly large expense returns, having lunched with senior Globecom executives on a monthly basis in an effort to win new business. The Globecom executives were tired of hearing the proposals, but enjoyed the lunches.

'Zey loved the deal I proposed,' Jean-Claude would claim in his heavy French accent when the suits in New York dared to question the outrageous sums. 'It's just the timing – zis was a bad quarter for them.'

This time Jean-Claude wanted to discuss with Rupert yet another of his hare-brained schemes to get Globecom to part with their cash. Unfortunately, he faced a major problem: mergers and acquisitions were out of fashion. It was difficult to pull them off in an overpriced market. Any banker who struck a deal – any deal – would be viewed within the bank as a hero. That made Rupert highly suspicious of Jean-Claude's motives.

'I hope he's not going to waste my time with one of his crazy ideas,' he said as the elevator doors opened.

The moment they stepped into the meeting room, they got down to business.

'Rupert, we need your help,' said Jean-Claude. 'We 'ave a deal. It's a dead cert. We'd like to make a proposal to Globecom. It's worth twenty-five billion dollars.'

'My people are already overworked.'

'Our fees would be well over two hundred million.'

'You guys have called quite a few false starts lately,' said Rupert drily. 'I don't want you sending us on another wild goose chase.'

'Zis deal is different. You'll like it, Ru. Trust me. And it's important to our New York office.'

'Yes, indeed. Very important,' added Mortimer.

There was a silence that lasted a few seconds until Rupert and Niccolo realised that Mortimer had in fact nothing more to add.

'So, what is this deal?' asked Rupert, filling the vacuum.

'Frankfurter Telekom has some cable assets for sale. They're worth five billion euros. FreeMedia has already bid for them, but the deal faces regulatory problems. I think Globecom should submit a bid.'

Rupert thought about the proposal. It had some commercial logic. Frankfurter Telekom was heavily in debt and needed cash. Globecom could put a German cable network to good use.

'What's the time frame?'

'Well,' began Jean-Claude, distributing copies of a pre-prepared timetable. 'Working backwards, I estimate the whole deal to conclude by December this year – at the latest. That gives us three months to help Globecom raise the cash. I've already lined up Paddy to brief the sales team and get our clients interested in taking a share of the pie on this one.'

'So you need Niccolo to work with you for three months?' asked Rupert.

'It'll only be part time, of course. And it depends if we get awarded ze deal. But hey, I don't lose deals.'

Niccolo and Rupert looked at each other, their faces remaining politely blank. Jean-Claude's flair for deal-making was fading fast. With nothing significant in the pipeline for over a year, he no longer had the Midas touch.

'How do you rate our odds, JC?'

'I think we have a fifty-fifty chance of being made lead adviser and a seventy-five per cent chance of being made co-adviser – maybe with Deutsche Bank.'

Rupert turned to Niccolo, pondering the stakes. He knew that this was one of the few avenues open to the bank to make a size-able advisory fee. He did not want to be known as the asshole who screwed up the deal.

'It's not worth our while to go for co-adviser. We'd need sole mandate.'

'A sole mandate, as we say in France, is like a beautiful woman,' said the Frenchman. 'Everyone wants her, but not everyone can have her.'

Nobody laughed.

'OK,' yielded Rupert. 'I'll give you Nicco for as long as you need him. But you'd better get the mandate!'

'*Mais bien sûr*,' confirmed Jean-Claude smugly. '*C'est certain.*'

'I have a few contacts in Globecom,' said Mortimer, justifying his presence for once. 'Perhaps I could test the waters, bounce a few ideas off some of my sources . . .'

All eyes turned to him. Perhaps this guy was worth the salary they paid him, after all. 'Who do you know, Morty?' asked Rupert.

'Well, John Roderick and I go back a long way.'

'You mean the Finance Director?'

'Yeah, yeah, of course. We're very close.'

'I thought their Finance Director was called *James* Roderick.'

'Yeah, that's the one. That's the guy.'

Niccolo looked at Rupert. Rupert looked at Jean-Claude. Jean-Claude looked at the ceiling. Mortimer wondered what all the fuss was about.

'OK,' concluded Jean-Claude. 'I think we're done.' He turned to Niccolo and smiled as they shook hands. It was a hard hand-shake. Neither man could afford to show any sign of weakness.

'Welcome aboard, Nicco. I've heard a lot of good things about you. They'd better be true or I'll fire you on the spot!'

Niccolo joined the others in an obligatory round of forced laughter and replied, 'It's a pleasure to be working with you, Jean-Claude.'

'That son of a bitch is full of shit!' Rupert swore on the way down to the trading floor. 'The bastard hasn't brought in a single deal for at least a year. He keeps wasting my fucking time. In the last six months alone he's used half the Equity Research Department to fund his dead-end projects.'

'So why couldn't we just say no?' asked Niccolo.

'Because *he* earns the fees; *we* don't.'

'What's our cut?'

'That's the problem,' said Rupert. 'JC's unit keeps a hundred per cent of the fees, even though they use our expertise to execute the deal. We get to pick up the crumbs.'

'We could charge him for our services.'

'It doesn't work like that, Nicco. Our bonuses depend on the number of deals that we help bring in. The problem is, nobody keeps track. So we rely on Mortimer's goodwill to fund our bonus pool. If we don't help him bid for mandates, we get no bonus.'

'It's a good thing you've got a Buy rating on Globecom, boss!'

'You wouldn't win that sort of corporate mandate without it,'

Rupert said, as if explaining something to a very stupid child. 'After all, why would Globecom appoint as advisers an investment bank that told its clients to sell Globecom stock?'

'Can I see the black one, please?' asked Donna, politely pointing to the uppermost shelf of the display cabinet.

The Louis Vuitton sales assistant pulled up a wooden stepladder, and climbed two rungs to fetch down an exquisite hand-made leather handbag. She carefully removed the tissue paper from inside, and offered the bag enticingly to her customer. Donna slung it over her shoulder, twirled around and admired herself in the mirror for a few minutes. Then she took a casual walk around the boutique. 'It feels nice,' she said.

'It suits you, madam,' the sales assistant agreed approvingly.

Donna walked up to the counter and placed the leather handbag next to a full-length Vuitton raincoat she had tried on earlier. 'I'll take them both,' she announced.

The assistant checked the price tags and scanned the barcodes. 'That will be £3,248.98, madam. How would you like to pay?'

Donna flashed a Visa card at the woman.

'Thank you, madam.' The sales assistant swiped the plastic, then directed Donna to enter her security code into a touch-screen keypad.

Donna examined the handbag, admiring its soft curves and near-seamless stitching. As she did so, an electronic message arrived on the touch screen. The sales assistant read it with a bewildered frown. 'I'm terribly sorry, madam. There seems to be a problem with your account.'

'Really?' enquired Donna calmly.

'Yes, madam. I believe your card has been rejected. Would you like to try another card?'

'This is ridiculous,' Donna snapped dismissively.

She grabbed her bag, rummaged inside for her mobile phone and hurriedly dialled Jack's direct line at the office. As she waited, counting the rings under her breath, she realised she had exceeded her £10,000 monthly limit. The call finally connected. 'Oh Jack, darling,' she burbled frantically. 'I'm in Louis Vuitton, New Bond Street. My Visa card doesn't work . . . I feel so embarrassed . . . I don't know what to do . . .!'

'Donna, Jack's gone to the gym,' said the voice at the other end of the line. Startled, Donna dropped the phone. When she picked it up again, the voice said, 'Hi, Donna. This is Larry Sikorski.'

'Oh my God! Larry, I thought it was—'

'I know. Jack's gone to the gym. His calls normally get diverted to Anne-Marie, but she doesn't seem to be around either, so you got me.'

'Larry, I'm so sorry – I didn't mean to disturb you.'

'Donna, my dear girl, don't apologise. It's a pleasure to hear from you. I was hoping to have the good fortune to meet you again after our brief encounter the other day.'

'You were a brilliant host, Larry. And I absolutely adored your home.'

'Now listen, Donna, what on earth are you doing with a Visa card? The bank provides an Amex to all staff – platinum, of course – and it can be extended to include spouses.'

'I do have an Amex card, Larry,' replied Donna curtly. 'It's just that I left it at home today.'

'Listen, I have an idea. Why don't you let me settle this bill for you right now, and we can sort out the details later?'

'You can't do that, Larry. Jack would blow his—'

'Jack doesn't need to know,' Larry cut in smoothly. 'Anyway, a beautiful lady like you deserves the best. Please allow me to be of service, just this once. It would be an honour – in fact, I would consider it a personal insult if you refused.' Donna's body quivered in anticipation. She paused to consider her response, but Larry continued. 'There's only one condition – you have lunch with me.'

'Larry—'

'It's settled. Let me speak to the shop assistant and I'll call you later about lunch. Is that a deal?'

Donna's brain almost shut down as ripples of anxiety and excitement shot through her. 'Thank you, Larry,' she said finally. 'I'll be eternally grateful.'

'The pleasure is all mine, Donna.'

Donna passed the handset to the sales assistant, who completed the transaction using a platinum American Express card registered in the name of Larry S. Sikorski.

'I'm not Superman,' groaned Niccolo. The sauna was excessively hot that day, but they had it to themselves. Jack nodded in sympathy and wiped the sweat from his brow.

'It's bad enough just working for Rupert. Now I've got two bosses to report to!'

'What's JC got you working on?'

'I'm drafting a proposal for his team to present to Globecom.'

'Is it a big deal?'

'It's a highly dubious deal.'

'Don't you think he can pull it off?'

'JC says he can pull off *any deal in ze world*. What he actually means is that everyone except him will be working their nuts off around the clock, making him look good. He's only great at lunching and covering his ass.'

Jack laughed and poured some more water over the coals. 'Listen, he has a bit of a reputation. When the ship goes down, he's normally the only one wearing a life jacket. You better be careful, Nicco. JC's good at taking credit for the successful deals and shifting the blame for the dud ones.'

'I know – I can't afford to fuck up my first M&A deal.'

'You look exhausted. Are you getting enough sleep?'

'Not really. None of JC's boys go home before nine o'clock. And that's when there's nothing on! Right now they're working till midnight!'

'Twats!'

'It would be OK if they were productive, but they're not. During the day they drink coffee, take long lunches and read the paper. Then at five p.m. they start work.'

'That bunch of clowns couldn't string a sentence together between them, let alone put together an investment proposal. They're bullshitters.'

'Yeah, but they're the most accomplished bullshitters I've ever seen. I'm just waiting till the deal's done. Then I'll kick JC's little Froggie ass all over the place.'

CHAPTER 8

The role of a compliance officer is to negotiate the labyrinth of rules and regulations laid down by the Financial Services Authority, some of which are so complex that the FSA itself has no idea what they mean. The FSA's primary objective is to protect ordinary investors from unscrupulous and inappropriate behaviour by banks and other financial institutions. And a bank's reputation and standing is dependent to a large extent on playing by the FSA's rules. In the event that a bank ever breaches the rule book, whether by accident or design, all fingers point to the Compliance Department. So it is up to them to foresee all possible risks, and prevent them. In theory, this gives the Chief Compliance Officer enormous power and, by association, enormous respect.

But Dudley Rabinowitz was of a different breed. He had more important things to worry about than the odd rule breach. If a major compliance issue arose on a Friday evening, it was no good expecting Dudley to deal with it – he had to observe the Sabbath. If Dudley was not home by dusk, his mother would call the bank to find out why.

Dudley was fifty-two years old, single and an unrepentant gambler. He would trade all kinds of stocks every day, but his pet favourite was a small alternative energy company called DBK. Nobody, including Dudley, could remember what the abbreviation stood for. Such information was provided in shareholder accounts, which few investors in start-up companies ever took seriously. In fact, the initials were short for Deutsche Brennstoffzelle Kompressor, though it was habitually referred to behind his back as Dudley's Bloody Kompany. DBK was run by Dudley's uncle Joshua Rabinowitz, who had spent a lifetime making gas turbines in East Germany. When the Wall came down in 1989, so did Joshua Rabinowitz's inhibitions. He became a serial inventor.

DBK made electrolysers and fuel cells for cars. Fuel-cell technology had been around since 1839, but had never really taken off because of cost. Dudley was certain that DBK had all the answers, that it would solve the world's energy problems at a stroke. Whenever the oil price spiked, he never failed to remind people how important it was to hold alternative energy stocks like DBK in one's portfolio. And enough punters felt the same way to turn DBK into a billion-pound company.

With petrol prices soaring, DBK – the alternative to petrol, Dudley would say – simply went from strength to strength. Dudley planned on retiring on his investment, and spent more time looking at DBK's share price than he did doing his day job. Soon, DBK began to take over his life. He cleared out most of the FSA manuals, which were taking up valuable space on his office bookshelf, and replaced them with books on alternative energy. Wind turbines, solar panels and tidal-wave machines gradually invaded his life: his walls were plastered with engineers' drawings of fuel-cell prototypes, and his computer screensaver displayed the Toyota Prius. Dudley Rabinowitz was, without a shadow of a doubt, slightly mad. Yet no one ever dared to suggest that the bank's Compliance Department was headed up by a lunatic.

To say that Dudley was obsessed with DBK's fortunes would

be doing him a grave injustice – he had dedicated his life to the subject. As Saracen Laing's Chief Compliance Officer, it was entirely inappropriate for him to provide any kind of investment advice to either colleagues or clients. But over the years he had informally tipped the stock to countless clients and duped scores of colleagues into investing vast chunks of their personal wealth in DBK shares. Professional fund managers wouldn't touch it because it failed every investment test in the book: useless management, lack of transparency, unproven technology and limited political connections at board level. Most importantly, it had no revenues – let alone profits – with scant prospect of any in the future.

Dudley's real aim, of course, was to ramp up the DBK share price. However, his preoccupation with the company carried the risk of clouding his overall judgement on other matters.

Larry rose to his feet as Donna approached the table. 'I'm so glad you could make it,' he said. He planted a kiss on her cheek and offered her a seat. Quo Vadis was always busy at lunchtime, but Larry had managed to secure a corner table.

'I've been looking forward to it all week,' said Donna.

A waiter arrived with menus and a wine list. Larry suggested that he order for both of them, and Donna agreed. Larry selected the best from the menu and pored over the wine list, finally settling for a bottle of Sancerre.

'Larry,' began Donna apologetically, 'I must ask you for a small favour.'

'Anything.'

'I haven't yet told Jack about your wonderful gesture the other day. He can be quite old-fashioned when it comes to accepting outside help. I was hoping you could give me a few weeks to pay you back.'

Larry laughed. 'It'll cost you.'

'Pardon?' retorted Donna, startled.

'A Russian art exhibition opens at the British Museum in a few weeks' time.' His eyes softly scaled her neck. 'I hate going to see beautiful works of art alone.'

Donna blushed. 'Larry, that's very kind, but I don't think Jack would approve.'

'Jack doesn't need to know. He's never left the office before nine o'clock. I'll have you back home by then.'

'Larry, I—'

'Are you going to disappoint a lonely old man?'

Donna flashed a smile. 'I suppose not.'

By the end of the month, the Saracen proposal was signed, sealed and delivered to Globecom's board. Niccolo had played an integral part in the final team presentation. Now it was a waiting game. The decision could take anywhere from twenty-four hours to two weeks, according to Jean-Claude. But that didn't matter. Finally Niccolo was able to say goodbye to the M&A team and return to his day job as a stock analyst. Now he could relax a bit, perhaps take some time off.

That afternoon he left the office early. On the way home he texted his Kloomberg account manager, informing her of his whereabouts.

CHAPTER 9

'If you have a problem, my friend, Karim can fix it for you,' Mubarak would repeat incessantly. 'I trust him like my own brother.'

Picton had worked with Karim once before, many years ago. He did not trust him, but then Picton did not trust anybody. Karim Rashid was a useful man to have around because his wages – and they were considerable – were paid by Mubarak. More importantly, he operated under full diplomatic status. His day job at the Usmani embassy in London was performed by local staff, leaving him relatively free to run errands for Mubarak.

Karim had received little formal education, but he learned fast and knew how to look after himself. He had joined the Usmani army as a teenager, but within a couple of years he had left to seek fame and fortune as a mercenary, circulating between Lebanon, the West Bank and Gaza. His loyalties switched from time to time to the highest bidder. Mubarak had come across him in Beirut. One evening in 1998, from the safety of his hotel room, he had watched as a fight between two rival militias broke out on the street below. He had seen Karim risk his life to save the Lebanese businessman for whom he worked. By the end of that day, Karim worked for Mubarak.

Since then, Karim had rejected numerous employment offers. He remained unquestioningly loyal to his new master, primarily because Mubarak paid him more money than all the other offers he had received combined.

'I'd like you to do something for me, Karim,' said Picton.

Karim straightened almost imperceptibly, and gazed intently at the Doctor, saying nothing. Picton went on, 'I want you to find out everything you can about Niccolo Lamparelli.' He showed Karim a photograph. 'Find out who his friends are, where he has worked, what makes him tick. Find out what sort of person he is.'

Karim nodded and remained standing near the door of the office above the Moneypincher's Inn, as Picton paced up and down the room, deep in thought. Finally the Doctor said, 'And find out who he's fucking, will you?'

The walk from Hampstead Underground station normally took Lucy fifteen minutes. She had made the journey several times over the last fortnight and had grown to like the leafy residential north London village with its quaint little high street and anti-quated buildings. She turned into a steep cobbled street, fumbling in her bag for the set of keys Niccolo had given her. She could no longer resist the urge to pull out her mobile phone and read the text message one more time – **Off early today c u at my place hurry!**

The house was built of weathered red brick partly covered by ivy. Lucy let herself in and sprinted up to the top-floor maisonette.

A trail of clothes and the sound of running water led her to the en suite bathroom. The door had been left slightly ajar, and Niccolo was standing in the shower with his back to her. Around his neck was a solid silver chain, which he never took off, and to which was attached a shark's tooth. Through the glass shower-screen her gaze rested on his bottom, taut as a gymnast's. His tanned skin glistened wetly, flawless but for the ragged series of scars on his right thigh. She had asked him about them a few times, and about the shark's tooth, but all he said was, 'One day, maybe.' Piqued that he wouldn't tell her, she was determined to find out.

She hastily shed her clothes, slid the glass screen open and wriggled into the shower with him. 'My boss is away today,' he said softly. 'I thought I'd take the afternoon off.'

'Me too,' she whispered, kissing him under the jet of water. 'So what shall we do with our afternoon . . .?'

Later, snuggled up in bed, wrapped tightly in Niccolo's arms, she enquired flirtatiously, 'So, Mr Niccolo, as a valued Kloomberg customer, may I ask whether you are fully satisfied with our service?'

He hesitated for a moment. 'To be honest, there's room for improvement.'

'*What?*'

'Definitely,' he went on, nuzzling her neck. 'You need practice. *Lots* of practice . . .'

Early the next morning, Picton logged into his bank to check for incoming funds transfers. Across a number of offshore accounts, nine large credits had appeared, a total of $426,334,912. He smiled. That was enough for starters, he thought.

He shut down the computer, and went downstairs to pour himself a cup of strong coffee in the restaurant kitchen.

Two weeks later, an email brought good news. Noting that Rupert's name was not on the CC list, Niccolo forwarded it to him.

Jean-Claude Bouvier had written:

Well done, guys. Congratulations are in order. I've just
come off the phone with Kenneth Oakes at Globecom.
Our proposal has his support and he is ready to
recommend it to his board.

He says that our credentials (in terms of our research)
are exceptional. We should get confirmation in the next
day or so. Thanks to all who helped in getting us involved
in the deal.

The hours of effort that Niccolo had put in to ensure the deal's
success had paid off. It was going to be a real revenue-spinner.
More importantly, he was likely to get noticed by John Sukuhara,
Head of Investment Banking in Europe, the most senior Saracen
Laing banker outside New York.

But the look on Rupert's face as he opened the email told a different story. He was furious that he had not been included in
Jean-Claude's original list of recipients. Jean-Claude later apologised personally to him for the omission, laughing it off as a
careless oversight by his executive assistant. But in a year when
M&A deals of this magnitude were likely to be few, it could have
been a costly omission for Rupert. Bonuses depended heavily on
fees emanating from such transactions. The Head of Telecoms
had no interest in developing other people's careers – there was
only room for one star per team when bonus time came round.

Now Niccolo had profited – albeit inadvertently – at Rupert's
expense, and Rupert did not like it one bit.

The first time Niccolo met John Sukuhara, he was struck by his
candour. There was nothing Japanese about the Head of
Investment Banking, Europe, apart from his looks and his name.
Sukuhara was a complex character. At times he could be reserved
and introverted; other times he came across as a hard-assed

Harvard-educated banker, who swore a lot and thought he was God. Some said he favoured sycophantic ass-lickers, but amongst others he had a reputation for being approachable, especially to those who made the effort to get to know him. The Globecom email gave Niccolo the perfect excuse.

The only obstacle was Sukuhara's personal assistant, April 'Bulldog' Drummond. April was endowed with neither talent nor looks but made up for that with a temper so ferocious that grown men crumbled before her. Her desk was strategically positioned right outside Sukuhara's office, and she operated a default policy of refusing entry to any person, at any time, for any reason, including genuine emergencies. She was the last filter and her word was final. So it was impossible to orchestrate any kind of unannounced visit to Sukuhara's office.

However, Niccolo had a plan. He stood patiently by the coffee machine around the corner and waited. And waited. And waited. Luck played its part, for soon nature called and Bulldog headed off to the ladies' room. Niccolo headed straight for the door to Sukuhara's office.

'I hope you don't mind my intruding, Mr Sukuhara,' he said. 'I'm Niccolo Lamparelli.'

'Not at all,' said Sukuhara. He offered Niccolo a seat on his plush new leather sofa. 'Call me John. You mind if I smoke?' He placed a huge cigar in his mouth and joined his guest.

Wondering whether anyone had ever dared say they did mind, Niccolo gazed around the holy of holies. Even by the standards of chief executives, Sukuhara's offices were large and lavish, consisting of a study area, a living room with a TV and leather sofa and a bedroom with an en suite shower. On the wall hung an antique Samurai sword, and beneath it a leather baseball signed by what could well have been the entire squad of the New York Yankees.

'Niccolo Lamparelli, eh? Larry and I were just talking about you.'

Sukuhara spoke perfect English, though his accent was unmistakably New York, and his overconfident style suggested that he considered himself more American than Japanese. 'That Globecom deal you're working on – fucking great job, Lamparelli!'

'Thank you, sir.'

Sukuhara inhaled deeply and blew out a thin stream of smoke. 'You know, kid,' he began, 'when I first started out, I worked for a Japanese bank, and I did the exact same thing you just did – walked straight into the boss's office and told him who I was and what I could do for him. Of course, it was a different era, different culture . . .' He blew out a cloud of smoke.

'What was it like working for a Japanese bank, Mr Sukuhara?' Niccolo ventured.

'Funny bunch, the Japanese. They know their weaknesses, but they normally want an insider to fix things for them. I studied in the States, but I speak Japanese, so I was the perfect trouble-shooter – *Nihon* on the outside, but *Gaijin* on the inside.'

Niccolo nodded. Sukuhara paused for a meditative moment to savour the cigar smoke.

'Japanese managers don't understand how to manage staff in Western countries,' he went on. 'So I did it for them. They don't know how to deal with corporate customers in the West, so I dealt with them on their behalf. It was great for them, and great for me. They promoted me so fast I couldn't attend all of my own cele-bration drinks – eventually gave me an ulcer.' He took another puff and exhaled in Niccolo's face. 'The Japanese never like to lose face. Make a cock-up in a Japanese bank, you're finished. Thing is, we're all human – everyone makes a mistake sooner or later. When you cock up, you take the heat, say sorry and move on, right? Not the Japanese. They just go round covering their asses all day. I hate ass-coverers. Drive me crazy. So I came here. You like it here, Lamparelli?'

'Yes, very much, sir.' He felt more comfortable with 'sir'.

'Good. Good. You married? Got kids?'

'No, sir.'

'Smart guy!' He elbowed Niccolo hard, ignoring the red-hot ash that fell on to the leather, and chuckled. 'Take it from me, kid, I know what I'm talking about – been divorced twice. And it's a dirty business. A wife is like an Aston Martin – you got one of those yet?'

'No, sir. Not yet.'

'Great cars. Anyway, you service an Aston Martin regularly, it'll last a lifetime. You get my drift?'

'I get you, sir.'

'John! Call me John!'

'I get you – John.'

'Well, look,' said Sukuhara, plugging the cigar into his mouth and rising to his feet. 'I gotta run. Seeing Silvermans at eleven – trying to get the fuckers to cut us in on some more deals.' He offered his hand and Niccolo grabbed it as fast as he could. 'Glad you dropped by, Lamparelli.'

'Me too. It's a pleasure to meet you, John.'

'You keep up the good work now.'

Niccolo shut the door on his way out and grinned victoriously at Bulldog, who had returned to her post and was looking daggers at him. There was something very likeable about Sukuhara, he thought.

Antonio Sanchez was the Head of Omega, the IT support team for all front-office staff. He was a marathon-runner, a gadget freak and a genius with software. At the age of sixteen, he had written the program that became the working foundation for a best-selling computer game, Lady Warrior. By nineteen, he was working for British intelligence, helping to make their systems hacker-proof. At twenty-six, he was poached by Saracen, who guaranteed him a million-dollar bonus if he stayed for five years. He stayed.

When he powered up his computer on his first day back after spending two weeks at his parents' villa with his boyfriend, he found he had 682 unread emails and a conference call on codecs with New York that afternoon. But his attention was grabbed by a notification of a malfunction on one of his home-made security programs. He had written the software a year earlier to enhance the bank's IT systems security. It was only a beta version – still being tested – but it had worked fine for nine months, so Antonio took the error message seriously.

System 22 security breach: PBX recording malfunction.
Check intrusion detection systems.

There had been insufficient time to draft a user manual. Antonio's memory had held all the answers but it wasn't being too helpful. He frowned, and went through the various permutations in his mind, trying to decipher his own code.

The malfunction was clearly something to do with the bank's digital telephone recording systems. System 22 referred to the north-eastern segment of the trading floor. Was someone trying to listen in to analyst conversations? Was it a malicious hacker? Perhaps an employee was planning a fraud. Perhaps a rival bank was up to some mischief. Or could it just be his own untested security software malfunctioning?

He printed off the error message, grabbed a key ring from his drawer and headed for the server room in the basement.

*

In the end, the Globecom deal failed to materialise. Jean-Claude churned out excuse after excuse, attributing each delay – as always – to 'external factors beyond my control'. Rupert had predicted such an outcome, but did not have the balls to take on Jean-Claude in public. The risk would have been too great: had the mandate been won, Jean-Claude would have branded all those who had opposed him deal-breakers, and Rupert would have been shown the door. So now, having invested at least two hundred man-days in the Globecom proposal, the bank had nothing to show for its efforts but a colossal waste of expensive time and expertise. Everyone involved was fully aware that Saracen Laing was not in the business of rewarding failure.

CHAPTER 10

By June 2007, two hedge funds run by Bear Stearns had collapsed unexpectedly. Investment banking business all over Europe was showing signs of drying up. Saracen Laing was in trouble, as were many of their rival global houses. On the first Monday of that month, a memo was distributed to all Global Investment Research staff within the London office. It was sent by George Gambatti, the New York-based Global Head of International Operations. Few London staff needed to open it to know what it said. The writing had been on the wall for many months.

> In the present economic climate, senior management in New York have had to consider a rationalisation of our global business operations.
>
> I regret to inform you that I have asked John Sukuhara to reassess his resource requirements within Europe with a view to making significant cutbacks. You will be informed individually by your HR manager of any management decisions that affect your employment with the bank.
>
> Kind regards
> George Gambatti

Chaos followed. No one in the London office had been informed of the decision prior to the memo's release, not even Larry Sikorski, the Head of European Research, who would be responsible for implementing a large chunk of the redundancy programme.

The sensible thing would have been to put in place an orderly change-management programme. Unfortunately, Larry Sikorski had no idea what an orderly change-management programme looked like. Neither did Daryl Walker, the Head of HR, nor any of the other heads of department. So nobody bothered. There was no plan, just a single objective. The redundancy programme was bulldozed through.

Rumour had it that Larry had been given twenty-four hours to submit to Head Office the names of those he would be making redundant. Word got out – from April – that he had been given authority to cut at least forty analysts from his payroll. In theory, Head Office did not care who they were, as long as the specified headcount target was met. In practice, bigwigs from New York were almost certain to interfere in the selection process for personal ends. Larry, alert to the potential for embarrassment, fired off an email to Daryl in Human Resources.

Daryl – Please advise me of all staff with strong personal connections in New York.

The next couple of days were stressful for everyone. Those staff deemed 'at risk' knew that the bank's management had never once handled a redundancy programme with any degree of competence, despite their extensive experience of sacking staff.

'We need to act now and talk later, John,' Larry advised his boss one evening as they stood side by side at the urinals. 'It's not good for my ulcers to have to worry about who I'm going to fire tomorrow.'

'OK, Larry,' replied Sukuhara, shaking off and zipping up. 'Let's make it short and sweet. Give me your list tomorrow. I need to send it to New York for approval.'

It took Larry two hours to draw up the list. Unfortunately, it took Sukuhara four days to approve it. In that time, staff morale took a nosedive.

Larry received numerous calls from Daryl Walker, who seemed to generate more questions than answers. 'Our procedures require that we operate a last-in, first-out methodology for redundancies,' he said pompously. 'We want to reward loyalty. So I recommend that Niccolo Lamparelli should be on your list.'

Larry spoke to Daryl with the same respect he would show a beggar on the street. 'You tick your little boxes any way you want, sonny. Just remember – I'm in charge here. And the reason I'm in charge and not you, Daryl, is because when this whole fucking mess is over, we still need to make money. Niccolo is of strategic importance to this company. He isn't going anywhere, you got that?'

At precisely 07.00 the following Friday, less than a week after George Gambatti's original email, Operation Facelift was launched. Its objective was simple – two hundred and ten employees from various departments were to be made redundant that day. The individuals in question did not yet know who they were.

Full responsibility for the administrative side of the operation was assigned to Daryl Walker. His job was to ensure that all employees on the list were informed of their rights, given a redundancy package in return for a signature, and escorted expeditiously out of the building. It was a horrible way to end a career at the bank, but it was the way Saracen Laing did things. Such operations were typically carried out just before the weekend. There was no recourse.

On the day of reckoning, Larry called in sick. 'If anyone asks for me, I'm seeing my physiotherapist for my knee injury. I won't be in again until tomorrow.' Anne-Marie didn't believe him for an instant.

That Friday, the trading floor looked like a graveyard. One by one, the wretched souls named on the list were summoned up to the Human Resources department on the fifth floor to be told their fate. By ten o'clock, several desks had become vacant. Niccolo, relatively new to the bank, considered himself at risk, even though Larry had already taken great pains to inform him on numerous occasions that his position was secure. 'The pricks in Corporate Finance like you,' he said. That counted for a lot. But it would take a great deal more than Larry's word to remove the lingering uncertainties in Niccolo's mind.

An Emerging Markets trader two rows away from him put on his jacket and allowed himself to be escorted to the main entrance with the minimum of fuss.

'I can't take this shit, Niccolo,' Jack declared. 'Let's go to the gym.'

Jack announced that they were each to do four sets on heavy weights. Jack always lifted around thirty kilograms more than his leaner gym partner. Niccolo was sweating heavily as he began his third set. He groaned as he lifted the seventy-kilogram loaded bar. Jack stood behind him, poised to step in to the rescue, if required.

Afterwards, sweaty and muscle-sore, they headed for the sauna. Niccolo sat back and closed his eyes. 'You know, Jack,' he said, 'I think Charlie's taken me under his wing.'

'Well, you couldn't get a better man to teach you the ropes. There's no better tech analyst than Popeye. He's outperformed the competition for twenty years. That guy's amazing; you know he's the son of a steel-welder from Pittsburgh? Yet the son of a bitch has made it all the way to the top. Now he looks after his dad as well as two or three wives and God knows how many kids. As long as he stays true to himself, Charlie'll always be number one.'

'What do you mean – true to himself?'

'Well, I don't know this for sure, but a long time ago – before my time – they say that he got caught up in some scam of Larry's. Nobody knows exactly what happened, except that Larry made a lot of money and Charlie refused to blow the whistle on him. Charlie may have profited too, but I really hope he wasn't involved. Though I think he should have put Larry away when he had the chance.'

'Doesn't sound like the Charlie I know. He doesn't bend the rules, and he doesn't take shit from anyone. Why'd he keep his mouth shut?'

'Why do people do what they do? Look at you, Nicco; right now you're single. One day you'll get married, then you'll have kids. Then you'll have school fees and shit like that. And then you'll do whatever you have to do.'

Niccolo sighed. 'Maybe, Jack. Maybe.'

But he doubted it. At least, he hoped he did.

By the time Jack and Niccolo returned to the office, a few more desks had been cleared out.

'Where's Charlie?' asked Jack nervously.

Just then Charlie appeared, as if from nowhere. 'I've been multitasking in a parallel universe,' he said coolly. 'Otherwise known as reading the paper in the loo.'

Rupert updated them on the casualty list. 'Two of our telecoms boys – Ian and Graham – have been marched out of the building like criminals. Charlie's lost a man, but it's not you, Jack. And here's the best bit: Jean-Claude still has a job – where's the justice in that, eh?' He turned to Niccolo. 'Your phone hasn't rung yet. I think you're OK for now.'

'I'd say we could all do with lunch. Singh from Punjab, anybody?' Charlie suggested.

James Heath pondered the invitation. 'But we need to be at our phones. What if one of us gets called up to the fifth floor?'

'What are they going to do if you're not here, sack you? You can stay if you like, I'm going for a curry,' announced Charlie, unperturbed. He walked off the trading floor, taking Niccolo, Jack, Odile, Anne-Marie and Rupert with him.

It was a Friday, so the Singh from Punjab was fully booked, but regular customers like Charlie received special service. Charlie was good for business; he always ordered the most expensive wine and he always tipped outrageously. Jagdeep the head waiter showed them into a private dining area reserved for just such occasions. They scanned the menu in sombre silence.

As the wine came, Jack said, 'Well, it's all downhill from here, guys. We're all fucked.'

'Not me,' announced Odile. 'Not lately, anyway. I haven't had a boyfriend for at least a year.' Odile rarely swore or made any sexual references at work, and she normally kept her private life to herself. Niccolo vaguely registered that this was a bit out of character.

'I can't afford to lose my job,' blurted Rupert, resting his head in his hands in despair. 'I'm building an extension.'

'If I lose my job . . .' began Charlie in a melancholy chant, 'I'll be forced to devote my time to something useful.'

'I cannot afford to lose mine, *mes amis*,' said Odile in her husky French accent. 'I haven't yet paid off the loan for my Aston Martin.'

The confessions had taken a clockwise route around the table, and it was now Jack's turn. 'I can't afford to lose my job because I've got a fucking high-maintenance wife.'

Niccolo sat back. 'I don't have a wife. I don't have a mortgage. And I don't have an Aston Martin,' he said proudly. 'If I get laid off, I'll become a ski instructor in Chamonix.'

Rupert diverted a piece of poppadom headed for his mouth and threw it at him. 'Smug bastard!'

Anne-Marie was looking more and more troubled. When all eyes eventually turned to her, she came clean. 'Look, I'm the boss's PA. I can't get sacked, OK!'

'Hey, look!' said Charlie, leaning towards the window. 'See that guy cleaning the street, yellow fluorescent jacket? He used to be a bond trader at Salomon on a million-pound guaranteed bonus. Now look at him!'

As his colleagues laughed, each knew that investment banks had overpaid their staff for far too long – not necessarily for exceptional performance, but simply for turning up at the office every day and staying there half the night. Now the good times were over.

The man from Saracen Laing was speeding down Park Lane listening to Pink Floyd when he received the call. The in-car music system automatically lowered the volume and Picton's distinctive voice monopolised the speakers.

'I hear there are some redundancies at Saracen. Does this change things for us?'

'Not at all, Doctor. A lot of people are going to get fired. But as far as you and I are concerned, there's nothing to worry about.' He switched lanes and carefully navigated the roundabout at Hyde Park Corner. 'I only require a handful of key people in key positions.'

'Glad to hear it. I expect to be fully funded within a couple of weeks. At that point we will start doing business with each other. Will you be ready by then?'

'I'm ready now.'

Jagdeep offered the Saracen party a complimentary round of 1984 Armagnac. This sorry bunch of bankers had already spent a fortune on wine, he thought, so it only seemed fair that they retire in style.

'Well, I know who I'd fire,' slurred Charlie, trying to hold his glass steady. 'Bulldog.'

'You can't do that,' snapped Rupert. 'She's the armature around which this bank turns.'

'Yeah, but she can't type!' retorted Charlie. 'That woman delegates her work, walks around the floor like she owns the place and picks fights with the traders. She's got thighs the size of tree trunks and an ass with so much cellulite it looks like an Ordnance Survey map. Sorry, girls and boys, she's got to go.'

'JC Bouvier?' suggested Rupert.

Charlie nodded. 'Bullet to the head.'

'What about Cuddly Dudley?' asked Jack. 'He's a walking liability.'

'Nah – every office should have its very own overweight Jewish eccentric,' concluded Charlie. 'It's Mortimer Steel that's the real liability.'

'Our big swinging dick? You can't fire him! He's married to the boss's daughter!'

'If *he's* our big swinging dick, then we've got bigger problems than I thought!'

By the end of the day, Operation Facelift had fulfilled its objectives. A total of two hundred and three staff had been informed that their services were no longer required and marched out of the building under escort. The Equity Research department suffered the smallest number of casualties with a loss of thirty-eight staff, whilst Equity Sales & Trading took the largest hit with the loss of seventy-two.

In Equity Research, the telecoms team fell from nine to six, whilst the technology team collapsed from twelve to seven. The media team was halved to five analysts, but the entire internet team of eight got the axe. Financial Services lost three analysts and Pharmaceuticals another two. Only the automobile and energy sectors emerged unscathed.

As the day drew to a close, those who had survived the butchery looked almost as miserable as the wretched souls who'd been fired. Another round of cuts was almost certain. Everyone on the trading floor knew someone who had just been axed. But life would go on, and in a week's time many of the old faces would be forgotten.

Before leaving for the weekend, Rupert addressed what remained of his telecoms team. 'Well, guys, if you're still here, your jobs are safe. That's the good news. The bad news is that our workload stays the same. And since we've lost a third of the team, you can each expect a bigger workload. I'll rejig our stock coverage and inform you of your new allocations on Monday. Have a good weekend, everybody.'

Late that Friday evening, Karim Rashid arrived unannounced at the Moneypincher's Inn. He was shabbily dressed, in ripped jeans and a fake Giorgio Armani T-shirt, and had not bathed in a week. He came without notes or photographs or evidence. He came alone. But he came with information.

Like a smelly, unwanted stray dog, he was led by the maître d' at arm's length to the private dining room in the basement, where he was told to wait. Picton arrived shortly afterwards, smartly dressed in a pinstripe suit and carrying a black leather diary.

'What have you got?' he demanded.

Karim rested a pair of battle-hardened forearms on the table and leaned forward, staring purposefully into Picton's eyes. He spoke perfect English, except for a deep Usmani accent and a mild stutter. 'Niccolo Lamparelli is thirty years old. His father's name was Feroz Guzdar – he was an officer in the Indian Navy. Stationed on the US naval base in Okinawa. Worked on a military technology exchange programme. Guzdar died when Niccolo was twelve. It looks like he was killed in some sort of training accident, but I could not find the records. Niccolo's mother, Isabella, returned to Milan after her husband's death, and he took her name, Lamparelli.' Picton made notes, nodding periodically.

'Lamparelli has a friend at Saracen – Jack Ford. They were both educated at St Mary's International School in Tokyo when they were children. Jack's father is a marine zoologist; at that time he was working for the Okinawa Institute of Science and Technology. After Tokyo, Jack went to school in Australia, whilst Niccolo was educated in England, at a school called Upp-ing-ham. However, every summer for many years they went back to Okinawa without their parents – yes, I know it is strange, but that is what I have found. They both ended up at Cambridge University at the same time. Jack is three years older than Niccolo. He started a Masters degree when Niccolo arrived as an undergraduate. The university records show they were both pretty good at karate, won many trophies. Jack left college and came straight to Saracen Laing. He is married now and earns a lot of money. Niccolo had many jobs after leaving Cambridge – in a bar, in a gym – and many women, then he went travelling around the world. He was a journalist for a few years at *Financial Telegraph* in London. Then he joined his friend Jack at Saracen Laing. He's been there for just over a year now. It looks like he's doing OK.'

Karim paused. Picton finished what he was writing and looked up. 'Does Lamparelli have a girlfriend?'

'Yes, boss. Lucy Grey. It looks like they started going out soon after he went to Saracen. She works for a company called Klum Bug.'

'Kloomberg?'

Karim nodded vigorously. 'Yes. Shall I find out more, boss?'

'Keep digging.'

'Is this Lamparelli your enemy, boss? Has he harmed Prince Mubarak? Do you want me to kill him?'

Picton thumped the table angrily. 'Don't be stupid, you fool! This man could make us all very rich!'

CHAPTER 11

The weekend provided welcome relief from a week of uncertainty. On Saturday evening, Niccolo asked Jack and Donna round for dinner. Gino and Olivia Martinelli were also invited with their two daughters, Teresa and Silvia.

Jack and Gino had first met through their respective wives, and over the years they had become inseparable, often spending weekends together, sometimes with their wives, sometimes as a tightly knit threesome with Niccolo.

Gino was born in Podenzano, a small industrial town near Milan. His father had died young and left his family in poverty. So Gino studied law at night school, consistently coming top of his class. Hand-picked by a Milanese law firm, he was given the opportunity to complete his legal training, initially on a stipend. Ten years later, when the firm had grown exponentially on the back of the Italian textile industry, Gino was sent to London to run their UK office.

His wife, Olivia, came from a wealthy family whose blue-blooded ancestry opened several doors for her husband. She and Donna would describe themselves as the best of friends, though friendship, of course, is a relative term. When they first met, as newly married young women, both viewed life as a competition for the acquisition of material possessions. True happiness, for them, was measured in Gucci handbags and Prada shoes. But as they grew older, their outlooks on life diverged. While Donna's materialistic tendencies grew more pronounced, Olivia's values were changed completely by the births of two daughters. A devoted mother, she contentedly wore fashions from two or even three seasons past, whilst her unassailably patrician background meant she was free to draw her friends from all levels of society. Donna, less socially secure, disapproved of Olivia letting her standards slip. However, with Olivia's superficiality abandoned, Donna's became exposed, and the two women lost what they had once had in common. Over the years, they had grown apart.

The friendship that linked the three men went far deeper. Niccolo and Gino had both lost their fathers at an early age, and Jack – though his father was still alive – had grown up in a broken home, seeing his father scarcely once a year. Robbed of the safety net of love and guidance that only a father could provide, they all learned their lessons in life the hard way, making mistakes in the process. They valued everything they had achieved, and understood only too clearly how easily it could be taken away from them.

'So, Lamparelli, what's for dinner?' asked Gino.

'Don't panic, it's all under control.' Niccolo produced a tattered little black notebook. The paper had turned yellow with age, and some pages had come loose from the binding and were clamped carefully between the covers. The notebook had been given to Isabella by her mother on her wedding day. The inscription inside the front cover was handwritten with a steady, generous flow of black ink from a beautiful thick nib in the graceful style of a bygone age.

*Cara Isabella – To help you
look after the love of your life.
Tanti baci, xx Mamma.*

As a boy, Niccolo had often watched his mother in the kitchen. When he came to England to study, she gave him the little black notebook. He treasured it. It served as a daily reminder of his mother. Each stain carried a memory. Each recipe embodied her love. Each line told a story.

Niccolo had decided to cook *risotto alla Milanese* and *osso buco*. Two hours later, dinner was served. The risotto might not have matched Isabella's high standards, but Olivia and Donna were impressed nonetheless. Niccolo poured the wine and they sat down to eat.

'So, when is young Niccolo going to get married?' enquired Olivia softly.

Niccolo took a moment to respond. 'Once I've seen the world, made my fortune and had my fill of adventure,' he replied confidently.

'That's not what Jack tells me,' said Donna, with her mouth full of food and her eyes full of mischief.

Jack and Niccolo exchanged glances as Donna continued. 'What about Juicy Lucy?'

'Who's Juicy Lucy?' asked Olivia with avid interest.

'Her name is Lucy, OK?' said Niccolo, slightly rattled.

Olivia hastily smoothed over the awkward moment. 'Well, I hope one day soon we will meet her. However,' she continued with her mouth full, 'marriage is one thing, but once you have kids, your whole life changes. You never get a minute to yourself. They take over everything.'

'Jack doesn't need kids to take over his life, do you, darling?' interjected Donna. 'You have the bank to do that for you.'

Jack bowed his head, guilty as charged.

'Tell me, Niccolo, does your Lucy know about Italian men? Because Gino has never changed a single nappy. He thinks I'm here to cook, clean and look after babies.'

'But *carissima*, you are! And to look after me as well, of course.' Olivia smiled as her husband's lips caressed her neck.

CHAPTER 12

Over the weekend, the north and south trading-floor walls had been updated with the latest in large-screen technology. It seemed ironic to many that management should have chosen to spend so much on non-essential gadgetry on the very weekend that so many had lost their jobs. Niccolo was pleased with his new desk because he had a good view of the cinema-sized video wall. It comprised ninety-six flat-screen video monitors stacked up side by side, forming a twelve-by-eight rectangle, giving the appearance of a single screen. Like the old projector-based system, its purpose was to provide traders and analysts with key information on the markets: some screens showed the main stock market indices, together with foreign exchange prices; others displayed news banners; but the bulk of the video wall was used to screen TNBC.

'Hey, Nicco,' whispered Jack. 'Popeye's on TNBC in a couple of minutes. He's doing the seven-thirty slot, pushing his theory on doom and gloom in the tech sector again.'

The TNBC news team loved to have Charlie on the programme because he spoke his mind. His performances were always controversial. Whilst many analysts hedged their bets, Charlie never did. He called a spade a spade. It made him newsworthy, and it made him a walking advertisement for Saracen Laing, too. But whilst he raised Saracen Laing's profile with the millions of retail investors watching TNBC, he also risked antagonising the bank's core client base – the big corporations. From an employer's perspective, that made him a double-edged sword.

A crowd gathered, and all work stopped. Analysts and traders always got excited when their colleagues were asked to speak on TNBC. It was a nerve-racking experience, as interviews were normally conducted live, leaving little room for mistakes.

Jacqui Hanson, a brunette with heavy make-up and a warm voice, was the show's anchorwoman and a highly rated trading floor pin-up.

'OK, viewers. It's just turned seven-thirty a.m. and it's time for our weekly look at the markets. After a three year boom, we ask two experts which way the tech sector is headed over the next six months. On the hot spot this morning we have two views. First there's Jeremy Lagerfeld, Chief Strategist from Silverman Ross. And next to Jeremy we've got Charlie Doyle, Chief Technology Analyst at Saracen Laing.'

Both men nodded good morning to camera.

'Starting with you, Jeremy,' continued Jacqui. 'Tell us how you expect the tech sector to perform and what advice you would give investors looking at a six-month investment horizon.'

'Well, by any measure, tech stocks are still undervalued,' Lagerfeld began. 'Trading at a Price to Earnings multiple of around twenty compared to a historical average over the last decade of at least double that, we believe tech stocks are now cheap. However, overcapacity in the semi-conductor market remains a big problem, so we would caution investors to hold rather than buy the sector at present.'

'Thank you, Jeremy. And now we turn to Charlie Doyle at Saracen Laing. Charlie, do you agree with Jeremy?'

'No,' said Charlie, staring pointedly into the camera.

Jacqui waited patiently for Charlie to continue. 'Would you care to elaborate?' she asked finally.

'Of course, Jacqui,' replied Charlie. 'Bulge-bracket banks will always tell you what their bulge-bracket clients want you to hear – that their clients' share prices are going up. In sectors such as natural resources and defence, that may be the case. In technology, it's not.' Charlie paused to flick his hair back before he continued. 'The tech sector's a bit like a rock star: it entered the market a nobody; it had a couple of big hits; it rose to the top on the back of a load of nothing special; then it crashed and burned spectacularly, checked into rehab, and now it's about to have a nervous breakdown.'

A tidal wave of laughter gently rocked the trading floor and was captured live on air. Jacqui appeared slightly flustered as she attempted to digest a host of conflicting hand signals from her bosses behind the scenes. Composing herself, she stiffened her posture and regained control. 'OK, I want to focus now on China's increasing importance as a manufacturer of high-tech goods. Turning to you first, Jeremy, how successful do you think China will become in tech?'

'I forecast that China's tech economy – if it continues to grow at current rates – could easily overtake America's tech sector in under two decades. Chinese tech stocks should rule the world by then. Chinese internet companies, such as Baidu, will have larger captive audiences than Google one day. Investors should buy China.'

Jacqui shrugged and flashed her teeth at the camera. 'That's an interesting perspective from Silvermans. Now let's turn again to Saracen's Chief Technology Analyst, Charlie Doyle. Do you agree, Charlie?'

Charlie flicked his hair back again and laughed. 'That sounds like another case of premature extrapolation by the boys at Silvermans. Great sound bite for a dinner party, but not much useful analysis.' Before Jacqui could intervene, Charlie continued. 'China might be the factory of the world, but it's not a particularly profitable factory. So why would you want to invest there? It might be the highest growth region in the world, but they don't respect shareholder rights. Again, why would you want to invest there? The only people who make any money are Party members. The search for Chinese profits could turn out to be the biggest wild goose chase in history. It's the 1999 bubble all over again, only this time with chopsticks.

'In this world, you get what you pay for. China is a brothel run by a bunch of gangsters in Party uniform . . . which leads me nicely on to something Chong Lee, the famous Chinese management guru, once said while addressing a bunch of Harvard MBA students. Referring to the US manufacturing sector, he said, "Hey, guys, brace yourselves. It looks like you're about to be bitch-slapped by the invisible hand of Chinese capitalism."'

Jacqui raised her eyebrows. 'I didn't know the Chinese believed in capitalism.'

'They don't, sweetheart. That's the bitch.'

As Charlie stepped out of the recording studio, he faced a standing ovation from the floor. 'Popeye, you're a fucking legend!' came the shouts. 'That was great!'

Back at his desk, a welcoming party was waiting to congratulate him for trashing the opposition in a way that only Charlie could.

'Hey, Charlie, who's this Chong Lee chap?' enquired Rupert.

'Give me a break, will you! Out of one billion Chinese, there's bound to be at least one Chong Lee with an economics degree!'

Later that day, Rupert initiated a reshuffle, and called the team in one by one. James went first. Niccolo waited outside, pacing the corridor, edgy. James did not take much more than a quarter of an hour. When he eventually stepped out of the meeting room, he and Niccolo brushed past each other like actors at an audition. Niccolo shut the door and sat down.

'I'm impressed with your performance, Nicco,' said Rupert.

'Thanks.'

'Larry has asked me to take on more of a managerial role. That means you and James get some of my stocks.'

'Cool.'

'How would you like to add Ultrafone and Globecom to your portfolio?'

'Bloody hell, Ru,' exclaimed Niccolo, flinching with a shot of adrenalin. 'That's great! I won't let you down.'

'You'd better not!'

By the time Niccolo had returned to the trading floor, the news was already out.

'I told the others,' offered James rather apologetically. 'I didn't think you'd mind.'

'Not at all,' replied Niccolo with a twinkle in his eye.

Odile was the first to congratulate him. 'Well done, Nicco. You got Ultrafone and Globecom! Wow! You'll never have a dull moment with them. Good luck ... I can't wait to read your research.'

Niccolo felt exposed. Until now his expertise had been in the smaller telecoms stocks. He could afford to make the odd mistake because those stocks were low profile. With Ultrafone and Globecom, however, the stakes were much higher. The great and the good would be watching his every move.

This was the lucky break he had been waiting for. But was he ready? Was it too early in his career? It was a once-in-a-lifetime opportunity to cover some of the greatest companies in the telecoms sector. He couldn't afford to refuse it. Nor could he afford to fuck it up.

He only had one shot at this game.

*

Arnaud Veyrieras peered out at London's spectacular skyline. Picton was up to something. He could sense it. He could *smell* it. He had to keep the investigation into the Doctor's activities alive. But without an official team working on the case, things looked bleak.

He heard a knock. 'Sir, it's Maurice,' came a faint voice from behind the door. Maurice was a software engineer. He had been working for Arnaud until Team 19 was disbanded. Now his face looked weary and drawn and his stubble was out of control. 'Sir, I've some bad news,' he announced, wiping his nose with his sleeve. 'We no longer have access to Saracen's telephone systems. It appears they've discovered the bug.'

'*Merde!*' Arnaud slumped in his chair, a hint of despair in his eyes. 'Did they trace it to us?'

'Highly unlikely, sir. I tested the encryption myself – there's no way anyone could tell it ended up here. Shall we put another tracker in place?'

'No, they're on to us – and this time we don't have clearance from the top. Digital technology always leaves a trail. Leave this one to me, Maurice. We've still got our man on the inside. We're going to have to do this the old-fashioned way.'

'Right, sir,' replied Maurice. He sneezed violently, wiped his nose again and stood to attention. 'Will there be anything else?'

'No. And remember, you stopped working on this case a month ago.'

Maurice nodded and turned to leave. 'And Maurice . . .' continued Arnaud.

'Yes, sir?'

'Do something about that cold!'

CHAPTER 13

Over the following days, Niccolo set himself a gruelling schedule. In a few weeks he would be ready to comment on the two additional telecoms stocks he had been allocated. He got on the phone and set up meetings to see their management. He asked Anne-Marie to prepare a file of broker reports, company press releases and Reuters newswires for both companies. He searched their websites for information and read their annual accounts and press releases. He made copious notes.

Then came some controversial judgement calls. His first move was to downgrade Globecom to Sell. In a research report entitled 'One Cable Too Many', he set out his rationale for the change in investment rating, arguing his case with conviction. At the close of markets, the Globecom share price was £4.35, valuing the company at one hundred and twenty-three billion pounds.

The following day, the phone on his desk refused to stop ringing.

'Nicco Lamparelli? Ricky Fernandez from the *Sunday Fortune*. I see on my Reuters screen that you've changed your Globecom rating to Sell. Brave call.'

'I would have phrased it differently.'

'I'm doing an article on Globecom,' continued the reporter. 'Can you run me through your rationale for the downgrade?'

'Sure. I take it you're familiar with the company?'

'I could always do with a recap. Tell it the way you see it.'

'OK, why don't I start at the beginning?'

'Hang on while I put you on the record . . .' The reporter fiddled with some buttons, then came back on the line. 'Carry on,' he said.

'Right. Kenneth Oakes founded Globecom in 1988. For the first few years it was just a struggling telco. Then the internet thing happened. By the late 1990s, everyone was talking about "bandwidth". Oakes had invested heavily in optical fibre networks so he could supply all the telcos with the extra bandwidth capacity they needed. He believed in the internet right from the start – in its ability to transform the economics of business.

'Oakes' business model was based on a view that saw exponential growth rates in internet traffic on the world's telecoms networks. That view was shared by just about everyone at the time. So he went on a building spree. He convinced all his investors that once these expensive pipes were built, the money would come rolling in.'

'You mean from leasing the pipes to other telcos?' asked the reporter.

'Exactly,' said Niccolo. 'But by March 2000, the internet bubble had burst. Growth forecasts were halved, and halved again in a matter of months. Analysts realised they had got it wrong by a huge margin.'

'And Globecom relied on internet growth, so its shares crashed too.'

'That's right.'

'But that was almost ten years ago. The shares have already fallen fifty per cent since the bubble burst. Why switch to Sell now? Isn't it a bit late?'

'Not if you think they're going to fall another fifty per cent.'

'And why would you think that?'

'Because I believe there is still a huge amount of overcapacity in Globecom's markets. There are too many pipes in the world. Prices for those pipes are still falling. So Globecom is still in trouble.'

'But Oakes doesn't agree with you and neither do most of the other telecoms analysts I've spoken to.'

Niccolo paused. 'They're wrong,' he said finally.

'All of them?' asked the reporter aggressively.

'Yeah, all of them.'

'Oakes says his revenues will grow by ten per cent over the next three years,' said the reporter confidently.

'I don't believe him,' retorted Niccolo.

'What do you think?'

'I think they'll *fall* by twenty per cent.'

'But that could mean Globecom's shares will crash!'

'Now do you understand why I rate it Sell?'

The man from Saracen Laing waited patiently outside Toni's Café. He paced up and down the pavement, checking his watch six times in under four minutes, swearing profoundly between checks. It was ten past two in the afternoon when Picton eventually arrived. They shook hands civilly and got straight down to business.

'I have something for you – pharmaceutical stock.'

'Tell me.'

'Sell GlazerStahlFine. Do it before markets close tonight.'

'How reliable is your information?'

'It will move tomorrow morning. That's all I can tell you.'

They shook hands and parted.

Back in his office, Picton made the trade. He sold six million GSF shares short at £15.33 per share. As the trade confirmation ticket printed out, he poured himself a neat Scotch and wandered downstairs into the restaurant, to stretch his legs.

*

A pristine 1988 Bentley pulled up outside an extravagantly refurbished nineteenth-century red-brick building on Pall Mall, and an elderly chauffeur opened the passenger door. A crowd of American tourists stopped to take a peek as Kenneth Oakes climbed out of the car, thanked the chauffeur and walked into the worldwide headquarters of Globecom plc.

On the penthouse floor his secretary folded her newspaper and headed for the coffee-maker in the kitchen. The boardroom, unused for most of the year, housed a marble banqueting table acquired illegally from an Italian museum, and twenty-four white leather chairs. Next door to the boardroom was a well-stocked library intended for clients, which housed a plethora of reference material covering precious stones, jewellery design, metallurgy and Renaissance art. Presented in alarmed glass cases stood some of the most unusual diamonds ever mined. Some were displayed roughs whilst others were set in rings and necklaces. A leather-bound book kept in the safe held the names of those to whom the jewels had been loaned over the years, a list that included movie stars and politicians, royalty and aristocracy; anyone who could afford the insurance.

The office of the Chief Executive spanned one whole side of the building with magnificent views of Trafalgar Square. The secretary brought coffee and served it quietly. A selection of broker reports on Globecom lay on the desk, along with a copy of the *Financial Telegraph*, which bore the blazing headline: *Globecom stock slips on Saracen downgrade.*

'Did you know Saracen had downgraded our stock?' asked Oakes.

'No, sir, but they did send a copy of the research report to Investor Relations as usual.'

'Hmmn. It looks as if they've changed the analyst. Who's this Lamparelli character?'

'I'll find out straight away.'

*

At a little after nine o'clock the following morning, a research report was published by Saracen Laing's Chief Pharmaceuticals Analyst, Lindsay Compton, in which he argued that the development of GlazerStahlFine's next big blockbuster drug was significantly behind schedule. He had moved his rating from Buy to Sell and lowered his price target by twenty per cent. The markets reacted immediately. GlazerStahlFine's share price moved sharply downwards. Within minutes, it had fallen almost eight per cent.

Over at the Moneypincher's Inn, Picton watched his screens like a hawk. When the share price fell to £14.05, he closed his position and bought back the shares, making a clean £7.7m profit. Smiling, he leaned back in his chair. Not bad for a morning's work, he thought. And it was still only nine-thirty.

The British Museum is an imposing building, with a richness of proportion that reminds visitors of the long-lost grandeur of British design and workmanship. Larry was enjoying the morning sunshine outside, admiring the building's finer features, when Donna spotted him and waved through the iron railings before hurrying towards the South Side entrance.

'I'm so happy you could make it,' said Larry, spreading his arms to greet her.

She kissed him on the cheek and keenly absorbed his scent. 'Forgive me for being so late,' she murmured apologetically.

He led her into the main hall, producing two tickets from his blazer pocket for the Russian exhibition. Exhibits had been flown in from private and public collections all over the world, the biggest contribution being made by the Russian Museum, housed in the Mikhailovsky Palace in St Petersburg.

They hastened through the first few rooms, leaving the crowds behind, to steal some privacy. Larry did most of the talking, impressing Donna enormously with his knowledge of Russia, its geography, its history, its culture, its art.

'There she is,' said Larry, pointing to a portrait of a slender ballet dancer. He hurried towards the painting and beckoned Donna to follow. 'This is my absolute favourite – Anna Pavlova, by Valentin Serov.' He spoke with a passion and candour that Donna found exhilarating. 'Isn't she beautiful? She was considered the greatest dancer of her time, you know, and he the greatest portraitist. Compared with his peers, Serov is much more sensuous, less nostalgic. He could do everything – oils, watercolour, pastel, lithography, charcoal drawings, everything. I wish I could paint like that.'

'Do you paint?' asked Donna. Behind them a group of Japanese women shuffled along like well-disciplined mice. All wore headsets and all looked equally serious.

Larry shrugged modestly. 'Oh, I'm not very good, but I find it relaxes me. I do portraits mainly.'

Donna's eyes lit up. 'Where do you paint?'

'I paint anywhere I can, sometimes in the country, sometimes in my Kensington flat. It's hard to find a model. I mean, I could go to an art school, of course, but I can't stand working with other artists. Art is such a private matter. And the models one finds at art school – Christ, you should see some of them! Awful, just awful. Finding somebody that you really want to paint . . . that's priceless.'

Donna smiled innocently. 'I think it's wonderful that you paint.'

Larry frowned slightly, as if about to speak, then hesitated. Finally he leaned forward and whispered, 'Donna, I was wondering . . . would you be willing?'

Donna looked perplexed.

'Willing to be my model, I mean. You would be absolutely perfect.' His eyes swept the length of her body.

Donna laughed awkwardly. 'Next you'll tell me I'd have to go nude.'

Larry gazed at her intently, one eyebrow raised very slightly.

Donna's heart pounded. She was shocked by his request, yet the shock was strangely delicious. She felt drawn to him, as she had never felt drawn to anyone else. 'I've never done anything like that before,' she confessed.

'I assure you, Donna, you'll be in safe hands.'

Niccolo returned home from his run to find the windows wide open and the flat smelling of lemon-scented detergent. The sound of running water led him into the kitchen, where he found Lucy halfway up a stepladder, cleaning his kitchen units. She was dressed in a pair of his boxer shorts and a lace brassiere. He turned off the tap, swept her off the stepladder and carried her into the bedroom.

Later they watched television in bed and lazed around for the rest of the afternoon. In the evening they shared a bottle of wine. He asked her to stay the night and she accepted.

CHAPTER 14

The alarm clock went off just after half past four. Niccolo's eyes opened immediately. Lucy groaned and rolled over.

Whilst shaving, Niccolo noticed a red mark on his neck. 'Oh, shit,' he muttered. The boys on the trading floor would love that. He squinted, moving his head from side to side. A polo-neck sweater would easily cover it, but the bank's staff had to dress formally. 'Shit!' he said again.

But last night was worth it, he reckoned, as he gazed at Lucy's naked body sprawled untidily on his bed. Anyway, there was nothing he could do about it now. He got dressed quietly, putting on a black Canali suit, white shirt, dark blue Gucci tie and black Tods. He kissed Lucy, who was still fast asleep, reset the alarm for 7 a.m. and left for work.

Odile was the only salesperson at her desk. It was six o'clock.

'You'd better get an email out pretty soon, Nicco,' she said, looking up from a *Financial Telegraph* article. 'Wire & Satellite were all over the weekend press – rumour of a takeover bid. Did you see it?'

'No, not yet.' Nicco blushed, remembering just how he had spent his Sunday.

'Get a move on. We need a view on this. Dickhead Dan at

Feldman has just upgraded WireSat to Buy. It's on Reuters. You need to make a call. Your coffee's on your desk.'

'I'm on it.' He grabbed her copy of the *Financial Telegraph* and sipped his latte. It was an unwritten rule that Odile took care of the 6 a.m. coffee round, leaving the 8 a.m. one for Niccolo.

Analysts dribbled in and the desks slowly filled up. Niccolo tapped away at his keyboard, relieved at Odile's apparent failure to notice the love bite. Larry walked on to the trading floor and offered his usual morning greeting, a vague raising of the eyebrows accompanied by a slight tilt of the left hand.

'Who's speaking this morning?' demanded Rupert.

'I've got something on WireSat,' cried Niccolo.

'Pass it to James,' came Rupert's response.

In Rupert's absence, James, Odile and Niccolo often reviewed each other's draft morning meeting scripts prior to speaking. This was to ensure first that they were speaking as one team, and second that what they were about to say had passed a reasonableness test.

James made a few stylistic changes and emailed the morning meeting note back to Niccolo with a nod of approval. 'Nice little love bite there,' he observed.

The tech team turned their heads in unison. 'A love bite? Really? Where?' asked Charlie.

'Right there on Nicco's neck.' James grinned smugly to himself.

'Nicco's got a love bite, guys,' Charlie shouted to the traders. 'Come and check it out!'

'Who is she, Stud? What's her name?' came the excited shrieks. 'Tell her to have an eye test! She needs a new pair of glasses if she's shagging you, man!'

Niccolo stood firm, and smiled.

'Sorry, guys, nothing as exciting as that,' he announced. 'I played squash last night. Got hit by the ball.'

'Nice try, Stud,' said Charlie. 'But this one's got *yeah, baby, yeah* written all over it. Give us a name.'

Jack took pity on him. He went to his desk, rummaged around in his rucksack and dug out a small tube of Colgate toothpaste. 'Here,' he said. 'Rub this on it, Stud. Then it won't look so fucking obvious.'

Later that morning, Charlie strolled confidently on to the trading floor.

'Good morning, guys,' he addressed his team. 'I've decided to change my image – what do you think?' He posed for a few seconds, one hand on the wall, the other resting on his hip, to show off his brand-new suit. It was charcoal grey, single-breasted and cut for a snug fit. A few of his junior analysts returned the greeting. Some of the others smelt weakness, and moved in for the kill.

'Makes you look a bit chubby, Popeye,' said James with mock seriousness.

'I think it's a great suit!' said Charlie, failing miserably to disguise his hurt.

'Nice ass, Charlie,' interrupted Odile. 'The cut suits you.' The comment carried weight. The crowd fell quiet.

'Yeah, that's what the sales assistant at the Richard James shop told me,' said Charlie.

'Richard James! Wow!' said Odile.

Niccolo turned to Rupert and James, comforted by the looks on their faces that matched his own – a look that said, *Who the fuck is Richard James?* He was clearly so exclusive that Charlie and Odile were the only people on the trading floor who had ever heard of him.

'Not bad for a tech analyst, I guess,' said Niccolo, nudging Jack conspiratorially.

'Not bad?' retorted Charlie. '*Not bad?* This thing is *hand-made*. It set me back three and a half grand – that's what you need to pay for a decent suit these days. But you lot are such a bunch of muppets, you wouldn't recognise a fashion icon if Armani himself walked past!'

Charlie's ego was an easy target, and damage limitation had never been his strong point. Anne-Marie finally took pity on him. She strolled over to his desk. 'Give me your scissors,' she insisted. And with the softest touch, ignoring Charlie's look of panic as he imagined his pricey new acquisition being reduced to rags by way of an expensive joke, she snipped the price label from his jacket. Then she bent down and whispered in his ear, 'So who is Niccolo going out with?'

'Why – you interested?'

'Of course not,' she lied. 'Just wondering.' She felt the texture of Charlie's jacket. 'By the way,' she added. 'I really do like your suit.'

On the south side of Finsbury Square, just outside the Kloomberg building, Lucy was dragging out the last remnants of pleasure from her cigarette when she heard her mobile phone beep.

'Lucy, my dear girl, I know you like Lamparelli, but was that level of violence really necessary?'

Startled, she said, 'I don't quite follow you, sir.'

'Oh, never mind, girl,' said the voice, which was male, middle-aged and powerful. 'I suppose I should congratulate you on a job well done. Keep doing what you're doing, but no need to get over-zealous. We don't want him dumping you for bad behaviour just when you're beginning to get some traction. Report back to me the minute you feel he's ready, OK?

The phone went dead.

*

At precisely five minutes past one that afternoon, Antonio Sanchez notified John Sukuhara in person that the security of the trading-floor voice-recording systems had been compromised.

'The identity of the intruder is not known,' he reported. 'However, the security violation has now been eliminated and Saracen have regained full control. I'd say it was the work of professionals.'

'OK, Antonio, I want you to draw up contingency plans in the event of a future breach,' Sukuhara responded. 'And April, can you gather all heads of department in this office within the next hour. They need to be aware of this breach.' Most importantly, Sukuhara added to himself, he needed to know whether any Saracen employee might have done anything to place the bank's reputation at risk.

Patrick O'Shea, Mortimer Steel and Larry Sikorski were summoned at short notice to Sukuhara's office to be briefed on the security breakdown within the voice-recording systems. 'We're not going to inform the police because we don't want a press leak,' Sukuhara made clear. 'Saracen's reputation is everything. So the matter is to be kept confidential until a full internal investigation has taken place.

'External forensic consultants have been hired,' he went on. 'In the meantime, senior staff need to remain vigilant. I want every trade, every telephone conversation, every report with the bank's name on it to be checked and double-checked. Most importantly . . .' He scowled at each of them in turn. '. . . under no circumstances is the Compliance Unit to be informed of this security breakdown. The last thing we need at this point is for those idiots to get involved.'

The meeting was short and to the point. By the end of it, O'Shea, Steel and Sikorski were clear on one thing. Any son of a bitch who messed with John F. Sukuhara would pay a heavy price.

CHAPTER 15

Finally, after weeks of diligent analysis, Niccolo decided to move his Hold rating on Telecom10 to a Buy. In doing so, he knew, he would be going against the consensus view. Virtually all investment banks had a Sell rating on Telecom10. They viewed it as a company on the verge of bankruptcy.

Telecom10 had expanded too fast. Its management had made two disastrous decisions in recent years: they had overspent on expensive acquisitions just before the telecoms market crashed; and they had invested billions of euros in third-generation mobile licences, which many analysts now considered to be worthless.

Niccolo and Rupert did not see eye to eye on this stock, and had not done so since coverage of it had been reassigned. Each thought he knew the company better than the other – Rupert because he had covered it until recently, Niccolo because he had done some heavy investigative reporting on it at the *Financial Telegraph*.

'It's already fallen ninety per cent in the last year, Ru,' said Niccolo. 'When a company's share price keeps falling, at some point it becomes cheap. That's the time to buy.'

'Well I say you're wrong. Sometimes companies are cheap because they're heading for bankruptcy. I think that's the case with T10.'

'I don't. I value it at six pounds per share. The market gives it a break-up value of three-fifty. Come on, Ru, this is a screaming takeover target. The shares are going to climb, damn it! We've got to catch it now.'

Rupert stuck to his guns as the discussion heated up. Finally, he yielded. 'Like I said, Nicco, I think you're wrong, but it's your stock. You make the call.'

By the end of the afternoon, Telecom10's share price had fallen another ten pence. That evening, after the markets closed, Niccolo published a twenty-page research report, switching the Saracen recommendation on Telecom10 from Hold to Buy. On the top left-hand corner of the report, in large font, the closing share price of £3.27 per share was recorded. It was against that price that investors would later be able to assess the merit of Niccolo's judgement call. Unlike Niccolo, they would, of course, have the benefit of hindsight.

Earlier that afternoon, a man in a suit had left the bank in a hurry. He walked down Bishopsgate and turned right on Artillery Lane. Halfway down, he turned into a narrow street that opened up into a pretty, secluded park with a finely manicured lawn surrounded by shrubs and flower beds. At one end stood an old Presbyterian church. Facing the church on a pathway across the gardens was a lone wooden bench. The man from Saracen Laing checked his watch. It was ten minutes past three. He circled the gardens and exactly five minutes later returned to the bench and sat down.

Another man in a dark suit stepped out from inside the church, headed towards the bench and sat down next to him. 'I got here as soon as you called. What's up?' he said.

'Saracen will raise T10 to a Buy,' came the answer.

'When?'

'After today's close.'

'Should I trade?'

'Normally I wouldn't hesitate . . . but this time I recommend you hold off. I just don't know which way the stock will move. Our analyst isn't a big name yet, so the market may not react. Anyway, I think he's wrong.'

'OK. Call me if things change.'

The two men stood up and headed in separate directions, having deliberately avoided eye contact throughout their conversation.

At the morning meeting the following day, Niccolo explained the reasoning behind his decision to the bank's sales team. A few minutes later, Odile and Paddy hit the phones hard. They called client after client, informing them of Niccolo's new rating. One by one, Saracen's clients were persuaded to move into Telecom10 stock. Odile and Paddy were professionals – they could sell anything – and the business came rolling in.

Within fifteen minutes of the research report being released, journalists had picked up on the fact that Saracen Laing was going against the market. Everyone wanted to speak to Niccolo, and Saracen's switchboard went haywire. For the rest of the day, Niccolo took endless calls, guiding clients and journalists through his rationale, taking the time to explain his views in great detail.

The following day, the *Financial Telegraph*'s front page announced:

TELECOM10 MAY BE A WINNER AFTER ALL, SAYS SARACEN LAING ANALYST

Telecom10, whose management team has justifiably acquired a reputation for financial recklessness, saw its share price decline further in late trading yesterday. However, according to Niccolo Lamparelli, an analyst at Saracen Laing, T10 could still be a winner after all. 'Now is the right time to buy T10 shares', he claimed in an interview last night. Lamparelli believes Telecom10 shares are fifty per cent undervalued at current prices.

Others disagree. Dan Alamanto of Feldman Finch and David Freedman of Silverman Ross both argue that Telecom10 will be unable to service its short-term liabilities to bondholders. That makes its shares worthless.

Yesterday Saracen Laing upgraded its investment rating on Telecom10 to Buy, whilst teams at Feldman and Silverman reiterated their Market Underperform ratings. Analysts remain bitterly divided on Telecom10.

Telecom10's share price held steady for a couple of days. Then rumours surfaced of a possible merger between the company and its rival Téléjeune, the French telecoms operator. Some in the industry saw Téléjeune as a white knight offering to merge with its British rival and save it from near-certain death. Others viewed it as an asset-stripper.

'Investors are remaining cautious,' Feldman's Dan Alamanto said on TNBC that day. 'There are well-founded fears that any deal may not necessarily be beneficial to Telecom10 shareholders, given the level of debt that the company is saddled with.'

The net effect of the news stories was to send Telecom10's share price up slightly. Niccolo commented on the stock every day that week. Clients were constantly on the phone, needing to be updated on events by the minute, since large amounts of money were at stake. To all of them he said the same thing. 'T10 is going up. Buy.'

By Friday, having staked his reputation on this call, Niccolo had little room left to manoeuvre out of the stand he had taken. There was no turning back.

Then disaster struck.

That weekend, Téléjeune unexpectedly pulled out of merger talks. By Monday morning the news was all over the trading screens. Those analysts who had not already written off Telecom10 shares as worthless were now downgrading their recommendations as fast as their systems would permit. Traders in all markets were dumping the stock. By eight o'clock, when the markets were due to open, Telecom10's share price chart would look very ugly indeed.

Niccolo did not relish the thought of speaking at the morning meeting. He thought about downgrading the stock like everyone else, but instinct told him the company was strong, that it would bounce back, and he trusted his instinct.

'Of course I expect the T10 share price to fall in early trading,' he insisted. 'However, I believe this will be no more than a knee-jerk reaction to the news that Téléjeune have pulled out of merger talks. And I believe it will prove to be temporary. The shares should bounce back in a day or so. At current prices, T10 still remains grossly undervalued. Therefore, despite this bad news, I retain my Buy rating on the stock.'

The looks on their faces said it all.

'This thing is going down,' whispered Rupert to Paddy.

'A fucking wally, your young analyst,' sneered Paddy. 'I give him three months.'

*

Dr Picton checked his records. He held around £400 million in cash; the rest was invested in the markets. He scratched his head. Too much cash. Too little market exposure. It took him less than a minute to make the decision. Let's see how good this fucker really is, he said to himself.

Picking up the phone, he called his broker. 'Buy one million T10 shares.'

Niccolo leaned back in his chair and closed his eyes. He recalled the tale Mizuno-san had told them, about the monk hanging off the edge of a cliff with a two-hundred-foot drop on to solid granite rock below him, and above him the tiger that had chased him off the edge.

Niccolo knew his case for supporting T10 stood up to scrutiny, but it was difficult to present a proper case in the three-minute slot allocated to him in the morning meeting. So after the meeting he took Odile and Paddy – the two specialist telecoms salespeople – out for coffee. Without their support, he would be in trouble. He recapped his main arguments for the ratings upgrade. But salesmen's minds are hard to change; Paddy and Odile gave Niccolo ten minutes to convince them. Then his time was up.

'I'll say one thing for the son of a bitch,' said Paddy as they headed back to their workstations afterwards. 'He's got balls.'

CHAPTER 16

'Nicco, look at your screen,' yelled James. 'T10's in free-fall!'

'Shit!' screamed Niccolo. His Reuters monitor showed the T10 ticker flashing red – down nineteen per cent and falling.

'*Merde!*' snapped Odile.

The unease on Niccolo's face became visible to the rest of the floor. Two traders who were holding large positions in T10 on his advice rose to their feet and swore blindly at their screens as their losses widened by the second.

Rupert joined in. 'Nicco, find out what the fuck's going on with T10! Now!' Giving orders to his team in public boosted his ego. It also allowed him to deflect bad news on to someone else.

Niccolo leaned over and scrutinised the screens. '*I know* what the fuck is going on with Telecom10,' he growled. 'The merger was called off. I warned everyone about it in the morning meeting. But the market's overreacted. I can't believe it's tanked by twenty-three per cent!'

'Twenty-four now,' James reported with relish.

'It doesn't make sense,' insisted Niccolo. He was twitchy and on edge, doing his best to hide his despair. But the tone of his voice remained decidedly upbeat. 'I still think this stock is a Buy.'

Rupert Southgate had been with Saracen Laing for nine years. The bags under his eyes and his pallid complexion were symptoms of a stressful job. He had encountered many scandals in his time, some of his own making, some a direct result of his own incompetence. But he had survived. Over the years he had learned that one never tries to save a drowning man, even if that man is part of one's own team. 'I don't think the market agrees with you, Niccolo. Look at your valuation on Telecom10 again. Let's talk in thirty minutes.'

'OK,' replied Niccolo, opening his model, praying that he had made no errors in his calculations. The computer file took a few seconds to stabilise. Niccolo checked the figures. Then he double-checked them. There were no mistakes. He was going against the market. He attempted to resist the urge to panic. But that was easier said than done. He had put his reputation on the line, and events over the last two hours had proved him catastrophically wrong. Share prices in the telecoms sector can rise just as fast as they can fall, he reassured himself.

A few rows down, Jack watched the commotion unfolding within the telecoms team, and sensed Niccolo was in trouble. At that moment the phone rang. He grabbed the receiver. 'Saracen,' he said curtly.

'Hi, darling. Are you busy?'

'Never too busy for you, baby.' The words came out snappily, almost automatically. The lack of interest was all too audible in his voice. He knew that. He knew she knew that.

'You sound tense, *tesorino*. Shall I call back?' *Tesorino* – little treasure – was an expression she had picked up from Olivia.

'No.'

'I just wanted to check we're still on for lunch today.'

Jack flinched. He wanted to go to lunch with his wife. But he

118

couldn't, not while Niccolo's career was in free-fall. 'Sweetheart, forgive me. I can't today. Something's come up. We're up to our ears in shit.' He glanced over at the telecoms team, and saw a train wreck waiting to happen.

'Oh baby, your job is driving me crazy,' his wife complained. 'We never have any fun.'

'I'll make it up to you . . . Donna, are you there?' Nothing. 'Donna . . .?'

He hung up, feeling guilty as hell. But he knew he had done the right thing. Donna's needs could wait; Niccolo's could not.

'OK, Nicco, show me what you've got,' Rupert grunted, wheeling his chair round to Niccolo's desk, his tired, bloodshot eyes ready for battle. 'We can't afford to fuck this one up. The whole god-damn market is watching us right now.'

Niccolo knew his job was on the line if he mishandled this stock. But he also knew that the share price would rise very soon. Unfortunately he did not know *when* it would happen. Moreover, having the entire market disagree with him did little to bolster his case.

'Show me the numbers,' demanded Rupert. Niccolo produced a scrap of paper with a few calculations. His boss barely looked at it. 'Let me think about it,' said Rupert. 'Let me think about it.'

At five minutes to midday, Rupert stood up and hoisted his gym bag on his shoulder. 'Right, I need a break,' he said. 'I'm off for a run.' He signalled for James to join him. Niccolo wondered how long he would have to wait before he too received an invitation. Eighteen months after joining the bank, he was still an outsider on his own team. As Rupert and James disappeared down the escalators, Niccolo took a deep breath. The trading floor suddenly felt claustrophobic. He had to get out.

'Charlie, do you feel like an early lunch?' he asked.

Charlie stood up and yawned. 'Sure. Shall we go to the Singh from Punjab?'

Charlie said nothing until they got to the restaurant. When they arrived, he ordered a bottle of wine.

'OK, I heard you two arguing back there,' he started. 'So I know what's on your mind.'

'The bottom line is that I want to keep Telecom10 a Buy and Rupert wants to switch back to Sell. Larry's with Rupert. I don't know if it's wise to go against them.'

'*You* are the Telecom10 analyst. Trust your judgement.'

'It's not so easy.'

'You and me, we're like actors on a stage. Whatever we say is in the public arena, for the whole world to hear. When we make a mistake, everyone knows about it.' Charlie tasted the wine and waved the waiter away. 'What does your gut tell you?'

'My gut tells me I'm right. The problem is I don't have Larry's support.'

'Larry doesn't know what he's talking about.'

'Maybe. But he's my boss.'

Charlie took a sip of wine and placed his glass down firmly on the table. 'Hold your ground and Larry will respect you. You won't last a minute without his respect.'

'I'm just scared that if I go out on a limb with this one, then I'm fucked.'

'You're fucked anyway, kiddo. Look, anyone who tries to predict the future is going to screw up at some point. But right or wrong is not what's important in this business. If you want to be a winner in this game, you need to follow my three little rules.'

A waitress glided over to take their order. Charlie dismissed her with a wave of his hand. 'Rule number one: stand up for what you believe in – your reputation is all you've got,' he declared. 'Rule number two: don't follow the crowd – if you can't think of anything original to say, keep your mouth shut. And rule number three . . .' He looked furtively right and left, leaned forward and eyed Niccolo with steely precision. '. . . never trust anyone in this business. They're all a bunch of dirty, lying motherfuckers.'

'What's this I hear about Telecom10?' The voice on the phone was husky, impatient, jittery.

Rupert considered his response carefully. 'Nicco's fucked up, Larry. I'm not sure he knows what he's doing. I might have to take over T10 myself.'

'I don't like bad news on my floor,' Larry snarled. 'Sort it out!' And he slammed the phone down.

Rupert pondered his next move.

CHAPTER 17

As they left the Singh from Punjab, Charlie and Niccolo were both the worse for alcohol. Niccolo decided to take the opportunity to confirm his and Jack's flight bookings for a week's skiing, whilst Charlie headed back to the office. On his return, the Head of Technology Research grabbed a bottle of Evian from Odile's desk, collapsed into his chair and put his feet up on a stack of papers on his desk. He leaned back, took a few sips and whispered to Jack, 'I'm checking out . . . wake me up if the world goes pear-shaped, DBK breaks the two billion pound mark or Rupert announces he's gay.' And he fell deeply and unattractively asleep.

Jack covered for the big guy as best he could in an open-plan office. It was not long before April was seen patrolling the trading floor on one of her random inspections. Jack did his best to sound an early warning, but Charlie was still out cold by the time April reached his desk.

She took no prisoners. Grabbing a ruler, she tapped Charlie's feet sternly. 'Busy, Charlie?' she demanded.

Charlie rubbed his eyes and slowly gauged his position. Taking careful aim, he fired back, 'Of course I'm busy. I'm meditating.'

April placed her hands on her oversized hips, but Charlie continued, unfazed, 'I'm reaching out to my karma, searching for a divine flash of wisdom to help me write my next note. How about you, Bulldog? Are you busy? You don't look busy.'

Traders, analysts and salesmen, who had until now been minding their own business, dropped their phones and pens and tuned in. Nobody had *ever* called April 'Bulldog' to her face.

'It is my job to make sure that this trading floor operates efficiently,' she barked. 'And that means keeping an eye on the likes of you. You're a drunken mess!' She pulled out a few sheets of paper from the mountain on Charlie's desk and examined them. 'Look at this – you haven't even stapled them together! You're a liability to this bank, Charlie Doyle!'

'Why not get straight to the point, Bulldog sweetie – you want to shag me senseless, right?'

April reeled back and gasped, 'How dare you!'

'Or are you just a silly sex-starved old hag with nothing better to do all day but make life miserable for your colleagues?'

'I'll make sure Mr Sukuhara hears about this!' screamed April. 'I'll tell him about your drunkenness, your ill manners and your insolence!'

'I love it when you take control, sweetheart . . .'

But Charlie was already regretting his outburst. He heaved a sigh of anguish, spraying the air around him with the smell of alcohol.

April scanned the trading floor, desperately seeking help. No one came forward. Finally she cried, 'If you don't apologise to me this instant, I'll have you dragged to the fifth floor first thing tomorrow morning.'

The fifth floor housed the Human Resources crew. In recent years, they had been coerced by Daryl Walker, their politically astute head, into taking a tough line on sexual harassment. The result was that the fifth floor bore a closer resemblance to a departure lounge than a conflict-resolution zone.

Charlie's voice was tinged with apparently genuine regret as he replied: 'Sorry, Bulldog old girl, no can do. My daughter's playing the big bad witch in the school play. Can't miss it. Come to think of it, maybe you could help her with her lines? I could see you in the afternoon. Is that good for you?'

By now, April's usually pale face had turned crimson and she was fuming. Like a woman on a mission, she stormed off the floor, heading for the main elevators.

When Niccolo returned to the office, he was cornered by Jack, who offered him an abridged version of the Bulldog story. When the laughs were out of the way, they got down to business. Jack pored over Niccolo's model with a fine-tooth comb. It was hard to judge the direction of Telecom10's share price, but events were overtaking themselves. Time was of the essence. The market needed to hear Saracen Laing's view. Finally they agreed that Niccolo should stick with his Buy rating.

Niccolo informed Rupert of his decision and was given the green light. He was surprised but pleased, since he needed Rupert's support now more than ever.

'So where are you muppets off to this time?' asked Charlie, slipping on his jacket.

'Just a few beers at the Warren – want to come? We'll have a quick drink and you'll be in bed before *Newsnight*.'

'I'm normally in bed before *Dougal and The Magic Roundabout*!'

Still far from sober, Charlie was escorted to the Rabbit Warren by Larry, Rupert, Jack and Niccolo. Larry went to get the first round and returned to find the conversation had taken a direction of its own.

'We're talking about who's shagging who in the office,'

explained Rupert. 'Popeye reckons Pierce has had half the girls in the copy room.'

'Who's Pierce?' asked Niccolo.

'Pierce Rattenbury. Prop trader. Ugly bugger,' replied Jack.

'Ugly certainly, but already on his third marriage,' said Charlie. 'He's going through a mid-wife crisis.'

'The guy drives a Maserati,' said Larry, joining in. 'I guess money makes the world go round.'

'So you're saying women are attracted to Pierce because of his money?' Charlie hiccupped. 'Not because he has phe ... phemo ... *phenomenal* sexual powers?'

'Look, women equate money with power,' said Larry authoritatively. 'They want powerful men. Ergo they desire rich men. Simple as that.'

'You're a powerful man, Larry,' said Jack solemnly. 'And rich ...'

'I am,' confirmed Larry. 'How else would I know women so well?'

He then embarked on a colourful account of his various extramarital affairs. He mentioned no names, but gave heavy hints that among his girlfriends were former and current Saracen employees.

'Larry, if you've screwed half the office, we don't want to know,' said Charlie.

'You'd be surprised whom I've screwed, Charlie.'

'Well, as long as you're not fucking any of *my* wives or kids, I don't really give a shit,' exclaimed Charlie.

The conversation was clearly leading somewhere, but nobody dared ask where.

'Are you going to tell us the sordid details then, Larry?' volunteered Jack.

'Take some advice from your Uncle Larry. Go for the married ones, because they don't bother you afterwards.'

Jack stared at Larry Sikorski. He could see why women might find him attractive: he was a divorcee who dressed well, oozed cash in a sleazy sort of way and – for an older man – had a sort of sophisticated sex appeal.

'Women want excitement,' explained Larry. 'And if they can't get it at home, they look outside.'

'Not all women are like that,' pleaded Jack, with a hint of desperation.

'Yeah, they are,' sniped Charlie. 'And here's a word of advice from your Uncle Charlie – if it flies, floats or fucks, it's cheaper to rent.' He drained his glass, picked up his briefcase and patted Niccolo on the back. 'Well, guys, here endeth another day of stunning underachievement in the upper echelons of Team Saracen.'

The conversation died abruptly; they all finished their drinks and left the Rabbit Warren together. Charlie made it unassisted all the way to Bank tube station, a few hundred yards away. 'I'll see you heroes of capitalism tomorrow,' he gurgled.

At the morning meeting the following day, Niccolo signalled to Dudley that he intended to speak. With Telecom10's share price having fallen so far in the last twenty-four hours, it was tempting to keep his mouth shut whilst the storm blew over, but he remembered Charlie's advice. He was determined not to hide in a corner. He had to follow his gut instinct, had to speak out loud and clear. His credibility depended on it.

When his moment arrived, he was focused, concise, confident. As they left the Oval Room afterwards, Odile patted him on the shoulder and walked up the trading floor with him. 'Your arguments on Telecom10 were crystal clear this morning,' she said. 'I think you've made a good call on this one, Nicco. Don't lose faith in yourself.'

Niccolo made some client calls and tidied up a few loose ends in preparation for his annual skiing holiday. He briefed Rupert on the status of his stocks and sent the team an email. 'I've emailed you and the team my contact details, Ru,' he said, putting on his jacket. 'Call me if anything comes up. If you can't get through on my mobile, try Jack's.'

'Excellent. Will do. Have a great holiday.'

Later that morning, Charlie was summoned by the Head of Human Resources to the fifth floor. He knew broadly what to expect. Of course his unwise exchange with April warranted a reprimand. Off the record, Daryl relayed a genuine heartfelt sympathy for Charlie. On the record, however, April's complaint was considered serious.

Appropriate remedial action was agreed. An entry was made in Charlie's personnel file to the effect that he acknowledged the folly of his actions and would make a written and verbal apology to April. Daryl formally warned him against making similar remarks about staff in future. And with that, the matter of April and Charlie was laid to rest.

CHAPTER 18

Each year since graduation, without exception, Jack and Niccolo had spent the last week of November skiing. They always went early in the season, they always went to Tignes, and they always went alone. Until this year.

It was Niccolo's idea to invite Lucy, leaving Jack no choice but to bring Donna. Lucy and Donna abandoned the men during the day, opting to divide their time between the slopes and the shops while sharing their most intimate secrets. They found they had more in common than they had first thought.

The week passed quickly. On the final night, Niccolo and Lucy decided to skip dinner and retire to bed early. Left to fend for themselves, Jack and Donna dined at Pascal's, the finest restaurant in Tignes.

The setting was exquisite, the lighting dim and the ambience romantic. The tables were laid with white lace-edged cloths, antique silver cutlery and home-made candles mounted in silver holders bearing the family crest. A well-fed Frenchman waited on them, providing for their every need. With the local speciality on their plates and the local vintage in their glasses, Jack toasted their future.

But Donna did not join him in the toast. 'I'm fed up with this life,' she moaned. 'I never see you.'

He sighed. 'Donna, we've talked about this before. I don't have a choice.'

'That's what you said five years ago.'

'Saracen can always get someone younger, hungrier and cheaper to take my place. Is that what you want? Look, I'm doing it for us.'

'You're doing it for yourself,' snapped Donna. 'I might die tomorrow. I want to enjoy my life now.'

They ate their dinner in two separate worlds. Donna's make-up did a poor job of hiding the tension on her face, her pale skin and her drawn, hollow cheeks.

'There's something I've been wanting to say, Jack.' She attempted an uncomfortable smile.

Jack reached out and took her hand. 'What is it?' he asked gently. The waitress heading towards their table with an offering of complimentary chocolates read the signs and embarked on a detour. But the moment was lost.

'I do love you, Jack.' Donna sighed. 'That's all.'

Dudley Rabinowitz always put on weight when he was happy. And when old Cuddles put on weight, the entire trading floor took note, for his weight was an accurate and proven market barometer, a clear sign that he sensed a bull market out there – a bull market in one particular stock, that is. By the end of the week, he had put on half a stone.

Traders took one look at Dudley's expanding waist measurement and piled into DBK. They piled in on their own account, their wife's account, their mistress's account, their kids' account, the bank's proprietary account – any account.

Dudley leaked so much inside information on DBK that John Sukuhara felt, not for the first time, obliged to launch an internal enquiry to investigate any possible compliance breach. There was only one problem – apart from the obvious one, that Dudley was the bank's Chief Compliance Officer: Sukuhara himself was personally up to his eyeballs in DBK stock.

Dudley loved the adulation that came his way whenever he walked the trading floor in the aftermath of a rally in DBK's share price. The more the traders cheered him on, the more Cuddly Dudley ate. The more he ate, the higher DBK's share price would rise. The more DBK's share price rose, the wealthier Dudley became. And so it was that Dudley Anthony Rabinowitz, Saracen Laing's Chief Compliance Officer, ate his way to riches.

They landed at Heathrow late on Sunday afternoon and shared a taxi home. Once Jack and Donna had got out, Niccolo directed the cab-driver to his flat, inviting Lucy to stay the night. Whilst Lucy unpacked, he checked his inbox. There were 223 unread emails, but one immediately grabbed his attention. It was a memo that had been sent two days earlier to all the bank's institutional clients. With palpitations in his chest, he read it quickly.

Telecom10 is downgraded from a Buy to a Hold . . . by Niccolo Lamparelli.

'That son of a bitch doesn't even have the balls to print his own name on the goddamn report!' he screamed. There was no reply. Lucy had already fallen asleep.

Niccolo lay awake for hours, exhausted, with one thought on his mind. He wanted to beat the living daylights out of Rupert Southgate.

The following morning it rained heavily. Shortly before dawn, Rupert walked on to the trading floor soaking wet. He grabbed a couple of tissues from the box on Odile's desk and wiped his forehead. Then he cleaned his shoes.

'I noticed you downgraded one of my stocks in my absence,' barked Niccolo.

'That's right,' replied Rupert. He hung up his jacket and loosened his tie, both of which were drenched. 'I had no choice. T10's management made a few announcements last week that were likely to hit their share price, so I thought it best to move to Hold on your behalf. I hope you don't mind.'

'I would have preferred it if you'd called me first.'

'I did think of calling you,' said Rupert apologetically, 'but I didn't want to disturb you on holiday.'

'I left you my contact details precisely so you *could* disturb me!'

'Come on, Nicco, holidays are for relaxing. Your friends wouldn't have appreciated it.'

'Next time you want to downgrade one of my stocks in my absence, Ru, I'd be grateful if you could discuss it with me first.'

Rupert reflected for a moment. Then he nodded. 'You're absolutely right, Nicco. Now that I think about it, I'd be pretty pissed off if I were in your shoes.' He offered his hand. 'Quits?'

Niccolo forced a smile. 'Quits,' he agreed.

This little fiasco presented the sales force with two problems: first, they had an analyst who did not believe in the rating on one of his stocks; and second, they had a Hold rating on a stock that was highly volatile. If there was one thing that a company on the verge of bankruptcy was *not*, it was a Hold.

Analyst stock ratings are public knowledge. They are published daily by Reuters, Kloomberg and other news agencies. The world of equity research is a small one, and everyone talks to everyone else's clients about everyone else's stock ratings. In the process, stories spread like wildfire around the City, normally via the sales teams.

Saracen Laing's sales team were amongst the best storytellers in the business, and word spread fast that Niccolo had been double-crossed by Rupert whilst on holiday.

'Hey, Odile,' shouted Paddy. 'Sean Moloney from Elsenheim on the line for you.'

Odile picked up the transferred call. 'Seanie,' she purred to Elsenheim's Senior Fund Manager. 'How *are* you?'

'Odile, darling, what's the story with T10? I hear Saracen has downgraded to Hold. I've bought loads of the stuff on your man's advice. Should I dump it now?'

'Sean, you know me. I wouldn't bullshit you . . .'

'That's why I love you, baby.'

'Good. Well, there's some politics in the background here. Lamparelli thinks T10 is going to shoot up and Southgate thinks it's going to collapse.'

'What do you think?'

'I'm with Lamparelli.'

'So you think I should hang in there?'

'Yes.'

'OK. Put me down for another two hundred thousand at best price.'

'Why has Nicco got a tan?' asked Anne-Marie.

Charlie arched over her desk to grab a pencil. 'He's just back from a week's skiing.'

'He didn't go with that little tart, did he?' she enquired anxiously.

'Of course he did.'

Anne-Marie slapped Charlie's arm. 'You don't even know who I'm talking about!'

Charlie grinned. 'Oh yes I do – Juicy Lucy.'

Anne-Marie snarled. 'What does he see in her?'

'Apart from big tits and a great ass?'

'The tits are fake.'

Charlie eyed up Anne-Marie's. 'You're right,' he said sympathetically. 'More plastic than ICI.'

Anne-Marie shook her head in disgust. 'So what's she got that I haven't?'

Charlie scrutinised Anne-Marie from head to foot. Finally, he answered. 'Niccolo Lamparelli.'

Anne-Marie turned bright red, and marched off the floor.

Charlie heaved a sigh of relief as he slumped into her leather chair. He swivelled round and peered through the glass wall that shielded Larry's office from the rumpus of the trading floor. Larry had just answered a call on his mobile phone. The glass walls were soundproof, but there was an intercom button on Anne-Marie's desk. Larry walked over to the window, his back to Charlie. With equal measures of guilt and curiosity, Charlie weighed his options. Carefully he slipped Anne-Marie's headphones on to his ears and switched on the intercom.

Larry's voice was faint. 'I told you before, Doctor, you can't rush this . . . He's not ready yet . . . *When* he's ready, I'll let you know. You'll have twenty-four hours to make the trade before we release the information to the public . . . Yes . . . Yes, I *know* what's at stake, for fuck's sake . . .'

Charlie swiftly switched off the intercom and grabbed a magazine lying on Anne-Marie's desk. Curiosity had got the better of him and now he felt guilty as hell. He leaned back and flicked through the pages, checking on Larry's movements from the corner of his eye. Nothing out of the ordinary. Charlie threw the magazine on the desk and strolled casually across the trading floor. By the time he reached the other side, he had broken out in a cold sweat.

*

At a few minutes past ten, TNBC started to broadcast live pictures of a major explosion in London that had killed dozens. Information was scanty and coverage of the story clumsy, as the cause of the explosion had yet to be established.

As analysts, traders, secretaries and IT staff watched the carnage on their screens in horror, Pierce Rattenbury, head of Saracen's Proprietary Trading Desk, leapt into action. Even as the death toll was being calculated, on the off chance that the explosion had been caused by terrorists he shorted everything he could lay his hands on. It took the markets just a couple of hours to stabilise, once it was confirmed that it was a gas main that had exploded, but in that time Pierce had netted the bank a profit of twenty-nine million pounds, more money than he had made in the previous two years.

Whilst Pierce preened and crowed and strutted around the office, Niccolo checked his own screens. Telecom10's share price had fallen another two per cent. It closed the day at £2.86.

Within days, Niccolo heard the news he had been waiting for. Telecom10 announced that its existing CEO would be replaced. The incoming CEO, Morgan Purcell, had built up a reputation from his previous jobs as a tough cookie, a hard man who talked dirty, meant business and never budged an inch. His appointment was instantly viewed as positive for Telecom10. He was expected to cut costs, fire inefficient managers and turn the business around. By the end of that day, Telecom10's share price had risen by nine per cent.

Purcell immediately announced a focused strategy for the British company based on selective asset sales. By the end of the week, the Telecom10 share price had almost doubled, as markets reacted positively to the new CEO's strategy. Those investors who had bought Telecom10 when Niccolo had first moved the stock to

Buy reaped potential gains of almost ninety per cent over two months.

The rest of the telecoms sector continued to move sideways. But one telecoms stock in particular fell much faster than the others. Globecom shares were now trading at £3.40, having fallen forty per cent since Niccolo switched his rating to Sell three months earlier. That dramatic collapse branded Globecom the worst-performing stock in European telecoms that year.

With Telecom10 and Globecom, Niccolo had correctly picked the best and worst performing stocks in his sector. Those investors who had followed his advice profited significantly. Those who had not immediately added his name to their list of favoured analysts. Saracen Laing's switchboard was bombarded with telephone calls. Everyone wanted to speak to Niccolo Lamparelli.

Saracen's sales team suddenly snapped to attention whenever Niccolo spoke in the morning meetings. They were quick to sell his views to clients, often displacing other analysts in the pecking order. The bank's institutional clients now wanted direct and early access to Niccolo, and the TNBC news desk took an ever-greater interest.

The bank's brokerage business increased dramatically as institutional clients switched their execution business to Saracen Laing in the hope of climbing up Niccolo's call list – obtaining a stock tip a few minutes earlier than the next man can make a big difference to performance figures. Niccolo could hardly believe that the gut-wrenching apprehension of the past few weeks had suddenly resolved itself, that he really had been right all along. He was suddenly everybody's blue-eyed boy, and it would take some getting used to.

Niccolo looked up to see Larry striding down the trading floor, armed with the November management report.

'Well,' Larry said, pulling up a chair. 'It looks like you've made your mark. Our trading volumes for telecoms stocks have increased spectacularly, just as the other guys are going tits-up in the sector. You've established your credibility in the markets and you've done it in a remarkably short time frame. Well done.'

'Thank you, Larry.'

'Every client I meet talks highly of you. You've got the potential to go far. How you handle it, though, is up to you. I told you on your first day in the office that the only person you need to keep happy here is Odile. Well, she loves you. I know that because she's breaking her back for you – marketing your research to all our clients at the expense of some of my other analysts.'

Niccolo blushed. 'We're all part of the same team . . .'

'Of course, but let me give you some advice, son. You're only as good as your last call.'

For a moment, Niccolo detected an undertone in Larry's words. But Larry went on, 'I just got an email from my old buddy Sean Moloney, who's Senior Fund Manager at Elsenheim. I've forwarded it to you and Rupert. Keep up the good work, Nicco.'

He slapped Niccolo's shoulder and moved over to Rupert's desk. Niccolo checked his screen and opened the email.

Larry

Just thought I'd let you know that I've requested our traders to shift a large chunk of our brokerage business your way on the basis of some damn good research from your boy Lamparelli.

He made a great original Sell call on Globecom, which prompted us to close our position. His update note 'Zero Sum Game' in September removed the temptation to change our current underweight position despite other analysts' bullishness and despite a company visit by our own analyst to see Kenneth Oakes at Globecom last week.

Also appreciated the T10 call. Lamparelli's coverage easily best in market and prompted us to go overweight on T10 post a detailed conversation with him.

Don't ever take me off your research distribution list for this guy's work!

Let's do lunch at the club next week. Perhaps you can ask Lamparelli to come?

Sean

The Cane Bar was empty, as it usually was on Mondays. Paddy O'Shea came straight to the point. 'Whenever you ask me out for a drink on a Monday night, I know there's something on your mind.'

Charlie hesitated, wondering how to respond. Finally he replied, 'Larry's up to his old tricks again.'

'What old tricks?'

Charlie edged closer and lowered his voice. 'Share-rigging, or something. I don't know what exactly.'

'Can you prove it?'

'I overheard a conversation – well, part of a conversation . . .'

'What exactly did you hear?'

'Nothing concrete. I mean – it's just a gut feeling I have.'

'What do you want me to do?'

'I'm thinking of going to Dud with this.'

'Going to Dudley with what? A conversation? A hunch? A feeling? You've got nothing.'

'Don't you think I can trust him?'

'Of course not. Dudley does things strictly by the book, and the book is the Old Testament. If he catches you bad-mouthing Larry, it could get very messy very quickly. Anyway, Dud isn't even

137

coming in tomorrow. He's spending all day at the Mercedes show-room.'

'What's he doing at the Mercedes showroom?'

'Have you *seen* the price of DBK lately?'

'TNBC on the line,' Odile shouted to the telecoms team.

Rupert stood up and called out his extension.

'Sorry, Ru,' replied Odile. 'They want Nicco. What's your number, Nicco?'

'Five-six-two-six.' The reply came from Charlie. 'Same as it was yesterday and the day before that. You know, Odile, you remind me of a girl I used to know at Silverman – Wendy Wong. Whenever I called her, I always got the Wong number!'

Amidst a chorus of groans, Odile transferred the call.

Rupert turned to James and laughed nervously. 'Well, I guess Nicco's the man.' He sounded as though he was feeling slightly sick.

CHAPTER 19

By early December, Anne-Marie and April had begun their annual contest over diary clashes and the ranking order in the *Who's Who* of important bankers. By the time the ritual was over and they had managed to agree on a date for the office Christmas party, most of the venues had already been booked. Anne-Marie used her charms – and the bank's money – to secure a booking at one of London's finest hotels.

The swanky black-tie event was held at the Park Lane Plaza, in the Ball Room with its high ceilings, intricate cornices and overbearing chandeliers. Jack was there with Donna, Charlie escorted Odile, Rupert and Jean-Claude came with Daisy and Geneviève, while Larry came alone. Niccolo and Lucy arrived as a couple, but vehemently denied reports that a serious relationship was brewing. The food was rich and the dessert richer. The conversation around the dinner table was the same as it always was, almost word for word.

'Get a good bonus?'

'Yeah, not bad. What about you? Better than last year?'

'*Much* better than last year.'

'Hmmn.'

Many around the table had sacrificed everything for Saracen Laing. Some had done it for years, some for decades. Their wives, their children, their hobbies, their holidays, their evenings, their weekends – their lives – all were dispensable when it came to the bank. For years they had set the alarm clock for five o'clock in the morning. For years they had put up with shit at work – shit from colleagues, shit from bosses, shit from clients, just shit generally. For years they had seen hotshot bankers – self-proclaimed high-flyers – start below them and end up above them. But none of that mattered so long as the bonus cheque they got was higher than the year before. This year, for the first time in a decade, it was not. Yet to admit as much was not an option. The problem with getting obscene bonuses every year is that everyone thinks everyone else's bonus is even more obscene. Before long, a million-pound bonus is investment-banker-speak for basic salary.

The conversation moved on to holidays and cars and private art collections. When coffee was served, the guests left their seats and mingled.

By eleven o'clock, Charlie was approaching his natural limit, swaying from side to side, slapping the backs of those who got in his way as he roamed aimlessly from table to table in search of intelligent conversation. Eventually he stumbled uninvited into a private discussion between Rupert and Niccolo.

'You made the greatest call I've seen for a while, Nicco,' he slurred. 'You went against the market on T10 and you were right . . . Give the herd the bird, that's what I say . . .'

Rupert scowled. But Charlie would not take the hint. 'You should tell your boss to give you a stonking great pay rise,' he continued. 'Or a promotion. Or both.'

Rupert chipped in curtly, 'Charlie, you're embarrassing yourself and corrupting my teammate.'

'Corrupting him?' retorted Charlie, hiccupping a cloud of

alcohol. 'I'm saving him from turning into a boring little depressive like his colleagues in the telecoms library.'

'Behave yourself, Charlie,' insisted Rupert, with as much self-confidence as he could muster.

'*Me?* Behave *my*self? Oh, Rupie Rupes . . .' Charlie leaned back and laughed, almost falling off his chair. Steadying himself, he said, 'We had young Niccolo strapped to the main rocket booster wearing a Saracen Laing T-shirt . . . and *you* cut him loose right before the action started! T10 went sky-high! It went into intergalactic fucking orbit, and *you* put the damn thing on Hold! When will you learn that you don't interfere with another analyst's recommendation? When will you learn to be-have your-self?'

'You run your team, Charlie, and I'll run mine.' Rupert rose to his feet furiously, and elbowed his way past Charlie, heading directly for the bar.

'You really don't like Rupert much, do you, Charlie?' enquired Niccolo.

Charlie stared blankly at the bar. 'I hate the bastard's guts,' he growled.

The party went on till late. Jack drank a lot that evening and lost sight of Donna as he engaged in unarmed combat with Anne-Marie, debating the pros and cons of Juicy Lucy's strategy for targeting discerning young men. Halfway through, he felt a tap on his shoulder. 'I'm tired, honey.' It was Donna's voice.

Jack stopped mid-conversation. 'OK, sweetheart,' he said. 'I'll call us a cab.'

'But you look like you're enjoying yourself. Why don't you stay and I'll see you at home?'

'Don't be silly. I'm not sending you home by yourself.'

'You won't be. I was just talking to Larry. He says he's leaving in a few minutes and he'll give me a lift. It's not much out of

141

his way. And he's got a Porsche – I've always wanted to ride in one!'

Larry winked at Jack from the doorway, flashing his car keys. All Jack could say was, 'I really appreciate this, Larry.'

As Larry escorted Donna out, Jack turned to the bartender. 'Another Scotch, please,' he said wearily. 'And make it a double.'

CHAPTER 20

The glare of the spotlights and the eyes of the cameras made him nervous. He sat on the sofa where he was told to sit, and waited.

After a mere twenty-one months at the bank, Niccolo Lamparelli's profile had risen stratospherically as he continued to make one good judgement call after another. Together with Charlie, he began to appear with increasing frequency on television shows and in newspapers. It drew business into the bank and therefore pleased Sukuhara and the other senior bankers who ran the London office. The only person who wasn't pleased was Rupert, who began to wonder whether he should have kept the higher-profile stocks for himself and retained more control of public appearances.

Someone turned the studio lights down and the spotlights up. The legendary Jacqui Hanson, prepped and ready to go, spun round to face the cameras.

'The time is twelve-thirty. You're watching TNBC. It's time for *PowerLunch* – the lunchtime news programme that tells you what you need to know about the markets. This afternoon I'm going to focus on the telecoms sector – a sector that appears to be going from bad to worse. Here in the studio with me is Niccolo Lamparelli, Senior Telecoms Analyst at Saracen Laing, and the man our viewers have rated as their number-one stock picker. He has a track record in European telecoms that needs no introduction. Welcome to *PowerLunch*, Niccolo.'

Niccolo felt a shot of adrenalin rush through his veins as the cameras turned on him. 'Thank you, Jacqui.'

Jacqui winked casually at Niccolo as if she had known him for years.

'Niccolo,' she began, 'so many telecoms companies seem to be in financial trouble – can you tell us how this has happened?'

Niccolo tried to look confident, and to persuade himself that he felt confident. 'Fifteen years ago,' he began, 'Europe's mobile phone sector was seen as a high growth sector. Two reasons: first, less than ten per cent of people had a mobile phone, so it was a relatively untapped market; second, new cellular technology made it feasible to make the mobile phone a mass-market product.'

'So you're saying that anyone who went into the telecoms sector in the 1990s stood to make lots of money?'

'That's right, Jacqui. Then things changed. In 2000, European governments sold 3G licences. By 2003, the operators had built brand-new 3G networks. 3G is a third generation of mobile technology that provides customers with greater bandwidth for transmitting data. By 2005, 3G technology had unleashed a whole catalogue of multimedia services, including video calls and high-speed internet access, but anyone who wanted to use the radio spectrum that the government had put aside for 3G use, anyone who wanted to provide 3G services, had to own a licence. Back in 2001, many governments had demanded crippling amounts of money for the licences. The British government sold theirs for around five billion pounds apiece. The Germans charged even more.'

Jacqui wisely didn't interrupt, but let Niccolo continue to explain.

'Yes, they were expensive,' he went on. 'Europe's phone companies borrowed over eighty billion euros to pay for these licences because they thought they could make lots of money from them. But that eighty billion was just for the licences alone. Building the 3G networks cost them another fifty billion minimum. Then they hit two problems. First, 3G technology didn't perform as well as expected. Second, subscribers weren't willing to upgrade unless they were offered huge discounts. So the operators made losses on their 3G investments and wrote off billions from their balance sheets. Stocks like Ultrafone and Telecom10 collapsed. Now the competitive advantage has switched back to the fixed-line players. Investors should move out of mobile stocks.'

'That's a big call. Isn't the mobile industry worth a trillion dollars?' Jacqui prompted.

'That's right. It's a trillion-dollar switch.'

'So, Niccolo, which stocks would you move into?'

Niccolo smiled. 'That's the trillion-dollar question, Jacqui. And I'm afraid the answer's only available to Saracen Laing clients.'

'Niccolo Lamparelli, it's been a pleasure.'

With a smile stretching from cheek to cheek, Karim marched down St Swithins Lane clutching a large brown envelope. As the Doctor had instructed, he entered the Moneypincher's Inn by the kitchen entrance, scaled two flights of stairs to the offices and knocked three times.

Picton had been glaring at his Reuters screens for some time. He rubbed his eyes and yawned, focusing lethargically on the envelope.

Karim grinned even more widely. 'Please look, Doctor.'

Picton ripped open the envelope and pulled out a set of photographs. They had been taken in quick succession, and were very explicit. All captured the same two subjects. Picton flicked through the set quickly, then a second time at a more leisurely pace. He leaned back in his chair.

'I'm very pleased, Karim. Well done. These will come in very handy.'

'Thank you, sir.' Karim beamed with the air of a man who had exceeded his employer's expectations.

'But how the hell did you stumble across this? It was Lamparelli that I asked you to track – not this guy.'

The winter sales were almost over. The most exclusive stores had sent their most exclusive customers all sorts of exclusive incentives to turn up at exclusive openings. Donna headed for Knightsbridge, where she was tempted. Several times. And she gave in to temptation. Several times.

When she got home, she threw away the price tags and tried on her newly acquired outfits all over again. By the time Jack arrived home it was late evening, and the clothes had been neatly hidden away in Donna's wardrobe.

CHAPTER 21

By March 2008, Globecom's share price had fallen another fifty per cent to £2.12, just as Niccolo had predicted. But he expected it to fall further.

The Globecom call was one of the best calls Saracen Laing's telecom team had made for years. It had saved their institutional clients – at least those who followed Niccolo's investment advice – a lot of money in a difficult market. More importantly, by going against the consensus view of the market, the call had enabled Saracen Laing to stand out from the competition.

Larry congratulated Niccolo both privately and in public. But over lunch with Charlie, he sounded anything but pleased.

'Lamparelli's been upsetting Globecom's management far too much lately. I'm not sure what to do about it,' he said. 'He's been highly vocal in his criticism of Globecom's corporate strategy. Christ, our relationship with Oakes and his CFO is verging on total meltdown.'

'I would get upset if an analyst put a Sell rating on my company, Larry. The problem is – he's been right! In other words, he's done exactly what you hired him to do. Look, analysts sometimes upset CEOs. That's the nature of the job. Maybe Ken Oakes should have

147

written the Globecom note instead of Nicco. I suspect, however, that Ken spells Sell with three letters, starting with B!'

'This is a serious matter. He could cost the bank business.'

'Larry, you can't compromise an analyst's position on a stock like Globecom just because some prick in Corporate Finance is about to win the bank some business. That's blackmail. More to the point, it's short-sighted and stupid, because none of our institutional clients would ever trust us again. Oh, and I almost forgot – it's illegal!'

Larry grimaced at Charlie's sermonising. 'You're as naïve as he is, Charlie. Lamparelli's just trying to make a name for himself. Nothing wrong with that, but he thinks he can do it in ten minutes. It took me ten years to make my name in the markets.'

'Yeah, but *cunt* isn't a very good name, is it?' said Charlie, chuckling. 'I'll be honest with you, Larry. I like the kid. He speaks from the heart. He won't bend. And that's why people listen to him. We need *more* guys like him.'

Larry picked up his knife and fork. 'We'll see, Charlie. We'll see how good he really is.'

For her part, Odile made it a priority to market Niccolo's research, and would regularly take him to see her biggest clients, leaving less time to market the work of other analysts.

Working so closely together, Odile and Niccolo developed a strong bond. They would swap secrets and exchange their most intimate thoughts. One evening Odile asked him out for a drink. She chose the Blag Club, a lively jazz bar near her Notting Hill flat.

Odile bought the first round – Bloody Marys. 'Do you believe in love?' she asked, sitting down close to him.

'Of course,' replied Niccolo, wondering where this would lead.

'I want to find love,' she whispered seductively.

Though mesmerised by her French accent and husky voice, Niccolo was apprehensive. 'You'll find it when you least expect it,' he said confidently.

'You really think so?'

'Well, take my parents – they met under the most amazing circumstances.'

Odile sipped her drink and gazed interestedly through her long eyelashes.

'It was during the Six Day War, in 1967.'

'The Yom Kippur War. Long before I was born,' Odile simpered prettily. 'But my father was the French ambassador to Iran, and talks about it often. The Israelis inflicted immense damage on neighbouring Arab states, didn't they? The Arab states threatened to invade Israel, so Israel launched a pre-emptive strike.'

'Correct,' said Niccolo. 'My parents met in Jerusalem shortly after that war. Dad was a weapons expert with the Indian Navy. He was sent by the UN to the Jordanian part of Jerusalem to monitor what the Israeli forces were doing there, and to enforce a UN Resolution that instructed Israel to withdraw unilaterally from the occupied territories.'

'Resolution 242,' Odile murmured.

'That's right,' said Niccolo, rather surprised. 'Anyway, Dad's UN team got caught in the crossfire. He ended up sandwiched between a maul of Israeli tanks and two rival Arab militias. In the fighting he got separated from his team and was shot in the leg. Some Arabs stole his clothes and identification papers, and left him to die. The Israelis found him and mistook him for an Arab. Their commander had actually given the order to shoot him. But my mother saved him.'

By this time, Odile was genuinely fascinated, rather than merely pretending. 'How?' she asked.

'Mamma was a journalist working for an Italian news channel.

She saw the Israelis training their weapons on an unarmed man, and recognised him; a few days earlier he had warned her not to enter the occupied territories, that the UN could not guarantee her safety. She screamed, 'Don't touch my cameraman!' She told them that Dad worked for her. She showed them her Italian passport and press pass and told them his had been stolen. She kept telling them until they finally believed her. Then she arranged for him to be taken to an Italian hospital, and looked after him until he had recovered fully. They married six months later. She told me they fell in love at that very moment, when he was facing death with a gun held to his head.'

'That's so romantic,' Odile sighed enviously, 'a real love story. But I don't understand why – if your father's Indian – you have an Italian surname. Or shouldn't I ask?'

'That's OK. They were married, and very happily. But my father . . .' Niccolo hesitated. Then he said purposefully, 'He died suddenly, when I was still very young. We were living in Japan at the time, and my mother had to return to Europe. She wanted to live in Italy, so she arranged for me to take her surname – I suppose she thought it would make life easier. But my father was educated in England, and he wanted me to be educated here too. So here I am – half-Italian, half-Indian, childhood spent in Japan, educated in England. Where is home for you?'

Odile sighed. 'Home is wherever you decide to live, where you marry and have children. Your parents' story is rather moving. It's not that they found happiness, rather that happiness found them. My trouble – probably it's my father's influence – is that I have always been attracted to powerful men, men with money, men with status. Do you find that shallow?'

'There has to be more to a relationship than that, surely?'

Odile laughed ruefully. 'How long has Jack been married?'

'For ever.'

'You and Jack – you're very close, aren't you?'

'Like brothers. Since my father died, Jack has done more for me than any man on earth.'

'That's sweet.' Odile fiddled with the Jaeger-LeCoultre on her wrist. 'So is there any special woman in your life, Nicco?'

'Well, there's Lucy.'

'Lucy! Juicy Lucy? Oh, come on!' scoffed Odile. 'You can't be serious about her!'

'Why not? Though actually I'm not ready to be serious about anyone just yet.'

'Do you remember, months ago, I said I hadn't had a boyfriend for ages?' Odile's soft brown eyes had lost their usual lustre and were looking sad. 'Well, I wasn't being honest – there is someone.'

'Tell me,' Niccolo invited.

'He's rich, good-looking, everything I ever thought I wanted.'

'But . . .?'

'There's a problem – there's always a problem. At first, he was married. He said he would leave his wife for me, but he never did.' She began to cry. Niccolo offered her a napkin. She took it, wiped the tears from her face and composed herself. Then she continued. 'But even once he was divorced, he still wouldn't admit that we were a couple. He still wanted everything kept secret.'

'But Odile, you're lovely. Attractive, intelligent – any man would be proud to have you by his side.'

Odile blew her nose firmly, and took a gulp of her Bloody Mary. 'And I think – no, I *know* – he has other women.'

'He doesn't deserve you,' Niccolo assured her.

'That's what I keep telling myself.' She smiled wryly. 'Dear Nicco, you're very sweet. I wish I could fall in love with someone like you. But – yes, you will tell me I'm stupid – I think I still love him.'

Niccolo saw a woman who was in danger of wrecking her life.

151

How could she run after a man who clearly didn't value her in the slightest?

'Do you know the story of the scorpion and the frog?' he asked.

'No – I hope it has a happy ending!'

'A scorpion has to cross a river, but he can't swim. So he asks a frog for a lift. The frog's first instinct is to run, but the scorpion persuades him that he is not in danger. The frog succumbs and carries the scorpion on his back. Once they reach the other side, the scorpion thanks the frog, and then stings him. As he dies, the frog asks the scorpion, "Why did you sting me?" And the scorpion replies, "Because it's in my nature." Some people are like the scorpion, Odile. They can never be trusted.'

'You're right, I know.' The worry lines melted away. 'But I guess I still love this scorpion, even now. I can't help it – it's in my nature.'

Niccolo lay on his bed, staring at the ceiling, thinking of Odile and the pernicious relationship she was in, and wondering if he would ever find true love. Just then, Lucy walked out of the shower with a skimpy towel and a bottle of body lotion, and lay face down on the bed. 'Rub this on my back,' she demanded. He sat astride her bottom, as instructed, and began rubbing in the lotion, his mind fixed firmly on Odile.

Lucy groaned with pleasure and writhed beneath him. 'They're talking about you all the time at the Kloomberg news desk,' she told him. 'They think your Globecom call was sheer genius.'

'I was lucky, that's all.'

'They wonder when you're going to switch it to a Buy.'

Niccolo stopped massaging Lucy's back. 'Lucy, you're drop-dead gorgeous and I fancy you to bits. But you work for Kloomberg and I work for Saracen Laing. We both deal in confidential information. Sharing it could get us both in trouble.'

Lucy flicked the bottle out of Niccolo's hand, grabbed him by the neck and pulled him down towards her. 'Maybe I want to get you into trouble, big boy.'

Niccolo checked his emails. Two new ones had just come in from Shingo Shimada, Saracen Laing's telecoms analyst in Tokyo. Shingo covered the four main stocks in the Japanese telecoms sector: Nippon Telepost, Nippon Wireless, Softofone and Yamaguchi Telecom. He maintained a permanent Hold rating on all four telecoms stocks under his coverage, and had never once had the courage to change it since he'd inherited them from his predecessor three years earlier. As a Tokyo-based analyst, he would never dream of doing anything to upset a corporate customer of the bank, and Sell ratings did tend to upset them. For Shingo, it was more important to cover his ass than to provide useful investment advice to the bank's institutional clients. However, given that all four stocks had fallen by well over fifty per cent over the last two years, few of Shingo's clients were impressed by his stock-picking abilities.

In his first email, Shingo asked for the London team's forecast of European mobile subscribers over the next ten years – and he wanted it yesterday.

'Sounds like he's throwing his weight around,' Niccolo muttered, and looked at Shingo's second email.

There are rumours in Tokyo that Yamaguchi Telecom is selling off some of its domestic fixed-line assets. These assets comprise 42,000 km of high-speed optical fibre networks with rings round eight major cities in Japan. They would be ideal for a European telco looking to buy an internet backbone network in Japan.

Are you aware of any potential buyers? If so, this could

be an interesting opportunity that we could refer to our
M&A team. We are well placed, with our expertise in the
Japanese telecoms market, to advise a European telco
seeking to acquire such assets.

One company immediately sprang to mind – Globecom.
Globecom's global telecoms network had a few holes in it, most
notably in Japan and Australia. Their need to acquire a Japanese
fibre network matched Yamaguchi Telecoms' desire to sell such
assets. It was a perfect fit. If Saracen Laing were to broker this
deal, Niccolo told himself, its M&A team stood to make significant advisory fees. But first they needed to win the mandate.

He forwarded the email to Rupert, who read it carefully. 'What
do you reckon the deal's worth, Nicco?' he asked finally.

'Hard to say, but Shingo mentioned forty-two thousand kilo-
metres of fibre. I'd put a price tag of, say, two billion dollars on the
network.'

'Telecoms are down. Every telco in Europe is worried about
debt. Haven't you heard of the credit crunch? Why would they pay
so much to get into Japan?'

'Because the Japanese market is the second biggest in the
world and is far more technically advanced than anyone except
perhaps the Koreans. That means prices are pretty high.
Potentially there's a lot of money to be made. Wire and Satellite
is the only foreign company with a decent footing in the Jap
market right now. They're likely to bid for these assets. That'll
push up the price.'

'Good point.'

'Let's say the deal's worth two billion dollars. If we win the
mandate, it could pull in fees of fifty million. Shall I call JC?'

'No, I'll do that. I'll need a briefing paper from you. I need to
know how the deal benefits both parties – Globecom and YamTel.

Put in all the numbers. I need it on my desk by lunchtime. I'll let Larry know what we're up to.'

'I'm on it, Ru.'

Lucy sat alone on a park bench in the middle of Finsbury Square. As expected, he joined her at a few minutes after ten.

'Give me a progress report,' he demanded.

She lit a cigarette and exhaled timidly. 'Things are going as planned,' she said. 'Niccolo likes me – he likes me a lot.'

'But when will you have him in a position where he might be useful to us?'

'That might take a while. He's too straight. He refuses to talk about work. I think I can get him to loosen up. But you'll have to give me some more time.'

'You need to stay on schedule, girl. We're getting close to the big one now. Can't afford any fuck-ups. I want to know what he thinks, how he thinks, why he thinks. And I want to know *now*. Do you understand?'

She nodded obediently, and he left her to finish her cigarette in peace.

By noon, Niccolo had prepared the briefing that Rupert would use to present his case to Saracen Laing's M&A team, outlining the benefits to Globecom of acquiring YamTel's fixed-line assets and suggesting a bid price of $2 billion.

Rupert read the briefing paper and smiled. He knew this could be the bank's biggest deal this quarter. He made a few superfluous adjustments, then emailed it to Mortimer Steel, Head of Corporate Finance, with a copy to Larry Sikorski.

Dr Picton sipped a cup of mint tea and listened to the wind wrestling playfully with the palm trees. The sky was a beautiful clear blue, and the sea glistened like an emerald against the golden-white sand. He could see as far as the Straits of Hormuz. The copper dome above him sheltered him from the fierce afternoon sun, the marble floor beneath him cooling the air around him. He felt refreshed after his massage by the swimming pool.

The Prince arrived an hour later, surrounded by an entourage of guards and mistresses and local wannabes. The latter two groups were dismissed, and the Prince walked up to Picton with his guards. They embraced each other, exchanging three kisses. The guards created an outward-facing ring around the two men.

'Was Leila's service adequate?' asked the Prince, displaying a healthy curiosity.

'Yes, of course. She gave me an excellent massage.'

'And your quarters – is everything to your satisfaction, my friend?'

'It is always an honour to be welcomed with such munificence to your home, Your Highness.'

'The honour is mine.'

Picton cut the courtesies short. 'Your Highness,' he said, 'I know you and your associates are anxious to be kept informed of progress, and I know you don't like discussing such things by phone . . .'

'My father taught me that business is best done face to face. We live in a small world. You never know who is listening. The old ways are still the safest.'

'Indeed. Shall we get down to business?'

'Proceed,' said the Prince majestically.

'The total amount you promised to invest with me through the various syndicate accounts was to have been one billion dollars. Yet so far you have invested only six hundred and fifty million.'

'But that, my friend, is because you appear not to be keeping your promise. When we talked last, you mentioned tripling my money.'

'Indeed,' Picton said again. 'But the markets have been tough. Allow me to explain my strategy. So far we have been dabbling a bit here and a bit there in advance of the big one. Preparations have been simmering in the background for over a year. We are almost there. A few more things need to be put in place, then we will invest most of the funds in a single stock.'

The Prince waved his royal approval. A guard turned his head to check all was well.

Picton continued, 'Over the next few weeks, we shall discreetly build up a long position in a certain UK blue chip. The orders will be channelled through nominee accounts so that nothing can be linked to you and your associates.'

'I would expect no less of you.'

Picton gracefully nodded acknowledgment of the compliment. 'At the appropriate time, we will instruct our contact at Saracen Laing to move his rating on the stock. The rating change will have a significant impact on the price. Once it rises, we will exit.'

'Saracen is only one bank – what about Silverman Ross, Keegan Seidmann, Feldman Finch and all the others?'

'All the major brokers already have a Buy on this particular stock. But they've all been wrong. Saracen's analyst has got it right. He carries a lot of goodwill in the markets. When *he* switches to a Buy, the stock price will move up.'

'How can you be sure he will play along?'

'Our contact at Saracen can be relied upon. He's helped us several times before. There's no reason to doubt him. It's just a waiting game now.'

The Prince threw his hands in the air. 'I leave the details to you – you have my full trust. Just remember one thing, my friend.'

Picton eyeballed him.

'If you lose my money, I will not be a happy man.'

'This thing is foolproof, Your Highness. You have my word.'

'I will take your word, Doctor, and I will hold you to it. Now that business is over, my friend, I have a present for you. Her name is Katarina. I flew her in from Moscow only last night . . .'

The maître d' welcomed his valued customer to the restaurant with a smile. 'Good afternoon, sir.'

The smile was returned. 'Has my guest arrived yet?'

'Yes, sir, about ten minutes ago.' The maître d' led the way to the corner table, where another suit was waiting.

'Good to see you again, Ken,' said the suit.

'Likewise,' replied Kenneth Oakes. 'Listen, we've got to move now.'

'That's not possible. I'll need a little more time.'

'I thought your end wouldn't be a problem.'

'My end is not a problem – I just said I need more time.'

'Opportunities like this don't come along every day. I can't delay the deal for ever. You need to switch now.'

The man from Saracen Laing loosened his collar. 'OK. I'll try to speed things up.'

'You do that. After all, it's in both our interests.'

CHAPTER 22

By half past seven the following morning, a mutiny had been reported on the trading floor – the entire Pharma team had failed to show at the morning meeting. This was particularly surprising since GSF had just announced the results of a drug trial for a potential blockbuster, and its share price had edged up three per cent in pre-opening trading. The Pharma team's failure to present the market impact of this news at the morning meeting was not only highly unusual, it was highly unprofessional. Trading volumes in GSF were certain to be high that day, and Saracen Laing stood to lose business if they remained silent. Neither Dudley Rabinowitz nor Larry Sikorski referred to the Pharma team's absence, indulging instead in coded exchanges of schoolboy antics, as if sworn to a pact of secrecy.

The Pharma team huddled together beside the coffee machine just outside the Oval Room. They looked tired, angry, miserable, disillusioned. When the morning meeting ended, their colleagues filed out of the Oval Room and walked straight past them. Without a word. Without a glance. The trading floor was no place for sad faces. Those who did not like it could always leave. Those who could not cut it would be shown the door.

The tension on the trading floor was contagious. Everyone knew something was wrong, yet no one wanted to give the impression they cared. Back at their desks they went about their business, but a sense of unease gripped the floor, and with it a feeling of guilt. Guilt by association.

Finally Charlie wheeled his chair to within whispering distance of the Telecoms team. 'What the fuck's the problem with the Pharma guys?' he hissed.

Rupert had been waiting for the question. The analysts around him had been waiting for the answer. Like the Pied Piper, he led them off the trading floor, down the escalator and into the office canteen. They requisitioned a table, callously ousting a spectacled computer geek along with his half-eaten bacon sandwich and his copy of the *Sun*.

'Listen up, motherfuckers,' began Charlie. 'If anyone knows what's going on, now's the time to spill the beans.' He looked intently at Rupert, who simply sat staring down at the table, gazing at the crumbs from the computer geek's bacon sandwich.

'Well?' Charlie barked aggressively.

'I don't know how much of this is true . . .' Rupert began meekly. 'But it looks like Lindsay Compton walked out yesterday. He and Larry were having a slanging match . . . it was pretty vicious.'

'You mean he resigned?' Jack wanted to know.

'He just walked out . . . no one's seen him since.'

'Do you know where he's going?' demanded Charlie.

'No idea,' said Rupert, shaking his head unconvincingly.

'So when's his leaving party?' asked Niccolo.

There followed an uncomfortable silence.

'He didn't resign.' Odile's tone was very matter-of-fact and her voice so self-assured that it left little room for doubt. 'He was fired.'

'What do you mean, *fired*?' Charlie snarled.

'His performance had been poor of late,' explained Odile. 'He made some bad judgement calls, pissed off some major clients.'

Every pair of eyes in the room met all the others in a matter of seconds. Their brains cranked up a notch.

'Hang on a minute,' insisted Charlie. 'Didn't Lindsay get voted number one in the Extel Survey for the last three years running?'

'That may be so,' Odile conceded, 'but his recent performance has been poor. Well, that's what I've heard.'

They left it at that. Unfinished business. As they returned to their desks in bewilderment, nobody believed that the performance of a man of such calibre could deteriorate so fast. There were more pieces to this jigsaw, but no one would dare search for them, for that would amount to a direct challenge to Larry's authority. And such a challenge – innocent or not – would be severely sanctioned by management.

They had all known Lindsay Compton over the years, yet none of them really *knew* him. A family man who was good at his job, he came in early in the morning and left early in the evening. He rarely went to the pub, but when he did he would be the first to buy a round. He showered credit on his teammates whenever the situation warranted it. He refused to play office politics, and sometimes paid the price at bonus time. He was a decent, hard-working man, one of the good guys. Now he was gone.

The subject of Lindsay Compton and his unexplained disappearance was not raised again.

That afternoon, a meeting had been scheduled between Jean-Claude Bouvier and Rupert. Jean-Claude had already pencilled in lunch with Kenneth Oakes the following week. The bank's negative stance on Globecom stock was bound to come up in conversation, so Jean-Claude required a briefing from Rupert. Rupert brought Niccolo to the meeting. It was Niccolo's stock now. Jean-Claude attended with his own number two, David Woodland.

Saracen Laing's unwritten dress-down Friday rule encouraged cream chinos, blue Oxford shirts and colourful Burlington socks, the brighter the better. Whilst most Europeans followed the rule, their American colleagues ensured that a few designer labels were easily visible on their outfits. This year Gucci, Prada and Burberry were all acceptable. Ralph Lauren, YSL and Christian Dior were out.

Rupert and Niccolo followed the rules. Jean-Claude and David ignored them, as did the rest of the Corporate Finance Unit, whose own unwritten rule stipulated three-piece pinstriped suits from Brioni, shirts from Thomas Pink and cufflinks by New and Lingwood.

When Rupert and Niccolo arrived in the meeting room, the suits from Corporate Finance had already poured themselves coffee. They offered no refreshments to the late arrivals. Instead, they brandished their new business cards.

Rupert poured two fresh cups, whilst Niccolo checked the latest job titles. Corporate Finance changed their designations more often than Anne-Marie changed hairstyles. Jean-Claude was now 'Managing Director' and David Woodland was 'Executive Director'.

'Right, we 'ave to change the entire structure,' began Jean-Claude, standing up and pacing the room.

'What structure?' asked Rupert. Niccolo looked equally confused.

'We 'ave to completely restructure the company. I've already got my boys working on it.'

'We've looked at the deal,' David continued seamlessly. 'There are a number of problems, but we can fix them. Our boys have the expertise. It's a big operation, though. We've got to get the derivatives team to devise some type of SPV for the Bridge to Bond –

we reckon that's the best way to structure the debt. Then once it's in a jumbo facility we can get the average blended credit spread down to below LIBOR. If need be we can use a Yen/Sterling FX swaption.'

Niccolo and Rupert did a double-take. The self-styled 'elite team' often talked bullshit. The trick was to know when. Rupert gave an extended yawn, then said, 'OK, guys, slow down.'

Jean-Claude began fidgeting nervously with a pen, as if unsure whether Rupert's comment should be construed as an insult. The Corporate Finance team had a reputation for moodiness, unusually short tempers and a penchant for giving orders, and Rupert often described them as 'a bunch of prepubescent school-girls having a premature midlife crisis'.

'Let's see where we are now.' Rupert took over the conversation. 'We haven't yet spoken to Globecom's management; we don't have exact numbers for the deal; and there are significant regulatory hurdles. So let's not get ahead of ourselves, OK?'

'What do you suggest?' David Woodland asked politely.

'Step one: discuss this deal with Ken Oakes at Globecom,' began Rupert. 'Step two—'

This time Jean-Claude did take Rupert's remarks as an insult. 'This is a Corporate Finance deal,' he cut in rudely. 'You guys are here to help – not to tell us how to run the fucking operation!'

But Rupert was undeterred. 'True,' he said tersely. 'But you might do well to remember where you get most of your leads from.'

Just then Mortimer Steel walked in. 'Sorry I'm late. Have I missed anything?'

Jean-Claude and David stood to attention like junior cadets in the presence of their commanding officer. 'We were just concluding, Mortimer,' said Jean-Claude, helpfully. 'I can brief you afterwards.'

Mortimer was wearing a black woollen suit with red pinstripes. His shirt was yellow with blue stripes, and his tie was light brown, with the Gucci 'G' symbol splattered all over it. Niccolo wondered how the hell his wife could have let him out of the house looking like that.

The two Telecoms analysts jumped to their feet and headed for the door.

'Just one last thing,' said Jean-Claude, pulling out a Saracen Laing research report from his briefcase. 'Niccolo, I note you've still got a Sell recommendation on Globecom.'

'Glad you read my reports,' said Niccolo.

'By our calculations, your valuation of Globecom looks pretty harsh. We believe that the company's worth around a hundred and twenty-five billion pounds.'

Niccolo looked at Rupert. But Rupert was minding his own business.

'I don't like to shoot from the hip,' explained Niccolo. 'I don't have enough ammunition to switch my rating to a Buy.'

Jean-Claude scowled like a child on the verge of a tantrum. 'How much ammo do you need, exactly? We're about to do a fuck-off deal with Oakes, and it's going to send the share price sky-high. I'd say that's enough ammo to shoot your rating off its stupid Sell position.'

'Not the kind of ammo I had in mind.'

Jean-Claude turned to Rupert. 'The problem with *your boy*,' he sneered, 'is that he doesn't have the balls to—'

'Really?' Rupert's voice was glacial. 'The only thing you're good at shooting off, JC, is your mouth.'

The situation was becoming toxic.

'OK, guys, that's enough,' Mortimer said, uncharacteristically showing some authority. 'We're on the same side here. JC, you go and meet Oakes. See what sort of deal you can broker for us.' Turning to Niccolo, he said, 'Why don't you review your recommendation, old

164

chap?' Then, clasping his hands like a born leader, he added, 'Let's work together, guys. We're a team, so let's bloody well act like one, shall we?'

On Mortimer's instructions, they all shook hands. Then Niccolo and Rupert left the room.

In the lift, Niccolo asked, 'Are they going to put me under pressure to switch the rating, Ru?'

Rupert mulled over the question. 'It's a tough call,' he confessed. 'This is one that we may have to refer upwards. I'll book some time to see Larry.'

Back on the trading floor, several analysts and traders were unable to contain themselves. Their eyes were on the screens, their fists patriotically punching the air. Charlie was speaking live on TNBC. Niccolo and Rupert caught the final leg of the interview.

'Just one last comment from you, Charlie, before we go over to *PowerLunch*,' said Jacqui Hanson. 'We've seen a number of false starts in the technology sector in recent months. Some industry commentators say that the sector is back and that it's back for good. So my question to you, Charlie, is this – in your opinion, how likely are we to see a full recovery of the tech sector this year?'

Charlie smiled, taking a few moments to compose himself. He was chewing gum, in direct contravention of the bank's rules governing media appearances. 'A recovery of the tech sector, sweetheart,' he said, 'is about as likely as finding a drunken blonde bimbo in a miniskirt at the Taliban Christmas party.'

That sent the traders wild. They climbed on to their desks and whistled at the screen. 'Legal will be shitting themselves over this,' James said with malicious glee.

Jacqui Hanson looked flustered. Without warning, her producer marched on to the set, yelled orders at the crew, then said directly to camera, 'I'd like to apologise to any TNBC viewers who found those remarks offensive. It's just a bit of light-hearted humour from our friendly Saracen Laing tech analyst, Charlie Doyle. However, TNBC takes no responsibility for Charlie's remarks.'

The screen went blank for a few seconds, then the commercials came on. Charlie strutted out of the recording studio to a hero's welcome on the trading floor.

'We love you, Charlie!' someone called.

Odile patted him on the back as he returned to his desk. 'Now you've really pissed off Osama Bin Laden,' she said.

'Nah.' Charlie grinned. 'The old bin liner's got no time for the Taliban. He's in bed with Alky Ida!'

Meanwhile, no one noticed Rupert heading in the direction of Larry's office.

Had he been found guilty of gross misconduct, his dismissal might well have made the headlines. Perhaps if he had been exceptionally good-looking or flamboyant or sexually promiscuous, his story would have had more media appeal. But Lindsay Compton was none of those things.

Lindsay Compton was nothing out of the ordinary. He was just a good analyst, with a good track record, earning a good package. Such traits seldom created headline news. As a result, his dismissal only made a footnote on page 34 of the Companies and Markets section of the *Financial Telegraph*.

Arnaud Veyrieras read the *FT* every day during his morning coffee break at Carluccio's, just outside Canary Wharf station. The Lindsay Compton story intrigued him, if only because so many questions remained unanswered. Why was Compton fired? How much did he get by way of a pay-off? Why was there no official press release? Who had stepped into his shoes at Saracen Laing?

The article, however, did answer one of the many questions troubling Arnaud. Compton was the third analyst to be fired in dubious circumstances in the last three years on Sikorski's watch. On his return to the office, he asked his assistant, Claudine, to reconvene Team 19 for a meeting.

An hour later, she had managed to track down the seven men and women who had once comprised Team 19. Without the slightest hint of smugness, she informed Arnaud that, with one exception, they had all refused to attend the meeting. The reason was simple – Team 19 no longer existed.

'Well, at least I have one devoted admirer,' sighed Arnaud.

When Maurice finally arrived, he looked like a train wreck. Unshaven, shabbily dressed and clearly overworked, he seemed in no mood to take orders from anyone. He made it clear that he had neither devotion nor admiration for Arnaud and felt extremely uncomfortable attending clandestine meetings for officially disbanded teams. He was there because he needed an outstanding performance appraisal report from Arnaud in advance of the forthcoming promotion rounds – his last two bosses had graded him 'below average'.

Arnaud piled on the charm immediately, and dismissed out of hand any reservations Maurice might have had about attending clandestine meetings. 'History is riddled with such cases,' he declared. 'I'm thinking of your Lord Nelson and Sir Francis Drake, who saved Britain from the brink of disaster by choosing insubordination over due process.' His shameless flattery achieved its object and he moved on to what he wanted.

'Find out everything you can about this Lindsay Compton character,' he said, handing Maurice a clipping of the *FT* article. 'He was fired by Larry Sikorski, yet he is neither incompetent nor a criminal. And nor is he a moron. Sikorski is up to something – I can feel it in my bones, Maurice – and I want you to find out what it is.'

*

The sauna was empty, so after their workout, Charlie and Niccolo dumped their exhausted bodies indiscriminately on the hot pinewood bench and collapsed like two sacks of potatoes.

'JC is going to propose a big M&A deal to Globecom this week,' Niccolo said to Charlie, who lay back with his eyes closed. 'We should get the mandate soon. It's big money for us. But the problem is I have a Sell rating on Globecom and I suspect Larry may put some pressure on me to switch it.'

Charlie didn't open his eyes. 'It's already fallen quite a bit, hasn't it?'

'It's down sixty per cent since I first published my Sell note.'

'So don't you think it's cheap now?'

'No. I think it's still got a lot further to fall.'

'Everything has a bottom.'

'But Oakes' strategy is all wrong. He's risked the company's future on his hunch that data traffic on his networks will take off exponentially. But he's said that every year for the last four years and it hasn't happened.'

'What's *your* hunch?'

'I think data traffic *will* rise fast but data prices will fall a lot faster because there's huge overcapacity on the world's networks. That means revenues will fall. The company won't become profitable until around 2010. In the meantime, its share price will tank.'

'Fine. So the share price tanks. But if Larry asks you to switch to Buy to save the M&A deal, what are you going to do?'

'I'm going to stick with my Sell rating.'

'Let me rephrase the question – if the guy who pays your fucking bonus tells you to switch the rating . . .?'

'I won't do it.'

Charlie's eyes sprang open. He was lost for words.

'I have a fiduciary duty to my clients to give them the best investment advice I can,' Niccolo insisted.

'Fuck the investment advice – this is your job we're talking about!'

'I know.' Even in the intense heat of the sauna, Niccolo shivered. 'I'm scared, Charlie.'

'No shit you're scared, you dumb fuck! Our M&A boys are proposing one of the biggest deals in European telecoms. If the bank loses the mandate just because you have a Sell rating, you're going to be looking at a P45 this time next week. How many times do I have to tell you, kiddo – nobody at Saracen gives a fuck about your stock-picking abilities. They don't want independent thinkers. They want analysts who do as they're told – analysts who don't rock the boat. Stop trying to save the world, Nicco. Just look after yourself.'

'Someone once told me to stand up for what I believed in.'

Charlie leaned back and sighed. 'Don't get all emotional on me now, kiddo. I'd had half a bottle of Chardonnay and was trying to impress the new kid on the block. You know the effect drink has on me – delusions of grandeur and bouts of self-righteous idealism.' He paused, staring at his pale feet. 'This is the City. And it's the twenty-first century. We're here to make money. Principles are for wimps; they're what losers cling to when the battle is long over. Listen to me, for Christ's sake! I was young and brave once, but it got me nowhere. Now I'm old and wise – and for once I'm sober too – and I'm trying to save your sorry little ass.'

CHAPTER 23

The weekend saw the first signs of spring. Charlie, who was looking after his younger children for the weekend, burned a roast on the barbecue. Donna disappeared on a girls' golfing weekend, while Jack came into the office for most of Saturday. Lucy tried her damnedest to capture Niccolo's attention – she pulled out her skimpiest bikini and sunbathed topless on his terrace – but his thoughts were elsewhere. The Jean-Claude Bouvier meeting was messing with his mind. Friday night, Saturday afternoon, even Sunday morning, he was able to think of nothing else.

When he arrived at the office on Monday morning, he found a message from Kenneth Oakes, recorded at 21.09 on Friday evening on the bank's voicemail system: 'Niccolo, I read your recent Globecom report with interest. It seems that the market listens to you. So I have a request. I'd like to ask you to address my senior executives early next week, prior to our next board meeting. I'd like you to tell us why you believe Globecom's shares are performing so badly and what we, as management, should do to rectify the situation. I would really appreciate your help on this one, Niccolo. Please call me as soon as you receive this message.'

Niccolo was flattered and astounded. The chief executive of a major FTSE 100 company had asked *him* for advice! This was more than a surprise – this was an honour. A privilege. An achievement. He switched his terminal to speakerphone. 'Listen to this, Ru,' he said, and relayed the recorded message.

Rupert listened carefully. 'Well done,' he said. 'You've earned yourself the privilege, Nicco. I think you should go.'

'I thought Oakes hated your fucking guts,' said Charlie, tuning in from the sidelines. 'I'm coming along to watch! Hell, this'll be fun.'

'What about the compliance issues?' enquired James. 'And legal?'

'Good point,' replied Rupert. 'Nicco, make sure Compliance and Legal approve every word you intend to say.'

'That's right,' confirmed Charlie. 'Some of our friends out there want your blood. Don't give them the opportunity. Get Cuddly-sorry-can't-talk-now-gotta-check-DBK's-share-price-Dudley to look over every fucking word. Speaking of which, I just bought some DBK shares the other day. The guy's a genius.'

'Dud's a fool!' snapped Rupert.

'Listen, you muppet, DBK is hot! It's going to make Dud filthy rich. He's going to bitch-slap the market and then fist-fuck it into oblivion. If you don't get on this horse and ride it, you're going to be left by the wayside! Trust me.'

Niccolo caught Rupert's eye. Both men decided to stay shtum.

Maurice entered Arnaud's office, this time clean-shaven, with a dossier of evidence.

Lindsay Compton lived with his wife and two children in Barnes, in a detached Edwardian house with half an acre of land, overlooking the river. They led a modest life and kept a low profile. Lindsay coached his son's rugby team on Saturdays and attended church with his family on Sundays.

No one at Saracen Laing was willing to talk about Lindsay Compton on record. His clients rated him as a formidable pharmaceuticals analyst. He had covered GlazerStahlFine and rated the stock a Buy. The day after he was fired, Saracen downgraded GSF to a Sell. The shares promptly fell six per cent. There was an immediate and furious increase in trading activity as every offloaded share found a buyer. If someone somewhere had sold the shares short, then someone somewhere stood to gain a great deal of money.

Two days prior to Compton's dismissal, his mother and father, who were on holiday in Usman, were kidnapped while travelling in a taxi along the Sultan Majid Highway to the capital city of Shahaan. They were badly beaten by their captors. After their release, an emergency operation was performed on Mr Compton Senior, who had suffered severe brain damage. Rumours in the local press indicated that a local Arab benefactor had paid a sizeable ransom for their release. The *Gulf Times* was the sole newspaper to carry the story, but its account was low on facts and high on praise for the Sultanate's police force.

In a bizarre coincidence, Lindsay, the Comptons' only son, had received news of their ordeal on the very day he was fired from Saracen Laing. He had caught the first available flight out. Mr and Mrs Compton were being cared for in a private room in Al Mattar Hospital, with an armed policeman standing guard outside. Lindsay refused to comment when quizzed by British journalists as to whether there was any link between his dismissal and his parents' abduction.

Arnaud studied each of the documents in detail, requesting that Maurice add colour where necessary. Then he called Claudine in.

'Book us two tickets to Usman, first thing tomorrow morning. Charge them to the suspense account.'

'But that's against protocol,' Claudine protested. 'The suspense account is strictly for temporary projects.'

'Just do as I say, Claudine.' Arnaud returned his attention to Maurice. 'Pack your bags, my friend – we're going to the Middle East.'

Later that day, Rupert decided to consult Larry on the wisdom of sending a rookie analyst into an arena full of hungry lions.

'Fine by me,' said Larry impatiently.

'I mean, it's an honour for one of our analysts to be invited to present to the board of a big corporate—'

'So go with him. Make sure he doesn't fuck up. Anything else?'

'Um . . . I don't think so.'

'Good. We're done.'

'Sure. Hey, Larry, you've caught the sun.'

'Playing golf at the weekend. Had a great time.'

Rupert returned to his desk and gave Niccolo the thumbs-up. Niccolo put in a call to Oakes' secretary, and the presentation was scheduled for Friday of that week. Niccolo had four days to prepare.

'Shoe-shine?'

The soft, warm Eastern European accent brought a smile to Niccolo's face. He glanced at his shoes. The black leather looked impeccable. But he needed a break, so he rolled his chair around to greet her.

'Hi, Ella.'

'Hi,' she replied. With her back to Niccolo, she applied the finishing touches to Charlie's brogues. 'There you go, Mr Popeye Doyley. Now they look good like new.' She stood up and held out her hand. 'Two pounds, please.'

'Keep the change, darling,' said Charlie, handing her a five-pound note. 'You did a great job.'

Ella turned to Niccolo and placed her shoe box in front of him. Gently she placed his foot on the box, undid his laces, rolled up

173

his trousers and got to work. Charlie sauntered up to Niccolo's desk. 'Hey, Nicco, have you checked out the new girl in HR? Legs like a racehorse! Face like a racehorse too, but you can't have everything.' Ella smiled, minding her own business.

'Why venture up to the fifth floor when you've got Odile to look at all day?' Niccolo sighed. 'She's got sex appeal written all over her.'

'No, guys, you've got it all wrong,' added Jack, swivelling round in his chair. 'Jacqui on TNBC. She's got a great personality. Or should I say a great pair of personalities.'

'What about Anne-Marie?'

'Hmmn . . .' They considered.

'I'll tell you something, guys,' said Charlie. 'My all-time numero uno babe is Juicy Lucy. All that style and she chose to go out with Nicco!'

'Why you guys talk about girls behind her backs?' said Ella. Her audience suddenly looked as though they were stuck for words. 'Why you don't do something about it?'

This was a direct challenge. Jack took on the mantle of spokesman. 'It's a question of how to approach them.'

Ella stood up. 'OK, you approach me,' she said. 'Chat me. Give me one of your lines. I tell you if it work.'

'OK,' replied Jack, straightening himself out before delivering his line. 'Hi, I'm a love commando and this is a raid.'

Charlie and Niccolo both sniggered.

'No,' said the shoe-shine girl unflinchingly. 'Is rubbish. Mr Popeye, what about you?'

'Me?' said Charlie, cutting short his laughter. He pondered for a moment, then let her have it. 'Those jeans would look good on my floor, baby.'

Not bad, thought Niccolo.

Fifty-fifty, thought Jack.

But Ella shook her head scornfully. 'No. Never. Not a chance. Nicco?'

Niccolo leaned forward. 'Ella, I'm no jeweller, but I recognise a diamond when I see one.'

Jack and Charlie nodded in approval.

Ella picked up her box of shoe-cleaning equipment. 'Hopeless,' she announced. 'You *all* hopeless.'

Then she strode off the trading floor.

That evening, Jack bought Niccolo a drink at the Rabbit Warren. By the time they left, it was past nine o'clock and Jack quickly realised he had broken a promise to be home for dinner.

Mozart was playing in the background and Donna was eating alone at the dining table when Jack entered the flat with a voluptuous bouquet of white lilies.

Donna ignored him. He went to the bathroom to freshen up, returning to find the flowers lying on the floor.

'Dinner smells great, honey,' he said, attempting a kiss.

But Donna turned away to look aimlessly out of the window.

'You're all sweaty, and you stink of alcohol,' she said coldly. From her tone of voice, Jack knew she was in a bad mood, and that no amount of romancing would bring her out of it.

He backed off, cracked open a beer and slumped on the sofa. He didn't need this shit. Not today. He shut his eyes and sighed. The empty beer bottle dropped out of his hand as he eased into a deep sleep.

Al Mattar Hospital was equipped with every piece of advanced medical equipment that money could buy. Like most things in the Sultanate, the entire contents of the hospital was imported – from the doctors and nurses and the MRI scanners to the chocolate bars in the vending machines.

The hospital janitor overheard the visitors at Reception describe themselves as British law-enforcement officers and immediately led them to a private room occupied by two frail bodies and a lot of machinery. Mr Compton was deeply asleep, his wife conscious but in excruciating pain. She gripped the steel bed frame tightly as her two visitors greeted her.

'Mrs Compton, my name is Arnaud Veyrieras, and this is my colleague Maurice. We are law-enforcement officers. We represent the Financial Services Authority. We've just flown in from London. We would like to ask you some questions.'

'It's about time someone started asking questions,' said Mrs Compton. Her demeanour was apprehensive and her hands were shaking, but her voice, though faint, was spirited.

'I understand this may be difficult for you, Mrs Compton, but I need to ask you about what happened to you and your husband. Can you tell us who did this to you?'

Mrs Compton shook her head adamantly. She gripped the bed frame so hard that her knuckles turned white. 'I want Lindsay – I want my son,' she insisted.

'Mrs Compton,' persisted Arnaud. 'You have nothing to fear. You are safe now. We have contacted the British Embassy and they inform us that you will be flying back to London just as soon as the doctors confirm that you are well enough to leave.'

The door opened and a middle-aged man entered the room. He wore jeans and a white office shirt. Arnaud and Maurice stood up like soldiers at a barracks inspection. 'Who are you?' demanded Arnaud.

'Who are *you*?' replied the man defensively.

'My name is Arnaud Veyrieras and this is my subordinate Maurice. We work for the FSA.'

The man appeared stunned. Finally he said, 'I'm Lindsay Compton.' He offered his hand and they each shook it. 'What's this got to do with the FSA?' he asked crisply.

'Nothing, at the moment,' explained Arnaud. 'However, we believe that you were ... shall we say, released from Saracen Laing under suspicious circumstances, and we believe that may have something to do with—'

Compton stepped back, holding his left hand up as if warding off evil. Arnaud observed the platinum wedding ring and the Rolex watch. 'I'm not saying anything to you about Saracen.'

'Whatever you tell us will remain strictly confidential, sir. We may be able to help you.'

Lindsay swung open the door. 'I think you should leave,' he said firmly.

Arnaud and Maurice obliged without fuss. They marched towards the hospital entrance, the sound of their shoes on the marble floor echoing off the clean white hospital walls.

As they stepped out into the scorching heat, the hospital driveway was deserted. In the car park stood a selection of expensive-looking sedans, some with drivers in them. But no taxis.

'Shall I call a cab from Reception?' suggested Maurice.

'Good idea,' replied Arnaud. 'I'll wait here.'

Just as Maurice disappeared inside, a rusty old Toyota Corolla veered around the corner at high speed and stuttered to a halt. The driver leaned over and rolled down the passenger window. Arnaud immediately recognised him. It was the hospital janitor. 'I have the information you are looking for,' he said. 'Get in the car.'

CHAPTER 24

During the taxi ride to Globecom's worldwide headquarters, they talked about everything but the imminent meeting. Once in the lobby, the Saracen Laing contingent – Rupert, Niccolo and Charlie – developed a sudden case of nerves.

Charlie decided to pay a visit to the men's room. Once he was out of sight, Rupert cornered Niccolo and demanded angrily, 'Who the hell invited him?'

'I did,' replied Niccolo.

'Why?'

'Because he covers Coretel and Celltalk – they're both big equipment suppliers to Globecom. Any change in Globecom strategy would have a big impact on his stocks.'

'You should have cleared it with me first.' Rupert frowned. 'I thought we were just giving him a lift somewhere.'

A few minutes later Kenneth Oakes greeted them. Using a private elevator, he escorted them to the top floor. Before leading them to the boardroom, he made a detour to a tiny meeting room, barely large enough to hold the four of them. 'Guys, I just wanted to brief you personally before we went in,' he said, shutting the door behind him as he turned to face Niccolo.

'Of course,' responded Rupert emphatically, as if to clarify who was in charge.

'Everyone on the board is upset at our share price performance,' continued Oakes. 'Many of them blame you guys – they feel your Sell rating is short-sighted and unjustified. Your job here is twofold. You need to explain why you have a Sell recommendation. And you need to tell us what it would take for you to rate our stock a Buy.'

'I assume this is an informal discussion,' enquired Niccolo.

'Sure. They don't hate you *formally* – it's just a casual thing!'

Niccolo's smile was clumsy. His throat felt dry. Oakes motioned them to follow him down the corridor to the boardroom. Niccolo wondered if he had been wise to accept the invitation. Too late now. He wanted to turn to Rupert for moral support, but Rupert was way ahead of him, right behind Oakes.

Charlie squeezed Niccolo's shoulder. 'As the bishop said to the choirboy . . .' he whispered, 'you might find this one hard to swallow.' He felt the tension ease and heard the barest hint of a chuckle. 'You'll be fine, kiddo. Just stand your ground.'

The four men entered the boardroom. For a company that had accumulated £58 billion of debt, one thing could be said of Globecom's management: they did not scrimp on their own offices. The boardroom was enormous, and its decor lavish in the extreme. The white Italian marble table was seventeenth century. The backs of the chairs – all made of ostrich leather – were taller than the tallest person in the room. From secret compartments hidden under the table, each board member had access – at the press of a button – to a personal pop-up minibar, and a personal video monitor linked directly to the main projector. The sound of the projector running in the background echoed off the walnut-panelled walls.

The board comprised five executive directors and six non-executives. The chairman, Niall Windsor, was days away from his deathbed. He sat at the head of the table in a wheelchair, barely able to commit to a handshake.

Kenneth Oakes started proceedings at once. 'Thank you all for attending this board meeting. And special thanks to Niccolo Lamparelli for agreeing to present his views. This young man, I'm sure you'll agree, needs no introduction.' With an element of sarcasm in his tone, Oakes turned to his guest. 'I hope, Niccolo, that you can explain to us the logic behind your theories of doom.'

'Thank you, Kenneth,' said Niccolo, standing up. He took a sip of water. He had no script. And no Jacqui Hanson to pilot him through the pitfalls.

'I've been asked by your chief executive to answer two questions. Why do I rate your stock Sell? And what can you do to improve your share price performance?' He paused to gauge the response. Apart from the chairman, who was asleep, he had every other director's clear and undivided attention. He went on, 'During the late 1990s, everyone in this room – including me – believed that corporate revenues for anyone associated with the internet sector would grow at exponential rates. Companies such as Globecom put large pipes in the ground to carry the flood of internet traffic that they expected to arrive on their doorsteps. Your corporate strategy was based entirely on IP traffic. But the internet boom was not as big as everyone expected – certainly not in revenue terms. Today the industry suffers chronically from overcapacity. Forecasts have come down. IP growth rates have come down. And IP prices – the prices for your services – have fallen off a cliff. Some of your competitors have already gone bankrupt. Your debt levels are high and credit is becoming expensive. Your business could be the next pack of cards to fall. The question is: what are you doing about it?'

A pause.

'From where I'm sitting, you're doing nothing: your strategy remains the same, you refuse to respond to market conditions and you're losing market share fast. Some analysts believe that you will somehow be able to rescue your company despite today's harsh trading environment. They believe the telephone market will show more signs of life. I don't. Barring a dramatic change in your strategy, I believe that your future looks bleak. I don't believe Globecom's revenues will rise for the next three years, and I don't believe the internet division will become profitable for another four years. That is why I have a Sell rating on your stock.' Niccolo paused for breath. The silence that followed sent a shiver down his spine. 'So what *are* you going to do about it?' he continued, flicking on the projector. The slide that hit the screens contained two words and not much else.

EXIT IP.

It was a bold statement that hit at the very heart of Globecom's strategy. Niccolo sat down as a storm of chatter broke out around the boardroom table. The presentation was over. An irate director stood up, threw his pen on to the table and stormed out of the room. Before things descended into chaos, Oakes stood up and regained control of the meeting. 'If you think our strategy is so flawed, Niccolo, what do you suggest we do?'

'That's for you to decide. Your current business model doesn't work because you have taken no account of the damage that the internet can do to you. It might be better simply to return the assets to your shareholders.'

The chairman chose this moment to wake up. 'Bloody silly idea,' he barked. 'Are you saying we should shut the company down, young man?'

Niccolo refused to be cowed. 'That's one option, sir. This time next year, you may have nothing left to sell.'

Further rumblings spread amongst the ranks. One of their number muttered, 'Fucking City boys!' though he did a good job of hiding his identity.

Kenneth Oakes interjected once again. 'Now is the time to buy telecoms assets, Niccolo, not to sell them. The telecoms sector is the cheapest it's been for a long time. We can buy other networks at knock-down prices.'

'There's no point in buying assets if you can't make money from them.'

'The wholesale telecoms market will recover very soon,' Kenneth Oakes shot back angrily.

'Sir, I believe that your business could well go bankrupt before that day arrives.' Niccolo's heart was pounding and his own voice sounded strange to him.

Another director rose to his feet and stormed out. Rupert shook his head in despair.

'Gentlemen, I think this meeting is over,' declared Kenneth Oakes. With that, he left the room, followed by the rest of his board.

Niccolo turned off the projector. For a moment the vast expanse of the boardroom and the silence that had suddenly engulfed them felt threatening.

Arnaud opened the door of the beaten-up Toyota Corolla.

'What is your name?' he asked the hospital janitor.

'My name is Sahir. Jump in. I can give you information.'

'Can you wait a minute – my friend will return shortly.' Maurice was nowhere to be seen.

'No! I take risk just talking to you. Get in now or I go!'

Arnaud climbed into the car. Without a word, Sahir drove out on to the main coastal highway. On the left was the sprawling, bustling metropolis of Shahaan with its skyscrapers and wide roads and luxury villas. On the right was the sea, calm and serene and placid.

They travelled for a mile or so. Then, without warning, Sahir swerved off the road and on to the beach, skilfully manoeuvring the car over the slippery sand, bringing it to an abrupt halt underneath the shade of some palm trees. He switched off the engine and turned to his passenger.

'It's a pleasure to meet you, Sahir,' said Arnaud graciously. 'We would be willing to pay for any information you have.'

Sahir laughed like a man who has just been insulted. 'I did not come to you for money, Mr Policeman. I spoke to you back there because I saw honesty in your eyes, I heard truth in your voice, and because you are British police, you have power to change things, maybe.'

'I'm not exactly a policeman,' Arnaud said cautiously. 'I work for the FSA, the Financial Services Authority. We're like the police, but we do special work – we go after financial criminals, money-launderers, that sort of thing.'

'You mean you go after rich people who rob poor people?'

'I suppose you could say that.'

'What happened to Mr and Mrs Compton, it happens all the time here. It is always the same. The same people who do it, the same reason, the same cover-up afterward – it is always money.'

'What do you mean?'

'My family and I – we are Egyptian. We are *poor* Egyptian. The people here treat us like shit *because* we are poor Egyptian. The Indians, the Bangladeshis, the Filipinos, they don't even speak the language here, but they work for nothing. They take our jobs, they make it hard for me to feed my family. Now I cannot afford to keep my family. There is no justice in this country. Nothing.'

Arnaud nodded sympathetically, unsure where Sahir was leading.

'My son was killed in a car accident last year by one of the Prince's men, Karim. This is a bad man. Very bad man. He kills people for fun. For fun! Karim was drunk when he drove his Jeep over my son. Abdullah was only thirteen years old. He was playing on the street with the other kids. Karim did not even stop. I could not recognise Abdullah when I saw him. His face was . . . crushed.' On the verge of tears, Sahir clenched his fists and punched the steering-wheel, taking a moment to compose himself.

After a minute or two he went on. 'They do whatever they want in this country. They are connected to royalty, so no one can touch them. The man who killed my son did not go to jail. He did not go to court even. Fifteen witnesses see what he did. *Fifteen*! I plead with police to give me justice for my son, but it no use. Police serve only locals. After begging for three days, I manage to get five minutes with Chief Inspector of Shahaan police station. He tell me Prince Mubarak give me justice.'

'What happened?'

'My family got two thousand dirhams. Do you know how much is two thousand Usmani dirhams? Not one month's salary. Not one year's school fees. The Prince spends more on a birthday present for one of his sons. This man, he take away my son and throw dirt in my face. No apology. There is no justice for my family in this country.'

'Can your consulate help?' asked Arnaud.

'Have you not heard what I say? I am poor Egyptian. Egyptian consulate – they help rich Egyptian, not poor Egyptian. The outside world see Usman as great. They see trade, oil, jobs. Only the British are fair. I have seen British police, British army. They are fair people. When you say you are British police, I want to help you.'

Arnaud smiled. For the first time in his life, the Frenchman took it as a compliment to be thought British. 'I will do whatever I can to help you,' he said. 'But you must tell me what you know about Mr and Mrs Compton.'

Sahir nodded eagerly. 'This is the work of Karim. So it is the work of Prince Mubarak. I know it.'

'How do you know this?'

Sahir hesitated. The beach was empty, but he checked around nonetheless. 'My cousin brother, Amir – he works for the Prince. I mean, he supply him – he supply alcohol. You see, Prince – he Muslim, so he pay Amir to smuggle liquor into his palaces.'

'But I thought it was against the law in this country for a Muslim to drink alcohol.'

Sahir sighed. 'Mr Policeman, you have ears, but you not use them. Prince Mubarak does not follow the law. He *is* the law. I cannot complain. With the money Amir makes, my daughters can go to good school. I know smuggling is wrong. But Mr Policeman, murder is more wrong.'

'Don't worry, Sahir. You have my word that this conversation is confidential. I will not report Amir to any authorities. I just want the man who kidnapped the Comptons.'

'Amir never goes to Prince Mubarak's palace. He delivers liquor at a place near Shahaan airport. It is empty desert, where no one comes. One day Amir deliver liquor to two of Mubarak's men. He help them load car with many bottles. On the floor he notice a British passport. He read name. When he came home he told me the name.' Sahir enunciated carefully. 'The name was Mr Andrew C. Compton.'

Arnaud absorbed the information. Outside, the sun was fearsome, and even under the shelter of the palm trees with a soothing sea breeze, the car felt like an oven.

'What would Mubarak want with a retired English tourist like Mr Compton?'

Sahir shrugged. 'Mr Policeman, that is your job. I tell you only where to look.'

'What a fucking disaster!' screamed Rupert.

'Hang on a minute,' declared Charlie. 'Our man Nicco is here by invitation. *Their* invitation. He was asked to justify his Sell rating and that's what he did. He was asked to provide a critique of their strategy and that's what he did. We all knew damn well that none of them would like it.'

'He could have done it more *diplomatically*, for Christ's sake!'

'Tell me a diplomatic way of informing the CEO of a FTSE 100 company that his strategy is a piece of shit, Ru.'

'The bottom line,' said Niccolo, 'is that this company will go bust unless it changes its business model.'

'It's too embarrassing for Oakes to do a U-turn now.'

'Then maybe Oakes needs to go.'

'We've got to get out of here, guys,' said Charlie. 'These walls might have ears.'

During the taxi ride back to the bank, Charlie was unable to keep his mouth shut. 'You know, guys, I've been thinking . . . these plonkers just don't get this internet thing, do they? They need some help. I mean, the internet is growing like a triffid, yet Globecom's share price is getting it up the jacksie! And it looks like it's going to get worse before it gets better. Globecom's headed for a Monica Lewinsky moment – it's going down.'

'Charlie,' snapped Rupert, 'if you don't have anything sensible to say, shut up.'

But Charlie was not to be silenced. 'Think this through, mother-fuckers. Globecom are in trouble. They don't know how to get out of it. Maybe we can help them – and charge some hefty advisory fees while we're at it.'

Rupert's eyes lit up. 'Maybe JC's team will give us a cut.'

Charlie smiled. 'Why pass this one to them? I was thinking of bypassing JC's department altogether.'

'We'd have to think about that carefully,' Rupert warned. 'Compliance would go apeshit.'

'Oh, and one more thing . . .' insisted Charlie. 'I just thought of a great title for your next research piece on Globecom, Nicco.'

'What?'

'Tommy Telco Goes Tits Up.'

CHAPTER 25

'Any news?' asked Anne-Marie.

'Apart from Odile auditioning for the summer edition of *Dykes on Bikes*?' Charlie enquired facetiously. 'Well, Cuddles has made more money from DBK this month than all of us put together, Nicco's gone into intergalactic orbit with his Globecom call, Jack's pushing two twenty-five on the bench press and I'm about to have a nervous breakdown. Why do you ask?'

'What I meant . . .' giggled Anne-Marie, 'is, any news from the meeting at Globecom?'

'Hmmn . . . well . . . it was a bit of a fuck-up.'

'So they didn't like what Nicco had to say?'

Charlie leaned back, prepared to hold forth. 'Let's just say Nicco doesn't mince his words. These guys desperately need a bit of sere-nading, a bit of TLC – so what does young Nicco do? Gives them a punch in the face and tells them they're asleep at the wheel of a multi-billion-pound juggernaut.' Charlie allowed himself a smile. 'The funny thing is, twenty years ago I'd have done the same. I guess that's why I'm still an analyst and Larry fucking Sikorski is my boss.'

'But Charlie, you're the greatest analyst this place has ever seen.'

'I know, sweetheart, I know,' sighed Charlie. 'But my career is over. Nicco's is just beginning. If Boy Wonder doesn't watch himself, he'll get his sweet little ass into a lot of trouble. But don't you worry, baby – I'll watch his back.'

'Isn't Ru supposed to do that?'

'The only back Rupert watches is his own.'

Anne-Marie laughed, and changed the subject. 'Have you seen Antonio?' she asked. 'April says Sukuhara wants to see him in his office, urgently.'

Charlie shrugged. 'Not a clue, but if I were April – and that's a disturbing thought – I'd check in the server room. The system's down at the moment and I suspect young Antonio's wrestling with the mainframe along with the other propeller heads. Why – what's up?'

Anne-Marie leaned across and whispered, 'Apparently we've had some major lapses in security – someone's tapping our lines. April says Sukuhara's told Antonio to sort it out. She says they're targeting you guys in Research. But keep it hush-hush, Charlie.'

'Why the hell would anyone want to target Research?' Charlie bellowed, discretion thrown to the winds. 'We're a bunch of good-for-nothing deadbeats, conning the world into thinking we should be paid lots of dosh for rejigging old information into a couple of spreadsheets and calling it analysis.'

'Keep your voice down, Charlie!'

'There's only one thing in this department I'd want to target, and that's you, sweetheart. If I was still in my prime, and you weren't young enough to be my daughter, we'd be having this conversation horizontal.'

Anne-Marie giggled again. 'Charlie!' she warned. 'Fifth floor!'

Larry was munching on a sandwich – pastrami on rye with Dijon mustard – with his feet up on his desk, when Rupert burst in unannounced. Startled, Larry lurched forward, and coughed mustard down his shirt.

'Anne-Marie!' he screamed. 'I need a new shirt!'

Anne-Marie was used to this. She put down her novel and sauntered elegantly into Larry's office. 'White, classic collar, regular sleeves, size sixteen?' she enquired with cutting-edge precision. 'Hilditch and Key, or Thomas Pink?'

'Pink's. And shut the door, would you?'

Larry left the sandwich half eaten on his desk. 'Good thing you passed by, Ru. I just got off the phone with Kenny Oakes. He's screaming his fucking head off, demanding an apology from Lamparelli – in writing – copied to the whole board. What the fuck did Lamparelli do, exactly?'

'Oakes invited him in and told him to be provocative. Nicco did just that.'

'Well, he overdid it. And now he's going to apologise.'

'That might set a bad precedent – and it might be a bit embarrassing for us. Is there no other way we can keep Oakes happy?'

'Rupert, I'm only going to say this once. Investment banking is a zero-tolerance game. A cock-up like the one Lamparelli just made could cost this bank millions of dollars. I don't tolerate cock-ups.'

'You're right, Larry. What do you want me to do?'

'You write the apology letter, then get Nicco to sign it. And I'll tell Oakes that we're pulling Lamparelli off the stock.'

'What did Larry say?' asked Niccolo as Rupert returned to his desk.

'The bottom line is that you'll have to apologise.'

'Apologise for what?'

'Nicco, I did my best for you back there. I always look after my boys – everyone knows that – but Larry doesn't like it when you piss off a potential client of the bank.'

'Did you ask whether he'll back me up against JC?'

'You mean the Sell recommendation on Globecom? Sorry, I forgot.'

'Shit! In that case, can we delay our meeting with JC?'

'What meeting?'

'The one he's called for four o'clock today to discuss Globecom. You've got an email about it.'

'Why do you want to delay the meeting?'

'Because I don't feel comfortable defending my Sell rating if I can't be sure that Larry will back me up.'

'Let's see what they say, Nicco. No need to panic. When has Larry ever let us down?'

Once back in London, Arnaud instructed Maurice to follow up the leads Sahir had given him. After some preliminary investigative work and some discreet calls to his private intelligence contacts, Maurice came up with two pieces of information that he knew Arnaud would find interesting.

First, Karim. He was currently attached to the Usmani Embassy in London. But MI6 had put him under observation because he spent so little time there. He had been spotted on no fewer than three occasions at the Moneypincher's Inn with Dr Picton.

Second, the Comptons. It was no accident that Mr and Mrs Compton had gone on holiday to Usman. They had won a free trip in a bogus travel competition. It was a set-up. Within hours of their arrival in Usman, they had been kidnapped. Two days later, their son Lindsay was fired. And the very next day the Comptons were miraculously released.

'If you ask me, guv,' Maurice sniffed, 'someone's leaning on that Compton bloke.'

Arnaud was sure they were on to something. But Maurice had a day job and Arnaud was not authorised to cover the case. So the only question now was whether or not to go ahead without Amanda Sanderson's express approval.

The meeting with Jean-Claude was rescheduled for six o'clock, as it clashed with a personal gym training session and Jean-Claude refused to pay the cancellation fee.

'I had lunch with Kenneth Oakes last week,' he said, kicking off the meeting with a grin.

Rupert and Niccolo glanced at each other briefly. Both wondered what the French idiot had gone and done now.

'We discussed the YamTel acquisition,' continued Jean-Claude. 'The numbers he has given us make a lot of sense. We've reviewed broker reports from other analysts covering Globecom. It looks like most of them disagree with your valuation of the company, Rupert.'

'It's not my valuation, JC,' Rupert said hastily. 'Niccolo is the lead on Globecom.'

'Analysts always disagree with each other,' said Niccolo. 'That's what makes a market—'

Jean-Claude cut in abruptly. 'I accept that you represent the bank's official view on Globecom. However, I've done some research of my own. And my calculations show that Globecom is worth around one hundred and twenty-five billion pounds. So—'

'So that would make the stock a Buy? Is that what you're saying, JC?' Niccolo interrupted in his turn. 'I value Globecom at forty-six billion pounds. Today's market value is around fifty-five billion. That's why I rate the stock Sell. And that's why it'll remain a Sell.'

'Perhaps you could review your numbers, Nicco. I suggest you discuss the matter with Sikorski. He has the final say, doesn't he?'

Rupert finally came to the rescue. 'Larry's position, under normal circumstances, is to allow the analyst covering the stock to make the call. I doubt he's going to interfere on this. After all, Nicco has called it correctly for eight months.'

Jean-Claude leaned forward. 'Niccolo, maybe you're getting a bit too emotionally attached to this stock. I hear your ego talking. We all know that valuations are subjective. A little tweak of your cost of capital, a little tweak of your revenue forecasts – these things can make a big difference to the outcome. There's no mileage in being too rigid. In a situation like this, we need you to be fluid.'

'Are you asking me to fiddle my numbers, JC?'

'Come on, Niccolo. Don't put words into my mouth.'

Niccolo stuck to his guns. 'My job is to produce independent valuations based on the information I have available to me. Yours is to win big mandates from clients for advisory work. Sometimes our jobs can conflict.'

'So I guess we'll have to compromise, right?'

'I can't compromise my independence.'

Jean-Claude hammered the table. 'You're not being very helpful!'

'I'm not sure I'm in a position to be very helpful.'

'All I'm saying is that I would be . . . *grateful* if you reviewed your negative stance on Globecom.'

'Undue influence on a stock analyst is in breach of FSA regulations, JC. Were I to comply, it could get us all fired.'

David Woodland stepped in. 'Look, let's be commercial here. We could lose a fucking big deal! Doesn't anyone in the research department have any business acumen?'

'My business acumen is telling me not to break the law.'

'Niccolo,' said Jean-Claude, patronisingly. 'I don't think you see the big picture here.'

'I think I see the big picture just fine,' retorted Niccolo. 'You guys have your sights on a big deal and you're willing to do anything, sell anyone, break any rule so you can get yourselves a nice big bonus. Well, I'm not for sale, so you find a way round that.'

Jean-Claude got to his feet. 'I think you've made your position very clear, Mr Lamparelli. I don't believe there is anything more to discuss.'

Niccolo gathered his things and, without any handshakes or goodbyes, left the room. Rupert followed, with an uncomfortable look on his face.

In direct contravention of the bank's non-smoking policy, David and Jean-Claude lit up a couple of Marlboros and vented their anger at the young analyst in his absence.

'Does that little shit really think we pay him a bonus so that he can speak to us like that?'

'He was out of line, JC,' agreed David. 'But technically speaking, he's absolutely right.'

'*Quel con*!' raged the Frenchman.

'We'd better take it easy. The SEC and the FSA are coming down very hard on corporate bankers who pressure analysts to change their stock ratings.'

'Pressure? *Pressure*? That stupid shit could cost us this deal. Who ze fuck does he think he is?'

Kenneth Oakes instructed his secretary to make the travel arrangements. He and his wife would be flying first class to Tokyo. British Airways, of course. They would be staying in the presidential suite at the Okura Hotel. A modest supper of caviar, melba toast and oysters would suffice for the first night. Mrs Oakes hated travelling and would require a full body massage the morning after their arrival to help her adjust. Mr Oakes would meet his wife at the BA lounge at Heathrow, so a second Bentley would need to be booked to pick her up from their Knightsbridge residence.

Mr Oakes' corporate finance and advisory teams would make their own way to Tokyo. They would, of course, adhere strictly to company policy and guidelines in respect of travel and subsistence on overseas business trips.

After the meeting with Jean-Claude, Rupert and Niccolo headed straight for Larry's office.

'He's out for the rest of the afternoon,' Anne-Marie informed them.

'OK, book us in, first available,' Rupert said brusquely.

Anne-Marie scanned Larry's electronic diary for openings as Niccolo arched over her desk to take a peek at her screen. 'This issue has to be resolved. Fast,' Rupert fretted. 'Jean-Claude's likely to escalate it to New York. Larry needs to be warned.'

Niccolo thumped Anne-Marie's desk and shouted, 'Fuck! Fuck! And double-fuck!'

'What's up?' enquired Anne-Marie, concerned.

'Guess who's got the ten-thirty slot? Jean-Claude fucking Bouvier!'

'Fuck!' Rupert echoed bleakly. 'We've been outmanoeuvred.'

Jean-Claude might be an idiot, but he was no fool. Clearly he had foreseen the outcome of their meeting and had pre-booked some time with Larry. No doubt he would attempt to 'rectify matters' before Rupert or Niccolo could put their case. What worried the two Telecoms analysts was that the Frenchman had a reputation for playing the game well, and for getting what he wanted. Niccolo's olive complexion turned pale. Rupert, pale on the best of days, exhibited a whiter shade that afternoon.

'All hell's going to break loose next week,' he said.

Jack got off the train one stop early and walked the extra mile home so the fresh air could clear his head. Once in the house, he headed for the kitchen and grabbed a bottle of Budweiser from the fridge. Donna was not at home.

An envelope lay on the kitchen table, addressed to him in Donna's handwriting. He took a sip and opened the envelope.

My dear Jack,

I have tried for a while now to speak to you but you are always busy. Life recently has been all about you. You never stop to look at me. You never ask me how I am doing or how I feel. We never talk any more. I'm sorry to tell you this in a letter, but I have found someone else. I don't love you any more, Jack. There is no easy way for me to tell you that. Don't hate me. Please just understand that we have drifted apart over the years. I've moved out. I'm staying with a friend. Please don't contact me, Jack. It's over.

Donna

Jack placed the beer bottle on the table and reread the letter. Donna's habitual ending – *All my love* – had been crossed out. Without taking his eyes off the piece of paper, and with his hand as his guide, as if blind, he found a chair and sat down. The second item in the envelope was a petition for divorce, signed by Donna and witnessed by someone who appeared to be a co-worker at the hospital.

A million thoughts rushed through Jack's mind, none of them making much sense. If he was honest, he had seen this train wreck coming for months. Yet he had chosen to ignore the warning signs.

He gulped down what remained of his beer and poured himself a generous slosh of vodka.

Back at his desk, Niccolo opened his Globecom model. Models are based on forecasts of future profits, so they are inherently subjective. Different analysts make different forecasts. Niccolo stared at the screen, and ran through the various changes that might be made, looking for any minor adjustments that could allow him to switch his Globecom rating to a Buy.

Weary suddenly, he closed his eyes. If only there was some sort of sign . . .

Young Niccolo was drawn to the top of the mountain by the smoke. The smell of the burning incense engulfed his body, but it was the sound of the prayers that captured his mind. Mizuno spoke so clearly when he prayed. His words flowed like a meandering stream, always following the same path each day, never reaching its destination, full of life, full of love.

Young Niccolo clenched his fists, walked cautiously up towards Yoshiro's grave and knelt quietly on the ground beside Mizuno. The old man rocked gently back and forth, his eyes closed, his body acknowledging Niccolo's presence. When he had finished his prayers, he kissed Niccolo and led him down the mountain path.

'Sensei,' asked the boy, 'what were you praying for?'

'I pray for my grandson's soul, Nicco-san.'

'Where is Yoshiro's soul, sensei?'

'In heaven.'

'How do you know, sensei?'

The old man shut his eyes as though the question was too painful to answer. 'Because he lived a good life,' *he said eventually.* 'And he died with honour.'

The eleven-year-old Niccolo nodded, remembering. 'Will I go to heaven too?' *he asked.*

Mizuno laughed heartily and gently patted young Niccolo's shoulder. 'You will go to Michiko's hut to fetch some goat's milk.'

'But sensei,' *insisted young Niccolo*, 'when I die, I want to go to heaven and be with Yoshiro.'

'That is up to you, Nicco-san. If you obey your parents, work hard at school and live a good life when you grow up, then you too will go to heaven.'

Niccolo thought for a minute. 'Sensei,' he said again, 'sometimes it's hard to know if I'm being good. Do grown-ups always know?'

The old fisherman answered quite seriously. 'No, not always. Sometimes it can be hard, even for grown-ups. But if you live your life with honour, you too will go to heaven, Nicco-san.'

'But how will I know what to do, sensei?'

Mizuno stopped in his tracks, lowered himself to young Niccolo's level and looked sternly into his baby-brown eyes. 'Listen to your heart, Nicco-san. Your heart never lies. If you follow your heart, if you do what is right, then you too will have honour, like Yoshiro. If you achieve your goals in life without trampling on others, if you stand up for truth and fight injustice, if you help people less fortunate than yourself, you will have honour, Nicco-san – in this world as well as in the next.'

'If I do all these things today, sensei, will I have honour tomorrow?'

Mizuno chuckled. He picked up a nearby pebble from the ground and showed it to young Niccolo. 'Take this stone,' he said, offering him the pebble. 'Pretend it is your honour. Feel it – so smooth to the touch. It has become so only after thousands and thousands of years. Honour takes a lifetime to build, Nicco-san. And it can be lost in an instant. Like this . . .' All of a sudden, Mizuno grabbed the pebble from the palm of Niccolo's hand and threw it out towards the sea. 'Now do you understand how easily something you have struggled to attain can be taken from you? Honour is like that.'

Young Niccolo tried to spot where the stone had landed, but he could not. 'But what I don't understand, sensei, is how I am supposed to know what the right thing to do is.'

The old fisherman smiled. 'When your time comes, Nicco-san, you will know,' he said. 'Just as Yoshiro knew.'

Young Niccolo reached out earnestly for the old man's hand. When he *found it, he grabbed it and squeezed. 'I want to die with honour, sensei, just like Yoshiro.'*

'Little boy, you talk too much. Go fetch me some milk. And hurry back. I am hungry!'

Young Niccolo snapped to attention and bowed. 'Hai, sensei!'

Niccolo opened his eyes and looked around him. The usual culprits were busy beavering away at their desks, the cleaners were lurking in the shadows, and TNBC was playing on the big cinema screen.

Without saving any changes, he closed the model and allowed himself a smile. Then he got up, switched off the computer, put on his jacket and made his way home.

CHAPTER 26

Well into his third shot of Smirnoff, Jack paced the room. He leaned his aching head against the windowpane, and gazed unseeing into the street. Suddenly his eyes focused and he straightened up. The car was still there. So she must have taken a taxi. He picked up the phone and speed-dialled the minicab office.

'Hi, it's Jack Ford,' he said. 'I'm supposed to be at a party with my wife, but she left without giving me the address. One of your guys dropped her. Can you tell me where?'

'Ah yes, sir.' The operator shuffled some papers. 'Ali took her to . . . let me see . . . Onslow Square at three-thirty this afternoon, sir.'

'What number Onslow Square?'

'Sorry, sir, we don't have the house number. Shall I send a car round for you?'

'No thank you.' Jack placed the receiver down gently. His mouth was dry, his head heavy, his blood polluted with alcohol.

In the late hours of the evening, a courier arrived at the Money-pincher's Inn with a message for Dr Picton. The message was typewritten in pre-agreed code. Picton paid the courier a generous tip and returned to his offices upstairs, where he deciphered the code.

The message was unambiguous. It was time to start buying up Globecom stock, as much as the market could bear.

They had just made love. She felt guilty for what she had done. But only for a second. There was no turning back now. A new man. A new future. A new life. It was exciting.

Her gaze rested greedily on him as he stepped into the shower and turned on the tap. His lightly tanned skin was the colour of pure virgin olive oil. The creases in his skin, softly multiplying as the years passed, were the only reference to his age. Silently she let go of the satin sheet covering her naked body, allowing it to fall gracefully on to the marble floor, and slid into the shower behind him. Her shoulder-length golden hair, like silk to the touch, streamed down her back, heavy with water. She nuzzled the dip at the base of his neck and let her hands drop down to cup him. The groan of pleasure that escaped him made her look up and smile.

It never ceased to amaze him how horny the sound of running water could make him. With a practised motion he caressed her back as her full breasts beckoned his mouth. He pushed her against the tiles and she gasped at the shock of the cold. He kissed her, one hand tangled in her wet hair, the other resting between her buttocks. She felt a shiver down her spine, but at the same time she felt totally secure and safe with this man. He was a man of power. And he was in charge.

Later, he said, 'It's getting on. Perhaps you should go home?'

She smiled. 'But I've left him, just like we agreed.'

He stared at her, surprised by her timing. Finally he unleashed a cool grin. 'I have a bottle of Moët – lightly chilled. Shall I open it?'

*

The balcony doors were wide open and a cool breeze swept through the apartment. On the kitchen table, a Nokia handset vibrated incessantly, its owner otherwise occupied only a few yards away.

A few hours later, Niccolo emerged from his bedroom to fetch two glasses of water. When he checked the phone, he found six missed calls and four text messages, all from Jack. He was clearly drunk. Each message was garbled and distressed, but conveyed much the same story: Donna had left him for another man, the man in question lived somewhere in Onslow Square, and Jack didn't know what the hell to do. Niccolo took a deep breath and sat down.

'Come back to bed,' shouted Lucy. 'You're not playing with that silly video game again, are you? It's two in the morning, for God's sake!'

'Lucy, I need to go out. Jack's in trouble.' Niccolo slipped on whatever clothes he could find, grabbed his running shoes and kissed her. 'I'll be back as soon as I can.'

In the luxurious suburban comfort of his newly built seven-bedroom, six-bathroom Surrey home, Rupert was watching television with his family when his mobile phone rang.

'Rupert? It's Ken Oakes. Your boy Lamparelli – he's being rather difficult. I'd be grateful if you could have a word.'

'We're dealing with it,' Rupert assured him. 'Lamparelli is not someone you need to worry about, Ken. He won't cause you any problems. I can personally assure you of that.'

'I hope so. There's a lot at stake.'

By the time Niccolo arrived, Jack could barely stand up straight. The stench of alcohol leaked from every pore, and his eyes were bloodshot. Niccolo froze, as if staring at a ghost.

'I'm glad you're here, Nicco!' said Jack incoherently. He

lurched forward and collapsed into Niccolo's arms. Niccolo held him tight. It was a while before either spoke.

'Who is he?' asked Niccolo.

'I don't know,' whispered Jack. 'I just know that he lives in Onslow Square.'

Niccolo brewed some coffee, and they ordered a takeaway pizza. Jack talked. And talked. He talked of family, and love, and memories he and Niccolo shared.

Niccolo shared Jack's pain. He had known Donna for almost a decade, and while he had never really liked her, he had to admit that he had never seen her even flirt seriously with another man.

Now he felt every bit as betrayed as Jack.

CHAPTER 27

At precisely 08.30 on Monday morning, Rupert and Niccolo shut themselves in one of the soundproofed meeting rooms on the edge of the trading floor to discuss the Globecom rating. Niccolo presented the facts. Rupert listened. Then Rupert put forward a view. Niccolo listened. They argued. They listened to each other. They argued again. They went out for coffee. They returned. They argued some more. Then they reached a decision – for now, the Saracen Laing rating for Globecom would remain Sell.

At twenty-five minutes past eleven, they marched down the trading floor towards Larry's office.

'Do you want to do the talking, Ru?' asked Niccolo.

When Rupert smelt trouble, his policy was to distance himself from it. He would wait and see which way Larry was batting before taking sides. 'Why don't you handle this one?' he countered.

When they entered Larry's office, Jean-Claude Bouvier, who'd had the 10.30 slot, was nowhere to be seen.

'OK, guys, what seems to be the problem?' asked Larry.

Rupert chuckled. 'Nicco's made himself some new friends in Corporate Finance.'

'I've just had a little chat with JC. He mentioned something about your Globecom valuation being a little on the low side.'

'JC has been putting pressure on me to change my rating,' explained Niccolo.

'Oh, come on! We all have to deal with pressure in this job, Nicco.' Larry's reply conveyed anger and irritation.

'I was hoping to get your support, Larry.'

'JC has a good case. He put some very convincing arguments to me earlier this morning.'

'Larry, JC's views are biased,' Niccolo protested. 'His interests are conflicted.'

'JC is an experienced banker. You should listen to his views. You might learn something.'

'I need you to back me up, Larry.'

'Now listen.' Larry adopted a distinctly conciliatory, fatherly tone. 'Nobody really knows which direction share prices will move. They can go up and they can go down. Sometimes there's not much to be gained by being too rigid in one's thinking. Perhaps it's time for Globecom's price to go up. What do you think, Rupert?'

'JC *may* have a point,' Rupert said, reluctantly entering the debate. 'In my view Globecom stock is probably cheap now. Perhaps it's time to upgrade to Buy.'

'See here, Nicco,' said Larry, calmly leaning on the table. 'It's worth remembering that JC plays a significant role in determining your bonus. So we need to be as helpful as we possibly can.'

Niccolo pondered his predicament. In most industries it was awfully unwise to confront one's boss; in an investment bank it was downright stupid; and in an American investment bank it was certain suicide. He was tempted to follow instructions. It was the easier option. There was only one problem. In his heart, he knew he was right. Caving in to pressure would amount to cashing in his honour; it would amount to cashing in everything that Mizuno-san had taught him to hold dear in life.

He took a deep breath. 'Larry, I'd feel extremely uncomfortable changing my recommendation. I simply don't believe that Globecom's share price will go up.'

Larry began tapping his fingers on the desk.

Rupert recognised the signal and decided to proceed with caution. 'Nicco, Larry and I have been concerned at the way you've been handling Globecom lately,' he said. 'Especially the board meeting the other day. We both feel you should apologise to Kenneth Oakes. I've taken the liberty of drafting a letter on your behalf. I'd like you to read it and sign it.' He hurriedly pulled out a document from his pocket. 'Larry, clearly this whole thing is taking a toll on Niccolo. Can I suggest that I relieve him of this stock for now? It's probably time for a fresh look at it anyway.'

Larry nodded amicably. 'I think that suggestion is wise under the circumstances. OK, Nicco, I'm pulling you off Globecom.'

Niccolo's jaw dropped. 'Larry, you can't be serious—'

'Thank you, gentlemen,' said Larry abruptly. 'I think we're done.'

Rupert led a stunned Niccolo out of Larry's office. No sooner had they got back to their own desks than Rupert's phone rang.

'Rupert, it's Larry. Can you come back in for a couple of minutes?'

'Sure.'

As Rupert retraced his steps to Larry's office, Niccolo watched helplessly. He counselled himself against falling into the dark abyss of paranoia. Then, without reading it, he crumpled up the letter of apology and threw it into the bin.

The Head of Research was on the phone. His eyes flickered with an uneasiness that made Rupert queasy. Larry left the caller on hold as he turned to Rupert, tapping his fingers agitatedly.

'What the fuck's going on, Ru? I expect you to sort these problems out before they hit my desk!'

'To be fair to Nicco, his calls on Globecom have been accurate ever since he took on the stock . . .'

Larry slammed the phone down and paced the room. From outside, Anne-Marie monitored events closely from the relative safety of her desk.

'Rupert, that sort of attitude is just not helpful. Just take over the fucking stock yourself and switch the bloody thing to a Buy!'

'That could be tricky right now. You see, Nicco's Sell argument is based on the premise that the stock will continue to fall unless the CEO changes his strategy or gets sacked, or the market suddenly rallies. None of these things have happened yet, so we might look a bit silly tampering with the recommendation. Perhaps we could move it to a Hold?'

'For Christ's sake, Ru, take a stand! Just fiddle the fucking model or something. Make it up. I don't care. We can't lose this deal. It's the biggest fucking telecoms deal this year!'

'Leave it to me, Larry. I'll sort it out.'

Rupert scurried out of the room, annoyed at himself for being so timid, and stormed across the trading floor.

In his office, Larry sank into his leather chair and pondered his next move. In a masochistic sort of way, the Head of Research loved problems. He would deal with this one in the way he dealt with most – with the use of disproportionate force. That either eliminated the problem, or it eliminated the problem-maker.

The minute the man from Saracen Laing arrived at the Money-pincher's Inn, the maître d' escorted him up the narrow staircase, as instructed, and knocked twice on the office door.

Picton was staring at his Kloomberg terminal, a half finished

Cuban cigar in his hand. 'Come in,' he said coolly. 'I've been expecting you.'

His visitor took a seat, folded his arms and eyeballed his host.

'I'm long Globecom,' Picton said.

'How much have you got?'

'Two hundred and eighty million shares at an average price of £2.05 and I'm heavily geared.'

'Good.'

Picton jumped to his feet, spilling ash over his suit. 'It's not good at all. The stock's trading at £2.01 today. When the fuck are you going to act?'

The other man chewed on his lip. Finally he said, 'Everything is working as expected. We're just a little behind schedule. Another couple of days – a week max – should sort things out.'

'I could lose a fortune by then! I thought you were ready.'

'No one is going to lose money, Doctor. OK, Lamparelli is fucking us around. But I have a contingency plan for situations like these. He'll be eating out of our hand within a matter of days. Anyway, what the hell are you worried about? I've already delivered on a whole bunch of sectors – all our analysts have played ball, and you've made good money from Pharma, Banks and Resources . . .'

'Those other deals were small,' growled Picton. 'Telecoms is the big one. We have a fucking big position in Telecoms. I want Telecoms. *Get me Telecoms*!'

For the first time in a long while, the man from Saracen Laing felt unsure of himself. 'OK, Doctor,' he said meekly.

'You fuck up even by a teeny-weeny margin on this one and you can kiss your ass goodbye. You can kiss *everything* goodbye. Do we understand each other?'

It was nine o'clock in the evening when Larry arrived home. The door to his Kensington flat was unlocked. Two Louis Vuitton suitcases occupied the entrance hall. He followed the smell of sweet perfume into the living room, where he found Donna relaxing in an armchair. He headed towards the bar.

'Look, Donna, you can't stay here,' he remarked, pouring himself a Scotch.

'But I thought we agreed ... I've left him ... I love you, Larry ...'

'Sure, sure,' replied Larry. 'I love you too. But we can't do this straight away. It wouldn't look good.'

Doe-eyed, Donna feigned surprise. She gazed helplessly at Larry, as if mimicking a stray dog abandoned in the street.

'I'm thinking of your reputation, Donna.' He paced up and down the room, frowning. 'We can still see each other, but we'll have to be careful.'

'I thought you wanted us to be together,' she whispered.

'Of course I do, my darling. I want you more than anything in the world. But first of all, you need a good divorce lawyer. He'll want a retainer. I'll lend you some money to help you get the whole thing moving. You need to get a hotel room, hire a lawyer, get yourself sorted out. How about fifty thousand? That should be enough for starters, eh?'

'Larry, I couldn't possibly ...'

'Sure you could.'

Donna picked up the beginnings of impatience in Larry's tone, and smiled apologetically. 'I don't know what to say, Larry. You're truly an amazing man.'

Larry disappeared into the study and returned a few moments later with a brown envelope full of used fifty-pound notes. 'I only have twenty-five grand in the house – I'll get you the rest tomorrow.'

Donna shook her head in denial and protested with all the sincerity she could muster. Her sincerity lasted a full minute, until finally she let common sense prevail. Accepting the envelope graciously, she found a home for it in her handbag.

'Perhaps you should stay the night after all,' he said, unbuttoning his shirt. 'But you'll have to leave in the morning.'

For weeks Antonio had been working day and night on Sukuhara's 'special project'. He worked alone, delegating many of his day-to-day duties to his deputies, much to the disappointment of many on the trading floor, for whom Antonio had no equal. He wrote complex algorithms, queried tailor-made databases and sifted through files and files of data until one day he found what he was looking for.

Sukuhara promptly called in Peterson, Head of Legal, in case any ass-covering was required. Peterson, a tall, gaunt-looking man with a wiry frame and an unsympathetic manner, was a bachelor who worked late every night and was addicted to Marks & Spencer ready-made meals. He was rude and obnoxious and condescending to his staff, but to Saracen's board of directors he was worth his weight in gold. He was even more highly regarded by the boards of rival banks. It did his bonus no harm. Peterson was astute, and wonderfully adept at protecting the bank from all forms of legal liability, even where legal liability never actually existed. He possessed a photographic memory and a brilliant legal mind and, most importantly, he excelled at ass-covering. His genius was that he was able to cover not just his own ass, but also the asses of others senior enough in the bank to commandeer his services.

'So, Antonio, you found out who's eavesdropping on our trading floor?' Sukuhara asked.

'Well, who is it?' demanded Peterson impatiently.

Mindful of seniority, Antonio turned to Sukuhara. 'It's not possible to tell, sir.'

'Whoever the fuck it is – how did they get the bugs into the building?'

'They placed some surveillance software directly on to our own servers in the basement, sir. Access to our servers is almost impossible – we have strict security, both physical and digital.'

Sukuhara and Peterson exchanged glances. 'So?' demanded Sukuhara.

'There's only one way they could have done it, sir. They've got someone on the inside.'

CHAPTER 28

For the first time in eight months, Rupert walked around to the back of the building. When he arrived at Smokers' Corner, he bummed a cigarette from a stranger. He inhaled and basked in the rays of the sun. It felt good. So good.

When there was nothing left but a dirty filter, he flicked the butt on to the street and entered the building. From Reception, he dialled Niccolo's number. 'I'm in the lobby. Fancy lunch? It's on me.'

Rupert popped briefly into the gents' cloakroom. When he came out, Niccolo was already waiting outside the front entrance. They walked briskly towards St Paul's.

'Listen, Nicco, Larry was a bit pissed off at your intransigence back there. I respect your principles, but there's a place for all that shit and it ain't here.'

'I understand, Ru.'

Rupert placed his hand firmly on Niccolo's shoulder and said, 'I want you to know that I fought for you with the big guy. I've put things right between you two.'

'Thanks.'

'You know something, Nicco? In this place, you've got to know who your friends are.'

'I'm beginning to learn the hard way. I trust you, though, boss. Because if I can't trust you, it's all over.'

The presidential suite at the Okura Hotel in Tokyo had everything a corporate executive could possibly need. It also had everything a modern executive's wife could possibly need. Mrs Oakes always travelled with her husband, but knew when to make herself scarce. She was on her way down to the salon, having booked a masseuse, a hairdresser and a beautician back to back.

In her absence, Kenneth convened a meeting in the presidential suite with his Finance Director, two fellow executives, an external adviser, his executive assistant and a couple of bottles of sake. The purpose of their trip to Tokyo, he explained, was to clinch the deal that could save the company. Globecom needed a distraction from its failing business model and flagging share price. The acquisition of YamTel, its Japanese counterpart, could set Globecom on the growth path that its shareholders desperately sought.

The Finance Director described the nuts and bolts of the deal. YamTel had yielded to Globecom's initial demands and had agreed a sale price. Globecom could not raise enough cash on the capital markets to buy YamTel outright, so the bulk of the consideration would be in Globecom shares. The problem was that Globecom shares were trading at a four-year low, making any share-based deal appear expensive for Globecom's investors. For the deal to make commercial sense, the share price had to rise significantly. Most of the stock analysts covering Globecom already had a Buy rating, but the market wasn't listening to them. The market had rallied behind Saracen's analyst.

'Saracen is the only major house with a Sell rating on our stock,' said the external adviser. 'Their analyst is a relative newcomer, but he seems to have his finger on the pulse of the market. If he switches to a Buy rating, the stock will almost certainly shoot up. That could save us millions, gentlemen.'

Kenneth smiled. He was one step ahead of his team. For now, however, there was no need to let them know that.

Rupert allowed Niccolo some grace, but only a little, for his patience was wearing thin. As usual, Tatsuso's was busy, but Rupert had managed to secure a secluded table in the corner near the bonsai garden, where a miniature waterfall flowed peacefully, its uneven sound neatly blocking out much of the restaurant clatter. He waited until their chopsticks were down, then he let rip. 'Now, about this letter—'

'I'm not signing an apology letter, goddammit!'

'Nicco, you don't want to piss Larry off any further.'

'I gave Globecom's board my considered view of their company. I did so at the request of their own CEO. I have nothing to apologise for.'

'But Larry wants—'

'Larry should back me up. He should protect me from pricks like JC and from schizophrenic corporate bosses like Ken Oakes.'

'Just sign the letter, Nicco.'

Niccolo deliberated. He recognised the wisdom of playing the game. If he took Larry on, he would lose. Yet if he gave in, he would lose even more. 'No fucking way,' he said, picking up his chopsticks.

Back at the office, Charlie took Jack aside, using the staff coffee machine as a shield of privacy, and made a snap assessment. 'Are you OK, Jack? You look completely fucked.'

Jack's face was pale. His breath smelt of alcohol. His eyes looked tired. 'Charlie, I need to take some time off. Just a couple of days. There are some things I need to deal with – family issues . . .'

Charlie glared at him, as if expecting further explanation. 'No problem, Jacko,' he said finally. 'Take as long as you need.'

The Carrera had personalised number plates, low-profile alloy wheels and a Bose eight-speaker music system. Leather seats came as standard, but the built-in personal body-heating system was an optional extra. The man behind the wheel skipped a gear as he momentarily took his mind off the road to speak into the voice-recognition device linked to his car phone. He spoke clearly. The device recognised his voice signature and dialled the appropriate number automatically.

'Hi, Damien,' said the driver, as soon as the call connected. 'How's my portfolio doing today?'

'Very well, sir. You seem to have a knack for picking winners.'

'Listen, Damien, I'd like you to buy eight hundred thousand shares in Globecom. Do it immediately. And do it through my nominee account, offshore. The funds are already there. No limit. Buy at best.'

'I'll place the order right away, sir. I'll call you tomorrow, once the markets open, to confirm the price.'

'Fine. And don't call me at work.'

'Of course, sir. Have a nice evening, sir.'

The driver stepped on the accelerator hard, then changed down a gear, lurching forward as the clutch engaged. Wishing he had worn a seat belt, he swore. A speed camera had just flashed him.

Three miles away, in the basement of a government office block in South Kensington, a police computer printed a traffic offence report. It recorded the vehicle speed at 64 miles per hour in a 40 mph area. Below that it recorded the number plate of the offending motorist.

L 4 RRY.

*

215

When Jack arrived home, the house was empty, yet he felt Donna's presence, like a ghost, everywhere. He had to get away. He went into his study, sat down at his desk and began searching the internet for flights. When he found what he was looking for, he called Niccolo.

'Come with me. Please,' he pleaded.

'I can't. I just can't,' Niccolo explained reluctantly. 'I'm in a stand-off with JC. There's been an official complaint from Globecom, and Larry's insisting I sign a letter of apology – no way I can leave town.'

'*Please*, Nicco,' Jack entreated a second time. A sympathetic silence was all that greeted him. 'OK,' he sighed.

Jack went ahead and confirmed the booking. The next flight to his destination left the following day at dawn. He printed out the ticket and strolled into the kitchen. He opened the cellar door and switched the light on. Halfway down the stairs, he stopped to look at the photograph of Yoshiro, Niccolo and himself as young boys with Mizuno-san. With the tips of his fingers he caressed the old man in the picture frame. 'I don't know what to do, *sensei*,' he whispered. 'Help me.'

Then he rummaged around in the cellar, found a suitcase, dusted it off and took it upstairs to pack.

CHAPTER 29

Young Jack was apprehensive about going to St Mary's International School in Tokyo. Since the age of five he had been at a small school where he knew everybody, but now he was going to a much bigger school, in a new city, where the children would come from all over the world and speak all sorts of foreign languages he'd never even heard of.

'Why do I have to go to this school?' he demanded. 'Why did we have to come here anyway? Why couldn't we just stay at home?'

'I've explained it to you a hundred times,' his mother said wearily. 'Your father's been given an important job at the Okinawa Institute of Science and Technology, so of course we have to come with him. You wouldn't want him to leave us behind in Brisbane, would you?'

Jack wasn't sure that would be such a bad idea. His father, who he could remember playing with him, carrying him on his shoulders, patiently kicking a ball round the back garden for hours on end, had become distant and moody. He was hardly ever at home, and when he was, the air was thick with tension. Jack's mother, a pretty woman who used to laugh a lot, hardly uttered a word when her husband was around. She was much more fun to be with when she and Jack were on their own.

'Anyway,' she went on, *'there'll be so many kids of your age, you're bound to make one good friend.'* She smiled encouragingly.

Young Jack sulked the rest of the way to school.

The morning passed miserably. Little cliques formed based on language, and Jack began to think he was the only child in the world who didn't speak Chinese, Japanese, French or Hindi.

During the mid-morning outdoor break, a gang of bigger boys improvised a rather rough game, and somehow Jack found himself sprawling on the asphalt with scraped knees and hands. He sat gazing at the blood welling up, and felt like crying.

Suddenly a boy of about his own age, with dark hair and flashing eyes, shouted furiously in a strange language at the boys who had knocked Jack over. Shamefaced, they came over and hauled him apologetically to his feet, then wandered off leaving him standing alone and very close to tears.

'Come with me,' the boy said, taking Jack's hand. *'My name's Niccolo.'*

Once Jack had had antiseptic dabbed on his knees and Band-Aids applied, he felt better. *'I didn't think you'd speak English,'* he said. *'You don't look English.'*

'I'm not,' came the reply. *'My dad's Indian, and my mum's Italian. So I speak English, Italian and Gujarati. And I'm learning Japanese too.'*

Jack was deeply impressed. *'How long have you been here?'* he asked, imagining that his saviour must know all the ropes.

'Oh, this is my first day, same as you,' the other boy said airily. *'How old are you?'*

'Twelve,' said Jack proudly. *'Nearly thirteen.'*

'Wow! I'm not even eleven yet.'

That afternoon, Jack announced to his mother, *'This is my friend Niccolo.'*

'That's nice,' Bronwen Ford said. *'Hello, Niccolo.'*

Niccolo shook hands politely, then turned to the elegant and striking-

looking woman who was just bending down to kiss him. 'Mamma,' he said. 'This is my friend Jack.'

Within minutes the two mothers had introduced themselves and were chatting away like old friends, making arrangements to meet. They were amazed to find that they were both married to men who lived and worked far away on the island of Okinawa – Jack's father a marine zoologist at the Okinawa Institute of Science and Technology and Niccolo's an Indian Navy officer on loan to the US Navy base on the island.

After that, hardly a week went by without the two families going on an expedition of some kind. Despite the three-year age gap, the boys' friendship worked well, Jack's stolidity and caution balancing Niccolo's boisterous confidence, and they stayed over so often that they kept clean clothes and toothbrushes at each other's house. Isabella and Bronwen treasured each other's friendship too.

When the long holidays came, all four of them went up to Okinawa for the summer. Feroz Guzdar and Derek Ford both lived in cramped institutional accommodation, and the weather was intolerably hot. So Bronwen and Isabella found a seaside house to rent, intending to do nothing but rest, read and chat, while their husbands came for long weekends.

The house was fairly basic, but for Niccolo and Jack it was a wonderful adventure. They found fishing rods in the porch and immediately scampered down to the sea to try them out. But when the sun went down, they came trudging back up to the house empty-handed.

'You'll have better luck tomorrow,' said Isabella.

At that moment they heard a knock at the door. Bronwen went to open it, and found a diminutive Japanese boy on the step, holding out a fish beautifully wrapped in a single large leaf and tied with grass. He bowed, and said something in Japanese.

'Niccolo! Come and translate!'

Both boys came running, and a lively three-way conversation in Japanese ensued.

'His name's Yoshiro, and he says the fish is a gift of welcome from his

grandfather,' Niccolo explained. 'He's got a boat and he goes out every day to fish, and Yoshiro says he'll ask if we can go with him, so can we – please please please?'

The next day, both mothers went down to meet Yoshiro's grandfather. They found the fisherman – a slight, wiry man with an alert face – sitting out in front of his little house, neatly mending a pair of Yoshiro's jeans.

'I am pleased that my grandson has two new friends,' he said, bowing. 'It would be a great pleasure to take them fishing. I will look after them as though they were my own sons.'

'Mind you do what Mr Mizuno says,' Jack's mother warned.

'We will, promise,' came the reply.

Niccolo and Jack wanted the summer to go on for ever. They were blissfully happy working aboard Mizuno-san's boat, learning how to scan the surface of the water for shoals of fish, how to throw the nets wide of the boat, how to troll for horse mackerel, how to kill the fish cleanly once they were landed and how to gut them. Every day they came home exhausted and laden with fish for dinner.

Mizuno sold most of his catch locally, and made enough to live modestly, though he gave away as many fish as he sold. Intrigued by him, Niccolo's father Feroz made enquiries locally. He found out that Mizuno's son and daughter-in-law had died in a car crash when Yoshiro was just a baby, and that he had brought the boy up to Okinawa and looked after him ever since. And there was something else. 'Mizuno-san is a very great sensei,' Feroz was told. 'Like his father and grandfather before him.'

'Of course, Okinawa is the home of karate,' he said to his wife. 'The boys will probably learn as much from him as they'll learn at school.'

As well as how to catch fish, Mizuno did indeed teach them many other things. In periods of calm when the fish were not running, he would ship the oars and let the boat rock and drift, initiating earnest discussions in which the four of them explored all sorts of weighty moral matters. And when the sea was too rough to go out, he would teach them the many *ancient martial arts of Okinawa, and the absolute discipline necessary to master them.*

Niccolo and Jack revered and adored their sensei. *At home, every other sentence started, 'Mizuno-san says . . .' One day, when Bronwen Ford asked, 'And what would Mizuno-san say?' to some small dilemma, Jack, in all seriousness, told her exactly what he would say.*

During the six weeks they spent on Okinawa, Jack and Niccolo gained the sort of wisdom that cannot be learned in school, most importantly that honour and integrity were to be prized above all things. 'For without them, nothing is of any value,' Mizuno-san explained gravely.

A few days before they were due to leave, he said, 'I would be sad to think that I might never see you both again. So I shall hope and believe that one day you will come back to Okinawa. And wherever you are in the world, no matter how far away you travel, if there is ever a time when you need my help – well, I shall be here.'

CHAPTER 30

After a barrage of terrorist threats earlier in the week, airport security was tight. Jack passed through various checks and controls and found a seat at the departure gate. He instinctively thought of calling Donna to let her know where he would be for the next few days. Old habits died hard. Then he took a deep breath and heaved a long, tired sigh of relief. He was single again, he told himself, and he was going to enjoy it. He scanned the airport lounge for attractive females.

Just then he felt a tap on his shoulder. Niccolo was standing there grinning, passport in hand and a rucksack hitched over his shoulder.

'I'm coming with you,' he said.

'How the hell . . .?'

'Simple. I lied. I told Larry my mother'd had a stroke. He didn't believe me, but in the end he gave me four days' compassionate leave.'

'Hadn't you better tell *her* she's supposed to have had a stroke? He'd call her to check, the bastard.'

So Niccolo rang his mother. Without condoning his dishonesty,

Isabella Lamparelli agreed at least not to tell Larry she was in perfect health, should he happen to call.

'And send my fondest good wishes to Mizuno-san,' she added.

'So did you sign that letter of apology?' Jack demanded as Niccolo sat down beside him.

'The hell I did. It's in the bin.'

'You don't want to push Larry too far, Nicco.'

'Let's forget about the office for the next few days. Just let me take care of you.'

The final call for their flight sounded and they made their way through security and were ushered aboard like sheep. The flight was scheduled to take twenty-six hours, with a stopover in Hong Kong.

Jack had planned on sleeping through most of the journey, but Niccolo's unplanned arrival gave him an uncontrollable adrenalin rush. They chatted incessantly until breakfast was served. Afterwards, Niccolo took a nap.

Jack tilted his head back and shut his eyes too. A million thoughts ricocheted like bullets back and forth in his mind. He was happy to be with Niccolo, yet sad that it was not Donna sitting next to him. He was eager to see Mizuno, yet terrified of what his future might hold. For the first time in his adult life, Jack had lost his way. He had always been the rock that everyone held on to, but the rock was sinking into a bottomless pit from which there was no way out. His vision had become blurred and his thinking lacked clarity. After his father had left, only one man had been able to give him the guidance he had needed in times of distress. Jack summoned up a mental image of Mizuno-san, so slight and unthreatening, yet so implacably firm about right and wrong. Then, having found a peaceful tranquillity, he dozed off.

*

Armed with an incident report detailing his trip to the Sultanate of Usman, Arnaud marched uninvited into Amanda Sanderson's office. It was late in the evening and the FSA's Head of Enforcement was sitting at her desk with a pile of dossiers to her right and a bright table lamp to her left. She looked up and peered over her spectacles.

'I've got a lead on Picton,' he announced, giving her no opportunity to dismiss him. 'And there's someone we can link him to.' He pulled up a chair, made himself comfortable and took her through his activities during the past couple of weeks. He told her about his illicit tapping of Saracen Laing's phone system. He told her about the kidnapping of Lindsay Compton's parents in Usman and the global network run by Prince Mubarak. He told her how his recent surveillance had indicated that someone at Saracen Laing was somehow connected to this organised crime syndicate.

'It's a huge network,' he explained. 'And the Moneypincher's Inn is its London headquarters. Picton, who's an experienced financial fraudster with previous form, calls the shots from there.'

The instant he paused for breath, Sanderson launched her assault. 'I could have you fired, Arnaud. You acted without my authorisation. You diverted resources from their core function. You wagered the integrity of this organisation on little more than a hunch. And now you have the cheek to march into my office and just unload this stuff on me without an iota of shame!'

Arnaud carefully but unsuccessfully attempted to gauge his boss's mood.

Sanderson stood up and removed her spectacles. She was smiling. 'I wish I had ten people like you, Arnaud,' she said. 'If you were British, I'd have to reprimand you, but you're a foreign national here on loan, so I'm going to look the other way. I think you may just have saved my ass.'

'De rien, madame. C'est mon plaisir.'

*

Shortly after nightfall, the Boeing landed on Okinawa. With difficulty, Niccolo and Jack ruthlessly fought their way out of the labyrinth of airport officials, checks and paperwork that greeted them.

Outside, it was raining slightly. They searched for Mizuno. It took a few minutes before they spotted him, patiently sitting cross-legged under the shelter of a tree. It was twelve years since they had last spent a summer on Okinawa, and in that time he appeared to have shrunk, though he looked in good shape for his seventy-eight years. The lines on his forehead had deepened. He had lost much of his hair, and the few thin strands that remained had turned silver. He wore it tied back neatly into a ponytail. His dark brown eyes now required spectacles, and he squinted slightly as he recognised his two boys. They were men now.

'*Oss, sensei*,' said Jack as he embraced Mizuno. In a traditional karate dojo, *oss*, pronounced *ooooss*, is the only word that can be uttered by a student without the express permission of his *sensei*. It can mean virtually anything. The body language that accompanies the term allows most instructors to interpret its many meanings with remarkable agility.

'*Oss*, Jack-san. I see you have brought Nicco-san. I am honoured that you have both found time to see your old friend.'

'*Sensei*,' said Niccolo softly, 'the honour is ours.'

'Jack-san, you have a sad look on your face. I sense something is worrying you. There will be plenty of time to talk. And in the morning we will go fishing. I have found that there are few problems in life that cannot be solved by going fishing.'

Already, Jack felt as if the sound of Mizuno's voice had lifted much of the burden he was carrying.

They climbed into a Toyota Jeep that had seen better days, and set off along the winding road that led to Mizuno's house on the other side of the island.

When they finally arrived at his bungalow on the beach,

Mizuno set about making tea whilst all three talked about the old days. Mizuno would have been happy to talk all night, but the fatigue painted around Jack's eyes spelled bedtime. He and Niccolo slept on the hard tatami floor that night. The cool breeze from the north Pacific Ocean and the sound of the waves crashing against the shore seemed to take them back to their childhood. Though it was dark, Jack and Niccolo recognised everything in Mizuno's home. After all, once upon a time, it had been a second home to them both.

Larry walked down the trading floor to Rupert's desk and stood squarely behind him until his presence was felt.

Rupert was caught off guard. 'Forgive me, Larry,' he said, startled. 'I didn't see you.'

'Tell me, did Nicco sign that apology letter?'

'Not yet.'

Without another word, Larry stormed back to his office. Rupert watched him go, and James watched Rupert watching Larry.

Back at his desk, Larry shouted for Anne-Marie. 'Get me Daryl on the phone, would you? And shut the door behind you.'

Anne-Marie returned to her desk. When she had the Head of HR on the line, she gave the signal to Larry. He picked up the receiver, lay back in his chair and put his feet up on the desk. 'Daryl, I've got a problem. It's Niccolo Lamparelli. He's behaving irrationally, and I'm concerned about him; he may be having problems at home. Anyway, he's unstable and I don't want him making client calls right now. He's made enough fuck-ups already. I'd like to suspend him without pay.'

'On what grounds?'

'On the grounds that he's not performing.'

'We have to be careful in a situation like this. There are procedures that must be followed.'

'Fine. Follow them. Just do it fast. Before he becomes a liability.'

'What do you mean?'

'Look, why don't you do your job and I'll do mine? I'm trying to protect this bank. I need – *we* need – to get rid of Lamparelli. Do you understand?'

'You can't just suspend someone from office without good reason – especially not a highly rated analyst. Your motives will be questioned.'

'I'm running out of time, goddammit. Just push the process along, will you?'

'I'll email you form HR35 and you can record your concerns. It will need sign-off from Mr Sukuhara.'

'Oh, for fuck's sake! I don't want to get Sukuhara involved. I don't have time to fill out a bunch of fucking forms. I have a business to run!'

'Very well, I will record your concerns regarding Lamparelli and put him on negative watch.'

'Yeah, you do that.'

Jack had not slept well. He rose, yawned, stretched and walked out on to the veranda. The ocean beat at the battered, jagged boulders at the south-western foot of the beach where he and Niccolo used to play as children, and seagulls were dipping playfully in and out of the water. He walked a little way along the edge of the sea, to where Mizuno was tinkering with his boat. The letters engraved in Hiragana on the hull many decades ago had all but faded away. *Yo-shi-ro.* In those three ideograms, the old man had found a way of holding on to the memory of his grandson.

'*Ohayu gozaimasu, sensei,*' shouted Jack.

'*Ohayu,*' replied the fisherman. 'I was wondering when you would get up.'

They returned to the house to find that Niccolo had also woken up. Breakfast was fresh tuna, served raw with a fried egg and seaweed. Jack relinquished his share to Niccolo, who devoured it within seconds. Mizuno waited until Niccolo's plate was empty before he spoke. 'Yesterday, Jack-san, I could see sadness on your face. It is there still. It is time to tell me what has caused this sadness.'

When Jack finally spoke, his voice was weak. '*Sensei*,' he said timidly, 'my wife has left me. I've lost my way. I don't know who I am any more. I don't know who to trust. I'm scared.'

Mizuno turned to Niccolo, a look of enquiry in his eyes. Jack nodded permission, and Niccolo stepped in with a concise account of the last few days and the problems they had both encountered. When he had finished, Mizuno reflected for a few moments. Then he placed his hand gently on Jack's cheek and said, 'Jack-san, do you still believe in yourself? Do you still believe today in all the things you stood for yesterday? Things like honour, integrity and loyalty?'

'*Hai*,' confirmed Jack.

'Then you have lost nothing, Jack-san. You have lost nothing. Now let us go fishing.'

That afternoon Mizuno took his boys across to the other side of the island. They walked along the beach for a mile, then followed a path that took them up the tallest hill on the island. The sea breeze tempered the sun's strong rays and both men felt invigorated by the constant spray of water in the air. They arrived at the spot where Yoshiro was buried. Mizuno knelt down, and Niccolo and Jack followed suit, closing their eyes for a few seconds, and remembering their childhood friend.

When he was ready, Mizuno got up. The view from their vantage point was spectacular. In every direction one looked, one could see the ocean. To the north was the East China Sea, to the east the Pacific. In the distance, to the north-west, they could see the snow-capped mountains on the neighbouring island of Ryukyu. They could hear crickets in the fields below them, and the song of birds, and a soft breeze through the palm trees. A little frog leapt out of nowhere, only to disappear again. Mizuno noticed it, and smiled.

'Jack-san, when you feel that your life is falling apart around you, then you must forget about the past. You must forget about the future. You must only live for now.'

Jack stared numbly at the ground, the old man's words floating past him. Niccolo listened intently. Though Jack's needs were more pressing, Niccolo needed Mizuno to listen to his own predicament.

'Live only for now,' repeated Mizuno. 'Feel the warmth of the sun, inhale the sea breeze, listen to the birds. Breathe.' The old man set off down the hill, and they followed him without a word. Mizuno walked to the centre of a field, took off his shoes and stood with his shoulders back, his chest proudly out. Then, feet together and hands by his sides, he bowed.

'Ni-ju-shi-ho!' he yelled sharply. With deadly precision he performed the *kata* as his former students watched with awe. The old man had lost none of his agility over the years. Perhaps he moved a touch more slowly than before. Perhaps his strength and power were not what they used to be. But his focus was razor sharp, his stances were rock solid and his body flowed effortlessly from one move to the next like running water in a stream.

When he had finished, he bowed again and beckoned to Niccolo, who walked out and began the *kata* as instructed. The ground was uneven and he momentarily lost his balance but quickly regained it to complete a performance worthy of Mizuno's praise. Once he had finished, he too bowed.

Jack politely asked to be excused from the exercise. But his request was denied. Feeling weak, he walked reluctantly to the middle of the field, turned to face Mizuno and bowed. '*Ni-ju-shi-ho!*' he screamed.

He delivered a distinctly lacklustre performance. Though the actions came easily, the strength to execute them had deserted him. The pain in his gut was too intense. His mind was distracted, his concentration gone. He lacked focus and spirit.

'Clear your head, Jack-san!' snapped Mizuno. 'Clear your head!'

It was no use. Halfway through the *kata*, Jack gave up. Dejected, disillusioned and defeated, he flopped clumsily to the ground.

Niccolo and Mizuno exchanged glances. 'Time to go home, I think,' Mizuno said. He led the way back and Niccolo trailed in the rear.

'Nicco-san,' asked Mizuno from the front, 'do you remember the tale about the old man and the young man?'

Niccolo called from behind, 'Of course, *sensei*! Two men are sitting on the beach, watching life pass by. The sun is shining and the sea is calm. The view is the same for both men. Yet the old man looks sad, whilst the young man looks happy. The young man asks the old man why he is always sad.'

'And why is the old man always sad, Nicco-san?' asked Mizuno.

Jack had heard the story almost as many times as Niccolo had. Like all of Mizuno's tales it had meaning. He cut in, 'Because the old man looks back and the young man looks forward.'

'That's right, Jack-san. But today you look like the old man!'

A few hundred yards from the hut, Mizuno said, 'Nicco-san, please run on ahead and make us some tea.' As soon as he had gone, Mizuno turned to Jack and said, 'I'm tired now.' He found a place to sit down and motioned Jack to join him. Together they watched the horizon, neither uttering a word for several minutes.

'I don't understand why Donna left me, *sensei*,' said Jack, breaking the silence.

Mizuno took a moment to reflect before he answered. 'A marriage requires two people, Jack-san. If one person withdraws consent, you cannot have a marriage. It is not a failure on your part. You are not responsible for her happiness any more. She has chosen another path and now you must choose your own.'

'I don't know if I can ever find happiness again.'

'Her choices do not affect your happiness unless you let them, Jack-san. Once the bond of trust in a marriage is broken, it can never be fixed. Only when you realise that your destiny is not with her can you move on with your life.'

'But how do I know that my destiny is not with her, *sensei*?'

The fisherman placed his hard, callused hand on Jack's face. 'A marriage is like a porcelain vase, Jack-san. It can survive unbroken for centuries, but it is also delicate and fragile. It must be handled with care. When you marry a woman, you place your mark on the porcelain. The mark is the embodiment of your marriage vows. Over time you add a few more brush strokes, until your marks turn into a painting. As the painting takes shape, so your marriage vows become stronger and more beautiful. But once the vase is broken, it is broken for ever. No amount of repair can restore it to its former glory, because the cracks will always remain, and one day they will resurface. Do not waste your life putting together the pieces of a vase that has been shattered by another. Throw away the vase, Jack-san, and begin a new painting.'

Larry Sikorski was running out of time and running out of options. Globecom's share price continued its downward journey. And all the syndicate's eyes were on him.

An upgrade of Saracen's stock rating would send the shares up.

Yet in reality Larry was caught in a dilemma. Interfering with an analyst's independence could cost him his job; on the other hand, failing to deliver on his promises to Prince Mubarak and the syndicate could cost him a lot more than that. Lamparelli had turned out to be harder to manage than he had expected. Larry knew what he had to do, but it was not going to be easy, nor was it without risk.

He took out his mobile phone and called Picton to arrange a meeting. If he was going to take on greater risk, he was going to make damn sure it was worth his while. A couple of million was not enough when others were making a tidy fortune from his genius. He would stick to his end of the bargain, but he would demand a bigger share of the cake. And if the Doctor did not like it, the deal was off.

Jack was out cold. The hard tatami floor was surprisingly conducive to a good night's sleep. So was Mizuno's home-brewed sake. Jack had drowned his sorrows earlier at dinner and was now snoring off the excess.

Outside, Mizuno rocked in his chair. Cupped in his hands was the tiny wooden replica of his fishing boat that he still worked on from time to time. At his feet Niccolo relaxed on the sand. The lights in the village a few miles down the beach had gone out. For miles around not a soul could be seen.

'What is on your mind, Nicco-san?' asked the fisherman, inspecting his workmanship.

Niccolo described his job and a few of the characters at work. He explained what Saracen Laing was like. 'My boss wants me to do something dishonest, *sensei*. In my heart I know it's wrong, but I may lose my job if I disobey him. I'm frightened.'

Mizuno placed the wooden boat on the ground. 'Why are you frightened of him?'

'Because he has power and money and status. And because he won't hesitate to use them, *sensei*.'

'What can he do to you if you follow your heart?'

'He can take away my job and make sure I never work again. He can destroy me.'

Mizuno laughed and said, 'No man can destroy you, Nicco-san. You must do what is right. You must protect your honour.'

'You do not understand, *sensei*,' pleaded Niccolo. 'You and I, we live in two different worlds.' He shook his head in despair. 'Honour has no meaning in my world.'

'Nicco-san, men are the same the world over. There are men who have honour and men who do not. This has been true for centuries past and will be true long after you and I are gone. A man's honour is worth more than the most beautiful wife, or the grandest house, or the finest title, or even the most revered job. For honour will outlast all these things. A man of honour has nothing to fear because he will have truth on his side. Nicco-san, you must do what you believe to be right.'

'*Sensei*, I wish things were that easy.'

'When you are an old man like me, and your time in this world is coming to an end, Nicco-san, you will ask yourself one question – of this you can be sure. It will not be how much money did you make, or how many possessions did you acquire. Life is like a journey up a mountain in search of forbidden treasure. There are many paths to choose and many treasures to find along the way. In the end you will judge yourself not by how fast you reach the top, or by how much treasure you gather along the way, but by the path you choose to get there. And when it is time for you to leave this world, there will be only one thing you can take with you. Throw it away, and you will never get it back.'

Niccolo shook his head, dismissing the old man's words with a sigh. He had hoped his old *sensei* would understand, but clearly he

233

did not. Abruptly changing the subject, he said softly, 'I am worried about Jack, Mizuno-san.'

'Jack has looked after you like a brother since you were little boys. Perhaps it is time you returned the favour.'

'I know, *sensei*. The problem is I don't know how to help him.'

'When a man is betrayed by the one he trusts most, it is a hard thing to overcome. If Jack becomes weak, you must be his strength. If he is unable to think with a clear head, you must be his mind.'

'I don't understand, *sensei*.'

'What this woman did to Jack may be a good thing. Only he cannot see it yet. Jack trusts you. Help him see the truth – that what happened to him may be for the best. Help him see that his best days lie ahead, Nicco-san.' The fisherman leaned back and sighed all-knowingly. 'Jack will surely find happiness again, and it may be bigger and better and more beautiful than anything he has ever known. But you must help him find it.'

This time Niccolo nodded obediently. 'I will help him find it, *sensei*.'

Dr Picton and Prince Mubarak were a formidable team. And they knew it. For some years they had had a lucrative business partnership that mainly involved ripping off unsuspecting investors, first in the arms trade and later, driven by a need to diversify, through a plethora of complex financial scams. All that time, they had remained unquestioningly loyal to each other.

But things were beginning to change. The catalyst was the syndicate, a group of young men whose only common trait was that they all had fathers obscenely rich in petrodollars. Picton and Mubarak had always worked as a team. With the syndicate's money now in the picture, the duo became a trio, and the third party had their own commercial interests at heart. Now, persistent delays had focused attention, patience was turning into frustration, and suspicion had replaced trust. A seasoned relationship was in danger of being pushed to breaking point.

Unknown to Picton, Mubarak had instructed Karim to keep a watchful eye on Larry Sikorski. A highly diligent and resourceful one-man surveillance unit, Karim viewed a direct order from the Prince himself as the highest of all honours. Within hours of receiving his instructions, he was set up to eavesdrop on Larry's conversations. He used a short-range encrypted tracking device that could be decoded using equipment housed in his car. His vehicle was registered to the Usmani Embassy and, as expected, carried diplomatic number plates. Officially, that meant that any recording equipment inside it, whilst illegal under British law, was housed in property owned and governed by a foreign jurisdiction.

Unknown to Mubarak, Picton – under pressure to deliver the results he had promised – had already commenced lengthy discussions with Larry regarding the possibility of a significant bonus payment for his continued services to the syndicate. The bonus, if agreed, would be too large for Picton to cover personally and would mean raiding the profits of the syndicate, whose books and records he would later massage.

In the event, Karim's earlier handiwork – obtained almost by accident – had provided Picton with a far more straightforward strategy that involved simple blackmail. Photographs of Larry and Donna – taken in compromising positions in Larry's Porsche – were the bait. The problem was that Larry, when confronted with the photographs, was not the least bit intimidated.

'Hey, I look fantastic,' he professed confidently, tilting the photograph this way and that. 'What do you think?'

Astounded by Larry's reaction, Picton sat motionless in his

chair. Downstairs, the Moneypincher's Inn was heaving, but the clatter of cutlery from the diners below seemed distant, blotted out by the almost tangible silence in the room. Then, without warning, Picton leaned forward. 'See here,' he began aggressively, 'I can make these photographs public if you refuse to cooperate. You complete your end of the bargain – with a little more gusto than you've shown thus far, if you don't mind – and they will be destroyed,' he offered.

'Don't rush me,' said Larry coolly. 'And don't you *ever* blackmail me.' He eyed Picton deliberately, as if to establish who was in charge. 'These things have to be done discreetly. We don't want to attract attention. Give me a couple of weeks and I'll turn this whole operation around for you.'

Soon it was time to leave the island. The fresh air and sunshine had helped Jack and Niccolo to see things more clearly. Mizuno hated crowds, so when they arrived at the airport he made them say their *sayonaras* in the car park.

Niccolo and Jack got out of the Jeep like two children being sent off to boarding school. They bowed and hugged the old man and thanked him again and again. Just before it was time for them to enter the airport, Mizuno pulled out a small bamboo box. With great care he presented it to Jack. Jack accepted the gift with a bow.

'You may open it,' said Mizuno. Jack bowed again, and opened it eagerly. Inside the box was a wooden boat.

'This is your boat, Mizuno-san!' he exclaimed.

'Indeed,' admitted Mizuno. 'It took me twenty years to make it. I suppose it is finished now. I want you to have it, Jack-san.'

Jack stared at the inscription – *Yo-Shi-Ro* – trying to hold back his tears. It brought back memories of his childhood friend. Maybe this was the old man's way of finally putting it all behind him. 'It's beautiful,' he said, wiping his eyes.

'Yoshiro was everything to me,' said Mizuno. His voice was proud. 'When I lost him, I thought I had lost everything. But you, you both became my sons. One day your world may collapse around you, just as mine did when Yoshiro died. If that happens, I want you to stick together. Help each other. Fight for each other. Love each other. But above all, live your lives with honour. If you do so, then my job is done.'

'*Hai, sensei,*' they both replied.

'Now go back to your faraway land and let an old man rest in peace.'

On the flight back to London, Jack told Niccolo how Mizuno had described marriage as a porcelain vase. They went on to recall the many lessons they had received from him as young boys. Since then two decades had passed, yet Mizuno's tales remained little changed. His stories all had a hidden meaning, their purpose to teach right from wrong.

'The thing is, those stories were fine when we were kids,' Niccolo pointed out. 'But we're grown men. In Mizuno's world, ideals overshadow reality. He has no idea what we're up against. I mean, how long would he last in a big city like London? How would he survive in a shark tank like Saracen?'

'Don't you believe in Mizuno's idea of honour any more?' asked Jack thoughtfully.

Niccolo sighed. 'Listen, motherfucker. Mizuno's stories are fun to listen to. But that's all. In the real world, time is money, business is business, and honour is bullshit.'

'Why do you always have to be the tough guy, Nicco? Deep down you still believe in the same things Mizuno-san believes in because deep down you know he's right. Look, if you really thought he was full of shit, you wouldn't be on this plane. Would you?'

Niccolo did not answer. He was not sure what he believed in. All he knew was that it felt good to know that Jack was his friend, a friend who – he hoped – knew him better than he knew himself, and believed in him. He yawned, then slid down in his seat, switched off the overhead reading light and checked himself out for the remainder of the flight.

CHAPTER 31

In the days following their return from Okinawa, Niccolo caught up on the backlog of work at the office whilst Jack decided to take another week off. Before leaving England, he had got Charlie to sign off on an extended leave of absence. 'I'll cover for you, kiddo,' Charlie told him. 'You've saved my sorry ass more times than I can remember. Take as long as you need.'

Jack valued the chance to have a few days to himself. Work was the furthest thing from his mind; he contacted no one, he ate little. Instead, he went for long walks over Hampstead Heath and tried to put back together the jigsaw that was his life. By the time the weekend arrived, he felt he had regained some of the self-confidence he had lost. That Sunday he set out early in the morning for the Heath yet again. He walked, and walked, and walked. It was midday by the time he finally came to a halt. He lay down under a sycamore tree and shut his eyes. Barely a minute had passed before he awoke to the sound of his mobile phone.

'Mr Ford? My name is Arnaud Veyrieras; I work for the FSA.' Arnaud came quickly to the point. 'I'm investigating irregularities in analyst recommendations in connection with the dismissal of Lindsay Compton. I have been informed by Saracen's Human

Resources staff that you are on extended leave, so I am wondering whether you are perhaps under any kind of pressure.'

'I haven't been fired, and I certainly haven't committed any crime,' replied Jack, sitting up. 'I'm just working out some personal stuff.'

'I beg your pardon, sir. I don't mean to pry. But it would help my investigation greatly if you could answer some questions.'

Jack sighed. 'Sure,' he said reluctantly.

'It is perhaps not a good idea to discuss such matters on the phone. I was hoping to arrange a rendezvous with you.'

'I'm back at work next week.'

'These are sensitive issues. Perhaps we could meet outside work hours. Where are you at present, sir?'

Jack was growing increasingly uncomfortable with Arnaud's line of questioning. 'Why don't I come to your office, Arnaud?'

'It would perhaps be better for you if we were to do this away from our offices, sir. Where are you at present?' Arnaud repeated.

'I'm on Hampstead Heath.'

'I know Hampstead Heath – I live in Kentish Town. I can be at Jack Straw's Castle in twenty minutes. Could you meet me there?'

'I'll be there at twelve-thirty sharp,' Jack said.

He felt a cold shiver run down his spine. Something was out of place. The conversation had happened so quickly that he was taken aback by his own complicity. He was annoyed at himself for agreeing to meet a total stranger at a time when he had far more pressing things to deal with. But then again, what did he have to lose?

Arnaud Veyrieras arrived at the front gate to Jack Straw's Castle at precisely half past twelve. The Frenchman was dressed in red corduroy slacks and a tweed jacket. His intention was to look English, but it only served to make him stand out all the more. A

240

few minutes later Jack turned up and identified himself. They shook hands and walked down Spaniards Road.

'I work for the FSA's Enforcement Division,' began Arnaud. 'What I am about to tell you is confidential. Do you understand?'

Jack reflected at length. 'Yes,' he agreed finally.

The two men then spoke freely, in a way that neither had expected.

'We believe Larry Sikorski fired Lindsay Compton. Given that we are in the midst of an ongoing investigation involving Mr Compton, there is little more I can disclose to you at this moment, except to say that we are investigating a number of serious irregularities at Saracen Laing. Many of these irregularities seem to be associated with the Research Department.'

'I'm not sure how this involves me,' said Jack.

'You are one of Saracen's longest-serving analysts. You know the Research Department better than most. You have watched analysts come and go. We have asked several of your colleagues for assistance in our investigation, but none is willing to help.'

'So what makes you think *I* can help you?'

Arnaud stopped and turned to face Jack. 'We have checked up on you, sir. You have a clean record. You are respected by your peers. But most of all, you have a reputation for integrity. There is a lot of dirty laundry in your department. I thought you would want a part in washing it out.'

Jack gave nothing away. 'What is it you want me to do?'

Arnaud glanced over his shoulder as if he was being tailed. 'A few months ago I was working on a case involving your boss, Mr Sikorski. The case has since been closed due to insufficient evidence. I believe you may be able to provide me sufficient information to reopen it. I am not speaking to you in any official capacity. The conversation we are about to have is strictly off the record. Is this acceptable to you, sir?'

Jack nodded. 'What do you want me to do?' he repeated.

'We need you to report to us anything suspicious. We believe Mr Sikorski is close to completing a large deal. We don't know what or when. We just have a sense that it is big.'

'You want me to spy on my boss?'

'We are merely offering you a chance to show which side of the law you are on,' replied Arnaud. 'We are already spying on Mr Sikorski. You work for him. If we find something on him, you would be guilty by association. Your reputation would be tarnished, whether you are guilty or not. You are an analyst; your reputation is everything. All I am asking is this . . .' Arnaud presented Jack with his business card. 'If you have information that could help our investigation into Mr Sikorski, please call me.'

As was often the case on Sunday evenings, the Northern Line was riddled with engineering works and the Underground journey from Hampstead to Moorgate took twice as long as it normally did. Jack waited impatiently for the doors to open at Moorgate station. Then he leapt out and darted up the escalators. He strolled briskly towards the Saracen Laing building, flashed his card at Security and ran up to the dealing floor. It was empty. He headed directly for Larry's office. With no one to stop him, he walked straight in and shut the door.

Larry's desk was clear, his computer on standby and his leather swivel chair empty. A filing cabinet stood in the corner with the keys still in the lock. It was too appealing. Jack opened the drawers and scanned their meticulously labelled contents. Management reports. Human Resources reports. Compliance reports. Trading reports. Expense claims. Journals. Unsure what he was looking for, he flicked through them at random.

He paused, and scrolled back one. Expenses. He pulled out the filing section and spread the contents on Larry's desk. There were a few bar bills, some phone bills, some restaurant bills. Lunch at the Moneypincher's Inn. Drinks at the Long Bar at the Sanderson. Dinner at Le Gavroche. A weekend away at Le Manoir aux Quat'Saisons. There was a rental invoice for the London pad Larry used during the week. The invoice was addressed to Saracen Laing Bank. The amount was £6,000 per month.

The address was 19 Onslow Square.

Jack froze. The palms of his hands began to sweat. *Onslow Square*, he whispered. A bitter taste filled his mouth and his gut wrenched.

Without tidying up the papers, he sprinted for the exit. Outside, a chilly gust of wind caught him off guard, for he had brought no coat.

'Taxi!' he shouted.

A black cab swerved and headed towards him, narrowly missing an unsuspecting cyclist. The cabbie lowered his window and leaned towards Jack.

Jack jumped in. 'Onslow Square,' he said snappily.

The route was an unusual one, down tiny cobbled streets and narrow lanes where the lighting seemed poor and the air smelt foul. It was a part of London that Jack had never seen. The sharp bends and the heavy braking began to make him feel nauseous.

'I don't recognise this route,' he called to the cabbie.

'I'll get you there faster this way, sir. Miss all the traffic lights, you see.'

Just get me there in one piece, you prat, Jack muttered nervously under his breath.

When he arrived at his destination it was raining. He thanked the cabbie and stepped out, avoiding the puddles that lay along the kerb. The rain pelted down on his face but he ignored it.

He found a plaque that read, *Onslow Square, The Royal Borough of Kensington and Chelsea*. The houses all looked the same. White stucco fronts, grand entrances with large steps leading up to them, broad pillars, ornate terraces, rooms with high ceilings and large fireplaces.

Jack strolled down the pavement, halting outside number 19. Judging by the number of doorbells, he guessed this one-time family residence was now home to three households. The lights were on in all three flats.

Jack whipped out his phone and punched in Niccolo's number. The call was diverted to answerphone. He left a hurried message, summarising the last few hours as best he could in under sixty seconds – the clandestine rendezvous with the man from the FSA, the expense file in Larry's office and his best guess as to where Donna had gone the day she left him. Then he switched his phone off, strolled decisively towards number 19 Onslow Square and rang all three bells.

Niccolo and Lucy had been dating now for almost two years. In their first month they made love frequently, passionately, obsessively. They would make love anywhere they could – at work, at home, in Hyde Park, in Regent's Park, in cinemas, in nightclubs; once they even managed a quick one at the Burger King outlet in Piccadilly Circus. In the second month, their passion remained strong, but the venue became limited to Niccolo's flat. By the third month, work began to take a fuller priority in Niccolo's life, and after four months, Sunday nights were the only time in the week when making love was a preordained certainty.

Niccolo switched his mobile phone to silent mode as he led Lucy into the bedroom. In the midst of their passion, an incoming call was automatically diverted from his handset to the Ultrafone voice-messaging centre.

*

Flat A was the first to answer the intercom bell. 'Yes?'

Jack recognised the voice immediately. 'Larry, it's Jack Ford. Can I see you?'

'It's nine o'clock on Sunday night, Jack! Can't this wait until the morning?'

'No, Larry, it can't.'

An elderly voice interrupted. 'Hello? Who's there?'

Jack apologised for pressing the wrong buzzer and the elderly voice disappeared, leaving only the hiss of the intercom.

'Larry? . . . Larry?'

Larry's voice signalled irritation. 'All right, all right. Come in, Jack.'

Jack entered the building, found his way to the mezzanine floor and knocked on the door of Flat A. It was at least two minutes before Larry appeared. Jack pushed his way in and unleashed his fury. 'Donna came here a few days ago. I haven't seen her since. Where is she? And what the hell was she doing here?'

Larry gripped Jack's arms as if to calm him, but it only made him angrier.

'Where is she?' he demanded.

Larry didn't so much as flinch. He turned and walked down the hall. Jack followed him into the dimly lit drawing room. It was a large room with a high ceiling, a priceless Qashqai rug and some carefully chosen eighteenth-century French paintings. Only a pair of rather threatening-looking chesterfield sofas were out of proportion. Jack and Larry sat down opposite each other.

'Poor kid, she didn't know where to turn,' Larry said smoothly. 'I have no idea what went on between you two, Jack. I merely listened to her, then packed her off to a hotel.'

'So, there's . . . I mean . . .' Jack stumbled on his words. 'So there's nothing going on between you two?' he asked finally.

Larry roared with laughter. 'Christ, no! No offence, buddy, but she's not my type.' Then, almost tenderly, he enquired, 'What happened?'

Jack curled up like an abandoned child, hugging his legs and burying his head in his chest. Then, without warning, he broke down in tears. With much embarrassment, he pulled out the letter Donna had written him, dirty and smudged and folded several times, and handed it over. Larry read it. Then he went over to the drinks tray and poured two large whiskies.

'Here, have this,' he said, handing one to Jack and sitting down again. 'Yes, she did confide in me. I know who it is she's having an affair with.'

Jack jumped to his feet. 'Who?'

Larry's voice became more aggressive, almost threatening. 'I need a little favour from you, Jack. You help me, I'll help you.'

'Don't play games with me, damn it! I want to know what she told you!'

Unfazed, Larry said, 'Sit down, Jack. I need you to persuade your little protégé Niccolo to switch the rating on Globecom.'

'What the fuck are you talking about?'

'I need you to get Nicco to switch the Globecom rating,' Larry repeated, as if Jack were a slow-witted child. 'We're in business to make money. Your friend doesn't seem to grasp that. We need to serve our customers, keep them happy. Now and then they might ask us for a few extras. What's the harm in that, eh?' He eyed Jack's clenched fists and sensed his wrath, but continued unabashed, 'You're coming up to ten years at Saracen. That shows immense loyalty, Jack. Plus you've performed well this year. I'd hate to see anything happen to your bonus.'

'I don't give a fuck about my bonus! I want to know who my wife is sleeping with!'

'I cannot betray someone's trust. Trust is something I value.' Realising that Jack's already frayed patience was about to snap,

Larry changed tack. 'This is a complex situation,' he professed. 'I feel it my duty to help you – after all, you're one of my own – so I'll tell you everything she told me, just as soon as the Globecom rating is switched to Buy.'

'We could all go to jail for this, Larry.' Jack slumped down in the armchair and took a hefty swallow of Scotch.

'Oh, I don't think that will be necessary. Nicco may have to resign, but he'll be paid off handsomely – I give you my word.'

'What makes you think Niccolo will do as I tell him?'

'He trusts you. You're his friend. He looks up to you like an older brother.'

'That's why I won't betray him.' Jack shook his head deliberately, as if to illustrate his point.

'I'll offer you three million – sterling.' Larry got up and walked through to his study. 'I can give you a fifty-K advance right now, if you like. Just think what you could do with that much money.'

'I'd rather burn in hell than take your dirty money, you son of a bitch!'

Larry came back into the room with a bulky brown envelope in his hand. 'Jack, here's fifty thousand, right here. All you need to do is get Nicco to switch his recommendation. He trusts you. It'll be a piece of cake.'

Jack blinked a few times. 'The FSA won't . . . won't . . . take kindly to your . . . th-threats.'

'You want to get the FSA involved? Kiddo, are you off your fucking head?' For the first time that evening, Larry came close to losing his temper. 'Listen, Jack, I've made the careers of a helluva lot of guys in the City. Most of them had more greed than brains. But you – it looks to me like you've got neither.'

'Just tell me where my wife is, or I'll break . . . your . . . fucking . . . legs!' Jack drained the rest of the whisky, and blinked owlishly.

'For Christ's sake, use your head, man! You work for me! We're on the same fucking team! I go down, you go down. You're just as tied up in all this as any of us, Jack.'

Jack's eyes swam, totally unfocused. 'I don't . . . don't have a clue what you're talking about.'

'OK – you want the truth?' sniped Larry. 'I'll give you the truth. Donna's having an affair with Lamparelli.'

Jack stared blankly at Larry. 'No . . . not Nicco.'

'I have the photographs to prove it. They're in my safe. Just say the word and I'll show you.'

'OK . . . show . . . show me.'

'One step at a time, my friend. First you help me with my little problem. Oh, by the way, keep this to yourself for now. Wait until Nicco's made the switch – Compliance get twitchy if they spot a pair of analysts having a public brawl – then you can do whatever the fuck you want. Beat the shit out of him for all I care. Hell, I might even do you a favour and fire the little prick for gross misconduct. I never liked the guy, you know. Too goddamn sure of himself. Not like you, Jack.'

'If . . . you think I'm goin' to . . . to hand over Nicco . . . so you can use him as a sc . . . sc . . . scapegoat for one of your scams, you'd better . . . think again, Larry.' Larry must have poured him a hellishly strong Scotch, Jack thought vaguely. Words were running away from him.

'I think the important thing here,' began Larry smugly, 'is that whoever's arms Donna ended up in, they weren't yours.'

'You're such a . . . bas . . . bashtard, Larry,' Jack mumbled. 'I'm gonna . . . call . . . police. Now.'

Larry didn't move a muscle as Jack fell off the sofa, crawled towards the telephone and picked it up. He was rocking back and forth on his knees, unable even to see what he was doing, and his fingers were just jabbing at the buttons.

Before he could make any call, the telephone receiver dropped to the floor, and Jack collapsed, unconscious.

Larry walked over, picked up the telephone and punched in a number. 'Can you send your man down here immediately,' he snapped. 'There's a problem.'

Lucy stepped into the shower, leaving the bathroom door wide open so they could hear each other, but Niccolo was not interested in conversation. He switched the television on and raced through the channels. Nothing of interest appeared, so he jumped out of bed and walked naked into the kitchen. He grabbed a beer from the fridge and collected his mobile phone from the dining table. He hurriedly dialled for his voice messages. He was surrounded by steam from the bathroom and the smell of honey and melon, and under the sound of hot running water, he was vaguely aware that Lucy was making some very seductive suggestions. But Niccolo's mind was elsewhere. By the time he had heard Jack's message for the third time, his face had turned completely pale. He hurriedly called Jack's number and waited impatiently for a reply.

Bit by bit, Larry's plans were gradually falling apart. The change in Globecom's stock rating would trigger a chain of events that could net him a personal fortune beyond his wildest dreams, with the potential to generate vastly more for Picton and the syndicate led by Mubarak. But the timing was absolutely critical. And the timing had to be now.

Only one man blocked the path that stood between Larry and his fortune. He had no option. The time had come to brush him aside.

Permanently.

But there was something else he had to do first. Grabbing his mobile phone and the brown envelope, he hastily left the flat.

*

249

Niccolo Lamparelli answered the call immediately.

'I'd like to talk to you.' The voice was familiar, though unwelcome. 'Is now a good time?'

'Of course, Larry. Is there a problem?'

'Could be, could be. You've known Jack Ford for a while, haven't you?

'Twenty years.'

'So you know him well. Would you say he'd been behaving rather strangely lately? He's taking some unpaid leave, I understand. Do you know why? I mean, of course I know his wife's left him, but apart from that?'

'It's hard to tell,' replied Niccolo guardedly.

'She rang me a week or two ago, you know. She was worried about him. She said he'd been behaving oddly before she left, buying her expensive presents.' Niccolo was puzzled. Donna wasn't the type to worry about receiving expensive gifts. 'In fact, she asked if I thought he might have been taking bribes – you know, for front-running the bank's research.'

'Jack? Not in a million years! He'd be the last person to do that.'

'Well, I'm not so sure. And Donna was worried enough that she was thinking of going to the police. Of course, she had no idea what a stink that would cause . . . front page news . . . Anyway, I persuaded her not to. I said I'd rather talk to Jack myself. I have to think of the bank's reputation, after all.'

Niccolo was aghast. 'Larry, I don't believe it, any of it.'

'Well, I sincerely hope your faith in your friend is justified, Niccolo. I'll talk to him tomorrow. Hey, I have to go. I'm meeting some people for a drink at the Long Bar.'

Niccolo snapped his mobile shut, his brain whirling. The only thing to do was talk to Jack. Yet again, he punched in Jack's number. Yet again, he got no answer.

*

Larry left Jack's desk tidy, just as he had found it. Then he crossed the Saracen trading floor and took the stairs up to the fifth floor. In the eerie privacy of the HR office, he opened a filing cabinet and took out the dossier he wanted. Careful not to disturb their order, he flicked through the papers until he found what he was looking for.

Swiftly he pulled out Jack Ford's most recent performance appraisal form. He found a loose sheet of paper that he recognised because it carried his own handwriting. Printed on Saracen Laing letterhead and marked *Strictly confidential – not to be shown to appraisee*, it contained the Head of Research's private remarks, often used by Saracen's board when assessing year-end bonus payments to exceptional staff.

Pulling out his pen, he scribbled some more comments beneath the ones he had written a couple of months earlier.

Jack asked for a pay rise. I got the impression he wasn't happy with what we paid him. Jack's work is satisfactory. But given that he only covers the smaller tech stocks, where the bank's commissions are low, I do not recommend we raise his bonus this year.

His mobile phone purred in his pocket.

'Your problem has been dealt with,' his caller stated.

'Good. Don't say any more on this line.' And he hung up.

CHAPTER 32

Detective Superintendent Dan Harcourt was woken in the early hours of Monday morning, on his day off, and summoned to the scene of a suspected suicide. The body had been sighted by a young post office worker at 6.06 a.m., marooned on a pier halfway between Waterloo and Blackfriars bridges. By the time Harcourt got there, Uniform had sealed off the area with 'Police – Do Not Cross' tape.

'What can you tell me?' he asked a young WPC.

'Deceased's been identified as Jack Ford,' he was told. 'Investment analyst, early thirties, worked for an American investment bank.'

'Cause of death?'

'Drowning, sir. Time of death we think was around midnight last night.'

'What do Forensics say? Any sign of a struggle?'

'No evidence of that yet . . .'

Harcourt snorted derisively.

'. . . but a handwritten note in the back pocket of the deceased indicates that his wife or lover had just left him. Suicide seems the most likely explanation.'

DS Harcourt was a man of few words, and his face was often devoid of expression. Harcourt hated criminals in general, but he hated white-collar criminals more. He classified suicide victims as criminals because their actions consumed police time.

For Harcourt, a suspect turned guilty the moment Harcourt judged him so. He rarely played by the rules because the rules stood in the way of justice. He solved cases by instinct rather than procedure, preferring to rely on people leading him to the truth rather than on forensic science finding it for him. His instinct had never let him down. The problem was that instinct alone seldom sent a guilty man to prison; evidence did. So there had been times when Harcourt introduced evidence of his own. His hunches and white lies were tolerated because they delivered results.

But these days Harcourt's methods were a liability to his superiors. Six months earlier, a new police commissioner had taken over at the Met, and had made it clear he would tolerate nothing that wasn't carried out strictly by the book.

'Fucking political correctness,' Harcourt frequently sneered. 'What about justice?'

Harcourt slipped on some plastic gloves and examined the body. He took his time, making detailed notes as he went along. He noted that a strip of hair had been ripped from the deceased's wrist, as if it had been waxed – or perhaps his hands had been bound by tape. He examined the victim's wallet and mobile phone with care. The wallet contained twenty pounds in cash, a handful of credit cards and a crumpled business card. Harcourt made a note of the name: Arnaud Veyrieras, FSA Enforcement Division. He handed both items to the hovering WPC, and requested a full transcript of all calls made to and from the victim's mobile phone within the last seventy-two hours.

WPC McKeever was attractive, blonde and ambitious, and a considerable distraction to DS Harcourt. In fact, she excelled in distracting senior police officers from their duties with remarkable consistency.

'But Harry says it's a straightforward suicide, guv,' she protested.

Harcourt glared disapprovingly. 'Harry's a sergeant, and you're a police constable. I'm a detective superintendent. That means I decide whether it's suicide or not, and you and Harry do as you're bloody well told!' He checked his watch. 'Right then, McKeever, it's now ten past seven. I need those phone records, and I need any CCTV footage you can find . . . and I need it yesterday. So if you ever want to make sergeant, I suggest you stop loitering aimlessly at the scene of a crime and get a bloody move on!'

Niccolo knew something was wrong the minute he turned up at work on Monday morning. Jack was not at his desk. Nor was he at the morning meeting; nor did he make it in for the nine o'clock coffee round. At lunchtime his chair still remained empty. No call. No message. No explanation.

Unable to concentrate all day, Niccolo left several messages on Jack's mobile phone. He called Donna too, but received no answer. Larry had not turned up for work that day either. At lunchtime, Niccolo went for a walk along the river, to clear his head. Back at his desk, he checked his emails. One caught his eye – it was apparently a CC from himself to himself, of an email from himself to Kenneth Oakes. Disbelievingly, he scrolled through it.

Subject: My sincere apologies
Dear Kenneth
     Thank you very much for inviting me to speak to your board last Friday.

I should make it clear that the views I expressed were my own and not those of Saracen Laing Bank. However, after careful consideration, I have come to the conclusion that my views on your stock were unduly harsh, unfair and uncorroborated.

A detailed review of my model indicates that some of my forecasts were far too pessimistic. I have updated my model and am now happy to recommend that Saracen Laing upgrade its Globecom stock recommendation to Buy.

I apologise for any offence I may have caused by making unsubstantiated statements in the presence of your board.

Kind regards

Niccolo Lamparelli

Senior Telecoms Analyst

Angrily, Niccolo hit the print button, just as Rupert walked on to the trading floor. Striding defiantly towards the printer, Niccolo collected the document and marched in Rupert's direction.

'Are you aware of this, Ru?' said Niccolo, hurling the printed copy on to Rupert's desk. '*Somebody* sent it out in my name.'

'Ah . . . yes . . .' Rupert havered nervously. 'Larry assumed you had forgotten to send it. He asked me to do it on your behalf. I used your machine and copied you. Didn't know your password, so I got Antonio to get me into your email – hope you don't mind. Amazing what those IT guys can do, you know.'

'I never agreed to send Globecom an apology!' yelled Niccolo.

'Er – we all agreed that it was the best solution under the circumstances.'

'I prefer to write my own emails, Rupert.'

'Well you don't need to worry about it any more. I've asked James to cover Globecom as of last Friday.'

'*What!*'

'Don't act so surprised – I told you I was pulling you off the stock last week in Larry's office.'

'Fine. But moving the Globecom rating – that was stupid!'

'Globecom has fallen eight per cent this year already. After a performance like that, it's almost certain to start rising at some point. I've done you a favour, Nicco.'

'Ru, don't be stupid.' Niccolo's voice was icy with fury. 'This stock is going down and you know it. Revenues are falling, IP prices are falling and there's a fuckload of overcapacity in the market. Their internet business hasn't made a profit in five years and I doubt it ever will. It's going to drag the whole company down.'

'You're not covering this stock any more.'

'Would *you* buy this stock, Ru?'

'You are no longer authorised to comment on Globecom – either publicly or privately. If you insist on interfering with James' recommendation, I will have no choice but to discipline you.'

With difficulty, Niccolo composed himself. There was little he could do in the circumstances.

'Listen, Nicco,' said Rupert softly. 'You've lost Globecom, but you've still got Ultrafone. Look, you're a good analyst, but you've only yourself to blame. For your own sake, just do as you're told!'

On his way to work that morning, Larry had dropped by the Moneypincher's Inn to see Dr Picton.

'You appear to have lost control of your operation, Sikorski,' snapped Picton.

'Ford could have blown all our plans out of the water.'

'Well, he isn't in a position to do that any more, is he?'

'No, he's not. Thank you for your assistance,' added Larry graciously.

'It is Karim you must thank.' Larry bowed his head in a reluctant show of gratitude to their absent friend, and Picton continued, 'What other news have you for me?'

'Events are progressing as planned,' Larry said confidently. 'Now there's just one minor hold-up. A small commission payment needs to be made to a certain – er – participant.'

'You are proving to be an expensive partner in crime, Sikorski. How much?'

'Half a million.'

'And who, may I ask, is this participant?'

'Let's call it a political donation. Think of it as insurance money if things go wrong.' Larry wiped his brow. 'The payment needs to be legitimate – if you will – so I'll make it personally, from my onshore UK account. But I ask that you reimburse me using my Usmani account.' He produced a piece of paper, as if from nowhere, containing a single eight-digit number and passed it to Picton.

'As you wish,' conceded Picton, with only the merest raising of an eyebrow. 'The funds will be paid out of a numbered syndicate account held at the Shahaan branch of the National Bank of Usman.'

Larry smiled. He knew that according to the laws of the Sultanate of Usman, no law-enforcement agency, domestic or foreign, had the authority to trace the holder of a numbered bank account held by the National Bank of Usman without the express permission of the Sultan himself. And under His Majesty Sultan Majid's regime, no record of such a precedent existed.

Just as Larry was about to leave, Picton added mildly, 'By the way, you no doubt found your spare key where you usually keep it? Karim was most insistent that he had put it back where he found it.'

*

257

WPC McKeever desperately wanted to make sergeant. So she gathered the transcripts of all calls made to and from the deceased's mobile phone within the previous seventy-two hours. And she did it fast.

Outgoing calls:
Sunday, 20.58, Niccolo Lamparelli. Call diverted to
answer message.
Saturday, 16.45, Niccolo Lamparelli. Call duration:
18 minutes, 3 seconds.
Friday, 01.44, Gino Martinelli (international roaming
charge: Ultrafone, Spain). Call duration: 2 minutes 5
seconds.

Incoming calls:
Monday, 09.14, Niccolo Lamparelli. Call diverted to
answer message.
Monday, 07.19. Niccolo Lamparelli. Call diverted to
answer message.
Monday, 06.22. Niccolo Lamparelli. Call diverted to
answer message.
Sunday, 23.58, Niccolo Lamparelli. Call diverted to
answer message.
Sunday, 23.42, Niccolo Lamparelli. Call diverted to
answer message.
Sunday, 23.23, Niccolo Lamparelli. Call diverted to
answer message.
Sunday, 12.05, number registered to FSA. Call
duration: 3 minutes, 56 seconds.

As fast as she could, WPC McKeever conducted some background checks on the counterparties identified by the call records. The calls immediately before and after the time of death – estimated to be midnight on Sunday – were both made by Niccolo Lamparelli. With the help of network engineers at the Forensic Science Service, WPC McKeever traced the deceased's movements in the early hours of Sunday night, which she hoped would enable her to piece together a clearer picture of the chain of events that had led to the death of Jack Ford.

'Someone in the market has been buying up large amounts of Globecom stock.'

Mortimer Steel leaned forward and placed his elbows firmly on the table. 'Why?'

'Well, that's just it. We don't know why. On the face of it, there's no reason to do so. Nothing of significance has happened either at Globecom or in the telecoms sector in general. No positive news flow, no price changes, no M&A, nothing.'

'Really? That's unusual.'

'Precisely, sir. That's why the dweebs in Compliance picked it up.'

'What are we talking about here, JC?' barked Mortimer. 'Give me some bloody numbers.'

'Around one point two billion pounds, in various orders over three days.'

'All the same buyer?'

'Possibly. Probably. We don't know. The buyer could be foreign.'

'How do you make that out?'

'Our market-makers have been asking around. But they're hitting a brick wall. Nominee accounts. Cloaks and daggers. No one's giving the game away. Smells like a takeover or something. But too many smokescreens.'

'Have they hit three per cent?'

'Not yet. My feeling is that they're getting round the notification rule by using several nominee accounts. Compliance are getting nervous about it. They want all heads of department to sign something to say they are unaware of any large buyers or sellers of Globecom stock. The usual stuff to cover their asses – you know, market manipulation and all that shit.'

'Christ, why do I have to get involved? I'm Head of Corporate Finance! It's my *job* to manipulate markets. How the fuck does Compliance expect me to make money otherwise?'

Jean-Claude shrugged and smiled. '*C'est la vie, mon ami.*'

'What a fuck-up! I don't want the goddamn FSA breathing down my neck. I'm staying out of it – and you work for me, so you're staying out of it too. Understand?'

'I don't think we can get out of this one, boss. The orders come all the way from the top. Sukuhara's involved now.'

The police decided to treat Jack's death as suspicious. DS Harcourt sent WPC McKeever to find Jack's wife. When Donna Ford could not be located at her home address, WPC McKeever contacted the police control room. Using repeater triangulation techniques with the assistance of the mobile phone networks, the control room tracked Donna's location to the Park Lane Plaza.

At a few minutes past eight on Monday morning, WPC McKeever and a male colleague entered the hotel and discreetly had the duty manager summoned to Reception. WPC McKeever produced a picture of Donna Ford. 'Can you help us track down this lady?'

They found Donna in the hotel gym, pushing a clean seventy pounds on the bench-press, and wearing a tight white singlet and heavy make-up. WPC McKeever's male uniformed colleague made an on-site assessment of the situation, and decided that the breaking of bad news required a woman's touch, while preparing himself to act as a shoulder to cry on. Within seconds, his services were required. As soon as WPC McKeever informed Donna of her husband's death, the transformation from gym queen to tearful wreck was almost instantaneous.

WPC McKeever decided not to question Donna Ford formally at this point, but indicated that an interview might be necessary at a later date. Once she had calmed down, Donna agreed to accompany the officers to the morgue to identify her husband's body.

After the formalities had been taken care of at the police station, Donna was handed a box containing the personal possessions found on Jack's body. A police driver placed them in the boot of a marked BMW and drove her back to the Park Lane Plaza.

Most of the CCTV cameras around the Westminster area had been upgraded to digital format over the previous two years, as part of an ongoing modernisation programme funded by the Mayor of London. But the camera that recorded the murder of Jack Ford belonged to the London Traffic Control Centre; it was an older model dating back to the pre-digital age, so the footage was in analogue format. Mysteriously, the tape had been requisitioned by some unnervingly official-looking men with briefcases. By the time the police requested the footage, the tape was gone.

'No, we never made a copy,' the LTCC controller on duty on the night of the murder defended himself. 'Wouldn't have been allowed. If you ask me, they was from MI5 or some such.' One thing was certain – whoever they were, crucial evidence pertaining to the Ford murder had disappeared.

However, the LTCC controller claimed that he had been able to study the footage briefly before handing it over. When first questioned, he was only able to provide WPC McKeever with a few snippets of useful information. The video footage, taken from a CCTV camera on Westminster Bridge, showed two men getting out of a car parked on the middle of the bridge, he said. One of the men appeared drunk. That was at around midnight, claimed the controller.

'Did you actually see anyone jump?' asked WPC McKeever.

'No, definitely not.' His voice was reluctant, shaky, as was his body language. He stared at the floor, his fingers twitching. 'The blokes from MI5 stopped the tape and took it away.'

'Can you describe the men in the tape?'

The controller shook his head. 'One of them had on a baseball cap, not that that's of any use to you.'

McKeever sighed. 'Is there anything else you can tell me?'

The controller walked over to the door, checked it was shut, paced up and down a few times, deep in thought, then suddenly stopped. 'Now I don't want to get into no trouble, mind,' he said, 'but I did get one thing – the car had a D number plate – you know, a diplomatic plate. The MI5 blokes were in a hurry. As soon as they found what they were looking for, they took the tape and left. But I'd memorised the number.'

'And?'

The controller pulled out from his trouser pocket a crumpled scrap of paper and handed it to WPC McKeever.

'You're a star!' she beamed. 'Thank you!'

Outside, she immediately radioed DS Harcourt, who promptly set about calling in assorted favours and obligations amassed over the years. Within hours, they had the getaway car. It was a blue Ford Escort, registered to the Usmani Embassy in London.

Late on Monday night, as the Forensic Science Service were examining Jack's phone, it suddenly lit up like a firecracker, and hummed 'Eye of the Tiger'. The phone's memory chip identified

262

the caller as 'Nicco'. It was the sixth call from this caller within the last twenty-four hours. On the sixth ring, the call was automatically diverted to answerphone, prompting the caller to leave a brief message. 'Jack, where the fuck are you? I'm really worried. Call me.'

Within seconds, DS Harcourt was informed of the call in the incident room. A few hours later, at eleven, he debriefed his team on the day's events. 'OK, early tests reveal that whilst drowning was the actual cause of death, the deceased's body had been subjected to an overdose of heroin immediately prior to entry into the water. The heroin could have been self-administered, and he doesn't appear to have been a habitual user, so on the face of it suicide seems entirely plausible. But I'm not convinced.

'List of those required for questioning. First, Donna Ford, the deceased's wife. Her handwritten letter is being examined by the graphology team even as I speak. Second, Niccolo Lamparelli, co-worker of the deceased at Saracen Laing, the last person to call the deceased before his death and the first to call him afterwards. Third, Larry Sikorski, the deceased's boss. Jack Ford's work colleagues will also have to be interviewed, as will Arnaud Veyrieras of the FSA, whose card was found in the deceased's wallet.'

Harcourt ended the briefing as he always did, by threatening to fire every last one of them if they fucked up.

'Oh my God, Larry,' Donna wailed. 'Jack's dead! The police came to the hotel to get me, and they took me to identify him, and it was all so awful—'

'Dead?' Larry interrupted, stunned. 'My dear girl, what are you talking about?'

'He's dead!' she shrieked. 'Drowned! They found him this morning in the Thames.'

'Jesus Christ!' he whispered. 'My dear Donna, I'm so sorry,' he managed to say.

'The police want to interview me,' she whimpered.

'You must be very, very careful what you say, my darling. After all, you left Jack for another man – and you were foolish enough to put it in writing – so that's enough to make you number one suspect.'

Donna gasped. 'But I had nothing to do with his death!'

'I know that. But think how it's going to look to the police. And to everyone else. Of *course* you didn't mean to drive him to suicide . . .'

'Larry, what am I going to do? Oh, my poor darling Jack!' And she collapsed into sobs.

'Look,' he said firmly. 'Of course you had nothing to do with his death. But the police are going to want to know more than that. Didn't you say he'd been behaving rather strangely lately? No? I thought you did . . .'

'Well . . .' And gradually Donna began to think that her husband might indeed have been behaving oddly. Subtle hints and suggestions from Larry built up a plausible picture in her mind of a man driven to despair by . . . she couldn't guess what by. Then, skilfully, Larry calmed her down and brought the conversation round to what they should tell the police. Donna would admit her affair with Larry. She would portray herself as a wife neglected by a husband who claimed to work unusually long hours. She would tell them that he had been acting strangely, that he was flush with cash – more so than usual – and that she had no idea where it came from. Of course, it was possible that he had been mixed up in something shady, but she saw so little of him, how would she know?

'Well done, darling,' Larry said soothingly. 'After all, you have to think of yourself now.'

At nine o'clock on Tuesday morning, DS Harcourt pitched up in a marked Ford Sierra just outside the Saracen Laing building. He marched straight inside, armed with two sullen-looking sergeants. A fourth officer stood beside the police car, parked obtrusively outside the bank's front entrance.

Confronted with three uniformed Met officers, Domingo surfaced from behind his security enclave to greet them in the lobby. His entourage of security guards watched from a safe distance and gave the distinct impression that they were out of their depth. Domingo inspected DS Harcourt's credentials thoroughly, and nodded to his guards to let the officers through.

At DS Harcourt's request, Domingo called ahead to commandeer an interview room on the executive floor. Then he personally escorted them there.

In the meeting room, DS Harcourt explained his business. 'It's not my intention to make a scene by sending uniformed officers on to your trading floor,' he announced. 'But I'd like to talk to this person.' He passed Domingo a scrap of paper with a handwritten name.

Domingo disappeared in search of the name, and DS Harcourt's two sidekicks produced voice recorders from their inside jacket pockets and stationed themselves at strategic positions around the table.

Niccolo sensed it in Domingo's melancholy demeanour as he was informed by the big guy that his presence was required on the executive floor. He sensed it in the wall of silence on the way up in the elevator.

As soon as the police officers introduced themselves, Niccolo felt a rusty wrench twist in his gut. It took a good ten minutes to digest the information that he was given by DS Harcourt.

For a long while, he remained speechless. Then, when he finally regained some composure, he told the police everything they wanted to know.

'Jack was my closest friend,' he told them. 'We met at school in Japan – I was ten, he was nearly thirteen – and someone made him promise he would always look after me. All my life he's been like an older brother to me. It was Jack who persuaded me to go to university, Jack who always kept me out of trouble. And it was partly the fact that Jack was already here that convinced me to accept a job at Saracen.'

'Would anyone have had a grievance or grudge against him?' Harcourt asked.

'No, everybody loved him – everybody here, friends. Everybody loved Jack.'

'Why did you call Mr Ford six times between eleven p.m. on Sunday night and ten a.m. on Monday morning, the hours immediately before and after his death?' asked Harcourt implacably.

'Jack called me on Sunday night. It must have been around nine o'clock. He left a message – my phone was switched off – and he sounded troubled. Very troubled. I knew something bad had happened.'

Harcourt nodded, but said nothing.

'His wife had just left him,' Niccolo went on. 'He thought she had gone to Larry's house.'

'Larry Sikorski?'

'Yes, he's our boss. Jack thought Donna was having an affair with him. When he left the message, he was standing outside Larry's house. He was *very* angry.'

'And *was* Mrs Ford having an affair with Larry Sikorski?'

'I don't know,' Niccolo said numbly. He felt deathly cold with shock. 'All I know is that she'd left Jack. And I can't tell you why, because I don't know that either.'

'Mr Lamparelli, when did you last see the deceased?'

The deceased. *Jack*.

Niccolo described the trip to Okinawa to see Mizuno-san.

When he had unloaded all he wanted to say, he paused, waited for the uniformed officer to lift his pen, and made one final statement. 'Jack was the best friend I ever had. He was a truly great man. He believed in honour and integrity and all the things Mizuno-san taught us. He made me what I am today. And I don't know what I'm going to do without him.' He bowed his head, as if in shame, wiping a stream of tears from his face.

Harcourt's sidekicks exchanged glances. Neither recorded Niccolo's closing statement.

'Can you think of anything else at this stage, Mr Lamparelli?' asked DS Harcourt.

Niccolo shook his head. 'I don't think so.'

Harcourt thanked him, the police officers gathered their belongings, then they shook hands with Niccolo and headed for the door.

'Oh, there's just one thing . . .' interjected Niccolo. 'I don't know if it's important . . .'

'Sir, in a murder enquiry, everything is important.'

'Well, Jack mentioned a guy from the FSA – Arnie something? – who was harassing him for some information about work.'

'Perhaps the name you refer to was Arnaud Veyrieras?' suggested Harcourt.

'Yes,' replied Niccolo. 'That sounds right.'

'You've been most helpful. Thank you, Mr Lamparelli. Please stay in the country until this murder investigation is over. We may need to question you again.'

CHAPTER 33

When Arnaud Veyrieras first received the news of Jack's death, he had a damn good idea who was behind it. But he trod carefully in the presence of the two police officers, and asked to speak directly to the senior inspector in charge of the investigation. Surprisingly, the officers granted his request, and politely escorted him without fuss in a marked police car from Canary Wharf to Charing Cross police station.

WPC McKeever cautioned Arnaud and informed him that their conversation was about to be recorded, then DS Harcourt explained that the circumstances surrounding Jack Ford's death were suspicious.

Arnaud nodded eagerly. 'This is no suicide, Inspector,' he agreed. 'I met Jack Ford the day he died, and I think I know who was responsible for his death.'

WPC McKeever leaned forward, betraying her excitement. But DS Harcourt gave away nothing. He motioned Arnaud to continue.

'I am certain, absolutely certain, that there is a link between this poor young man's murder – yes, I believe it to be murder – and Larry Sikorski, who is Head of Research at Saracen Laing.' Arnaud proceeded to paint a scathing portrait of Larry Sikorski and pointed to a history littered with the carcasses of unexplained staff departures, culminating in that of Lindsay Compton, whose abrupt dismissal coincided suspiciously with his parents' kidnapping in Usman. 'And now Jack Ford has been found dead under suspicious circumstances. This man Sikorski has been linked to a number of financial crimes in the past by the FSA, but he has never got his own hands sufficiently dirty to be charged with anything serious. At one point, even your Serious Fraud Office had him firmly in their sights, but they had to let him go. No evidence, of the kind the Crown Prosecution Service needs, has ever stuck to him.

'My own interest in Sikorski's dealings spans not months but years. But I must confess to you, Inspector, that my boss – you may know of her, Miss Amanda Sanderson – has officially banned me from any further investigation into Sikorski. She fears the FSA may be charged with harassment. This lack of authorisation meant that my meeting with Mr Ford had to be arranged with the utmost discretion. Might I request that you observe a similar discretion?'

He went on to describe Larry's scam, as he saw it. 'Sikorski takes money from hedge funds to make unexpected changes in the bank's stock ratings. The hedge funds move into a large position – long or short – and then give the order to Sikorski. Sikorski can change stock ratings at a moment's notice. Analysts are normally responsible for their own calls, but Sikorski runs a tight ship. He's in charge. Mostly his guys fall into line. If they don't, they're out. A couple of the analysts are straight – they want nothing to do with this scam – but they're too scared to blow the whistle. So they have a deal. He steers clear of them and they keep their mouths shut.

'Sikorski's partners are part of a private Middle Eastern syndicate. Their funds have grown sky high because of oil prices – they have more money to invest than many governments. But they're amateurs, mainly young Arab princes playing with their daddies' money, trying to prove they are men. Yet for all their Harvard degrees, they are still idiots. The real wrongdoing lies with Sikorski and his minions. I will do whatever I can, Inspector, to help the police establish their guilt.'

The Frenchman spent the rest of the afternoon telling DS Harcourt everything he knew about Larry Sikorski's dealings with Dr Picton.

Niccolo needed time to grieve Jack's passing, so he submitted a request for compassionate leave. The request hit Rupert's desk and was promptly passed on to Larry, who shunted it up to HR. A memorandum bounced back from Daryl Walker, Head of HR, with a copy to Larry, stating in no uncertain terms that, despite recent events, the request for leave was denied, on the grounds that Jack was not a family relative. Moreover, annual leave was ruled out too, since Niccolo had already exceeded his quota by two days. His attendance at work over the next few weeks was mandatory.

The discovery that CCTV footage of Jack's death had been appropriated from under their very noses sent DS Harcourt into one of his rages.

'What the fuck are MI5 doing with the tape in the first place?' he demanded of WPC McKeever, pacing up and down the incident room. 'Who the fuck asked *them* to get involved?'

'Perhaps it has something to do with the Usmani Embassy being involved, sir. The getaway car was registered to them. Could be part of a bigger diplomatic incident.'

DS Harcourt detected hesitation and showed no mercy. 'Well, get some bloody uniforms down to the Usmani Embassy, woman, and find out!'

*

News of Jack's death made its way into the national press. It was front-page material – dynamite! Few reports showed Jack's alleged actions in a positive light. *Banker drowns in Thames . . . Police treat banker's death as suspicious . . . Banker overdoses before jumping to his death . . . Suspected rogue analyst takes own life.*

The trading floor was gripped by sadness of a sort it had not experienced since 9/11, when many of their colleagues at Saracen's Global Headquarters had lost their lives. Larry's office issued a company-wide memo, requesting all staff to observe three minutes' silence at nine o'clock that morning in Jack's memory. To the press, he described his former colleague as 'intelligent, hard-working and revered by all'.

'Jack Ford was a personal friend, a distinguished analyst and a dearly loved member of the Saracen Laing family,' he averred.

After the morning meeting, Anne-Marie followed Charlie out of the Oval Room towards the coffee shop. 'Charlie, a client called for you. White Stone. I took down their number,' she said, handing him a scrap of paper.

'Can't do it now,' snapped Charlie, ordering himself a coffee. 'I've just been called up to the executive floor. Some detective called Hard-cop wants to interview me.'

Charlie ambled off the trading floor without the habitual spring in his step or the joker's sparkle in his eyes. He missed his friend Jack. And he didn't quite know how to deal with it.

CHAPTER 34

Larry Sikorski was far too busy to see the police in the days immediately following Jack's death.

'Tell the bastards I have a tight schedule and I'm sticking to it!' he
ranted at Anne-Marie. 'Morning meetings, breakfast meetings, client
lunches, peer review meetings – plus, I happen to have a department
to run. So any fucking Plod that shows up, just get rid of him. Unless
he has a warrant. Oh, and get a couple of boxes and clear out Ford's
desk right away, would you? And put these in my expenses file.' He
thrust a few receipts at her, amongst them two taxi fares and several
rounds of drinks at the Long Bar for four bemused Germans who
hadn't a clue why a total stranger was being so hospitable.

Niccolo, Charlie and James did their best to take no notice as
Anne-Marie methodically went through Jack's desk, emptying
every drawer before taking it out and banging loose the accumu-
lation of dust, fluff and paper clips. But when she gasped, 'Oh my
God!' all three looked up sharply to see her staring, shell-shocked,
at the bulky brown envelope she had just opened. She walked
over and handed it to Charlie with an imploring look in her eyes.
Charlie, for once, was lost for words.

'What is it?' Niccolo enquired, getting up from his desk.

'Money. Shitloads of it. Look.' Charlie dropped it on his desk as if it had burned him.

'No,' Niccolo said, shaking his head in denial. 'No way!'

'It fucking is. Christ, where did he get it?'

'He didn't. I mean, there must be some explanation. Jack's straight . . . I know he is.'

By this time, a small crowd of excited traders was gathering round Charlie's desk. Anne-Marie pulled herself together. 'I'm telling Larry, right away,' she declared. 'He'll know what to do.'

Like many old-timers in the bank, Charlie suspected that Larry was in some awful way linked – through some shadowy money-minting deal – to Jack's untimely death. Yet he dared not blow the whistle, for he lacked hard proof and was unlikely ever to find it. All he had to go on was his hunch, a hunch based on many years of watching Larry operate, of working closely with him, of witnessing many good analysts come and go on his watch.

What could he say to the cops – 'I think you should arrest this guy'? Not a snowflake's chance in hell. Larry wore a Teflon jacket. He was a fully paid-up member of the City High-Flyers' Club. He had money and power and status. He was untouchable.

At the Usmani Embassy, the ambassador was informed that the police had linked a blue Ford Escort registered to the embassy to the scene of a serious crime. An official request was made for his country's assistance in the investigation.

His Excellency graciously agreed to waive diplomatic immunity, assuring the uniforms dispatched by WPC McKeever that the embassy would conduct a thorough internal investigation of their own and report their findings as soon as anything of note came to light. He very much regretted, however, that the vehicle in question had already been sent, as all the embassy cars were every week, to be washed and valeted.

'If only we had known!' he sighed with great sincerity.

Senior embassy officials, on discovering that the car had been signed out to Karim, had already acted fast. A driver picked him up from his flat in Holland Park in a black limousine and drove him directly to Heathrow. At the airport, a standby team in dark suits and sunglasses hurried him through the diplomatic channel, and accompanied him on board the Royal UsmanAir 777 once it was ready. By five o'clock that afternoon, the only suspect wanted for questioning by the Metropolitan Police in connection with the death of Jack Ford was tucking into a nice juicy eight-ounce sirloin steak, having just downed a half-bottle of Dom Perignon, and was looking forward to a safe landing in Shahaan.

It was late on Wednesday night, after Anne-Marie had gone home, when DS Harcourt finally caught up with Saracen's Head of Equity Research in his office. Although the trading floor was deserted, Larry insisted on closing the door as soon as Harcourt had taken a seat.

Harcourt explained his business concisely. 'Mr Sikorski, Mr Ford's mobile phone records indicate that he was at or very near your house just hours before his death.'

'Really? How strange. This is the first I've heard of it. I was out all evening, got back very late.'

Harcourt looked up sharply. 'And I suppose you can prove that, sir?'

Larry nodded.

'His wife's phone records are on the same account, so we looked at them too. I note that you made a number of calls to Mrs Donna Ford. What was the purpose of those calls, sir?'

Larry leaned back in his expensive leather chair. 'At Saracen

Laing, we take care of our employees. And we take care of their families. When Jack died, I called Donna to offer my condolences, of course, and to reassure her that the bank would meet its commitments – pension, final pay, all of that stuff—'

'No, sir,' interrupted Harcourt. 'That's not what I'm referring to. You phoned Mrs Ford on several occasions, sometimes nights, sometimes weekends – well before Jack Ford's death. Why?'

'I was worried about Jack,' Larry answered smoothly. 'And so was Donna. He'd been working too hard. I wanted to check that everything was all right at home.'

'Is it normal for you to check up on your employees' wives, sir?'

Larry leaned forward like a released spring. 'This is Saracen Laing,' he announced proudly. 'We were voted Employer of Choice three years running. Our staff are our blood. We look after them. I was concerned about Jack, had been for a while. He'd been acting . . . well, strangely.' Larry's voice tapered off.

'In what way, sir?'

'Look, I'm not saying Jack did anything wrong . . .' Larry rose, turned his back to his guest and surveyed the trading floor. A lone sales trader was glued to his desk; the rest of the floor was empty. 'He came to my office a couple of times, asking for a rise. Even reminded me at his last performance appraisal. That wasn't like Jack. He'd always been a good company man. His wife – Donna – she loves the good life. Expensive tastes, you know how it is. But I wouldn't have said Jack was the sort to bend the rules. And if he did, I'd have fired him. I don't tolerate that kind of shit.'

Attentiveness written all over his face, DS Harcourt let the silence settle. As he had hoped, Larry went on talking. 'But sometimes analysts can bend the rules. Big money is often involved – and I mean *big* money. At some point, temptation can take over. Everyone has a limit.'

'Are you telling me Jack Ford was taking bribes, sir?' DS Harcourt persisted.

Now it was Larry's turn to maintain a carefully timed silence. Finally he said, with a sigh, 'You know, Detective Superintendent, I've known Jack for ten years. And I'd have gladly given my right arm for him, until . . .' He paused, bowing his head down in shame. DS Harcourt motioned him to continue. '. . . until my assistant found something in his desk this morning.' He handed a carrier bag to the policeman, who peered inside and raised an eyebrow. 'I haven't counted it. I really don't know what to think.'

Harcourt put the carrier bag down on Larry's desk. 'How easy would it be for one of your analysts to front-run the bank's research?' he enquired.

'We have tried-and-tested procedures to ensure that sort of thing never happens,' Larry said disdainfully, as if to ridicule Harcourt's line of questioning. 'But it's possible; you can't be sure of anything these days. Ours is a high-tech business. It's impossible to control everyone. We rely on trust. And I always believed Jack was trustworthy. It just doesn't make sense.'

'I can see you're very loyal to your staff, sir.'

Larry looked the policeman straight in the eye. 'Detective Superintendent,' he said. 'I just don't know what to think any more.'

That evening, Niccolo arranged to meet Gino just outside Hampstead tube station. When they met, they embraced each other long and hard.

'They're trying to pin some dirt on Jack,' said Niccolo as they descended the hill. It was a beautiful clear night. Many of the shops were still open and the high street was buzzing. 'There was a stash of cash in his desk. Larry says he was on the take, that he was mixed up in an insider-trading ring. He says he took bribes, that he was front-running the bank's research.'

'What does front-running mean?'

'If you're a Saracen employee – on the inside – it's illegal to trade shares ahead of the publication of upgrades and downgrades by fellow Saracen Laing analysts. You'd know which way the stock would move, so you could place your bets beforehand and profit from any change in the analyst's view – that's front-running.'

Gino took a deep breath. 'Look, Nicco, I'm really sorry about Jack. I know how highly you thought of him. But Larry could be right. Where did the money come from? Maybe Jack *was* dirty . . .'

'Jack was straight down the line!' Niccolo exploded. 'He would never take bribes!'

'You just don't know that, Nicco. Neither of us knows that!'

Without warning, Niccolo rushed Gino, pinning him up against a GapKids shop window by the throat. 'Jack would never take bribes!' he repeated.

Niccolo stepped back, then swung. He managed to deliver a stinging jab that sent Gino reeling back against the shop window before collapsing in a heap.

A sales assistant came running outside. 'Oi! Mind our window!' she yelled. 'What's going on? You want me to call the police?'

Gino carefully felt his swollen nose. 'No need. I'm OK,' he said. He motioned Niccolo to continue walking. 'I think we both need a drink, Nicco.'

Niccolo did not answer, but followed his friend into the bar at Al Casbah. They ordered two beers and sat down at a corner table, ignoring shocked looks from the diners as Gino wiped blood from his lip.

'I'm really sorry, Gino. It's just that . . . Jack's death . . . I can't think straight any more,' confessed Niccolo. 'I really need to take some time off work.'

'This is no time for a goddamn holiday!' Gino retorted, taking a swallow of beer. 'We have to find out how Jack died. If Larry is behind this shitty mess, the only way we'll catch him is if you're on the inside.'

When the police questioned Antonio Sanchez, he volunteered so much information that they asked him to build them a custom-made database, which he duly did. Antonio knew more internal gossip than anyone, including Anne-Marie. Moreover, he had a far better filing system; as far as the police were concerned, electronic information was more reliable because it was harder to doctor. Whilst nothing turned up that provided them with any useful leads, Antonio's systems gave them some assurance that, if there was electronic evidence of wrongdoing by any of the bank's staff, they had the best tools at their disposal to uncover it.

'When this sodding case is over,' DS Harcourt told WPC McKeever, 'remind me to offer that little dago bugger a job in police forensics.'

'I don't think we could afford him, guv,' WPC McKeever shot back cheekily.

Niccolo had never imagined life without Jack. Apart from Mizuno, after the death of his father Jack had been the single biggest influence on Niccolo's life. More importantly, while Mizuno lived thousands of miles away, fate had kept Jack close at hand, like a guardian angel sent to watch over him.

Niccolo was truly indebted to Jack. At school, at college, at work and at home, Jack had opened doors for his friend, and had always steered him on to the right path. Over time, his debt of gratitude had mounted up, but Niccolo never fretted, because one day he intended to repay it in spades. He'd had grandiose plans for expensive holidays, and intentions to share huge chunks of his wealth with Jack when it eventually came his way. But Niccolo's plans were always for tomorrow. As a struggling young journalist at the *Financial Telegraph*, he'd had little choice but to defer showing his gratitude until such time as he made more money. But tomorrow never came, and the one thing that Niccolo hadn't expected was that time would run out.

That night he lay awake contemplating life without Jack, wondering what the future held. For this was not the first time he had lost his guiding star.

When Isabella heard that her husband had been killed during a routine training exercise at the US naval base in Okinawa, she desperately begged his commanding officers to tell her what had happened, how he had died, where he had died, why he had died. Yet neither the Indian Navy nor their US counterparts would release further details. The training exercise was covert and, on paper, it had never taken place. The Indian Prime Minister himself presented Isabella with the Param Vishisht Seva Medal, the highest decoration for meritorious service, and Feroz's body was cremated, in accordance with his wishes.

Isabella's sorrow plunged her into a prolonged silence from which not even her son could rescue her. She was used to being separated from her husband for long periods of time, but the flames crackling on his pyre brought home to her a cruel message: there would be no tender reunion this time.

Isabella returned from Japan a widow, and set about making a life for herself in her native Italy. She rented a small apartment in Milan, and through her father's contacts was able to secure a position as a journalist with a regional newspaper, returning to what she knew best, which offered a small respite from the crushing pain of her loss.

Feroz had always had a clear vision of the balanced education he wished for his son, and Isabella was determined that his military pension would pay for his vision to be realised. So she sent Niccolo to board at Uppingham. After completing his secondary education in England, Niccolo, encouraged by Jack, applied to study engineering at Cambridge, the same degree course in which Jack was enrolled. For three years, Jack nagged and chivvied Niccolo into attending lectures and seminars even with a pounding hangover, and getting his papers written and handed in on time. In the end Niccolo did get his degree. Not a very spectacular degree, but a degree nonetheless.

'Thanks,' he said, hugging Jack on the day he graduated. 'I'd never have done it without you.'

Over the following forty-eight hours, Larry set about praising Jack's name in public and trashing it in private. He ran his smear campaign very effectively. Anne-Marie booked up his diary to the limit. At charity balls, industry seminars and private art viewings, at Champneys and the Chelsea Harbour Club, he leaked dirt on Jack Ford. It was subtle dirt, and it was low-level dirt, but it stuck.

Larry systematically covered the City circuit, targeting those individuals with the smallest IQs and the biggest mouths, engineering leaks and placing stories. He was on first-name terms with the editors of the *Financial Telegraph*, the *Wall Street Journal* and the *Economist*, and he even made a point of reacquainting himself with their wives. He worked discreetly and diligently, secure in the knowledge that the object of his malice was in no position ever to fight back.

CHAPTER 35

'I've got to find out who did it,' Niccolo whispered.

Lucy leaned up on her elbow, astonished. 'What do you mean, Nicco?' she demanded incredulously.

'Jack was murdered, and I need to find out who did it.'

'But it was all in the paper! He committed suicide!' she insisted with conviction. 'He took an overdose and jumped!'

'No.' Rocking on the edge of the bed, his head in his hands, he said, 'Don't ask me how I know, Lucy, but I do. I just know.'

'Know what?' she demanded nervously.

'Larry had something to do with Jack's death.'

'*Larry*? But . . . why . . .?'

'I don't know. But I'm going to find out.'

'Oh my God!' Lucy jumped out of bed, her face as white as the sheets, and paced the room, her arms wrapped round herself as though she were in pain. 'Oh my God!' she exclaimed again. 'I can't believe what I've done!'

She came over to the bed and sat down beside Niccolo, trembling from head to toe.

'What *have* you done?'

'You're going to be furious . . .'

'Look, just bloody *tell* me!'

'You remember when we first met, at Larry's party?'

'Of course.'

'Well, I'd been told to get close to you, I mean close enough to find out anything I could about you.'

'I don't believe this!' Niccolo got up impatiently and grabbed his bathrobe. 'Who told you?'

'Larry,' Lucy confessed. 'I suppose I was being paid to spy on you . . .'

'*Paid?*'

'. . . to spy on you, and – if I could – to influence your decision-making. At first, I just did it for the money. But then . . .' She burst into tears. 'Then I fell in love with you, Nicco,' she hiccuped.

'Why are you telling me this now?' he demanded coldly. 'Jack might still be alive if you'd told me this before!'

She stared at him, shocked by his response. 'I thought this was just about stocks. They wanted me to convince you to change your rating on Globecom. I didn't know how bad it would get. I had no idea anyone would get killed! Please forgive me, Nicco,' she sobbed. 'I love you. Please believe me.' She grabbed his arm, but he pulled away sharply.

'I think you'd better go.'

'I swear to you,' Lucy pleaded, 'I didn't know anything about Jack's murder.'

'You lied before, Lucy. You can lie again.'

'Please, Nicco, I beg you. Give me another chance . . .'

'Get out!'

'Please say you don't mean that. I don't want to lie to you any more. I love you, Nicco. I've never loved anyone like this.'

'I said GET OUT!'

*

After Lucy had gathered up her things and gone, still weeping and begging for another chance, Niccolo sat down on the bed once more. He was shaking with anger, and feeling sick with shame.

As expected, the media rehashed Saracen Laing's past and present misdeeds, portraying their management as clowns and their analysts as crooks. They hypothesised endlessly on the ramifications of the scandal for rival banks and put forward their own ill-informed theories on the future of the City as a global financial centre. In the process, they dragged Jack Ford's reputation through the gutter. Within no time at all, his name was mud.

However, a white knight surfaced in the highly rated 'Dex' column of the *Financial Telegraph*. Every cloud has a silver lining, they reported – putting their own characteristic spin on things – and in this case the silver lining belonged to Larry Sikorski.

The other broadsheets followed the *FT*'s lead. One portrayed Larry Sikorski as the responsible boss who worked hard to build an honest team only to be stabbed in the back by one of his own and fed to the wolves by his Teflon-coated bosses in Wall Street. Another did a cover story on Larry, complete with well-placed quotations from the man himself. Larry Sikorski was the hero of the hour.

After allowing for a respectable grieving period, DS Harcourt and his team summoned Donna to the police station for an interview. She strongly objected to being questioned 'under the circumstances'.

'It's merely a formality, madam,' Harcourt assured her. 'You need not be concerned; after all, you're not a suspect. Actually, cause of death hasn't been classified as unlawful, so there aren't any suspects anyway.'

When Donna arrived at the station, with mascara smudged under red-rimmed eyes, she looked the very image of widowed grief. She was asked the usual questions. She gave the usual answers.

She admitted to having an affair with Larry, though not before letting it be known to the DS, the WPC and the tape recorder that Jack had been acting suspiciously in the previous twelve months. He had been working hard, she said, and he had been highly stressed. Perhaps all the allegations about him in the press might have been true. She didn't know. Jack had not taken the news that she had fallen in love with Larry well. She feared he had taken his own life. She prayed for his soul and would miss him sorely.

After the interview, DS Harcourt went to the list of names on the board in the incident room. He scored a black line through Donna's name, and stared fixedly at the one immediately below it.

'*Buon giorno*, Niccolo!'

'Hi, Toni.'

'Eh, *signore*, you 'ave a way with the girls, *non è vero?*'

Niccolo smiled reluctantly at the ebullient proprietor of Toni's Café. '*Due cappuccini*, Toni. *Grazie.*'

'*E la bella signora?* 'Er name?'

'Her name's Odile.'

'Odile, you come to my café all-a the time. You never tell-a me your name. I have to ask your ugly friend, eh?'

Odile smiled thinly and slipped on her Gucci sunglasses. Toni took the unsubtle hint and left them alone. 'So? How are you?' she asked Niccolo.

'I've been better.'

'I'm so sorry about Jack. None of it makes any sense.'

'Donna was having an affair,' Niccolo announced baldly.

'My God!' Odile nearly fell off her chair. 'But Jack was such a great guy – intelligent, good-looking, hard-working, loyal – and a high earner too. Why would any woman want to leave him?'

Niccolo shrugged. 'Maybe the money wasn't enough for her.'

'A woman who doesn't appreciate a guy like Jack – there must be something wrong with her. You don't think he killed himself because of Donna?'

Niccolo chose his words carefully. 'I don't think Donna had anything to do with his death,' he said.

'Jack was your best friend, wasn't he?'

Niccolo nodded.

'Well, I hope Lucy is showing you the tender loving care you deserve.'

Niccolo laughed sadistically. 'Lucy and I are finished. We broke up a few days ago.'

'Oh, you poor thing!' Odile leapt to her feet and hugged Niccolo. 'What happened?'

'I'd rather not say.'

They finished their cappuccinos in silence. Then they left Toni's and headed back to work.

CHAPTER 36

Jack's funeral was a subdued affair that took place in a quiet spot at the north end of Hampstead Cemetery. He had left no will, so Donna made the arrangements. Her mother and both her brothers were there; Jack's father had flown in from Sydney and his mother from Brisbane; friends from Cambridge days and from the City converged in dozens. In all, close to three hundred people came to pay their respects.

Members of Saracen's staff were not notified until the day before, and very few turned up. However, Larry, Charlie, Paddy, Odile, Dudley, Mortimer and Sukuhara all stood like soldiers neatly in the back row.

Niccolo hid his anger well. He watched closely, but said nothing, as Donna wept copiously throughout and dabbed her eyes with an old handkerchief of Jack's. Afterwards, she was going back to Hampstead with her own family, leaving the funeral party without a hostess. 'Would you like to come too?' she asked Niccolo. 'After all, this is a time for family, and you're family,' she insisted.

Surprised, he accepted. Jack's parents had also been invited, and Niccolo went in search of them.

'We'd rather stick around with these guys, thanks, Nicco,' Professor Ford said.

'It would be nice to get to know Jack's friends,' Bronwen added. 'We heard about so many of them, you see, but of course we never met them.'

For a couple who, Niccolo knew, had not spoken to each other for two decades, the Fords seemed very close now. They were bound together by the greatest grief any parent can know – the loss of an only child.

Niccolo drove up to Hampstead in his own car. Donna's mother made a fresh pot of coffee. Her brothers carried their cups out on to the balcony and stood there chain-smoking, leaving their mother to clean up a perfectly tidy kitchen.

Donna came over to the sofa where Niccolo was sitting, with a large cardboard box.

'I can't bear to go through these things,' she said. 'I thought perhaps you might want them – Jack would have wanted you to have something of his.'

In the box were some of Jack's possessions, some clothes, his wallet, his watch, a collection of old medals, a silver chain with a shark's tooth attached, and the photograph of Jack, Niccolo and Yoshiro as young boys with Mizuno-san standing proudly beside them, leaning on his beloved fishing boat.

'I'd like that very much.' Niccolo smiled. 'What are you going to do now, Donna?'

'Well, I thought I'd sell the house and look for something else. Too many bad memories here.'

'But we have to find out what happened, Donna. We have to find out who killed Jack.'

'Dear Niccolo,' whispered Donna softly. 'It hurts me to say this, but Jack killed himself. I have put this matter to rest. I think you should too.'

'How can you say that? Don't you want to know how he died?'

'I *do* know how he died, Nicco.' Her tone was confident, almost arrogant. 'I know *exactly* how he died.'

Niccolo didn't believe a word Donna said. He wanted desperately to wring the truth out of her there and then. He had so many questions. He needed to know more about her affair with Larry, about the letter she'd written to Jack, about so many things. How close was she to Larry? Was it her idea to get rid of Jack? But now was not the time to take her on. Instead, he made his excuses and left, clutching the box of Jack's possessions.

Driving down Spaniards Road, he glanced several times at the box on the seat beside him. Each item was something that Jack had treasured, and he wondered why Donna had not kept some of them for herself. Perhaps she knew how much Jack had meant to him. Perhaps she was just being kind. Perhaps.

When Niccolo arrived home, he parked haphazardly on the street, jumped out, dumped the box on the bonnet and examined its contents in more detail. He pulled out the silver chain with the shark's tooth and slipped it around his neck. He rummaged to the bottom and pulled out the photograph of Mizuno-san and the three of them as young boys. He gazed at it for a long while. Then he shut his eyes for a few moments, reminiscing.

All of sudden there was a crash as the box slid off the bonnet and fell to the ground. Niccolo scrabbled frantically in search of the various bits and bobs that now littered the pavement, cursing himself as he tossed them back in the box.

A business card had fallen out of Jack's wallet. He picked it up and examined it. It belonged to Arnaud Veyrieras, of the FSA's Enforcement Division. He recalled the name from the voice message Jack had left on his mobile phone the day he died. He knew the police were already on to it. What the hell was Jack doing talking to the Financial Services Authority?

Any publicity is good publicity, it is said. But for the third day in a row, the *Financial Telegraph* was running a front-page story denigrating Saracen Laing with the sort of venom normally reserved for liars, cheats and thieves. However, for the first time that week, media attention had moved away from Jack. This time it was Niccolo's reputation that was under the spotlight.

GLOBECOM STOCK SOARS ON BACK OF ANALYST APOLOGY

Globecom's stock is expected to rally in the coming weeks following reports that Saracen Laing analyst Niccolo Lamparelli has issued an unreserved apology to Globecom's Chief Executive Officer, Kenneth Oakes. In an email sent last week to the CEO of Britain's largest telecom operator, Mr Lamparelli 'regretted a number of statements' that he had made previously. Earlier this week Lamparelli was replaced as the bank's lead analyst on Globecom by James Heath, who immediately upgraded the Saracen Laing rating on Globecom to Buy.

Lamparelli had earned himself a top place in the City's unwritten league table of leading analysts by hitherto holding firm on his Sell recommendation in the wake of massive discontent at the London headquarters of this internationally renowned wholesale telecoms carrier. Many of the bank's clients expressed outrage yesterday at the actions of Saracen's management team, whilst heaping praise upon Lamparelli as an outspoken critic of the internet-related hype often spun to investors by Oakes.

Niccolo read the article on his journey into the City, and wondered who had leaked the information. He took the escalators up to the trading floor, and walked by Anne-Marie's desk on the way to his own. It was quarter past six and the trading floor was still empty. Anne-Marie had a piping-hot cup of coffee in her hand and a copy of the *Daily Mail* spread across her desk.

'What's up, my love?' she asked. 'Come on, tell Auntie Annie!'

Niccolo shook his head. 'Nothing to tell.'

'Teensy-weensy tiff with Juicy Lucy?' she enquired archly.

Niccolo's face turned pale and Anne-Marie immediately knew she had struck a raw nerve. 'I'm so sorry, Nicco,' she said hurriedly.

He shrugged. 'It's OK. I'll live.'

'Is it final?'

'Yeah.'

'Never mind, you won't stay on the market for long, baby.'

When the phone rang in Rupert's hotel room, he was deeply asleep. The phone kept ringing. Rupert kept sleeping. On the tenth ring, he yielded.

'Ru, where are you?'

'In my hotel room . . . in New York.'

'What the fuck are you doing there?'

'Telecoms conference hosted by Keegan Seidmann. Larry, it's two in the morning over here. What's up?'

'Lamparelli! That's what's up! The son of a bitch has got our name splattered all over the *FT* this morning. It makes Saracen Laing look like a bunch of idiots.' Larry read the second paragraph out loud.

'Shit,' Rupert swore, fumbling for the bedside light. 'Oakes must have leaked it.'

'I doubt that. Probably Lamparelli himself. I want you to fire

290

the bastard as soon as you get back to the office, Ru. I don't care how you do it. Just do it!'

'On what grounds, Larry?'

'Find something, damn it! I'm not paid to do your job!'

'It's going to be difficult to get him on competence. He's a damn good analyst. And our clients love him.'

'I don't pay you guys to be damn good analysts; I pay you to make money. That fucker is blocking a large deal. I want him out. Do you think you can handle it, Ru?'

Even if he was only half awake, in a second-rate hotel on the other side of the Atlantic, Rupert recognised a threat when he heard one.

Larry stormed across the trading floor with a sour look on his face. 'Have you seen this?' he yelled at Anne-Marie, flashing the *FT* in front of her before disappearing into his office.

'Yes, Dudley's sent you an email about it. He says it's serious.'

'Serious! It's a bloody mess, that's what it is. We're getting trashed all over the *FT*!'

Globecom's share price rose steadily all morning. By lunchtime it had reached £2.23, up twelve per cent on the previous day's close. Larry spent a few minutes at his computer screen, then smiled smugly to himself.

Twenty-four hours later, a black Mercedes S320 pulled up outside the Saracen Laing building, having left Heathrow airport an hour earlier. Rupert tipped the driver generously, and walked through the revolving doors looking like shit. His hair was dishevelled, his clothes wrinkled and soiled. What he really needed was a bath. But that could wait; he would be on holiday within a few hours.

A backlog of paperwork greeted him at his desk, but he ignored it.

'Listen, Nicco,' he said. 'You know I'm on holiday from tomorrow?'

'No, I didn't know, Ru.'

'I'm taking the family to the Alps whilst the builders trash my house. I'm having some work done on the kitchen and building a granny extension above the garage. Nothing major. Anyway, I need a favour. I need to change my recommendation on Telespaña. I've written the research to back it up, but I don't have time to run it past the Ratings Committee.'

Niccolo shrugged his shoulders. 'I don't know anything about Telespaña.'

'Don't worry. The report's done. All I need is for you to present it on my behalf.'

'Ru, I don't know anything about Telespaña. I'd need at least a couple of weeks to get up to speed . . .'

'You'll be fine,' Rupert insisted.

'But I won't be able to answer any of their questions.'

'For fuck's sake, Nicco! Stop being a pussy and help me out, would you?'

Perhaps he was being unreasonable, Niccolo conceded. He really did want to be a team player. 'OK, I'll do it as a favour, boss, but I do feel uncomfortable about it.'

'Here's the report. You need to present it tomorrow morning. Read it and ask me any questions before I go away tonight.'

Rupert's Telespaña report was twenty-six pages long, and it justified his decision to move the stock from Hold to Buy. Niccolo needed to satisfy himself that the report was robust enough to pass a formal review by the Ratings Committee, but there simply wasn't enough time. He would have to trust Rupert and read as much as he could about the company in the meantime. At dusk he took a break and went to the gym, leaving the report in two halves – read and unread – on his desk.

On returning to his desk a few hours later, he found a new version of the report with a Post-it note:

Nicco – I'll see you in a week,
hopefully with a tan. Ru.

Rupert had removed his own name as lead analyst on the report and replaced it with Niccolo's. Strange, thought Niccolo – Rupert normally took credit for just about everything. Perhaps it was a goodwill gesture, to say thanks for the favour. He flicked through the note. There were so many questions he needed to ask. But there was no time. By ten o'clock, he was struggling to keep his eyes open. He packed up for the day and went home to get some rest.

He could not let the team down. Tomorrow he would simply have to blag it.

The Ratings Committee meeting was scheduled for ten o'clock the following morning. Niccolo felt dreadfully unprepared. Larry chaired the meeting and pulled no punches.

'I don't agree with your argument, Niccolo,' he said, holding up a marked-up copy of the report, before throwing it down in a fit of rage. 'Your argument is flimsy, your analysis is flawed and your numbers don't stack up. You've wasted this committee's time! Go away and rewrite it.'

And he stormed out.

No one else said a word. One by one they left the room, reluctant to interfere with the Chairman's ruling. Niccolo gathered his papers together and ambled back to his desk, feeling somewhat hard done by. He hastily quashed any desire to land Rupert in the shit, partly out of loyalty, and partly because he knew it would do him no good.

CHAPTER 37

'April's been taking a lot of sickies lately. Sukuhara's worried about her.'

'She's put on weight. I wouldn't be surprised if she's pregnant.'

'She *is* pregnant.'

'What! Bulldog's going to pup! That's gotta be a case of immaculate conception.'

'Charlie, she has a husband.'

'Shit, that's even worse! I feel for the poor bugger. Are you sure Sukuhara hasn't been giving her a bit of a stroke and a poke himself? Christ, what would the poor brat look like?'

'Charlie, those kind of remarks will get you fired.'

'Take it easy, Larry. Behaving like a cock-sucking Puritan bastard doesn't suit you.'

'This is a twenty-first-century workplace and it's my job to ensure that dinosaurs like you don't upset the hard-working ethos that I've created here. You persist in this line of discussion, and I'll have no choice but to report you to HR for insubordination.'

'Insubordination, eh? What's the punishment for that? A damn good spanking, I bet. Do me a favour – get Louise Horsforth to do the honours, would you? I've always had a thing for old Horse-face.'

'Another word out of you, Charlie, and you're history.'

'I was history last year, Larry. Hell, I'm just living off my back catalogue.'

Charlie headed towards his own desk, whilst Larry made straight for Niccolo's.

'Nicco, I'd like to see you in my office. Right away, please.' The words were abrupt, formal and chilling.

Charlie peered curiously over the partition. He watched Niccolo slip on his jacket and gather a pad of paper and a pen. 'Hey, Nicco, you fucked up again? Don't worry, I fuck up all the time.'

Niccolo waited patiently outside Larry's office while the Head of Research finished a telephone call.

'Yup. Yup. He's just outside. I'll speak to him now.' Larry replaced the receiver and called Niccolo into his office. 'Shut the door, please, Niccolo.'

Niccolo's curiosity turned to anxiety. The door to Larry's office was only ever shut for two types of discussion: bonuses and sackings. And it was not bonus time.

'How long have you been working at Saracen, Niccolo?'

'Around two years. It feels longer.'

'I've been watching your performance closely. You've made a few mistakes recently. Some of them are pretty serious.' Larry took a photocopied email from a file on his desk and chucked it at Niccolo. It was from Kenneth Oakes, dated a few days after the Globecom presentation.

Dear Larry

   Following a presentation made to my board last Friday by your analyst Mr Lamparelli, and after full consultation with my fellow board members, I have decided to write to

you conveying my dissatisfaction with the calibre of Mr
Lamparelli's work.

I find the words used by Lamparelli in both his written
and oral communications about my company to be highly
offensive and a disgrace to his profession. I demand an
immediate written apology. Furthermore, I have taken the
unusual step of banning him from future analyst
conferences. Finally, I respectfully request that you review
his suitability to cover blue-chip stocks such as Globecom.

The Yamaguchi Telecom acquisition is now a distinct
possibility. In the run-up to this deal, it would be
regrettable for both parties if anything jeopardised your
strong advisory relationship with us.

Kind regards

Ken

'This was sent last week,' said Niccolo, surprised. 'Why didn't
you show it to me earlier?'

'You are informed of these things on a need-to-know basis,
Niccolo.'

'The email mentions me by name. I need to know.'

'It's addressed to me. And I decide what you need to know.'

'I don't agree with a single thing Oakes has said. Can we discuss
this with Rupert and Charlie – they were there.'

'There's nothing to discuss. I'm afraid the standard of your work
is substantially below what I would expect. I've come to the conclusion that you do not have what it takes to be an analyst, Niccolo.
I should never have employed you.' The tone of Larry's voice indicated that there was no room for discussion. 'Rupert and I are in
agreement. Your coverage of Globecom has been extremely poor.
You managed to piss off the CEO, the CFO and half the fucking
board with that presentation of yours. Your incompetence meant

you had to make a formal apology to the company, and that has triggered me to invoke our disciplinary procedures. Rupert and I both believe your position to be untenable.'

'But Larry, *I* never apologised to anybody. *You* issued an apology in *my* name – and against my wishes.'

'These procedures are outlined in the Saracen Laing employee handbook, which I suggest you read. Briefly they state that where an analyst's work is substandard, a disciplinary hearing should be convened to assess the competence of the analyst. I have discussed your performance with Louise Horsforth in HR and asked her to convene such a meeting early next week. The meetings are normally attended by your line manager – in this case Rupert – yourself and a senior representative from HR. At the end of the hearing you will be set certain objectives with a timescale to meet them. Failure to meet the standards required of you will result in immediate dismissal.'

Niccolo remained silent. 'You look surprised,' Larry mused.

Niccolo paused. A long pause. Then he broke the silence. 'I *am* surprised, Larry.' His voice remained calm, but his mind was in total chaos, searching the various available exit routes. None looked too appealing, so he stalled. 'I am totally surprised. Did you say that Rupert was dissatisfied with my work? He has certainly never indicated that to me. Anyway, he's on holiday.'

'I spoke with Rupert yesterday, on the phone. He agrees with me. Your performance is substandard.'

Niccolo was confused. Why couldn't Larry have waited until Rupert returned to the office? What was the urgency? Rupert and Niccolo got on well on a professional level. They disagreed on recommendations all the time. That was healthy. They argued about strategy. That was healthy. But this looked as though Rupert had set him up, and Larry was in on the set-up. '*Which* of my reports are substandard, Larry?'

'If it was just the Globecom thing, I could have let it go. Then I saw your Telespaña report – the one that failed the Ratings Committee. You are not cut out to be an analyst, Niccolo. Your research has no depth. What's more, I do not trust you to write good reports.'

'Larry, the last reports I wrote were all groundbreaking stuff – and pretty well received by the market.'

'I am aware that some people like your research,' said Larry with a cold glint in his eye. 'But you don't work for those people. You work for me. I am responsible for the quality of research that passes through these doors. And I am not a great fan of your work.'

Niccolo winced. Clearly external opinion *did* matter. Happy clients filled the bank's coffers.

'Rupert tells me that you're not a team player.'

'That's rubbish, Larry, and you know it.'

'I guess we'll have to call a disciplinary hearing to find out then.'

'Larry, I can't believe you're doing this.'

'At the end of this disciplinary process, should you be found to be incompetent, we would terminate your employment. The implication would be that you are unfit to operate as an analyst. I would therefore be unable to provide you with a good reference. In addition, I would have to inform the FSA that you were fired for negligence. You would be struck off. You'd never be able to find work in the City again.'

Then Larry went in for the kill.

'Of course, we don't need to go down this route if you don't want to, Niccolo. There are other options you could consider. One would be for you to resign now. That would save you the embarrassment of being found to be negligent in your duties.'

'If I resigned today, would I receive my contractual entitlements?'

'You would receive one month's pay. That is your contractual entitlement.'

'But I have a guaranteed bonus. What about—'

'That bonus is only payable to staff who are in employment on the thirty-first of December.' Larry's tone was strong, confident, rehearsed. 'I suggest that you take the rest of today and tomorrow off. You look drained. Think about what we've discussed. You have a lot to lose. The reputation of an analyst is everything. Once lost, it is difficult to recapture. It may be in your interest to resign. Nicco, I'm trying to help you do what is best for you.'

An analyst's reputation *was* everything. But reputations that take years to build can be destroyed at a moment's notice. In a dark corner of Niccolo's mind, red neon warning signs began to flash, and he had a sudden mental image of a fish being tossed irretrievably into the sea.

'I'm late for an eleven o'clock, Niccolo. Feel free to speak to Louise in HR if you have any questions. And please – take today and tomorrow off.'

Back at his desk, Niccolo found three new emails: one from a journalist asking for his views on Frankfurter Telekom; one from Anne-Marie arranging to go for drinks that night; the third a CC from Larry marked 'Discussions'. He glanced at his Speedmaster. Quarter past eleven. His meeting with Larry had only finished three minutes ago, and the email, addressed to Louise Horsforth in HR, was stamped *11.14*. That meant it must have been written *before* the meeting.

Louise

I have this morning informed Niccolo that his work is not up to the standard expected by his manager (Rupert Southgate), nor up to the standard that I expect of my analysts.

299

Niccolo was surprised that this was the case as some of his work has been well received externally and indeed some has been well received internally. However, the catalyst for today's meeting was a draft report on Telespaña that was submitted to the Ratings Committee this week, and refused by the Committee for publication. I have discussed this today with Rupert Southgate.

Rupert is of the opinion that Niccolo does not perform thorough analysis and that he requires too much involvement of Rupert's time. Rupert has come to the view that the situation is untenable.

In such circumstances, Saracen Laing practice is to invoke a disciplinary procedure. I would like you to set up a meeting between yourself, Rupert and Niccolo for Tuesday. At this meeting, objectives will be set and monitored, typically over two months. I have explained to Niccolo that the matter is serious and, if unresolved, could result in dismissal.

I have also explained to Niccolo that he can call you at any time to discuss the situation with you.

Larry

Niccolo flicked through the Telespaña report, trying to work out what was wrong with it. He was pretty certain that it had been robustly argued, and that the numbers did stack up. He looked around for the original draft that he had worked on before going to the gym, but it was nowhere to be seen. That was strange – he wouldn't have thrown it away. He struggled to remember sentences and sequences of figures, thinking to compare them with the copy he held in his hand, but his brain refused to furnish them.

He leaned back in his chair and shut his eyes. Was it possible that Rupert had doctored the figures, just to make him look incompetent? He really didn't want to believe that. Yet in the City, it was always the analyst whose name appeared on the report who carried the can if anything went wrong. And Niccolo's name was on the Telespaña report.

The irony was that Rupert – the man who had got him into this mess – would be judge and jury at the disciplinary hearing. He wondered how he would get himself out of this one.

He whipped out a pad of paper and began to prepare a To Do list. The bank's clients were key. What did they think of him? What did they think of his work? How much money had he made them recently? Choosing his words with care, he drafted an email asking a select few for their comments, explaining that it was all part of Saracen's annual staff appraisal process. He personalised the emails, then fired them off one by one. If the bank's customers were on his side, Larry's case against him would simply collapse.

Then he returned to Larry's email. He read it over and over again. He noted that Larry himself would not be attending the meeting. That was a bit strange, he thought, since it was he who had called it. He leaned back, sighed and wondered what tactics Larry had used to secure Rupert's backing.

Twelve days after Jack's death, and against DS Harcourt's advice, the coroner issued a verdict of suicide. The police investigation into the death of Jack Ford was officially over. DS Harcourt was both surprised and unhappy with the verdict, but unwilling to contest it. The coroner's decision was rarely challenged, since the chances of successfully overturning a coroner's verdict were very slender indeed. And in any case, DS Harcourt had no evidence. All he had was his instinct.

Since his return from Usman, Arnaud Veyrieras had delved deeper into the affairs of Larry Sikorski, past and present. He had also kept in close contact with Lindsay Compton. But all of his attempts – and there had been many – at persuading Lindsay to testify against Saracen Laing in a court of law had failed. Lindsay had bought peace by signing his resignation letter and he had no intention of starting a war in which his parents could once again become innocent victims.

Information about the death of Jack Ford had been far easier to acquire. DS Harcourt had emailed Arnaud the coroner's report, together with a note detailing his own concerns, the main one being that the verdict of death by suicide was almost certainly wrong. Arnaud had also received a phone call from the detective superintendent, informing him that the case was unofficially open. Harcourt let it slip that the last place Jack had been known to be alive was outside Larry Sikorski's London residence.

Arnaud went to Amanda Sanderson with yet another request to reopen the investigation of Larry Sikorski. In making his argument, he stressed that Larry, in addition to his other misdemeanours, was now a suspect in a murder enquiry. Sanderson listened, and agreed to respond within twenty-four hours.

She did. The request was denied. Sanderson did not divulge her reasons.

CHAPTER 38

'What's up, Nicco? You look like shit.' Odile enquired sympathetically.

'Louis Vuitton?' he parried, indicating the new handbag she was brandishing.

'*Bien sûr*. Smart, isn't it? In fact, I bought three!'

'Odile, can we talk?'

'You're thinking about Jack, aren't you?'

Niccolo sighed. 'I'm thinking about what *happened* to Jack.'

'What do you mean? He killed himself. He was mixed up in some insider trading ring. That's what I heard.'

'Jack didn't kill himself,' insisted Niccolo. 'And he certainly wasn't involved in any kind of securities fraud.'

Odile nodded understandingly, like a teacher handling a slightly retarded child. 'You were close, you and Jack. I understand how you feel.'

'Jack . . . He did everything for me. I never got a chance to pay him back. And now he's dead.'

Odile jumped to her feet, and dragged Niccolo out through the back entrance and they walked to Finsbury Circus. They found a bench under the shade of a sycamore tree. Odile lit up. 'Now, tell me. Tell me everything, Nicco.'

Niccolo began awkwardly. 'The thing is, I've got no evidence to support any of this, but I really believe Larry had something to do with Jack's death. Larry's turned his sights on me now, and before I can focus on clearing Jack's name, I've got to clear my own.'

With fear and paranoia in his voice, he described the events that had led up to his forthcoming disciplinary hearing. Niccolo did not consider it a risk to tell Odile his most secret thoughts. She had been at the bank for eleven years and had many senior contacts. She could help. More importantly, he felt she *wanted* to help. Not least, she was the one person he felt he could trust.

'It wasn't what Larry *said*, but how he said it,' he continued. 'The look in his eyes, Odile – it was unmistakable. He'd already made up his mind. He wants me out.'

'Why do you think he wants to fire you?'

'It all started when JC put pressure on me to switch my Globecom rating to Buy.'

Odile nodded kindly. 'But you were right! All my clients love you for it. You saved them loads of money. Apart from that blip when your apology letter got leaked to the press, Globecom's share price has fallen steadily since you published your Sell. It's down another five per cent so far today.'

'I know. That's why I don't understand what Larry's up to.'

'You know, Nicco, I've heard some things. Larry has been having lots of conversations with Globecom recently. Rupert's in on them too. I don't know the subject of the discussions, but they're being very hush-hush about it.'

Niccolo perked up. Odile knew everything about everyone. She always did. It was a puzzle to many in the bank where she got her information from. 'Hmmn,' he muttered. 'So Rupert's in on it too?'

'Come on, Nicco. Rupert is the innocent party in all of this. He's got a wife and kids to support and a mortgage to pay. I think he's even in the middle of a huge kitchen extension. He just does as he's told.'

'Yeah, I guess you're right.'

'Be careful over the next few weeks. Don't lose your temper. Don't threaten anyone.'

'As if I would.' Niccolo laughed bleakly.

'I'm not kidding. Larry's a veteran at this game. When he plays, there are always casualties. Look, perhaps it would be best for you to say sorry. You're no match for Larry. Do you remember what he did to Jennifer Colley?'

'No. Before my time.'

'She was Saracen's chief strategist. Larry got her fired. It was back in 1998.'

'What happened?'

'Jennifer was in charge of equity strategy for Saracen. The suits in America wanted to do some sort of derivatives deal in Russian sovereign debt, but Jennifer was sceptical of emerging markets. She warned Larry to stay clear. The rouble was about to collapse, she told him. But he just wanted to keep his American bosses happy. So he persuaded Jennifer, against her better judgement, to write a research note recommending a number of Russian stocks and bonds. He even told her he would back her against the suits in New York. She was a single mum with three young children, and she couldn't afford to disagree publicly with him.

'Well, several investors followed the recommendations. Two weeks later, the Russian government defaulted and the rouble went into free-fall. Investors scrambled to get out of Russian paper. Many of Saracen's institutional customers suffered huge losses as a result. Sales people like me were even angrier than our clients because our reputations were tarnished. We were ridiculed for marketing Jennifer's research so aggressively, but she took most of the heat. She was the obvious scapegoat. It wasn't her fault in any way, but someone had to take the rap. So she got fired.

'Larry never backed her at all. The sad thing was that they'd been friends for years. Loyalty prevented her from leaking the fact that Larry's views were in the research note. Unfortunately for her, to the outside world the advice was hers. She took the fall. The Head of Investment Banking fired her.'

Niccolo frowned. 'Sukuhara?'

'Yeah. Larry spun him a web of lies, and Jennifer got nothing. Oh, everyone suspected Larry of foul play. It was thought he made a lot of money when the rouble crashed, but no one had the courage to stand up and say so.'

'If your intention was to get me worried, you've succeeded, Odile.'

'So just do as you're told, *mon ami*! You have a great career ahead of you. Why do you want to rock the boat?'

To the untrained eye, Charlie came across on the television screen as a financial markets guru who had done it all. To the seasoned interviewer, who could see straight through the façade, he was nonetheless a gift from heaven because he oozed charm and flattered the ratings. He had an answer for everything, and nine times out of ten, audiences fell off their chairs when they heard it.

The markets had been jittery all morning, so the mood on the trading floor was tense. The show was *PowerLunch*. The game was point-scoring. The opposition was Jeremy Lagerfeld, Chief Strategist at Silverman Ross – they were old adversaries and sore losers. The referee was TNBC's anchorwoman, Jacqui Hanson. And the subject matter was private equity. 'Everybody who's anybody in the investment world is talking about the private equity sector,' Jacqui began. 'That seems to be where the smart money's heading. But cynics are questioning the industry's methods. Let's see what the experts think. I'm going to start with you, Jeremy. Is private equity a force for the better?'

Jeremy grinned, revealing a perfect set of incisors. 'Jacqui, my answer has to be yes. One in five jobs in Britain is now provided directly by the private equity industry. From businesses that could never get off the ground to those that have run themselves into the ground, private equity has come to the rescue. Even healthy businesses get a better deal with private equity funding these days. Things have changed since I was a teenager. For the first time in my lifetime, I see chief executives of strong, decent companies actively recommending private equity as a solution to many of their problems. Bids that were once viewed as hostile are today welcomed with open arms. That's a seismic shift in corporate thinking, Jacqui.'

'So there we have it, folks. Private equity is a force for the good – the white knight we've been waiting for. But not everyone thinks so. Let's hear a different angle from Saracen Laing.'

Charlie flicked his hair back, adjusted his lapels and followed his cue. 'PE guys are a funny bunch. Somebody once described these characters as barbarians at the gate. I have to say, I've never seen barbarians who are so well dressed! The game has moved on since RJR Nabisco. Today the barbarians don't just wear fancy suits and spray mud on pedestrians whilst driving by in their flash cars. Today they have more cash and fewer ethics than ever before. They hire the brightest minds, and bring down the mightiest companies without losing a night's sleep. Their spin doctors will tell you it's all kosher. There's only one problem with private equity. They're smarter than you or me. And that means that at the end of the day, when all's said and done – and done and said – they wind up sucking out all the yolk, whilst you and I are left holding the empty shell.'

'What do you mean by that, Charlie?'

'Well, I like to picture the relationship between senior company execs and private equity guys like a bout of guilt-free sex with a beautiful stranger . . . only you wake up the next morning to find you've lost your job, your home, your wife and all the family silver.'

'That's an interesting analogy, Charlie. Now let's turn to the question of staying power. Whenever something truly unique becomes mainstream, it tends to lose its charm. Will private equity lose its charm?'

'Jacqui, darling, this little baby's like Jerry Hall – it's an old story with long legs.'

Niccolo decided to take Larry's advice and head home for the remainder of the day. Before leaving, he found Louise Horsforth's number on the intranet.

'Louise, I've just had a discussion with Larry. Has he talked to you?'

'Yes, I'm fully aware of the situation.'

'Can we talk? Now?'

'Now's good. Come up to the fifth floor. I'll meet you at the doors – your security pass won't let you through.'

Niccolo rummaged through his desk to find a pad and pencil and headed for the elevators.

Antonio liked being summoned into Sukuhara's goldfish bowl at short notice. It made him feel respected, appreciated and very, very important. The 'special projects team' that he headed up at Sukuhara's request got involved in far more interesting things than the mundane software glitches that had routinely come his way before.

Sukuhara closed the door and got straight down to business. 'I want you to tap some phones. Start with Larry Sikorski, Rupert Southgate and Niccolo Lamparelli – in fact, do Mortimer Steel as well. And I think . . . yeah, I think we should listen in to Dudley Rabinowitz too.'

Antonio flinched. 'But, sir, that's illegal . . .' he stammered.

'One of my employees has been killed!' Sukuhara shouted. 'The press are spreading rumours that Saracen Laing is out of control. I need to get to the bottom of this.' He pointed at the trading floor like a ship's captain addressing his first mate out of earshot but in full view of the crew. 'If someone out there is involved, I need to know!'

Antonio stood fiddling anxiously with his shirt, too frightened to respond.

Sukuhara continued, 'Let me explain, Antonio. My job is to run this bank as smoothly as possible. If there is a fucking murderer amongst us, I need to flush him out, understand? So just do it. But keep it quiet. Listen for anything out of the ordinary. And report back to me the minute you find something.'

It was lunchtime, so the elevator stopped on each floor, which gave Niccolo time to gather his thoughts. Louise stood ready to receive him with a copy of the Saracen Laing employee handbook under her arm. She led him to a vacant room, shut the door and opened the handbook at 'Disciplinary, Competency, Grievance and Harassment Procedures'.

'Read that,' she instructed, 'and I'll get us some coffee.'

Disciplinary procedures would be instigated 'if, in your line manager's judgement, your performance has fallen below an acceptable standard'. The procedure was intended 'to help you reach the performance standard the Company requires' by 'clearly stating what must be achieved and ensuring that you have the appropriate training and support to enable you to achieve that standard'. Failure to achieve the required standard after completion of this procedure would, in most instances, result in dismissal.

Niccolo found himself yawning. He skipped a few pages to the section on bonuses: '. . . your eligibility to be considered for a discretionary bonus will be postponed pending completion of any investigation and any subsequent disciplinary hearing.'

He tried to think like Larry, but his concentration was weak. One single image haunted him – Jack's lifeless body washed up on the shore of the Thames.

'Are you OK, Niccolo?' Louise asked softly.

He relaxed. 'I'm fine,' he said. 'I'm a bit shocked at the conversation I just had with Larry. I can't believe this is happening. Last month I was a star analyst – the golden boy. Now, all of a sudden, my position has become *untenable*.'

Louise shrugged nonchalantly, like an experienced paramedic who deals with horrific accidents on a daily basis. Then she talked him through the disciplinary process. 'This is a routine process,' she advised. 'I'll sit in on the hearing as an independent third party. My job is to ensure that everybody plays it by the book. Do you wish to exercise your right to invite a colleague to attend the meeting too?'

Her tone had become somewhat icy, and it unnerved Niccolo. 'What for?' he asked.

'To act as a witness on your behalf and to ensure fair play. They would attend purely as an observer. Now, I advise you to go home and prepare for the meeting. You should state your case clearly, and suggest ways in which you could improve your performance.'

Niccolo did not have the energy to argue.

Like any government-funded body, the FSA was, from time to time, subject to the passing whims of the great and the good at Westminster. In the FSA's case, the great and the good worked for the Chancellor of the Exchequer, who bore ultimate responsibility for the City regulator. The problem was that the Chancellor was a meddler. Worse, he was a clever meddler. That meant that every so often, the FSA was subjected to yet another Treasury-led reorganisation. In theory, the game was cost-cutting; in practice, it was musical chairs.

Amanda Sanderson took pre-emptive action. She launched a comprehensive cost review. All department heads were instructed to slim down their teams. Budgets were validated and revalidated with a fine-tooth comb. New projects had to be justified. No department was exempt.

As the cost review progressed, Sanderson discovered more than she had bargained for. Her department had, in fact, been lean and mean all along. It had been so lean that it had allowed some of the biggest corporate frauds in the City's history to carry on right under its nose for years, and so mean that it paid its staff well below the market rate for their services. When the final conclusions of the review were laid bare, there was little in the way of surprises. The Enforcement Division had too few staff and it paid them too little.

Hidden in the fine print of the report's findings, however, a few anomalies emerged. One of them was that an employee of Saracen Laing was drawing a salary from the FSA's payroll. The Saracen insider used to work for Arnaud when he headed up Team 19, and was continuing to draw an FSA salary, which had merely been transferred from one cost code – Team 19's – to another.

Sanderson summoned Arnaud and demanded an explanation. Arnaud made no attempt to cover his tracks. He spilled the beans, and did so with pride.

'Two years ago, while we were investigating Dr Picton, I placed a man undercover as an employee of Saracen Laing. He managed to hack inside Saracen's trading system, although they have since closed this security breach. When Team 19 was disbanded, our man's identity risked being exposed. In order to protect him, and the information that he provided, I made a very simple accounting adjustment: I simply dumped his salary bill on to the Capital

Markets team's cost code. Their budgets are so large that the whole of Team 19's salary bill could easily have been lost in there.'

Sanderson listened to his confession with interest. Unofficially, she was delighted that Arnaud had disobeyed orders and kept the Picton case open.

'And more recently,' Arnaud continued unabashed, 'I tried to recruit Jack Ford as an informant. But a few days later he was killed. The coroner said it was suicide, but I believe it was murder, and that the Doctor was almost certainly behind it.'

'The trouble is that the coroner's verdict rather ties our hands,' Sanderson said. 'I'd like nothing more than to take all this to the police, but the matter's out of our jurisdiction. And since the Picton file was officially closed two years ago, any kind of surveillance or intelligence-gathering exercise is now technically illegal.'

These things always kick up a stink in Westminster, Sanderson thought to herself, and she had no intention of becoming one of the Chancellor's scapegoats.

That still left open the question of what to do with their informant at Saracen Laing. 'Technically, the Picton project no longer exists,' Sanderson mused. 'Arnaud, keep your man in place for now. Capital Markets can go on funding him. And by the way, this conversation we've just had never actually took place, OK?'

'*Mais naturellement*,' Arnaud agreed.

As he stepped outside the Saracen Laing building, Niccolo caught Charlie stuffing his mouth with an ice cream.

'Charlie, I need your help.'

'It'll cost you!'

'I'm serious. I really need your help.'

Charlie threw the ice cream into a bin, and wiped the smirk off his face. 'OK, shoot, motherfucker.'

'Larry's concocted some bullshit story to get me into a disciplinary hearing. I'm about to get fired.'

'Fuck me! Why am I always the last to know these things?'

'He's using the fact that I pissed off the CEO of Globecom as an excuse.'

'Wait a second – don't you have a Sell rating on them?'

'I did, only Rupert concocted some story about me screwing up the numbers, forged an apology in my name and changed Saracen's rating to a Buy. I'm no longer the Globecom analyst – James is.'

'But your Sell rating was one of the bank's best calls this year.'

'Unfortunately, Globecom didn't see it that way.'

'Of course, they wouldn't. How many CEOs do you know who like Sell ratings?'

'And . . .' Niccolo continued, 'Oakes has banned me from all future analyst meetings.'

'Oakes is simply trying his bully-boy tactics. It's illegal for them to ban you. Listen, kiddo, Rupert never lets a high-profile stock like Globecom leave the building without his approval, right?'

'Right.'

'So why didn't he review your work?'

'He *did* review my work. That's why I'm confused.'

'It's simple. It's always the analyst that gets fired, never the boss.'

Niccolo's shoulders sagged as if the world weighed heavily upon him. 'There's more. I just found out that he's now trying to pin the Telespaña report on me – remember the one I presented to the Ratings Committee on Monday for Rupert, the one that failed?'

'I thought Telespaña was Rupert's stock?'

'It *is* Rupert's stock. Rupert asked me to cover for him while he went on holiday. I told him I knew nothing about Telespaña and couldn't stand in at such short notice. But he insisted.'

'Why didn't you refuse?'

'Rupert told me to chill out and stop being so anal; it was just a case of covering for him while he was on vacation. I thought that was fine.'

'Are you sure Rupert approved the report before he went away?'

'Approve it? He *wrote* the fucking thing!' Niccolo was beginning to sweat.

'Calm down, kiddo. Is Rupert still on vacation?'

'Yeah, he is. But Larry said he spoke to him yesterday. He says Rupert backs his version of events.'

'You mean Rupert says Rupert's own report is shit?'

Niccolo nodded vigorously.

'You egotistical twat! You should never have allowed that report to go out in your name. Telespaña is one of the biggest fucking stocks in Europe. You can't expect to cover a stock like that at a day's notice! I made Jack research Celltalk for two and a half months before I let him near a pen.'

'Charlie, I know that. But I was just trying to help Rupert out. And I thought I had my ass covered because he wrote it and he signed off the final copy for print. Now, according to Larry, Ru is denying all responsibility for it. And *my* name's on record as lead analyst. So it looks pretty bad.'

'Well at least you've got the draft with Rupert's sign-off, right?'

'No. He left me an unmarked copy. There's nothing with his handwriting on file.'

'Let me get this straight. Rupert wrote the report, printed it in your name and then made you present it to the Ratings Committee? Nicco, it looks to me like you've been set up.'

'I know.'

'That turd-shovelling, ass-licking, anally retentive excuse for an analyst! I should have shat all over him when I had the chance. I told you never to trust that motherfucker. He's so far up Larry's ass, we'd need to call the fire brigade to cut him loose.' Charlie put his arm round his younger colleague. In Niccolo he saw his younger self, fired with noble aspirations. But he knew that the system would crush Niccolo's values to a pulp, just as they had crushed his many years ago.

'Larry's got a track record of getting rid of guys he doesn't like,' he said. 'The problem is – nobody's ever taken the bastard on and won. Know this, kiddo. Whatever disciplinary process he puts you through, you won't get out alive. Your only chance is to come out fighting. Go on the offensive. Show the fuckers in HR that Larry is a vindictive, egocentric maniac who needs to be stopped.'

'Any tips on how I should save the world from His Evil Smugness?'

'First thing: demonstrate that you're a fucking good analyst. I mean, you're the best telecoms analyst Saracen has had since yours truly! Rupert's just scared you're doing his job.'

'I don't want his job. I'm hardly a threat.'

'When you're shit at your job, Nicco, any old dick is a threat.'

'Listen, Charlie, I need a favour.'

'Just don't make a habit of it, kiddo.'

'I'm allowed to ask one other person to sit in on this disciplinary hearing. I'd like to call on you. You've got credibility. Back me up, Charlie. Tell HR what you think of my work. Can you do that for me?'

'Don't be fucking stupid! Of course I'll do it. It could be my head on the line next.'

When he arrived home Niccolo called Gino, who was away on an overseas business trip, and updated him. Gino promised that upon his return to London that weekend, he would help Niccolo devise a strategy.

Then he called Odile.

'Hey, Nicco, is that you? I'm in Egypt – Sharm el Sheikh. I'm on a diving holiday with my mother. What's happening at your end?'

'The disciplinary hearing's taking place pretty soon. I'll need written feedback from you by Monday latest.'

'That's cool, Nicco. You can count on me. And don't worry, sweetie. Everything will work itself out. Larry's not such a bad guy, you know.'

Niccolo was too tired to dispute that. 'Thanks, Odile. I appreciate your help.'

He went up to his bedroom and drew the curtains. He slipped between the sheets and shut his eyes, but he could not sleep. The voices would not go away.

The voices were talking about him as if he were not present, either in body or in spirit. Young Niccolo could barely hear the words. The pain was too great. Grown-ups peered down at him. Their faces were blurred, but he could hear the voices clearly.

'Carcharias taurus,' *said the first.* 'We call it the sand tiger shark. Some call it the grey nurse shark. The bites are unmistakable.' *The voice was cold and masculine.*

'Have you seen these types of wounds before?' *enquired a second voice. It was his mother's voice. It was warm and comforting, close and soft. It was a beautiful voice.*

'This is the first case I have seen in four years,' *continued the first voice.* 'Sand tiger sharks are commonly sighted around these waters, but usually they are harmless. This one seems to have been agitated.'

'What do they look like?' *It was Mamma again.*

'They have fang-like razor-sharp teeth and piercing yellow eyes.'

Arnaud Veyrieras sat patiently behind the wheel of his car, quietly eavesdropping on the comings and goings at the Moneypincher's

316

Inn. Maurice, sitting next to him, had said very little all night. The City felt like a graveyard. The last diner had left the inn just before midnight and the last member of staff had cleared off an hour after that. The maître d' had locked up soon afterwards.

Arnaud had no authority to sanction a surveillance mission on Picton. In fact, he had no authority to go anywhere near Picton. What he did have was Maurice.

Dressed in black from head to toe, the two men strolled casually down the narrow moonlit alleyway that led to the Money-pincher's Inn.

Usman had come a long way since the day oil was first discovered there in the late fifties. Unlike their Arab neighbours, Usman's rulers had invested the fruits of their windfall wisely. Within two generations, the sultanate had become the commercial hub of the Middle East. It boasted one of the largest ports in the world, a highly developed tourist trade, an attractive expat lifestyle, a booming internet city and a fast-growing offshore tax haven.

Uncharacteristically for an Arab country, Usman also offered one of the finest selections of liquor for thousands of miles around. For Picton, such choice was merely a distraction, as he was a straight vodka man. For the Prince, it was more of an irritant, lest passers-by report his drinking habits to his devoutly Muslim father, the Sultan of Usman.

The Prince ordered two Smirnoffs and a tray of hors d'oeuvres, and the two men waited in silence for their drinks to arrive. The view from the revolving restaurant on the fiftieth floor of the Shahaan Tower, even in the early hours of the morning, was as spectacular as the prices, which would go some way towards explaining why Dr Picton and Prince Mubarak were the only diners being served.

Two waiters fussed profusely over their guests until the Prince, infuriated by their lingering presence, waved them off. Then he unleashed his anger upon his former friend. 'My associates in the syndicate are not pleased with the results of your grand plan so far.'

'Your Highness, I am fully aware of the risks you and your associates are taking. I value the faith you have placed in me, and I will not let you down.'

'You have *already* let me down, my friend. Where are the profits you promised me?'

Picton leaned forward and lowered his voice. 'Our plans have hit a small problem. I am making arrangements to resolve matters.'

The Prince mirrored Picton's posture, but made no attempt to hide his anger. 'A small problem?' he snarled. 'You call a *murder investigation* a small problem!'

Picton's voice remained subdued and calm. 'With all due respect, Your Highness,' he whispered, 'it is no longer a murder investigation. The police have completed their enquiries. They now believe it to be a suicide. There is no comeback to us.'

'Do you really think the British police are so stupid? Even if they call it suicide, they will investigate this man's background. They will find out *why* he committed suicide. And where do you think their trail will lead them?'

'You have nothing to worry about, Your Highness. The coroner has already made his ruling. In any case, this is a Mickey Mouse police operation conducted by a Mickey Mouse policeman.'

'The *Gulf Times* has run the story every day for a week – and they have dropped hints of a wider scandal gripping London's investment banks. The press won't let it drop until they get answers from the police.'

'The police are not investigating us,' said Picton. 'They are investigating a straightforward suicide case. The dead man was an analyst employed by Saracen Laing. His wife was having an affair.

When he discovered this, he committed suicide. That is the end of the story.'

'I hope for your sake that is true.' The Prince leaned back in his chair and finished his drink. 'I want to hear about every development in this case, no matter how trivial.'

'You have my word, Your Highness.'

The Prince slammed his empty glass on to the tiny wooden table in front of them. 'I don't want your word, Picton. It's worthless. I just want to be kept informed. Do you understand?'

Picton nodded coolly.

Odile rolled over and lit up. 'He knows,' she said, inhaling deeply. 'Nicco knows everything.'

Larry took the cigarette from her lips and inserted it between his own. He got out of bed, slipped on a dressing gown, headed for the living room and poured two generous helpings of Scotch. When he returned to the bedroom, Odile was getting dressed.

'That silly bitch you hired fucked up,' she said.

'Lucy was the right girl for the job. She just got too close to him.'

'She's an amateur. Too soft. You used her because she was cheap.'

'She's also young and beautiful.'

'You should have got a professional.'

Larry placed her glass on the dressing table and took a sip from his own. 'Like who?'

Odile looked graciously at her reflection in the mirror.

Larry sat on the edge of the bed. 'You are indeed a professional, my dear,' he said, 'but you're expensive. Anyway, I want you in *my* bed – not his.'

'Prove it,' Odile growled.

He placed his drink next to hers, grabbed her by both buttocks

319

and whispered into her ear, 'You know, sweetheart, the best things in life are free.'

She thought about it for a second, and then succumbed once more to his desires.

Within the space of half an hour, Arnaud and Maurice managed to break in and out of the Moneypincher's Inn undetected. They went through every piece of paper in Picton's office, leaving the computers untouched.

They searched in every drawer and every file, but their efforts yielded no clues, no evidence and no leads. Picton was no fool. The office appeared to be the legitimate trading room of an international hedge fund. The office contained nothing incriminating. Except for one thing.

In a large brown envelope, the seal of which had been broken, were photographs of Larry Sikorski with an attractive young woman. The photographs were intimate, almost pornographic. Arnaud saw an opportunity. He pulled out a compact digital camera and photographed half a dozen of the images. Then, under the cover of night, he and Maurice slipped out the same way they had come in.

Arnaud drove like a model citizen down King William Street, careful not to attract attention. As the lights turned green at the junction with Gracechurch Street, Maurice could no longer hold back his curiosity. 'Boss, who was that woman photographed in Sikorski's car?'

'I don't know,' Arnaud replied. 'But it didn't look like his wife to me.'

CHAPTER 39

'James? I'm not coming in today,' Niccolo said. 'I'm feeling really lousy.'

'OK.' James' reply was characteristically indifferent.

Niccolo did not feel bad about the lie. There was much to do. He splashed some cold water on his face, switched on his computer and called Charlie to confirm that his wingman was in position.

'Listen, Niccolo, about the hearing,' began Charlie. 'I've been thinking about it – it's going to be difficult for me to back you up. I report directly to Larry too. I can't be seen to go against him. You do understand, don't you?'

Niccolo weighed Charlie's words, wondering what to read into them. 'I understand,' he said finally.

'Listen up, motherfucker, you ain't going down. I'm going to do three things for you. First, I'll have a word with Paddy O'Shea. As head of the sales force, he'll be in a good position to help you. He doesn't report to Larry. He doesn't give a shit about Larry. Christ, he fucking *hates* Larry! He's the guy you should call to attend the meeting. Second, some of my clients, especially the hedge fund guys, just love you. You made them a lot of money – they all shorted Globecom after your Sell note came out! So I'll ring round and ask them to get back to me with some opinions on you. And lastly, I'm happy to talk to that HR babe – what's her name?'

'Louise Horsforth.'

'Yeah, yeah, Horseface. I'll put in a good word for you. But only on condition that it's strictly anonymous. Like I said, I can't go against Larry publicly.'

'Thanks, Charlie. But can I trust Paddy?'

'I wouldn't go that far, buddy, but he's the right man to get you out of this mess.'

'He makes me nervous,' confessed Niccolo. 'He's a money-grabbing, cock-sucking son of a bitch who walks around like he's a big swinging dick.'

'Yeah, but he also happens to be the highest-grossing salesman at Saracen. Listen, kiddo, you're on the back foot here. Larry's outmanoeuvred you and you need to start playing dirty.'

'OK.' Niccolo nodded, then enquired, 'So what does that mean?'

'It means we turn up the heat on Larry. I mean, he's got more skeletons in his closet than Hampstead cemetery. And our man Paddy's already dug a few of them out. Paddy hates Larry's guts because Larry is a stuck-up, toffee-nosed wanker who has never, ever cooperated with the sales force. Paddy'd be only too happy to shaft Smug Slug Larry in public. Plus he's got a big mouth, and you need all the positive press you can get.' Charlie's tone was optimistic and gung-ho.

'OK,' said Niccolo, starting to feel better. 'You soften up Paddy. Then I'll ask him on Monday.'

'Done. Listen, I feel really bad that I can't sit in on this meeting . . .'

'I should never have put you in that position. It's just that I'm thin on people I can trust at the moment.'

'I understand you called in sick today. Feel like meeting at the gym later?'

'Thanks, Charlie.'

Niccolo knew that Charlie's absence from the disciplinary hearing spelt disaster. And he was in two minds as to whether Paddy was the smart choice. Yet his options were few and far between. If Charlie thought Paddy was the right man for the job, that was good enough for Niccolo.

By noon, Arnaud was on his fifth cup of coffee and buzzing. With the help of the Interpol database, he had identified the woman photographed with Larry. It was Jack Ford's wife. Arnaud wasted no time in calling DS Harcourt to relay what he had found.

'Thanks, but that's old news,' said DS Harcourt dismissively. 'We already knew Mrs Ford was having an affair with Larry Sikorski. Anyway, the case is closed – there's nothing I can do.'

'Yes, but these photographs showing Donna Ford in compromising positions with Larry Sikorski were not found at either of their homes, but in the offices of a third party I am not at liberty to name.'

'Were they now? That's much more interesting.'

'I've been thinking, Nicco,' said Charlie, making himself comfortable on the sauna bench. 'There's got to be a simple way out of this mess for you.'

'There's always a way out. I could swallow my pride, apologise to Larry, tell him I've learned the error of my ways, that I'll play ball next time, that I'll keep my mouth shut about all of this. Then he'd be off my back.'

'So why don't you?'

'I don't think you understand what Larry is capable of.'

'The hell I don't! The guy's a Jekyll-and-Hyde psycho – I know that. One minute you're the golden boy, the next he's trying

323

to get you fired. The only thing to remember with Larry is, he's always right. Don't ever fuck with his ego.'

'Jack fucked with his ego, and now he's dead.'

Charlie glared at Niccolo. 'Listen, motherfucker, Larry's a nasty piece of work, but he's no murderer.'

'I think he is, Charlie,' Niccolo said bitterly. 'Jack left messages on my mobile phone while he was standing outside Larry's apartment, only a few minutes before he disappeared. Larry tried to bribe me to change my Globecom rating, and Jack tried to warn me he was planning something worse. And on top of all that, Donna has been having an affair with Larry all this time. There – you put two and two together.'

'Look!' exclaimed Charlie. 'You're messing with fire, Nicco. You've got to let this go or you're going to end up just like Jack.'

'Charlie, we've got to make sure justice is done. For Jack.'

'Larry's a powerful guy. I'm not big enough to take him on, and neither are you.'

'Maybe not, but I'm going to see that Larry pays for what he did to Jack.'

'Maybe it wasn't *Larry* that killed Jack. Maybe *you* got him killed.' Charlie wiped the sweat from his forehead, and continued. 'Jack had nothing that Larry wanted – that slut of a wife of his isn't worth fighting over – but you've gone out of your way to pick a fight with Larry. Maybe Larry was trying to get at you through Jack. Ever think of that?'

Niccolo shut his eyes. Could Charlie be right?

'You know what your problem is, kiddo? You live in a dream world where everything is black and white. You think people will respect you for having the balls to stand up for yourself – to stand up for Jack, God bless his poor soul. The best thing you can do is to drop this. Forget about it. Take a vacation. It's over.'

'No!'

Charlie sighed. 'Why do you think Larry took you off Globecom?'

'Because he was under pressure from the pricks in Corporate Finance to up my rating to a Buy.'

'So why didn't you tell him what a great idea that was and just do it?'

'Because I don't think the company is worth anywhere near the amount that Corporate Finance are pushing for.'

'You know what your second problem is? You're too fucking straight. Lose some goddamn integrity, will you! We're investment bankers. We're here to make money. You make money by saying whatever it is your client wants you to say. You make money by bending the odd rule here and there. What the hell did they teach you at business school, man?'

'I didn't go to business school,' Niccolo said sulkily.

'What's rule number one in the capitalist's survival manual?'

'Preserve capital.'

'No, preserve yourself. Kiddo, Jack's dead. You don't have to get yourself killed to prove a point, goddammit!'

Niccolo shook his head. 'You don't understand, Charlie.'

'Oh, I understand perfectly. See here, I'm a stock analyst because they pay me. They pay me awfully well. I come to work for that bonus cheque we get each January. And do you know how I make sure I get it? When the shit hits the fan, I do as I'm told. I don't fuck with the egos of the big boys in their ivory towers. It's not worth it, Nicco. You can't change the system.'

'But I could never be happy with myself if I sold out.'

'Happy? *Happy*! Happy people don't fuck each other over; happy people hug you. These guys will fuck you over if you mess with them, just like they fucked Jack over. Will you be happy then?'

'I'll take my chances.' Niccolo smiled. 'I'm going to trash Larry's name, the same way he's trashed Jack's.'

Charlie finally relented, unveiling a long, soothing smile. 'Well in that case, we're going to need a plan.'

'Shoot.'

'Hell, I haven't got one yet,' said Charlie, shrugging his shoulders. 'I just know we need one.'

Niccolo went back to the office and opened up his email. It was time to do something he had been dreading. He had to tell Mizuno-san that Jack was dead.

A few years earlier, Mizuno-san's neighbour Daisaku had gone online, and had set up an account for Mizuno-san on his own computer. Every so often, Niccolo and Jack would send news-filled emails in English, which Daisaku would print out and translate for the old man. Brief messages would be sent in return.

Niccolo wanted to write this particular email in Japanese. He selected the Japanese-language software, and began hesitantly hunting for the right characters. He could still speak the language fairly fluently, but it was a long time since he had had to write it. But after a few minutes, he gave up. Communicating such momentous news by email felt quite wrong. He wanted to do it perfectly.

A Parker pen, still in its box, lay at the back of his desk drawer. He took it out, and scrabbled around for a black ink cartridge. Then he found a clean white sheet of paper and, carefully and painstakingly, began to trace barely remembered Hiragana characters.

Dear Mizuno-san,

This is a very sad letter I write. Please forgive me for sending bad news. Jack is dead. His body was found in the river Thames. The police say he killed himself. I do not believe it.

There are bad men in our bank and they want Jack and me to do bad things. But Jack always had honour. He would not do these bad things. I believe that is why he is dead.

I will do everything in my power to find out who killed him and why. I give you my word.

I send you my respect and love.

Your loyal student,

Niccolo

DS Harcourt was not the only police officer unhappy with the coroner's decision. WPC McKeever telephoned him to ask if she might ferret around in her own time. 'I'd really like to talk to that French bloke again,' she explained.

Bet you would, DS Harcourt said to himself. His response was less than overwhelming. 'OK. Let me know what you find. Don't get overzealous, though. The coroner's already made his decision. You'd just be tying up loose ends.'

At home that night, Niccolo worked non-stop on the case that he would present to the disciplinary hearing. Several fund managers had emailed positive responses. Critical information was still missing – Odile had not yet replied, and he still had to ask Paddy O'Shea to attend the hearing – but for the first time since his confrontation with Larry, he felt he had some sort of plan. He just needed to collate the evidence into a coherent document. The document was half complete. Niccolo read it. He read it again. Then he rewrote it. This was important. It didn't matter how long it took. What mattered was that his case should be clear.

The problem was that he couldn't think straight. He needed a fresh mind to look at it. He needed Gino. He would ring him in the morning. When it was clear he could do no more, he turned in.

*

The water was dark and turbulent, and he was being dragged down deep. A deadly predator had him in its grip, a predator he couldn't see and couldn't fight. There was no air to breathe, no one to help him . . .

He was floating now, inert with cold and shock, on the surface of the water. The predator was still close by, implacable and cruel, and he was its helpless prey. The monster's hideous head broke the surface of the water, and it glared directly into his eyes.

Niccolo awoke, gasping for breath, his heart pounding terrifyingly. For a few minutes he lay still, to reassure himself that he was safe at home in his own bed. But still the disquiet would not leave him. For the creature's piercing yellow eyes, agleam with catlike malice, had been unmistakably the eyes of Larry Sikorski.

CHAPTER 40

On Saturday morning, whilst Gino and Niccolo went through the presentation for the disciplinary hearing, Olivia fed breakfast to her two daughters. Teresa loved croissants and could eat a whole one all by herself. Silvia, at six months, simply spat hers out.

'It's a piece of shit,' pronounced Gino. 'What's the purpose of this meeting? What's your message? Who's your audience? Stop pussyfooting around and get to the point. Rewrite the whole thing.' He flicked the document over to Niccolo.

Niccolo scowled. He detested any kind of criticism, and he detested constructive criticism even more.

Gino thought for a moment. 'From what you've told me about your case, I'm pretty sure it's not the first time this kind of thing has happened. Weren't these sort of pressure tactics rife in investment banks a few years ago?' he asked pensively. 'Hang on – let me see if I can find anything on the net.' He shot up the stairs to his study, with Niccolo hot on his tail. They sat down and Gino slapped some key search words into Google. 'Bingo!' he yelled, finally. 'Here's a case similar to yours: The *Financial Telegraph*, 3 December 2002.'

EQUITY ANALYST FIRED BY
HIGH-FLYING BANKER

Rebecca Smith, the luxury goods analyst at Feldman Finch resigned under suspicious circumstances . . . Last week, Smith, who reportedly received a $2m bonus last year, was forced to leave the bulge-bracket investment bank shortly before she was entitled to this year's bonus. For the last few years, Smith had steadily acquired notoriety as one of the bank's rising stars. Then, days after Smith downgraded B Y Beauty, a leading, high-end women's fashion group, to SELL, Smith found herself at the centre of an internal battle between the Research Department and IBD – the investment banking division – which she ultimately lost. Friends of the former analyst have come forward to say that she was fired simply because she offended Feldman's investment banker, Michael Gonzales, a senior IBD Managing Director who was close to signing a multi-million-dollar advisory deal with B Y Beauty. Feldman Finch's actions raise questions about whether brokerage analysts remain under pressure from investment banking colleagues to issue 'buy' recommendations.

Last night, a Feldman Finch spokesman declined to return our calls and Smith herself could not be reached for comment.

'My fine legal brain tells me that Feldman's put their fees before their ethics,' Gino observed. 'But I thought the big banks cleaned up their act after Eliot Spitzer – the New York Attorney General – fined them a billion dollars back in 2002 for unethical working practices. Analysts were supposed to be insulated from pushy bankers after that fiasco, right? You're not telling me this Globecom thing is all about some Saracen banker trying to land himself a big deal, are you?'

Niccolo nodded. 'That's what this is all about,' he said.

*

WPC McKeever was sitting at a private table for two at the Royal China restaurant in St John's Wood. She was dressed in plain clothes and had informed neither her superiors nor her team of her whereabouts.

When Arnaud Veyrieras arrived, she stood up and waved the *Economist*, and a waitress escorted him gracefully to the table.

'I was surprised to receive your call this morning,' said Arnaud as he sat down. 'Your boss was dismissive of my findings when we spoke on the telephone the other day.'

'He received some photographs from you in yesterday's post,' McKeever said quietly. 'He asked me to file them. Officially, we're unable to investigate this case further because the coroner has already made his ruling and suicide cases don't warrant huge amounts of police time.'

Arnaud smiled. 'So why are you here?'

'I had another look at the photographs this morning. Something really puzzled me. Not the affair itself, but the fact that someone took photographs of it. I called you here to find out more. Of course, you understand that I'm here not as a police officer, but merely as a citizen interested in seeing that justice is done.'

'I mean you no disrespect, Ms McKeever, but can you make any difference to the outcome of this case?'

WPC McKeever sat up straight. 'It's difficult to reopen a case once a coroner has ruled,' she began. 'But if new evidence were to come to light – *material* new evidence – I could bring it to the attention of DS Harcourt. On the strength of that evidence, the coroner could be requested, even forced, to review his findings.'

Arnaud unfolded his napkin and placed it on his lap. 'I believe I can provide you with sufficient evidence to convince the coroner to reopen this case.'

Once the waitress had taken their order, Arnaud briefed WPC McKeever on his prior dealings with Larry Sikorski and the trail of collateral damage that seemed to litter his past. 'Sikorski specialises in financial fraud,' he told her. 'But he's too slippery an operator to have his name linked to any white-collar crime. Until now I would have said that murder was out of his league. But this – the death of Jack Ford – his fingerprints appear to be all over it. And Sikorski's is not the only name in the frame.'

Arnaud neglected to mention that all existing FSA investigations into Sikorski's activities had been culled. The FSA, he explained rather convincingly, was working hard to link Sikorski to a number of known City fraudsters.

There was Dr Picton, who ran a 'family office' for a well-known Middle Eastern syndicate. His clients could be loosely described as relatives of wealthy Arab oilmen who willed their money to grow faster than their families could take it out of the ground. Picton had built his reputation by cashing in on the terrorist attacks on the Twin Towers – he shorted airlines and insurance companies in the days immediately before 11 September 2001, and made a fortune for his investment partners. Prior knowledge of the attacks was the obvious explanation for such brilliant market timing, but was next to impossible to prove. Since then, Picton had been associated with market manipulation schemes and tax fraud, though he had so far escaped prosecution.

Sikorski's connection with Picton could be summed up by a simple but devastating scam: Sikorski provided Picton with inside information about analyst ratings. Saracen Laing's analysts, like those of a handful of the bulge-bracket investment banks, could alter the direction of a company's share price simply by changing their stock rating. Thanks to Sikorski's tip-offs, Picton received those rating revisions before the markets did and profited handsomely from the timing differences. In the City they called it front-running. At the FSA, they called it securities fraud, pure and simple.

Then there was Kenneth Oakes, the dynamic CEO of British telecoms giant Globecom, which, in a matter of twenty years, had grown by acquisition to become a national champion on a global scale. Oakes was a fat cat. His remuneration contract rewarded him generously for precious little. His bonuses were loosely linked not only to Globecom's share price, but also to the size of the company. Oakes' motivations were clear – he had to buy as many telecoms companies as he could to make himself richer.

Sikorski ran a tight ship. He had been in charge of Investment Research at Saracen Laing for over a decade. In that time he had moulded a loyal team, carefully selecting new hires and ruthlessly firing troublemakers. He bullied analysts into blindly following his advice. When they refused, he struck mercilessly at their most vulnerable points. Unsurprisingly, most complied, and were handsomely rewarded for their trouble.

Sikorski had a reputation for crushing dissent at birth with an iron fist. A few weeks earlier, for example, a Pharmaceuticals analyst by the name of Lindsay Compton had refused to change the rating on GSF when instructed to do so by Sikorski. A few days later, Compton's parents were mysteriously kidnapped on holiday in Usman and ended up in hospital, fighting for their lives.

The link between Jack Ford's death and Sikorski was, admittedly, extremely tenuous. Ford covered small tech stocks, where it was harder for market manipulators to make really big money, so he was of little use to Sikorski. 'But there are other connections,' Arnaud went on. 'Ford's wife was sleeping with Sikorski, and Ford's best friend, Niccolo Lamparelli, was the analyst covering Globecom. Lamparelli was hired personally by Sikorski two years ago, since when he has risen rapidly through the ranks. The bank's clients now consider him one of their star analysts. When he speaks, markets move.'

Having analysts of such standing on his team gave Sikorski enormous power to manipulate the markets, provided that power could be harnessed appropriately, Arnaud explained. He confessed that he did not know precisely where the lines of the Sikorski–Ford–Lamparelli triangle crossed, but he suspected that Sikorski was close to pulling off one of his biggest scams yet, and that Jack Ford's murder lay right at its heart.

Arnaud's narrative lasted as long as their excellent lunch, after which McKeever offered to split the bill. Arnaud insisted that he take care of it personally. As they parted, the Frenchman brushed the woman police constable's cheek with his lips.

WPC McKeever returned to her station armed with hard facts, a charming new contact, a cunning plan and a faint but lingering aura of Hermès aftershave.

When the phone rang, Donna knew instinctively who it was. She knew she was totally innocent of Jack's death, but she also knew Niccolo was never going to forgive her. At Jack's funeral, he had looked at her with contempt, and spoken to her as if she were a stranger. And he had left her house without his customary peck on her cheek. She had a shrewd idea what he was calling about now.

She was right.

'Jack's mum just rang,' Niccolo said, once the awkward pleasantries were out of the way. 'She says her allowance didn't come through last month. Do you know anything about it?'

Over ten years, Jack had collected sizeable investment banking bonuses, enabling him to put enough on one side for an ample retirement chest. The Hampstead house was now mortgage-free, and worth a small fortune. Even allowing for the possible invalidity of his life insurance policies, given the official cause of death – suicide – his estate would be substantial.

But Jack had died intestate. In the absence of a will, under English law, his entire estate passed tax-free to his wife. There was no provision for his mother. Jack had always supported Bronwen, making a monthly payment by electronic transfer to her Australian bank account to augment her pension. He paid for her to come to London twice each year, and arranged for flowers on her birthday, on Mother's Day and at Christmas, on all sorts of occasions and even on no occasion at all. The remittances had started the day he got his first job, and had never stopped since.

Until now.

'I don't know anything about it at all,' replied Donna. 'The probate lawyers are handling everything. Perhaps they've closed down Jack's accounts or stopped outgoing transfers or something – I don't know.' She did her best to sound as though it was all completely beyond her.

'Jack's mum depends on that allowance,' pleaded Niccolo. 'Please promise me you won't stop it, Donna.'

But Donna was careful to make no promise. 'I'll talk to the lawyers, OK?'

'Thanks, Donna . . .'

The line went dead.

On his day off, DS Harcourt whisked through WPC McKeever's report on her meeting with Arnaud Veyrieras. He wondered what motive Arnaud had for divulging so much information voluntarily. Was justice all he was interested in? Or did he have another agenda? If so, DS Harcourt was pretty certain what it was.

The FSA had not had a successful high-profile prosecution for years. Larry Sikorski was no small fry; he was a big ocean-going predator. Netting him would mean long-awaited success and recognition for the FSA.

DS Harcourt had risen through the ranks despite his aversion to following orders. Were it not for the fact that his instinct, the source of his insubordination, had often proved – with the benefit of hindsight – spot on, his career would have ended long ago.

It was his instinct that DS Harcourt turned to now. Something smelled funny about the coroner's suicide verdict, and Larry Sikorski and Donna Ford did not seem quite as innocent as they appeared, he thought. And then there was the interesting Sikorski–Picton link, as relayed by WPC McKeever.

Harcourt smiled to himself as he made a few notes, jotting down grounds for reasonable suspicion. His instinct had rarely – if ever – let him down.

By eight o'clock that evening, Niccolo and Gino had between them downed most of a bottle of wine.

'This is not bad now, Nicco, not bad at all.' Gino said at last, looking up from Niccolo's document. 'The content is all here. We just need to work on the delivery.' He pencilled in a few amendments. 'Make sure you stick to the facts. Try to keep things simple. It gives them less room to outmanoeuvre you. Will this meeting be with a man or a woman?'

'One man, one woman,' replied Niccolo. 'Rupert Southgate, my boss, and Louise Horsforth from HR.'

'Logic works with men. Emotion works with women,' Gino declared, ignoring the sceptical look on Olivia's face as she studiously focused on cooking dinner. 'Get this Louise on your side. She needs to see you as just one brave man fighting a big ugly machine.'

'She's not that gullible.'

'Larry Sikorski and your boss Rupert have already determined the outcome. She may be the only chance you've got of a fair

336

hearing. And if your boyish charm fails, be prepared for a trade-off. You give her something, she gives you something. It's a bit like when Larry took Globecom away from you – you agreed to apologise, and Larry agreed not to fire you—'

'I did not apologise!' Niccolo shouted furiously. 'Larry printed an apology in my name. He undermined the credibility of the whole bank by giving in to pressure from Globecom, and he bullied me into keeping my mouth shut. He might as well have asked them to write their own research report and printed it on Saracen's letterhead!' He emptied the bottle into their glasses and thumped it angrily back on the table.

'Lose your temper like that in the meeting, you'll come across like an idiot who deserves to be fired,' Gino said quietly. 'Remember, Louise knows nothing about you except what she sees in that meeting.'

'I know, I know.'

'Exactly when is this meeting happening?'

'Louise is arranging it for Tuesday. Rupert returns from holiday on Monday, so he needs time to get up to speed with things.'

'Aha! So you're ready. He's not,' Gino said. 'You must insist that the meeting takes place first thing on Monday morning. Tell them you can't do your job while the uncertainty is hanging over your head, and you need the whole thing resolved as soon as possible.'

'I'll request the meeting for Monday afternoon – that'll give me the morning to talk to my witness.'

'Who is . . .?

'Paddy O'Shea. He's Head of Sales and Trading. He hates Larry. And he's prepared to put his ass on the line.'

Gino knocked back the last of his wine and reached for a new bottle. 'Well, in that case, *amico mio*, it looks like it'll be *un pezzo di torta*!'

*

'The smart thing for Nicco to do,' Olivia said to her husband at three in the morning, 'would be to ask his boss for help. They're both on the same team. They should close ranks and protect each other. Doesn't he have any brains?'

'Sweetheart, no one in the City has brains. They only have egos. Except for Rupert – he's got no brain and no ego. He just does as he's told.'

'I wish you were more like that, darling.'

CHAPTER 41

James was number two in the telecoms team, at least by length of service, and his opinion counted. Niccolo knew James was impressed with much of his work, but doubted he would ever risk his own neck for anyone else. Still, he needed to know which way James would bat.

James arrived ten minutes early for Sunday brunch at Ed's Diner, and was flirting with the waitress when Niccolo showed up. James caught sight of him and hastily told the waitress, 'Full English for two. The works.'

'Thanks,' Niccolo said, sitting down.

James made small talk about the weather and work and food until Niccolo rudely interrupted. 'Listen, I need to talk to you,' he said. 'I need to be careful whom I confide in right now. Of all the people in Saracen, you're the only one I trust. All the time I've known you, you've always acted with the utmost integrity.' Niccolo kept a straight face as he delivered his lines, his feigned sincerity matched only by James' equally feigned concern. 'This may require you to make a judgement call. It's clear you're a man of principle, but I need to know where I stand.'

'I'm listening.'

'Larry's playing games with me. He's dreamed up some bogus charge and he's trying to make it stick. He says I fucked up on Telespaña.'

'Just because you failed the Ratings Committee?' retorted James, this time with a respectable dose of unadulterated astonishment. '*Everyone* fails the Ratings Committee. I've failed it. Rupert's probably failed more than the two of us put together. Maybe the suits in New York have given Larry the order to reduce headcount,' he suggested.

Niccolo tried to work out what James was thinking, who was pulling his strings. He decided to give him the reluctant benefit of a large doubt. 'Maybe . . .'

'Look, it's not a good idea to get on the wrong side of Larry.' James hesitated, pondering his next statement with care. 'Maybe you should have been a bit more cooperative in the past. Your stance on Globecom did you no favours. You upset JC's boys. Larry hates that sort of thing.'

'Upsetting JC's boys doesn't make me incompetent, does it?'

'Of course not. But remember what happened to Lindsay Compton . . .'

'Lindsay wasn't incompetent.'

'Oh, your competence is not in question. Your judgement calls are amongst the best in the market – no one disputes that.' James paused to sip his coffee. 'This is not a competency issue, it's a personality clash. And Larry's ego doesn't help matters. It just makes any path to reconciliation that much more treacherous.'

It was one thing to get James to come to this conclusion by himself. It was quite another to expect him to speak out when it mattered. 'James, there's a good chance that HR will ask your opinion of my overall performance. I need to know what you're going to tell them.'

James looked flustered. 'Of course I'll help in any way I can, Niccolo . . .'

'Can I count on you to back me up at the hearing?'

Providing public support for Niccolo carried the risk of guilt by association. At best it could adversely affect James' bonus. At worst he could lose his job. Niccolo watched him carefully weighing up the odds.

'Well, Larry's always been fair to me . . .' James temporised.

Niccolo persisted. 'Can I count on you, James?'

'I'm not sure my opinion really matters much,' said James, pedalling backwards in haste.

'Of course your opinion counts. Will you back me up?'

'Let me think about it over the weekend. I'll let you know tomorrow.' But Niccolo knew there was no need to wait for a response. James had never got off the fence in his whole life. He certainly wasn't going to jump now.

Later that evening, Niccolo went yet again to Gino's house. Olivia and the girls had gone to a birthday party in Tunbridge Wells and would be staying there overnight.

'OK,' Gino said, handing the document back to Niccolo. 'What's your objective for this meeting?'

'To show that I'm a damn good analyst and that all this is a waste of everyone's time.'

'I mean – your objective at the *end* of all of this? From what you've told me, this guy Larry has set you up. He'll probably assign you some impossible targets, and when you fail to meet them he'll fire you. Am I right?'

'Yeah, something like that.'

'I've spoken to a friend of mine who specialises in employment law, and he says this sort of thing is becoming increasingly common. An employer fabricates some sort of negligence case against somebody, and if they can make it stick, they can fire them. It's cheaper than making someone redundant.'

'I'm not surprised,' Niccolo agreed glumly. 'The big boys between them have laid off the population of a decent-sized city, and there'll be more. I suppose firing's a cheap alternative.'

'And the odds are always stacked heavily against the employee because the rules governing such situations are embodied in the employee handbook. And guess who writes the employee handbook?'

'Doesn't the law protect me if I'm innocent?'

'It should, but not everyone has the guts or the cash to fight.'

'How do you rate my chances?'

'Well, as a lawyer, it looks to me like Sikorski has made some minor procedural errors. He's effectively asked you to resign without just cause. That can be interpreted as sacking you. Unless he's got a damn good reason, he's acted illegally. It was also pretty stupid of him to call you in alone, without a witness from HR. I'd say it looks like you have a pretty good case against the bank.'

'So should I fight it?'

'Difficult to say. They hold all the trump cards. They can hire expensive lawyers while they suspend your pay. They can tape-record your conversations whilst you remain in the dark about theirs. They can smear your reputation. And if you fuck with them, they can ensure that you never work in the City again. If it goes to court, it could take months to settle and it would be difficult to win outright. If you lost, you might have to pay legal costs, which would almost certainly bankrupt you. Now I'm asking you one more time: what is your objective? Do you want to threaten them with unfair dismissal and hope they settle? Are you prepared for a lengthy litigation case? Or do you want to go through this disciplinary bullshit and keep your job?'

Niccolo deliberated. 'There's no way I can work for Larry now,' he said finally. 'I've no respect for the man. Anyway, he'd just find something else to trip me up with. I've got to go for unfair dismissal.'

'In that case, you'll need a damn good lawyer.'

CHAPTER 42

When the alarm went off at quarter past five on Monday morning, Niccolo felt like calling in sick. The initial paralysis that had crippled his body upon hearing of Jack's death seemed to be creeping back, and he felt a cramp in his belly.

He lay there for a few minutes, thinking. He suspected Larry was behind Jack's murder, but to prove it he needed to stay on the inside – at least for a little while longer. That meant he had to fight for his job.

The trading floor was virtually empty. Odile was away for the week and Rupert was expected back from his holiday some time that morning. James, already deep in paperwork, simply blanked Niccolo.

Niccolo opened his coffee, and made a list:

Louise
Paddy
Distribute statement
Gino's lawyer

Just then, Rupert swaggered on to the trading floor, waving to signal his comeback as though inviting admiration of his tan.

Niccolo pursued him. 'Can we talk in private, Ru?' he asked.

'First day back. Got a lot of shit on my desk.' Rupert yawned. 'Give me a while to catch up. How about nine o'clock?'

Nine o'clock came and went. The meeting was deferred. Rupert appeared to have other priorities. Niccolo had to get his version of events to Louise before the hearing, but he needed to speak to Rupert first. After scanning Rupert's electronic diary for that day, he drafted an email to Louise.

Louise

Last Thursday, Larry Sikorski asked me to resign.

He informed me that he considered my position to be untenable and that he felt I did not have what it takes to be an analyst. He added that Rupert Southgate believed my position was untenable too. Larry further stated that he did not trust me, but refused to elaborate. He stated that he had asked you to set up a meeting to assess my competence. At his suggestion, I spent the following day at home.

Three months ago, Larry personally conducted my annual performance appraisal review, at which time he indicated to me that he was delighted with my performance, as was Rupert. At that time no issue of competency or trust was raised.

All of a sudden this view appears to have changed, for no apparent reason. Given that Larry has asked me to resign, I find myself in a difficult position through no fault of my own. I'd like to sort this out. Can we meet at 15.00 today?

He checked his Reuters screen. Globecom's share price had fallen to £1.92 – it was worth fifty-four billion pounds.

The phone rang. The digital display showed Louise's extension number. Her manner was brusque and she spoke quickly.

'Niccolo – your email. This differs significantly from the situation you outlined to me on Thursday. I was not aware that Mr Sikorski had mentioned the R-word in any prior communication with you. This changes things. Can you confirm to me that he has indeed asked you to resign?'

'Yes, he has.'

'Why didn't you tell me this on Thursday?'

Niccolo gathered his thoughts. 'I was taken by surprise. At the time I was unsure of my legal rights – I didn't know what I could or couldn't say.'

'Hmmn. I see,' was all Louise said.

'I've copied Larry in on the email so you can confirm everything I've said with him,' Niccolo added. 'Are we on for three o'clock?' The meeting was confirmed and Louise hung up.

A few minutes later, the phone rang again. 'Niccolo, I've just spoken to Mr Sikorski. He disagrees with your version of events. He says your email does *not* represent an accurate account of the meeting you had with him last Thursday, and that he never asked you to resign.'

'Well, one of us must be lying – sorry, *mistaken*.'

'Do you have any written record or documentation at all?'

'No,' Niccolo admitted.

'Let's hold the disciplinary hearing and decide how we proceed.'

'I assume Larry will attend?'

'I believe Mr Sikorski has already informed you that he will not attend, Niccolo.' Louise's manner was becoming more and more prickly. 'Rupert Southgate will attend as your line manager.'

'Given that Larry called the meeting, don't you think he should be there?'

There was a pause. 'I'll ask Mr Sikorski how he wishes to proceed.'

Niccolo knew perfectly well that there was as much chance of Larry attending the meeting as there was of Donna donating Jack's life savings to charity. Should the validity of the disciplinary procedure ever be questioned, it would be Rupert who would take the fall.

But why was Louise so jittery? Had she recognised the first signs of a potentially damaging constructive-dismissal case? Or was she out of her depth?

Niccolo had a soft spot for the girl from Human Resources. He found it hard to think of her as the enemy. In fact, he found her rather attractive. Her understated dress sense, her serious oval face, her husky voice, even her jumpiness – he was attracted to all those things.

He fired off another email, this time to Larry.

Larry

Louise informs me that in your view, my account of events detailed in an email I copied to you this morning (see attachment) is inaccurate. Given my understanding that you will not be present at the disciplinary hearing at 3 p.m. today, please could you clarify to me which elements of my email below you disagree with?

In particular, please let me know your position as to whether or not you suggested I resign.

I would like to know your position prior to my hearing.

Then he sent the statement that he and Gino had prepared over the weekend to the print room, with instructions to make six bound copies. Included were copies of emails he had received in the previous seventy-two hours providing internal and external feedback. He was conscious that Odile had not yet replied.

He checked his watch. Time to speak to Paddy O'Shea. Taking the scenic route around the edge of the trading floor, he tried to keep a low profile. Paddy's desk was vacant.

'He's in there, Nicco.' Anne-Marie pointed to one of the quiet rooms on the mezzanine floor that provided a refuge from the numerous distractions – flashing prices, breaking news stories and sexy Kloomberg sales girls – of the trading floor. 'Something wrong, my love?' she enquired.

'No, nothing's wrong. Thanks.' He winked at her.

Paddy was talking to Charlie in one of the glass-fronted meeting rooms. Both men looked serious. They invited Niccolo in.

Paddy came straight to the point. 'Charlie tells me you're in the shit,' he said, a glint of mischief in his eyes.

Charlie relaxed back in his chair and placed his hands comfortably behind his head. 'Up shit creek without a Paddy.' It wasn't one of his better puns, but they laughed anyway.

'This is just typical of Larry,' Paddy said sternly. 'There are two ways to manage staff – you get hold of their respect or you get hold of their balls. Balls is Larry's way. He likes yes-men. When an analyst gains the respect of the market, Larry sees it as a threat to his own career, rather than an opportunity for the firm. So when a chief exec complains about one of our analysts, Larry bows to corporate pressure instead of protecting his man. Nicco, you gave Saracen Laing a greater level of credibility in the market than we've ever had before. That fucker just threw it away. Someone needs to tell Larry that we are his customers and you are his product. I've got some good salesmen on my bench, but none of them can sell a dead man.' He leaned forward and added, almost paternally, 'Nicco, I want you to know – I'm going to back you all the way on this one.'

Niccolo got to his feet. 'Thanks, Paddy. The meeting's at three.

I'd like you to read this statement first. It says that they have no basis to challenge my competency. It's backed up by forty pages of supporting documents.'

'Good for you, kiddo,' said Charlie. 'Will the others get copies?'

Niccolo smiled grimly. 'Not a second before five to three!'

When Niccolo had gone, Charlie said, 'Thanks for coming good for the boy, Paddy. I really appreciate it.' A feeling of nostalgia overcame him, and he grew pensive. He had never been able to hide his fondness for Niccolo. He saw in him a man prepared to lose everything to defend his reputation, a young man with the fiery cocktail of ethical and maverick qualities that he once had in such abundance himself. As sole breadwinner for several households, constrained by political correctness at work, Charlie longed for the old days when he would say whatever he wanted to say, do whatever he wanted to do, screw whomever he wanted to screw – and take the rap for his efforts. Not any more, Charlie old boy, he chastised himself. It's the real world for you.

'This is more than just a headcount issue,' stated Paddy, interrupting Charlie's musings. 'I think it's personal – Larry doesn't like Nicco.'

'That's an occupational hazard – he doesn't like me either. In fact, he doesn't like anyone with an opinion.'

'So what about Globecom?' asked Paddy. '*Is* someone putting pressure on Nicco to change his rating? Larry'd have to be a complete idiot to try to pin dirt on him. The kid's hot property right now.'

'So he's got the support of you guys in Sales?'

'Are you kidding? He's the best thing we've had since . . . well, since you, Charlie.'

'Hang on, Paddy; you'll have me crying in a minute!'

'There's just one problem – Larry doesn't really give a shit about what I think. The sales force doesn't report to him. Technically we have no say in such decisions.'

'You know something, Paddy. Nobody gives a fuck about nobody in this business. We're all just waiting for the day when we have enough in the bank to retire. We've sold our souls. We're prostitutes. We just bend over whenever the M&A guys tell us to bend over, and take it up the ass without a word of complaint. The world's gone pear-shaped, my friend.'

'Yeah – and so has Dudley. It's all those free profiteroles in the executive dining room.'

'Hey, Paddy, stick it to Larry for all of us, will you?' Charlie dug his finger under his collar and tugged at it. It had chafed yesterday too. Perhaps he had gone up a size. His chest was sagging and his waistline protruding again. A funny sinking feeling gripped his senses. He shrugged his shoulders. Middle age had finally caught up with him.

In an unbearably hot warehouse in Mumbai, Raj Sanghavi was about to start his afternoon shift. Raj had achieved a first-class degree in mechanical engineering from the Indian Institute of Technology, but upon graduation had found to his surprise that he was unable to secure a single offer from a reputable engineering firm, because his father did not know the right people in the right companies. So he'd taken the call-centre job as a stopgap. That was eighteen months ago.

The company for which he worked provided outsourced services to State & County Bank. When the red light on his desk lit up, he answered his first call of the day. The caller's details were displayed on the screen, and a digital clock reminded him that it was 10 a.m. in her country. Raj took the caller through the security routine. Then he accessed her account details.

'Good morning, Mrs Ford. My name is Robbie. How can I help you today?'

Mrs Ford spoke in a brusque voice. 'I'm expecting a large sum to be credited to my account.'

'How much are you expecting, Mrs Ford?'

'About seven hundred and fifty thousand pounds.'

Raj raised his eyebrows and searched the account. 'I'm afraid the funds have not arrived yet, Mrs Ford.'

'I see. Well, do you think you could ring me up when they arrive? I need to know as soon as possible.'

Raj followed protocol to the letter. 'Of course, Mrs Ford, I will surely do so. Under UK money-laundering regulations, we are obliged to identify the source and nature of all transfers of this size. May I ask what the funds relate to, madam?'

'My husband recently passed away. He had some life assurance policies. I can give you the policy numbers if you like.'

'Thank you. It may help us to track down the funds if they are stuck in the system somewhere, madam.' Raj made a note of the insurance policy details. In a softened voice, he said, 'Please accept my sincere condolences for your loss, Mrs Ford.'

The caller ended the call abruptly. She did not sound old, so she could not have been married for very many years, Raj thought to himself. Yet she appeared to show scant grief for her loss.

Raj had no life assurance. His wife Sanghita had told him many times that she had no need of it, for if he died, she would join him in heaven. Perhaps, he reflected, marriage meant something different to people in the West.

Niccolo collected his documents from the print room, and packed them neatly into his satchel.

He got back to find an email waiting from Larry.

Discussions of this kind are never easy, and I regret that they have become necessary.

Last Thursday I sought to be direct and honest with you. I explained that your work was not satisfactory in either your manager's judgement or mine. I explained to you that in these circumstances we would go down the disciplinary route as outlined in the Saracen Laing employee handbook. I explained to you what the two possible consequences of this could be and that it was for you to decide whether you wished to go down this route, but that this was the process, designed to protect employee rights, that Saracen Laing had put in place for these situations.

I did not ask you to resign.

Oh yes you fucking did, you bastard, Niccolo muttered.

Just then the phone rang. 'Nicco? Gino. I've found you an employment lawyer. Duncan Witherspoon-Harper. He's good – the best. I've briefed him, and he's expecting a call.'

'Thanks, Gino. I owe you.'

He looked at his Speedmaster. It was 13.23.

Niccolo stepped out of the building, rang the lawyer and made an appointment to see him at noon the next day. Then he grabbed his gym bag, ambled down to the basement, changed into his shorts and went for a run along the Thames.

When he had showered, he returned to his desk with a roast beef sandwich and a can of Coke. With fifteen minutes to go before the HR meeting, he took a bite of the sandwich and checked his emails.

He grinned as he saw his trump card: Odile had sent an email entitled *Feedback on NL*. It was addressed jointly to Rupert and Niccolo and copied to Larry. Silly girl – she should have had more sense, damn it! But there was something else – she had copied in Louise Horsforth.

Wait a second! Odile was on holiday. How could she know which HR director was dealing with the matter? Other than himself, only Larry, Rupert, Charlie and Paddy possessed that information.

Maybe he was being paranoid. Odile's friendship was beyond question. Of course it was. She was the nearest thing he had to a sister. He had told her things about his personal life – things about Jack, about Lucy – that he had told no one else. And she had done likewise. Just print the email off, damn it!

As he hit the print button, his eyes moved to the main text. His mouth dried up and he felt nauseous.

Dear Rupert/Niccolo,

I have been asked to give my opinion of Niccolo's professional competency, having worked closely with him for two years. Over this period, Niccolo has fallen far short of the high standards we expect at Saracen Laing.

Most of the clients to whom I spoke as specialist saleswoman for the Telecoms Research Team took note of Niccolo's research and were always keen to discuss it and speak with him. His research is provocative and interesting, but his attention to detail weak. His research lacks factual and solid evidence to back his arguments. His knowledge of industry-related issues is poor. Thus I believe his position to be untenable.

I believe this to be a fair and balanced opinion of Niccolo Lamparelli.

Best regards.

From the corner of his eye, Niccolo caught Rupert opening the same email. His self-assured smile told Niccolo all he needed to know. The red neon warning signs that had sat dormant in his brain for a while now began to flash wildly again.

The style was not Odile's. She'd used the word 'untenable' – the same word used by Larry in his email on Thursday. She'd said that this was her 'fair and balanced opinion'. She would never use those words. And the phrase 'fallen far short of the high standards we expect at Saracen Laing' was taken directly from the Saracen employee handbook; he was sure of it. But it was the grammar that gave the game away. Odile's written English was normally so appalling that it was routinely the subject of ridicule. Yet this memo had no grammatical errors. Not one.

Niccolo hastily snatched the email printout, left the sandwich half eaten at his desk and marched over to Rupert's desk with two copies of his prepared statement. 'Ru, I intend to go through this at the HR meeting. Here's a copy, in case you'd like to flick through it beforehand.'

'I, er . . . thanks, Nicco,' Rupert stuttered. Once Niccolo was gone, he began frantically turning the pages.

The insurance clerk dealing with the probate lawyers acting on behalf of the estate of Jack Ford had just received confirmation of the coroner's verdict on the cause of death. Suicide.

With a wry grin of satisfaction, he drafted a letter to the probate lawyers notifying them that the life assurance policy on which they had just made a full claim was now declared null and void. He signed the letter, placed it in a brown envelope, and tossed it into his out tray. Then he posted his final computer entry in respect of life assurance policy number RD6658470.

Claim rejected.

Outside the office of the Head of Investment Research, Niccolo checked the time. One minute to three. He knocked on the glass door like a policeman with a search warrant. Larry was strutting up and down, talking via a Bluetooth headpiece and laughing uncontrollably. He pointed to his headphones, indicating that he was busy. Niccolo persisted, holding the document up against the glass. Rather reluctantly, Larry waved him in.

'Can I put you on hold for just a second?' he said to his caller.

'I've prepared a statement, which I will be submitting as part of my case at this hearing,' Niccolo said. 'I've got your copy here.'

'That's not necessary, Lamparelli,' said Larry nonchalantly. 'Give it to Rupert. He's your line manager. He's handling this meeting.'

'*You* called the meeting, Larry. So I'd like *you* to attend. Here is your copy.' He tossed the document on to Larry's desk.

Larry folded his arms. The two men glared at each other, contempt in the eyes of one, disgust in the eyes of the other. Larry glanced at his mobile phone. So did Niccolo. The call was still in progress. The display read, *Od mob*.

It took a moment to register.

The anger and betrayal that Niccolo felt did not surface – it just detonated a fuse deep in his gut. As he stormed out of Larry's office, the bomb was ticking.

Larry left the Saracen Laing building by the back entrance. He pulled out his phone and called a very old friend on one of the major daily newspapers.

'That piece you wrote about Lamparelli a few days back – about the Globecom apology letter?'

'One of my best features. The editor thinks I'm a genius.'

'If you're interested, I have an even bigger scoop for you.'

'I'm interested.'

'Lamparelli's not as good as everyone says he is. I've put him under negative watch. I suspect he'll be fired soon.'

'Shit! You serious?'

'You didn't hear it from me.'

'Goes without saying, my friend. Goes without saying.'

'Our usual terms?'

'Of course. Your Singapore account?'

*

355

'Miss Sanderson? I have the Chief Secretary for you.'

The call from the Treasury was put through. The caller wasted little time on pleasantries.

'Amanda, we've been looking through your stats – you know, the latest ones for March – and they're not too good, are they?'

'I'm . . . I'm not sure what you mean, sir.'

'Oh, I think you know very well what I mean, Amanda. Your performance is unacceptable. The Enforcement Division is not meeting its targets.'

'Sir, we're only halfway through implementing my new strategy. It's really too early to judge.'

'The public are getting restless. This whole credit crunch thing might blow up in our faces. The Chancellor needs results, Amanda, not strategies. I'm sure you understand. Well, I'll let you get on . . .'

But Amanda sensed the conversation had not yet ended. 'Oh, while I've got you on the phone . . .' continued the Chief Secretary. 'I've heard through the grapevine that you've reopened the old Sikorski case.'

Amanda took her time in answering. 'That's not true, sir,' she lied.

'Oh? Perhaps my sources are misinformed. They seem to think the FSA is helping the police with a murder enquiry. That young analyst chap who fell into the Thames . . .'

'Jack Ford, sir.'

'That's the one.'

'Sir, to my knowledge we do not currently have a file open on Larry Sikorski.'

'Very good. Very good. Sikorski's a man of impeccable character – does lots of work for good causes. I just want to make sure you don't open up past wounds. After all, you've had no evidence in the past. All you've managed to do is embarrass the hell out of us with the United States – Saracen is, after all, America's finest banking institution – and we don't want a repeat of that sort of thing, do we?'

'Of course not, sir.'

'Jolly good, then. I'll pass on your regards to the Chancellor, shall I?'

'Please do. Thank you, sir.'

Amanda replaced the receiver. She immediately dialled Arnaud Veyrieras' extension.

Niccolo was running late. It was four minutes past three. He collected the four remaining copies of his statement and scurried across the trading floor to the lifts, where Paddy was already waiting.

As the doors closed, he wondered what sort of hand Paddy would play. He was up against America's largest investment banking machine, and all he had on his side was Charlie's wild card.

Louise and Rupert were already in the HR offices with – to Niccolo's surprise – Dudley Rabinowitz, Saracen's Lang's corpulent Chief Compliance Officer. They were tucking into tea and biscuits, and Niccolo's entrance broke up the party. All five attendees shook hands, and spaced themselves round the table.

Dudley kicked off the show with the authority of a headmaster. 'The purpose of today's meeting is to assess whether Niccolo Lamparelli is capable of performing his duties as a telecoms analyst to the high standards expected by Saracen Laing. Louise Horsforth is here to act as mediator, so I shall hand over to her with no further delay.' And he sat down.

'This is a disciplinary hearing,' repeated Louise. Her plain beige two-piece looked as though she meant business, but she spoke like a fledgling administrator. 'Both sides will be given an opportunity to make their case. I will ensure that there is an atmosphere of fair play. I will adjudicate in the event of any disputes. My decisions will be final.' She turned to Paddy. 'Patrick O'Shea is in attendance as Niccolo's witness. Witnesses are here to observe and only to observe.'

'Can I take notes?' asked Paddy, uninvited.

'I will make notes. At the end of the meeting I will set Niccolo some objectives. Failure to meet these objectives will result in his immediate dismissal. Do you understand, Niccolo?'

Niccolo nodded. 'Before we start, can I say a few words?'

Louise agreed.

'I would like it on record,' said Niccolo, 'that I do not believe a disciplinary hearing is appropriate in these circumstances. I have done nothing to warrant any type of disciplinary review. On the contrary, my performance has been exemplary, and I have a document here that will prove it. I further wish it to be noted that I attend today under protest, and that I will not submit to any arbitrary list of objectives unilaterally imposed upon me by you as a result of this meeting. I consider this entire process to be unfair, unwarranted and illegal.'

He sat down to deafening silence.

Louise coughed delicately. 'Thank you, Niccolo,' she said. 'Rupert, perhaps you can explain to Niccolo why he is here.'

At first Rupert appeared nervous, uneasy, apprehensive. However, after a few moments during which he shuffled some papers, he spoke professionally, laying out very clearly the bank's case against Niccolo. His argument centred on events leading up to the sending of the apology letter to Kenneth Oakes – something that had been 'highly embarrassing for the bank'. He described Niccolo's work as 'of poor quality' and Niccolo himself as 'the new kid on the block who simply can't cut it as an analyst'. Niccolo had to sit and listen as Rupert denigrated the Telespaña report published in his name, reminding the panel that it had failed the Ratings Committee. He cited support of his assessments from Larry and Odile and others in the bank, and summed up by saying, 'Our Telecoms team is half the size it used to be. Our reputation is everything. I can't afford to have my analysts issuing any more letters of apology.'

Throughout Rupert's speech, Niccolo's mind worked overtime. He knew beyond all doubt that Rupert had set him up, but not why. And he also knew that his name on the Telespaña report meant that he, not Rupert, would have to take the rap. There had to be something he could say or do. But as the web of spin slipped effortlessly from Rupert's lips, Niccolo began to feel he had been outmanoeuvred.

Try as he might, he simply couldn't understand why so many of his colleagues had turned against him.

Larry, for instance. Larry, who had hired him, had rated him the golden boy, now wanted him fired for incompetence. Had Globecom's management been putting pressure on him? Were the M&A guys upstairs on the verge of securing a deal? Would they back off now that the bank had taken him off the stock and switched the rating to Buy? Or did they want his head on a platter no matter what?

Or Rupert, who had never voiced a single complaint regarding Niccolo's work, until now. Was he scared for his own future? Was he merely preserving his own bonus? Or was this revenge on the 'new kid on the block' who had stolen his glory?

And lastly, Odile – Odile, who had been a pillar of strength to Niccolo throughout his two years at Saracen Laing. He still believed that that damning memo was out of character for her. What had caused her to switch sides? And why now?

He stood up. 'In support of my case,' he said, 'I have prepared a statement that I would like you all to read now.' He handed out copies of the document to Dudley and Louise. 'Unlike the Telespaña report, I wrote it myself.'

'What do you mean, Niccolo?' Louise asked.

'Rupert wrote the Telespaña report. Didn't you, Rupert?'

'Really?' enquired Rupert. 'Whose name is on the report, Niccolo?'

'Mine, but . . .'

'But what?'

'Do you deny writing the Telespaña report?' persisted Niccolo.

'Yes.' Rupert folded his arms.

'You're lying!'

'Will you please stop this – now!' Louise interrupted. 'The only name I can see on the report is Niccolo's.'

'In that case, read my statement!' Niccolo almost shouted. 'Read the newspaper cuttings, the client statements, the external reviews – everything describes the rising career path of a star analyst, not the dud you lot say I am. So who is it who's lying?'

By the end of the meeting, two things were clear. First, Louise did not appear to have a clue about how investment banking worked. And second, Niccolo, Rupert and Dudley were equally clueless about all matters related to HR. It made the notion of any sort of reconciliation seem rather remote.

Paddy, the wild card, turned out to be not so wild after all. He repeatedly ignored Louise's pleas to be quiet and was twice reprimanded by Dudley – to Niccolo's delight – for opening his mouth out of turn. He protected Niccolo's corner like a Rottweiler, tearing Rupert apart over the slightest slip and arguing Niccolo's case with conviction. Rupert challenged Paddy with vigour, but mustered only a fraction of the eloquence.

In a final assault, Paddy struck at the very core of the process, depicting the hearing as a waste of time and money. 'Here,' he declared, 'we have five – *five*, count them – senior members of staff, discussing a non-issue, at an average of three hundred pounds per hour, for two hours. We have just cost the bank three thousand pounds. And that's just the start. This sorry saga could drag on for months. Which means Saracen Laing could lose hundreds of thousands of pounds. And for what?' he asked rhetorically.

Heated arguments promptly broke out. Louise struggled to keep control, eventually raising her voice to declare, 'Look, I am not – repeat *not* – going to tolerate any shit, OK?'

Silence fell. 'Whatever that means,' Rupert mumbled.

Dudley said little, giving the outward impression of genuine impartiality. Afterwards, when the formal discussions were over, he reverted almost by default to DBK's share price performance. 'Fucking thing's tanked thirty per cent this week,' he grunted. 'Probably going to fall a bit more yet.'

Later, in the elevator, Paddy said to Niccolo, 'Rabinowitz only had half his brain in gear. Bloody DBK! This time next week, you'll probably find him sitting on the loo sawing his wrists with a blunt razor!'

As the elevator doors opened, Niccolo burst out, 'Lying bastard!'

'Who?' asked Paddy.

'Rupert.'

'Well, as they say in Belfast: why stab a guy in the back when you can stab him in the stomach and watch his face crumple before you?'

Later that afternoon, Charlie sauntered round to Niccolo's desk. 'So how did the hearing go?' he asked impatiently.

'It went OK.'

'Did Larry turn up?'

361

'Nope.'

'Aw, shit, he was never going to turn up, was he? Nothing sticks to that fucker. Teflon's his middle name.'

'Dudley was there.'

'Duddles? That's good. He's an easy one to play. He's got no agenda except his own. He sees every meeting as an opportunity to offload his theories about global warming and get DBK's share price up. You just need to convince him that you're a born-again believer in fucking DBK, and you're home and dry. The thing is, kiddo – Dud may be totally mad, but he's also totally Head of Compliance. And we need his sorry ass on our side, *comprende*?'

That evening, Larry had an important engagement at Number 11 Downing Street. The entire trading floor knew about it because Anne-Marie told them.

'The Chancellor's very keen to meet Larry,' she explained earnestly. 'He wants to learn all about how American investment banks have made London the financial centre of the world in an age where British investment banks have all but disappeared.' She sounded like someone who had learned her spiel by rote, and under duress.

'Do I hear a chorus of *fucking Yanks*?' growled Charlie, as Anne-Marie faded into the distance. 'I mean, things were jolly different, what-ho, before *we Yanks* came along in a thundering herd. In the old days, you guys got up at a decently late hour, put on your tailor-made pinstripes, came in to work and had a jolly good natter. At ten o'clock the tea lady would come round with a hot cross bun or a bacon sarnie. If the markets went up three per cent by lunchtime and you made two per cent, you were doing well – at least you hadn't lost any money. Then you'd have a few drinks at half past twelve and write off the afternoon. Damn civilised, what! But then those dreadful upstart Yanks invaded London, and the

362

fun stopped overnight. Pinstripes replaced by polo shirts and chinos! Lunch was for wimps! If the markets went up three per cent, you had to make five per cent. Me, I guess I kinda preferred it the way it was before my countrymen came and spoiled the fun. The English gentleman's bond was ripped up and chucked on the rubbish tip of history. So if Larry tells you his word is his bond, my advice is – take the bond.'

CHAPTER 43

The following day, at precisely 9 a.m., Treasury officials, accompanied by uniformed police, marched into Amanda Sanderson's office at the FSA to deliver documents carrying the seal of Her Majesty's Government informing her that she was to be immediately relieved of her position. Her replacement – a steely middle-aged career civil servant – arrived with the invading entourage.

They found the Head of Enforcement in the midst of a meeting with one of her senior managers, Arnaud Veyrieras. The officials told her that their instructions were to escort her off the premises forthwith. They gave her permission to take her handbag and overcoat, but nothing else.

Amanda was taken utterly by surprise. She did not put up a fight. She simply asked, 'On whose authority are you acting?'

'On the authority of the Chancellor of the Exchequer, ma'am,' replied the steely middle-aged career civil servant.

'On what grounds?'

'I cannot discuss this matter on grounds of national security, Ms Sanderson.'

'May I at least inform my staff?'

'That will not be necessary,' came the reply, as if her replacement had anticipated every conceivable eventuality. He pulled out two typed documents and presented them to Amanda. 'Your resignation letter and a press release have already been prepared.'

Amanda looked at Arnaud. Arnaud looked back at his boss. Neither knew quite how to interpret the Treasury official's statement, but both recognised the futility of further debate.

Saracen Laing's senior management took great pride in the way they looked after staff and their families, and publicised the generosity of their employee benefits schemes with much fanfare. The third-party suppliers who serviced these schemes, however, showed markedly less regard for the substance of the HR policy directives they were employed to fulfil.

On paper, the Saracen Laing death-in-service scheme was exceptionally generous. In practice, it had not paid out a penny for years, and for good reason. Taking care of dead employees' families was a costly business. Earlier, the claims department at Farmers & General, the insurance company subcontracted to cover DIS risk, had refused to pay out on Jack's death. Death by suicide, they argued, was not covered by their policy.

But in view of the adverse publicity attached to this particular case, Saracen Laing decided after careful deliberation to pay *ex gratia* a sum of £1.2 million from the bank's own balance sheet to Jack Ford's widow, 'in recognition of his ten years' distinguished service'. The last thing they needed was the widow of a disgraced employee selling her story, warts and all, to the press.

The full amount was credited that very morning by telegraphic transfer directly to Donna Ford's bank account. Later that same morning, a letter was sent to her, by first-class post, detailing the bank's decision and expressing their sincerest condolences. *The bank recognises the stresses an analyst's career can place on family life*, the letter began. It went on to say that the *ex gratia* payment represented a full and final settlement of the bank's liabilities to all dependents of Jack Ford, and asked Mrs Ford to sign it and send it back by return post to show her acceptance of these terms. The final paragraph of the letter made it crystal clear that if Donna so much as uttered a word to the outside world about either the amount or the terms of the settlement, Saracen Laing would use every means at their disposal to claw the money back. And with that, Jack Ford's personnel file at Saracen Laing was closed.

Before the letter arrived, Raj – aka Robbie – at the State & County Bank call centre in Mumbai notified Donna, who found it difficult to hide her surprise.

'But I was told the insurance company had rejected my claim,' she said, trying not to sound too thrilled.

She heard Raj fiddle around with his keyboard. 'This credit came from Saracen Laing, madam,' he said eventually. 'The reference I have states that it is an *ex gratia* payment only.'

'I see,' said Donna, who didn't see at all.

'May I help you with anything else, madam?'

'No thank you,' said Donna, replacing the receiver.

She racked her brain for a few moments, but came up with nothing. She had no idea why the bank had paid her £1,200,000. But she wasn't about to ask too many questions. She slipped on a jacket, picked up her handbag, left the house and took a black cab to Bond Street.

Charlie was right, thought Niccolo. Paddy had turned out to be trustworthy after all. But things had gone too far. Niccolo knew he could no longer work for Larry. Nor could he stick around, waiting to be fired.

He sensed Rupert's presence just behind him.

'Fancy a drink?' asked Rupert, as if they were the best of friends.

'I don't think so.'

'Come on, Nicco,' pleaded Rupert. 'I did what I had to do up there.'

'So did I.'

'Good. So we're cool?'

Niccolo let his face do the talking. It wasn't a very pretty face, and it told Rupert to get lost.

But Rupert failed to read the message. 'At least let me buy you a drink. I want to help you, Nicco.'

'You could start by telling the truth.'

Rupert carefully surveyed the trading floor. A few late-nighters, mainly Americans, were still at their desks. He closed in, and whispered into Niccolo's ear, 'Listen, Nicco, you can get yourself out of this mess, if you play your cards right.'

'What cards?' Niccolo asked coldly.

'Just apologise and agree to Larry's terms, for Christ's sake!'

'Don't you see, Ru? I could be the best analyst in the world, but Larry is still going to fire me. You know why? Because he can.'

And with that, Niccolo slipped on his jacket and left the Saracen Laing building.

At the police station, Niccolo pleaded with DS Harcourt to reopen the Jack Ford case. Unfortunately, explained the detective superintendent matter-of-factly, the police investigation into Jack's death had been closed by the coroner and there was nothing the police could do unless new evidence came to light.

Finally the DS agreed to give Niccolo some face time. Within seconds they were in a police interrogation room and WPC McKeever had been called in. The conversation was taped.

Niccolo poured his heart out to the two police officers. He explained in detail why he felt a verdict of suicide did not stack up. He told them of Donna's affair with Larry and the motive it provided for murder. He told them about the message Jack had left for him the night he died. Jack was on to something – something big and nasty and dirty – and it almost certainly involved Larry. That provided a second motive.

He harassed them, begged them to reopen the case, at least to do a bit more digging. He asked them to search Larry's Kensington flat. To no avail. Their hands were tied. Nobody was above the law, they explained sympathetically, but due process had been followed and a judgement had been made. And in the absence of further evidence – substantiated evidence – that was the end of it. Go home, they said, feeling sorry for him. Go home.

That night, Niccolo strolled down to Kensington in search of answers. He wandered up and down Onslow Square, passing by Larry's flat many times. He peered in through the windows. No one was in. He wondered if Jack had stood there when he left that final message on his mobile phone. He wondered whether Jack had been killed inside that flat, and even whether Donna had been mixed up in the whole mess from the very beginning.

Finally he called it a night. He drifted east and then north, cutting through Hyde Park towards Mayfair until, a few minutes before midnight, he found himself at the Hilton, walking down the stairs to Trader Vic's. He ordered a Mai Tai, slumped over the bar, dropped his head in his hands and groaned.

Another Mai Tai followed, then he moved on to Scotch. Quite a lot of Scotch.

He remembered the bouncers putting him into a black cab. That was all he remembered.

In the morning, he found on the doormat a letter that had arrived the day before. He felt tears coming to his eyes as he read his own name and address, painstakingly transcribed by a man who could not read English. The letter was beautifully written in Japanese.

> *Dear Nicco-san,*
>
> *My heart was saddened by the news of Jack-san's death. Jack-san was like a son to me, as you are. And it is as a father that I mourn him, as I mourned Yoshiro.*
>
> *I remember when the three of you played as little boys. Then my life was full of happiness because your friendship was stronger than anything I had ever seen. Jack-san was always the responsible one, do you remember? Yoshiro-san, he was the mischievous one, always playing pranks. And you, Nicco-san, you were the tiger – carefree and wild. The three of you would do anything for each other. Now you are the only one I have left.*
>
> *Protect Jack-san's honour, Nicco-san. Find out who killed my boy. I know you will not fail me.*
>
> *Please tell Bronwen-san of my great sadness. And send my respectful greetings to Isabella-san.*
>
> *With much love,*
> *Mizuno*

As he read the letter out loud, Niccolo felt Mizuno's presence ingrained unmistakably in each and every word. Without hesitation, he made a solemn vow that he would carry out the old man's wishes. It wasn't going to be easy, but somehow he had to prove that Larry was behind Jack's death.

Once Amanda Sanderson had been removed from her post, it became increasingly clear that several other careers within the Enforcement Division were also in the firing line. Arnaud was quick to realise that his was one of those in jeopardy. He had broken the rules too many times. The steely middle-aged career civil servant who now headed up the Enforcement Division was unlikely to be as lenient as Sanderson.

Arnaud applied for a transfer to the Serious Fraud Office. Given the circumstances of Sanderson's departure, his application was likely to be approved fast. The new man from Whitehall would, if he had any sense, want to clear the decks.

When Picton informed Mubarak of the size of Larry Sikorski's expenses bill, the Prince was none too pleased.

'The money is to be used to grease the wheels of power – to limit our downside risk, should something go wrong, Your Highness,' said Picton, repeating word for word what Larry had told him.

'Something already *has* gone wrong, you fool,' snapped Prince Mubarak. 'A man is dead!'

Picton immediately deflected the blame. 'With respect, Your Highness, I am trying to put right Sikorski's mistake.'

'By bribing British government officials?' the Prince snorted. 'I thought bribes were illegal in the United Kingdom.'

'It's not a bribe; it's a political donation. Lots of people make political donations. It's quite normal.'

'Bribe? Donation? What's the difference?'

'Well, Your Highness,' Picton answered, as if it were blindingly obvious. 'If you call it a political donation, no one goes to jail.'

CHAPTER 44

'Hi, Domingo,' Niccolo said breezily as he stormed through the large glass revolving doors of the Saracen Laing building on Tuesday morning with a skinny cappuccino from Toni's Café.

But there was no answering smile. In its place was the sullen gaze of a man ordered to do someone else's dirty work.

'Mr Lamparelli, please forgive me,' Domingo said, blocking Niccolo's path. 'I have been instructed to collect your security pass and mobile phone.'

Niccolo handed over his pass and phone without fuss. So Larry was one step ahead of him. Perhaps that was why the slippery bastard had made it to the top. 'Sure, Domingo. Who gave the orders?'

Domingo smiled nervously. 'Mr Sikorski, sir. He says that you are to be escorted to Meeting Room Two on the seventh floor as soon as you arrive. He will meet you there.' Domingo summoned a tall blond security guard across the lobby. 'Yuri will take you up, sir.'

On the seventh floor, Niccolo was asked to take a seat. 'Mr Sikorski will arrive shortly, sir,' said Yuri. The door shut and the lock clicked. As the guard's footsteps petered out, Niccolo surveyed his surroundings and contemplated his fate. He was about to face the full wrath of a maniac – a maniac in charge of an awesome investment banking machine – ready to crush anything and anyone in his way. He felt like a bird in a cage, awaiting his tormentor.

A quarter of an hour passed.

Finally the door flicked open and Louise came in, apologising profusely. 'I'm really sorry to keep you waiting,' she said nervously. 'Larry sends his apologies; he has some important meetings to attend to. He's asked me to stand in for him.'

It was the oldest trick in the book. Keep the other side waiting, and then send someone junior to do the talking. Wear the other side down before you move in for the kill. 'I assume Larry gave the order to call in my security pass and mobile?' Niccolo double-checked.

'Yes. I'm sorry things have turned out—'

Before she could finish, Niccolo interjected rudely, 'It's Larry that I should be having this conversation with. If he's in another meeting right now, he's in the wrong meeting!'

'Look, off the record, I don't know what's going on. But Larry won't actually be turning up at all. He's given me instructions to offer you a deal.'

'I already have a deal. It's called my employment contract.'

'I'm afraid your actions may have invalidated that, Niccolo.' Before he could answer, Louise hurried on, 'When Larry read your email yesterday, he said that your boneheaded refusal to comply with our disciplinary procedures could be construed as nothing other than gross misconduct. It puts you in breach of your employment contract. He has asked me to inform you that it would after all be in your interests to resign.' By now, Louise's voice had become rather hostile. All the coltish awkwardness that had seemed rather endearing now began to irritate him, and he noticed flaws in her appearance that had never bothered him before. 'He also says that he cannot run the risk of allowing you back on the trading floor. But he is prepared to offer one month's pay in addition to your contractual one month's notice. I believe that is very generous. Our employee handbook states that dismissal for gross misconduct allows us to remove you from office without compensation.'

Bullshit, thought Niccolo. But his knowledge of employment law was insufficient to counter her statement with any authority. What the hell. He would counter anyway. 'The employee handbook also says that you are required to ensure that all parties act in a fair manner. Do you think Larry is acting fairly, Louise?'

Louise clasped her hands as if to bolster her own courage. 'I think that you are in a regrettable position and I strongly advise you to take this offer, Niccolo. It's the best you'll get.'

'Louise, it's a ridiculous offer!'

'I am duty-bound to inform you that in the event that you do not resign and Saracen Laing is forced to fire you for gross misconduct, you may be struck off the FSA register.'

'I suppose I need to see a lawyer, then.'

'That might be wise. I have taken the liberty of preparing a termination agreement, which details the generous package that we are offering you.' She pulled out some papers. 'As I said, we will be offering you two months' pay. This offer is conditional – you are not permitted to discuss its terms or the circumstances surrounding your departure with anyone other than your employment lawyer. If you do, you will be in breach of both your employment terms and the conditions of this termination letter. The offer will be withdrawn by noon tomorrow should you fail to accept by then.'

Niccolo collected the papers and got to his feet. Louise wished him well and called Security. 'Please escort Mr Lamparelli off the premises,' she said.

Niccolo found his mind wandering. Clear thinking evaded him. Then it occurred to him that he might never return to the building. Yesterday's dirty gym kit was still underneath his desk, and then there were his CDs. He was very attached to his CDs. 'If you don't mind, I need to pass by my desk to pick up my personal stuff,' he said to Yuri.

'I'm sorry, sir. I have strict instructions from Mr Sikorski to keep you off the trading floor.'

'Well in that case, why don't we go and see Mr Sikorski and ask him to change those instructions, because I'm not leaving this building without my CDs.'

'But sir, you are to be escorted directly out of the building.'

Niccolo folded his arms and looked the guard in the eye. Yuri was taller and heavier than Niccolo, built like a professional rugby player. But to Niccolo's surprise, the security guard merely said, 'I guess there's no harm in that, sir. We can pass by your desk if you make it quick.'

When they arrived at the trading floor, none of the analysts were at their desks. The big clock on the wall said it was twenty to eight. Everyone was still in the morning meeting. Niccolo glanced at the video wall. The FTSE 100 had fallen seventy-five points on the previous day and New York was down three per cent overnight. But what did he care?

Pierce the Prop trader sat quietly sipping coffee at his desk, monitoring his positions. He noticed Niccolo's uniformed escort, but remained uncharacteristically quiet. In an investment bank, no one ever admits to being friends – or even acquaintances – with someone who is about to be escorted out of the building.

As Niccolo collected his CDs and gym kit, unplugged the docking station for his iPod and packed it away, his mind travelled back two years, and he remembered why he had joined the bank. He had been awestruck by the legendary Larry Sikorski. He had wanted to emulate his every move, learn from him, pay homage to him, breathe the same air as him. And, of course, Jack was already working there. Two years later, the dream was shattered. Larry had turned out to be a slippery, murdering bastard. Niccolo Lamparelli, the golden boy, was discharged, disgraced and dishonoured. And Jack was dead.

After waving one last goodbye to the empty trading floor, he nodded to the security guard, who escorted him to the front entrance and, as politely as such things can be done, threw him out on to the street.

Niccolo breathed in the City air. Even the carbon monoxide fug of the street smelt fresher than the clinically air-conditioned atmosphere of Saracen Laing.

The young man in the Hampstead estate agent's office was impressed by the address the new client gave him.

'That sounds like a highly desirable property, madam. I'm sure we can handle the sale successfully for you.'

He wondered whether the crisp-voiced caller was perhaps downsizing. If he was quick, he might be able to pull off the sale of a nicely located flat as well. But even as he opened his mouth to ask, she cut in. 'If I were to buy another property through you, what sort of offer would you make me as regards your commission?'

The young man floundered for a moment. 'I'd have to look into that, madam. What sort of property are you looking to buy?'

His heart sang when she answered airily, 'Oh, something a *lot* bigger!'

Later that morning, Niccolo was officially suspended by the bank. His instructions were to get some 'rest and recreation' at home whilst negotiations over his settlement continued in his absence. As soon as he arrived home, the phone rang.

'Nicco?' He recognised the voice at once.

'Hi, Donna. Where are you calling from?'

'I'm calling from a friend's place.'

'Cut the crap, Donna. I know you're sleeping with Larry.'

It was a few long moments before Donna responded. 'Nicco, I know you blame me for Jack's death. Sometimes I blame myself. But Jack and I never got on. I've found happiness now – with Larry. Can't you be pleased for me?'

Niccolo laughed. It was an angry laugh. He wanted to say many things to Donna, nasty things. He wanted to call her all sorts of names, vile names. But he did not. Instead, he simply enquired why she had called, and left it at that.

'I'm calling because I want to help you. Look, Larry tells me everything. He trusts me. If he knew I was talking to you, he'd kill me.'

That wouldn't be such a bad thing.

'He's up to something, Nicco. He has friends in high places. He says he'll crush you like a bug if you mess with him. He'll make sure that you never work in the City again. Why don't you just take whatever settlement they offer you and walk away?'

'What do you care?'

'Whatever happened between me and Jack, I still care about you, Nicco. I am still your friend.'

'You stabbed Jack in the back. You're no friend of mine.'

She ignored him and performed on cue, like an actress rehearsing her lines. 'Just take the money and run, Nicco. Please!'

'Has Larry promised you a nice juicy bonus if you twist my arm?'

'That's not fair, Nicco. Money means nothing to me.'

'That's easy to say when you're about to clean out Jack's entire estate and trade up to Larry's.'

'Fuck you, Niccolo Lamparelli! Have it your way. Just remember it was me who warned you!'

Duncan Witherspoon-Harper was a partner at Jefferson Harper White. The marketing brochure for the company showed a photo of him on a yacht. His CV had all the right credentials – a first-class law degree from Exeter University, then Guildford Law School. After ten years at Clifford Chance, in 1991 – in partnership with two of his Guildford classmates – he set up Jefferson Harper White, a firm specialising solely in employment law. Niccolo stared morosely at the floor, wondering just how expensive Duncan Witherspoon-Harper was going to turn out to be.

'I charge by the hour,' said the lawyer without preamble once they had sat down. 'My rate is eight hundred pounds plus VAT. Expenses are extra. There's a five-thousand-pound retainer.'

Niccolo had come prepared to pay extortionate rates. It did not make sense to negotiate with a negotiator, he kept telling himself, particularly since the clock had already started. So he summarised what had happened over the last month while the lawyer scribbled everything down.

Niccolo mentioned Jack's death and his theories about who was involved. He retold the stories of Lindsay Compton and Jennifer Colley, and somehow tried to link them to Jack's murder. He described Odile, Charlie, Paddy and Rupert. He described his affair with Lucy. When it came to Larry, he let himself loose.

He ended by recounting his meeting with Louise, and passed the lawyer the termination contract. 'What I'm looking for,' he concluded, 'is a quick settlement, rather than a lengthy court case.'

Mr Witherspoon-Harper read the contract slowly and carefully, circling a few paragraphs with a pencil.

Niccolo then pulled out some more papers. 'These are copies of all relevant correspondence between myself and Larry Sikorski.'

The lawyer read the material in silence. 'You and Jack Ford were very close?' he enquired at last. 'Larry Sikorski knows that, I take it?'

'Yes, Jack was my closest friend for twenty years – more.'

'Have you discussed your theories with anyone in the bank – your theories about Larry being involved in Jack's murder?'

'Yes . . . well . . . sort of. I've told Charlie and Odile.' Niccolo fidgeted in his chair, then added, 'Charlie I trust; Odile was a mistake.'

'Has Jack's death affected your work?'

'It's totally fucked up my mind.'

'I see.' The lawyer did not look too pleased. 'Could you handle a tough legal battle in your present state?'

'I'd rather avoid one.'

'From what you've told me, Niccolo, I'd say the likelihood of a successful claim by you for constructive dismissal is very high.'

'But they haven't fired me yet. I've only been suspended.'

'You don't have to be fired to be *fired*, if you see what I mean. Constructive dismissal means that your employer continues to employ you, but you are *effectively* dismissed.'

'I'd rather quit.'

'That's exactly what they want you to do. Legally, that's by far their safest option. It means their liability is limited to your contractual entitlement. If you bring a constructive dismissal case against them, it may get messy. Banks hate messy situations.'

'What are the risks?'

'Too many to cover today. Suffice to say, you'll need balls of steel to see this thing through. Mr Lamparelli, think about what you're letting yourself in for. Your girlfriend's just left you. Your best friend is dead. Your job is on the line. And your reputation could be ripped to shreds. They're probably betting that you don't have the stomach for a fight.'

'Let's assume I have – what are my options?'

'Option One is to see if you can keep your job and get through the eight-week disciplinary process. Option Two is to accept the two months' notice they're offering and resign. Option Three is to negotiate a better deal but to settle before taking any formal legal action against Saracen Laing. Option Four is to sue their asses off.'

'There's no way I can work for Larry Sikorski after this. I don't stand a chance. I need to get out now.'

'That leaves Options Two, Three and Four. I don't recommend Option Two. Their offer is an insult. It implies in effect that you are guilty as charged. So that leaves Option Three for now, and Option Four as a last resort.'

'What would I get if I won?'

'Legally, according to your employment contract, you're entitled to one month's pay, accrued holiday and any guaranteed bonus.'

'My contract says the guarantee is invalidated if I'm ever called into a disciplinary hearing.'

'They always try that. OK, I'll rule out the bonus for now. Second, there's compensation for constructive dismissal. If Saracen Laing have effectively terminated your employment without good cause, you're entitled to compensation.'

Witherspoon-Harper examined the employment contract. 'Let's say a year's pay. Chuck in the fifty per cent guaranteed bonus and a quarter of a mil for general bad behaviour on their part—'

'How easy is it to win a constructive dismissal case?' enquired Niccolo.

'I'd say the odds are in your favour. A tribunal would probably consider that those emails demonstrate clearly that Sikorski had prejudged the outcome of the disciplinary process. You have kept copies of all the emails, haven't you? Good. Investment banks

379

have a tendency to lose important electronic documents when it suits them.' The lawyer leaned back and flicked through Niccolo's file. 'You say Larry asked you to resign?'

'Yes. But I've got nothing in writing.'

'Doesn't matter. Employment tribunals hate it when employers threaten employees.'

'Larry's got a history of bullying employees. The problem is, no one's likely to come forward. He's paid them all off.' Niccolo thought hard about what he was about to say. 'Or killed them.'

Witherspoon-Harper looked up sharply. 'Do you have proof of that?'

'Of course not.'

'In that case, let's not get carried away, Mr Lamparelli. We have enough to be getting on with.' The lawyer leaned back, twiddling his pencil. 'These types of cases – where an employer tries to get rid of an employee on bogus disciplinary charges – are becoming more and more common.'

'Don't employers worry about being sued?'

'Of course,' the lawyer said drily. 'Which is why many in my profession have made a good living by drafting employment contracts handbooks designed specifically to allow employers to fire the likes of you on what most of us would call highly dubious grounds. They effectively legalise bogus dismissals. But very few employees have the courage to take on such powerful institutions. If I were you, I'd request a further clause in the termination contract to protect your rights. After all, Saracen have done an excellent job of protecting their own rights whilst denying you many of yours.'

After the meeting, Niccolo got a cappuccino from a local café and sat in a nearby park to read his notes and formulate the next leg of his strategy. Then he phoned Louise.

'Louise, I've just seen an employment lawyer. We need to talk.'

'Talk.'

'Well, after giving it a lot of thought, I feel that I have no option but . . . to follow Larry Sikorski's advice. I will resign. However, I need to discuss my terms with you. Do you have sufficient authority to negotiate a settlement?'

'Of course. Why don't we meet at five today?'

'Fine.'

The Prime Minister ushered in the chief fund-raiser for the party and got down to business. 'So, where are we?'

'Well,' said the chief fund-raiser, 'it looks as if things have taken a turn for the better. Have a look at this,' he said, offering the Prime Minister a sheet of paper containing several names with monetary amounts beside them.

'Who's this one?' asked the Prime Minister, pointing to the largest amount.

'Ah, that's Larry Sikorski. One of the country's finest bankers.'

'Yes, I thought I recognised the name. Doesn't he work at . . .'

'Saracen Laing? Yes, PM. I met him at Number 11 the other day. The Chancellor was holding a dinner for the banking sector. They're going through turmoil at the moment, but Sikorski is an experienced hand. His unit at Saracen remains profitable whilst others are reporting record losses.'

'Impressive. Is he looking for a peerage?'

'He's been a supporter of the party since '97. We could certainly use him in the second Chamber, PM.'

Louise came down to the lobby of the Saracen Laing building within forty-five seconds of being notified of Niccolo's arrival. She led him to a private meeting room on the seventh floor. Once they were seated, Niccolo began. 'As I said on the phone, I feel I'm left with no choice but to resign.'

'That may be best for all parties,' replied Louise carefully.

'However, the proposal you made to me earlier is unacceptable.'

'It's a final offer. It's not up for discussion.'

Niccolo looked puzzled.

Louise continued, 'Larry and I are not prepared to discuss the matter any further. Under the circumstances, I must tell you that our offer of one month's contractual notice plus an additional month's grace is an extremely generous one and I advise you to take it.'

'My lawyer believes that I have a strong case for constructive dismissal. I would like to discuss a settlement.'

Louise sat up. 'I must warn you that making threats is a dangerous business and one that the bank will not entertain. You should understand that Saracen Laing will do everything in its power to defend itself against false and malicious allegations.'

'Listen, Louise, we both know that Larry's resignation is the one that should be on the table, not mine. This guy gets rid of anyone who gets in his way. He's done it before – with Lindsay Compton, and with Jennifer Colley. He runs the research department like a child throwing a tantrum. You've got to stop him!'

'There's nothing I can do unless you issue a formal complaint,' Louise said finally. 'If I receive a complaint from you, then I can launch an investigation.' There was a glint of encouragement in her eyes.

'Then what?'

Louise spoke with great care. 'My findings would be presented to Mr Sukuhara, who would ultimately decide Larry's fate.'

Niccolo deliberated for a few moments. Banks never fired incompetent heads of department – that made their internal controls look weak. Moreover, a formal complaint would turn Niccolo into a whistle-blower. He would become unemployable overnight. No deal.

'I'm meeting a friend for lunch tomorrow who works for the enforcement arm of the FSA,' he said. 'I'll be asking him for advice on how to handle this matter. In particular, I'd like to ask him his views on conflicts of interest within the Equity Research divisions of investment banks. Of course, it'll just be an informal chat.'

Chats with the Financial Services Authority were never informal. Louise was clearly aware of this. 'I think you should have a word with Mr Sukuhara first.' She picked up the phone and dialled John Sukuhara's number, diverting the call to speakerphone.

Niccolo heard Bulldog barking down the other end of the line. 'Mr Sukuhara's in a meeting just now.'

Louise stood up to April. 'I'd like you to interrupt him. Please tell him that Louise Horsforth wishes to see him, concerning Mr Lamparelli.' She spoke slowly, as if talking to a retarded child.

Bulldog put them on hold. Five long minutes later she returned. 'Today's your lucky day. He'll see you right away.'

DS Harcourt went through his notes once more. He simply couldn't square up the evidence in the Ford file. Jack Ford's wife had a lover. The lover had a work-related dispute with the deceased, though Harcourt had not managed to get to the bottom of that line of enquiry. Then there was the lover's past form. No convictions, but a chequered history, and a reputation for getting rid of disloyal staff; according to Arnaud Veyrieras, his methods could sometimes be brutal, often illegal.

He rang Arnaud at the FSA.

'I'm sorry, sir. No one of that name works here,' the operator informed him.

'Amanda Sanderson, then?'

'Miss Sanderson's on sabbatical, sir.'

'Her replacement?' This prompted the operator to put up her defences like a barricade. Harcourt fielded all her security questions until, in the end, she reluctantly put him through.

'What can I do for you, DS Harcourt?' asked the steely middle-aged career civil servant who now headed the Enforcement Division.

'A member of your staff was helping me with some enquiries on a case I'm investigating. His name is Arnaud Veyrieras. I'm unable to trace either him or his boss Amanda Sanderson. Could you tell me where I can find him, please?'

'May I ask the nature of your investigation?'

'The unexplained death of a young stock analyst. The deceased's name is Jack Ford.'

'I understand that the case you refer to is closed. And if my memory serves me correctly, the coroner issued a suicide verdict, did he not?'

DS Harcourt lowered his tone. 'Sir, I just need to know where I can find Arnaud Veyrieras.'

'I'm sure you understand, Detective Superintendent, that I cannot forward staff contact details without their permission.'

'In that case, may I have access to the files Arnaud kept on Larry Sikorski?'

'That sort of information is highly confidential, as you well know, Detective Superintendent. I'm afraid I cannot release any FSA files without the appropriate authority.'

'You're the Head of Enforcement. How much authority do you need?'

'I'm afraid I cannot help you, DS Harcourt.' He hung up.

DS Harcourt kicked his desk hard and unleashed an avalanche of swear words.

*

As he and Louise approached Sukuhara's office, Niccolo beamed with confidence. The fact that the most senior Saracen banker outside New York had seen fit to meet him at a moment's notice gave him all the courage he needed. They walked straight past Bulldog unchecked and into Sukuhara's suite. The Japanese-American rose from his desk, lowered the television volume with his remote control and offered them a seat.

'Thank you very much for seeing me, John,' Niccolo said. 'I'm sorry to have to meet you under such circumstances.'

Sukuhara smiled flatly. Louise provided a succinct explanation for their presence. 'Mr Lamparelli is not happy with the offer we have made him.'

'I see. What do you have to say for yourself, Niccolo?'

'Mr Sukuhara, in the two years that I have been with Saracen Laing I have performed exceptionally well. I'm a good analyst. Your sales force love my work. Your traders rate me highly. And your clients make a lot of money off me. Only one man wants me out – Larry Sikorski.'

Sukuhara nodded sympathetically, but said nothing.

'My lawyer tells me that I have a very strong case for constructive dismissal. But I love this bank and would never want to do anything to bring it into disrepute . . . unless I had to.'

Still Sukuhara remained non-committal.

Niccolo continued. 'The fact is, sir, I'm leaving not because of my own mistakes, but because of Sikorski's. I request you to improve on the bank's offer so that we can settle this amicably.'

Sukuhara maintained his poker face.

'The figure my lawyer mentioned was in the region of a million.'

'That's ridiculous!' cried Louise, feigning horror.

Suddenly Sukuhara jettisoned his serenity. 'I'll think about your request. Now I need a favour from you. Tell me what I should do with Sikorski.'

Niccolo drew back suspiciously. Why was Sukuhara asking him to comment on his superior? Deciding he had nothing to lose, he answered, 'I believe Larry follows some pretty flaky practices that could get us into trouble with the FSA. First, he's too cosy with the M&A boys on the sixth floor – there's a clear conflict there. Second, he's too subservient to our clients – when Globecom told us to jump, he made us all jump – and that compromises our independence. Larry Sikorski is a litigation disaster waiting to happen. More to the point, he's created a culture of fear. That's no way to produce creative independent research. Nor is it the way to retain good analysts.'

'Hmmn.' Sukuhara rose to his feet and paced the room. 'OK,' he said after a minute or two. 'I'll get back to you later today.'

That night, Gino and Olivia invited Niccolo round for dinner. Teresa and Silvia were fast asleep upstairs. The conversation all evening centred around Jack.

'How can you be so sure Larry was behind it?' asked Gino.

'I don't know,' mumbled Niccolo incoherently. 'I just feel it. I can't rest until I know Jack's killer is behind bars.'

'OK,' said Gino. 'What have we got on Larry?'

Niccolo knocked back his glass and held it out for a refill. 'The night Jack died, he said he'd found out something bad about Larry. Second, Larry was the last person to see Jack alive.'

'You don't know that, Nicco. You weren't there.'

Niccolo became agitated. 'Listen, I got a voice message on my phone at nine o'clock the night he died. Jack was standing outside Larry's place when he made the call. He told me he was going in to have a chat with Larry. The police say the time of death was around midnight. How much more do you need, for Christ's sake!'

'That still leaves three hours unaccounted for, Nicco.'

'Third,' stressed Niccolo, 'Larry's done this sort of thing before – Lindsay Compton's parents mysteriously got kidnapped and beaten up when Lindsay refused to follow Larry's orders.'

'Those are just rumours, aren't they?'

'Whose side are you on!' snapped Niccolo. 'Fourth, Larry's trying to fire me. Maybe he was trying to get at me through Jack—'

'I'm sorry, Nicco,' interrupted Gino. 'Now you're beginning to sound paranoid. Look, I'm playing devil's advocate here.'

Olivia finished her dessert and began to clear the table. 'Promise me you won't do anything stupid, Nicco.'

'She's right,' agreed Gino. 'Don't lay a finger on Larry. Jail is not a pretty place, believe me. I've put people in there.'

Suddenly Niccolo's mobile phone rang. He checked the time. Twenty to eleven.

It was Louise. Her voice sounded tired. 'I've just come out of a meeting with Sukuhara,' she said. 'I've missed an old friend's birthday drinks on your account.'

'I could make it up to you . . .'

'I don't think that would be appropriate under the circumstances.'

Niccolo sighed.

She continued, 'Mr Sukuhara has considered your request and has decided to improve upon it. The bank will pay you one million.'

'Dollars?'

'Sterling. The offer is final. I urge you to accept it. If you don't, he's more than happy to see you in court.'

'I'll think about it.' Niccolo put the phone down. The money was obscene, but this was just the beginning. He wondered how more many times Louise would make a final offer.

'Well, a million is more than I expected,' said Gino. 'It's an admission of liability. They're scared. They want this whole thing buried.'

'They killed Jack. A million isn't good enough,' decided Niccolo. 'I'm sending her a text.'

> **Louise, thnx for offer. My answer**
> **is no. Going to FSA tomorrow.**
> **Something not quite right with**
> **Larry's dept. Maybe they can**
> **advise me what to do. Nicco**

He showed it to Gino before clicking the send button.

'Why the hell are you going to the FSA with this?' Gino demanded.

Niccolo pulled out Arnaud Veyrieras' business card. It was filthy, tattered and worn, and the print was barely legible. 'Jack had this card on him when he died. This guy, Arnaud, could be the only chance I've got.'

CHAPTER 45

Niccolo hardly managed to get an hour's sleep before the phone went again. He looked out of the window, noticed the full moon and gazed at his Speedmaster. Half past one. His head felt heavy with wine. The phone rang.

'Hi, it's Louise. I'm sorry to disturb you so late at night.'

'You're pretty keen for me to buy you that drink, aren't you?' He immediately regretted saying it.

'Mr Lamparelli, you are still technically an employee of the bank. I could report you for that.'

'Forgive me, Louise. It was uncalled for.'

But Louise giggled suddenly, like a sixteen-year-old who'd had a drink too many. 'After everything I've done for you, Nicco Lamparelli, you're buying me dinner!' It took a while for her words to register. 'You're not going to believe this, but Mr Sukuhara's spent the last couple of hours reading your research reports. He's impressed. He's not going to reinstate you – officially, that's Larry's call – but he wants you to leave on good terms. He's decided to raise the offer to two million. He won't go higher, so don't bother trying. There are three conditions. First, you sign tomorrow. Second, you agree never to disclose details of the settlement or the circumstances of your departure to any third party – if you do, we'll sue your ass off. And third, you'll have to cancel your meeting with the FSA tomorrow.'

Niccolo deliberated for a few moments. The offer was obscene. Why not quit while he was ahead? He could use the money to do something in memory of Jack; he could help Jack's mother back in Brisbane, or buy Mizuno-san the fishing boat of his dreams. Finally, the deal was struck.

'You'll need to sign an amended termination agreement,' Louise told him. 'Come in tomorrow at eleven.'

Lying awake, Niccolo wondered why Sukuhara had given in so easily.

Niccolo's compensation package was large enough to require the signature of one other senior Saracen executive in London, together with a further two in New York. And the signatures could be obtained only after a board resolution had been passed to that effect.

So an extraordinary board meeting was convened at short notice in New York with Sukuhara attending via videoconference. The Japanese-American made it clear that he expected a prompt decision.

'All analysts report directly to Larry Sikorski, the Head of European Equity Research,' he declared. 'However, in the interests of damage limitation, I myself take personal responsibility for the Lamparelli case. This fuck-up happened on my watch. As of now, I am assuming control of the situation from Sikorski.'

As expected, the resolution was passed unanimously.

Later that morning, Larry Sikorski was summoned to Sukuhara's office.

'My sources tell me that you had no grounds whatsoever for

initiating disciplinary proceedings against Lamparelli. Do you have some sort of a personal vendetta against him?' Sukuhara demanded.

Larry answered coolly, 'I relied upon the advice given to me by Rupert Southgate. As Head of Telecoms – and as Niccolo's line manager – Rupert was given full responsibility for the conduct of the disciplinary hearing. I did not feel that my presence was required. With hindsight, that was an error of judgement. I will, of course, investigate how Rupert managed to fuck up such a simple administrative task. I clearly overestimated his people-management skills.'

'Perhaps you should take a closer look at your own people-management skills, Larry. Most of the guys on the floor hate your guts.'

Larry remained unfazed. 'I'm a results guy, John. I didn't take this job to be popular. Everything I do has one objective: to make money. Over the last twelve consecutive quarters all the numbers that I'm responsible for are off the clock: sales are up, profits are up, everything is up. I rely on my staff. Those whom I deem to be incompetent get fired. It's just a numbers game, John. And I always meet my numbers.'

'Unfortunately, Larry, our numbers aren't going to look too good once Lamparelli walks out of the door with a blow-out settlement.'

'What have you offered him?'

'Legal tell me he can hit us for at least five million, maybe more. On top of that, we may be facing a hefty FSA fine if this gets into the public domain. We have to settle. I've offered him two mil and he's taken it. We're doing the paperwork now.'

'I think you're off your head, John. I recommended that he be fired, but you pulled the plug. You overruled me.'

'That's right, Larry. I did – on the advice of Peterson in Legal. He informs me that Niccolo has a remarkably strong case against us. And it goes something like this: according to anyone who's anybody, Niccolo's a fucking good analyst, so we'd have to come up with a damn good reason for firing him. But you don't need a reason to fire people, do you, Larry? You just fire them because you can. It doesn't matter that they're good at their job. They have to be good to you, don't they? Tell me, what kind of scam are you cooking up this time?' Sukuhara lit a cigar and took a few puffs, enjoying his assault. 'And another thing – this guy Oakes, the Globecom guy, I hear you're getting too close to him. Keep your distance. The last thing we need is for our Research Department to get a reputation for sucking corporate ass.'

'Who did you hear that from?'

Sukuhara puffed a few times, considered his response, then confessed. 'Lamparelli, Doyle and Rabinowitz.'

Larry laughed out loud. 'Lamparelli is not the Head of Research. And neither are Doyle or Rabinowitz. I am.'

'Legal don't like the way you run your department either, Larry. They have a list of reservations as long as my arm. They say you could get us into trouble with the FSA – big trouble.'

'John, I have to make tough decisions on a daily basis. The only interests I take into account are ours and our clients'. Legal have never made a decision in their life. They just sit on their fat asses and criticise after the event. Rupert's call to initiate disciplinary proceedings in respect of Niccolo was the correct one, and I supported it. But his execution was weak. I'll be looking into ways to improve our disciplinary tribunal process in due course.'

'I am amazed at your total reluctance to accept any form of responsibility for your actions. You lead an army of men, yet you command the respect of none.'

'My staff respect my decisions—'

'Because you fire anyone who disagrees with you!' shouted

Sukuhara, thumping his desk. 'I want this whole mess buried by the end of the week. Do I make myself clear?'

As Larry marched out of the room, Sukuhara dialled the Human Resources department. 'I need to see the employment contract for one of my subordinates,' he growled.

'Certainly, sir. And who would that be?'

'Mr Larry S. Sikorski.'

At eleven sharp, Niccolo arrived in the lobby, where Louise was waiting for him with two Starbucks coffees. They went upstairs to a private room.

Louise picked up a handful of papers, separated them into two sets, pencilled in a few crosses and handed the first set to Niccolo. 'Sign there,' she demanded.

'May I have a few moments to read through them?'

'Of course.'

There were a lot of words, but the deal was simple. They were buying him off for two million pounds. In a businesslike manner, Louise explained that she would sign on behalf of Saracen Laing, with her secretary as witness.

As Niccolo took the pen in his hand, he felt nauseous. He thought of all that had been good in his life. The summers spent with Mizuno-san – with Jack. The years studying engineering at Cambridge – with Jack. Whenever anything important had happened to him – the day he passed his driving test, the day he graduated, even the day he got the job at Saracen – Jack was there. He didn't say much. He didn't take the credit. He simply made it happen. He was always there.

'Louise, you would have to formally investigate Larry Sikorski if I put in a written complaint about him, wouldn't you? You said you would.' Louise looked confused. 'Well, I've decided to make a formal complaint.'

'What!' Louise almost screamed.

'I would like you to formally investigate Larry Sikorski.'

Louise had trouble giving a measured response. 'I'm sorry, Niccolo, I thought I'd made it clear – this settlement is being offered on the basis that you drop any claims against Saracen Laing.'

'But it's in your own interests to investigate this man. He's a crook!'

'That's not part of our deal.'

Niccolo ripped up the contract and tossed it on the table. 'We don't have a deal, Louise. I don't want your money. I want Sikorski. Either you look into this, or I'm going to the FSA.'

Niccolo marched out and headed for the elevator. Louise came running after him clutching what remained of the contract. 'Don't be a bloody fool, Niccolo!' she yelled as the elevator doors closed. 'If you don't take this deal, I can't help you!'

The traders triggered off a whispering campaign that spread like wildfire. Unperturbed, Niccolo walked across to Larry's office. The door was shut and a meeting was in progress. Anne-Marie was not at her post. A few yards away, a nervous-looking Bulldog scented trouble and rushed over. 'Niccolo, you can't go in. He's in a meeting . . .' Her swift arrival alerted Larry, but it was too late. Niccolo kicked open the door. The chairs swivelled round and he found himself face to face with Odile and Rupert.

Larry jumped to his feet, his face bloated with anger. 'You've got a bloody nerve, storming into my office like this!'

Rupert and Odile wore the look of tourists caught up in a civil war.

'Get out!' Niccolo told them.

Nobody moved.

'I said, get out!' he repeated furiously. Some of the traders edged towards Larry's office to take a closer look. Larry calmly signalled to Bulldog through the glass wall.

April wasted no time. She dialled Security. 'Domingo? Please send some guards up to Mr Sikorski's office.'

'What's the problem, ma'am?'

'Do it now, Domingo!' she screamed, and slammed down the receiver before bursting into tears.

Niccolo grabbed Rupert by his shirt, causing a button to fly off.

'OK, OK,' pleaded Rupert. 'I'm going.'

Niccolo let him go, and turned to Odile. She stood up, avoiding eye contact, and also left the room.

Niccolo slammed the door shut and turned to Larry. 'It's game over, you bastard! I know you're behind Jack's murder. I don't know what you did or how you did it, but I know it was you.'

'Are you taking something, Niccolo?' Larry enquired smoothly. 'Perhaps you should see a doctor. You look a bit pale . . .'

'You killed Jack because he was trying to protect me, didn't you? You're making money out of his death, you son of a bitch.' The bland look of innocence melted from Larry's face and Niccolo knew he had made no mistake. 'You piece of shit!' he shouted.

As he pounced on Larry, a voice behind him cried out, 'Mr Lamparelli! Don't do it!' Domingo was at the door with two security guards. 'Please, Mr Lamparelli, sir, don't do it.'

The two security guards rushed into Larry's office, pinned Niccolo to the wall, clamped his arms back and cuffed him, whilst Odile and Rupert watched from the safety of the corridor.

But Niccolo looked only at Larry, his eyes blazing. 'You're a murdering piece of shit!' he hissed.

As the security guards marched him out of the building, with all the ceremony that surrounds the sentencing of a guilty man, Niccolo felt tears streaming down his face. He had been bitterly betrayed. And he didn't know why.

*

395

'I can't fire the son of a bitch, can I, Peterson?' Sukuhara snarled, flinging Larry's employment contract at the Head of Legal. 'Getting rid of him would cost me too much.'

'And more than merely money,' said Peterson mildly.

There was no need for him to elaborate. Though John Sukuhara's commercial judgement was beyond reproach, his standing in New York was being irreparably damaged by getting rid of Niccolo Lamparelli. A non-contractual pay-off of the kind Peterson had indicated Saracen Laing might be liable for implied that the bank had caved in to blackmail.

But getting rid of Larry Sikorski would cost far more in monetary terms, and – worse – would cause a seismic shock throughout the financial world. Saracen Laing could not come out of such a showdown looking good. And Sukuhara, as the most senior Saracen banker outside New York, would inevitably have to pay a heavy price.

Once the dust had settled, Domingo made his excuses at Reception and left for a cigarette break. Outside, he pulled out his mobile phone. 'Sir, Mr Lamparelli has just been thrown out of the building.'

'So it's all going as planned?' asked the voice at the other end.

'Yes, sir. Sikorski's back in control . . . Sir?'

'Yes?'

'If we're going to act, we've got to act now.'

CHAPTER 46

When Niccolo arrived at Jack's house, there was a 'For Sale' sign nailed to the garden gate. He sat on a street bench nearby and watched life drift by. A few pedestrians strolled past as though he was not there. There was no visible activity in the house and he suspected, after a while, that Donna was not in.

Suddenly he caught sight of the boat. The lovely carved boat – the *Yo-shi-ro* – so carefully crafted by Mizuno's own hands over twenty painstaking years had been the old man's last gift to Jack. Now it lay neglected on the ground beside the rubbish bins at the side of the house. Niccolo opened the gate and went over to pick it up. It seemed smaller than he remembered. The rudder was broken off and one of the sails was torn, but the hull remained intact. And Yoshiro's name was as bold as ever.

He held the wooden boat close to him, like a baby discarded by its parents, and searched in vain for the rudder.

At home, he placed the boat on his kitchen table, fetched his tool kit and set about repairing it as best he could. Carefully and slowly, he brushed off the embedded dirt. He pulled apart some of the loose pieces and washed them gently in warm water, then placed the broken boat and its parts carefully on his kitchen

397

windowsill to dry. He stood back and looked at it. Almost his whole life, and Jack's, was in some way bound up with that boat, and with Yoshiro.

It was just a simple little wooden boat. It was priceless.

Arriving fashionably late, Donna found that Larry was there ahead of her, and had already ordered himself a Bloody Mary. It was nine o'clock and Hakkasan's was buzzing. Larry rose to his feet, buttoned his blazer and kissed her hand, before ordering a Kir Royale for his guest and another Bloody Mary for himself.

'You look very lovely, Donna,' he said. 'But I get the idea you have something on your mind. Why not tell me, then we can relax and enjoy the evening?'

Donna unloaded her worries without much coaxing. 'I've seen lots of stuff about Jack in the papers . . . bad stuff. They say he was involved in some kind of insider trading ring. They say he took bribes, he falsified his research reports, printed lies. Is it true?'

Larry caressed her thigh. 'Calm down, darling,' he said, sounding concerned. 'I have no idea whether Jack was on the take, but you don't need to bother yourself with that kind of thing. It's in the past. And you weren't involved. You must move on now. You have your whole life ahead of you.'

Donna bowed her head meekly whilst placing the napkin on her lap. 'I couldn't bear the thought of life without you, my darling,' she whispered. 'I love you so much—'

'I think it's best we lie low for a while,' said Larry, cutting in. 'We mustn't see each other for some time.'

'But Larry – I left Jack for you. I risked *everything* for you.'

'Oh, I don't think you've done too badly out of this, my dear. I'm sure Jack left a sizeable estate. And I heard the bank saw fit to make an *ex gratia* payment to you to the tune of one point two million pounds.'

'Yes,' said Donna, blinking owlishly.

'You deserve it, my dear. Being a banker's wife is a tough job.'

Donna's eyes sprang wide open, as if she'd had a brain wave. 'That was hush money, wasn't it?' she snarled. 'You're hiding something about Jack and you want me to keep my mouth shut, don't you!'

Larry leaned forward and said sternly, 'Don't think too hard, child. It doesn't become you. I suggest you continue playing the grieving wife. Keep a low profile. Saracen gave you that money on condition that you keep your mouth shut.'

Donna fidgeted uneasily. 'What do you mean?' she asked, confused.

'Read the letter again, darling. Just remember they can claw it back just as fast as they gave it away.'

'You bastard! I wouldn't be surprised if you'd had something to do with my husband's death.' She shed some crocodile tears. 'My poor darling Jack!'

Larry chuckled. 'Come, come, Donna,' he said, with a glint of mischief in his eyes. 'Were you mourning Jack when you were lying in my bed last night? Or the night before, or the night before that, eh?'

Her tears dried up. 'You're sick, Larry Sikorski.'

'Perhaps. But *you* are a very rich woman. And you'll *remain* a very rich woman for a long time to come, provided you play your cards right.' He passed her a menu. 'Shall we order?'

Two days later, Charlie and Niccolo met in secret at the Bleeding Heart. Niccolo turned up in a pair of Levi's and a T-shirt.

'Look at you,' said Charlie, who looked as if he had slept in his hand-made Richard James suit. 'Dressed like a bum, and you think you can take on the world's biggest investment bank! Give me a hug, Nicco!'

They embraced. Charlie ordered for both of them, then leaned forward eagerly. 'So, what's the score? What's happening? Spill the beans. Hit me with the gossip. Give me the dirt, man.'

In a split second, Niccolo remembered everything he missed about the office, and everything he didn't. What he missed was sitting in front of him, and what he didn't would soon be behind him.

'Charlie, you once told me never to trust anyone in this dirty business,' he began.

'Did I? What amazing foresight I had in my younger days.'

'Did you include yourself?'

'*What?*'

'Jack trusted us both. Now he's dead – murdered. And Larry's trying to kick dirt on his memory. It's down to us to clear his name.'

'Fuck a dead ferret! We're not back to that again, are we? You just don't give up, do you, motherfucker? Jack's dead, and I'm sorry. But it's over. Drop it.'

'I can't,' said Niccolo. 'I know Larry's behind this. But I just can't figure out his angle.'

'His angle? His *angle*? That bastard's got more angles than a dodecahedron!'

'We owe it to Jack to come forward, tell the police everything we know. They can put Larry away for a long time.'

Charlie took his time before responding. 'Larry is even more powerful than you think,' he said. 'Sure, I know where the bodies are buried – some bodies, at any rate. But even if I come forward, it's our word against his.'

'If we don't do anything, he'll walk away.'

'What the hell do you want from me, Nicco?'

'*I* don't want anything from you, Charlie. Do this for Jack.'

'Look, kiddo, I've got a family, for fuck's sake! Several families, actually.'

'Charlie, what are you afraid of?'

Charlie scratched his forehead, agitated. 'Look, we've all done things in the past that we're not proud of. A full-blown investigation into Jack's death would open up a whole can of worms – for you, for me, for the bank, not to mention for Jack's wife.'

'Leave Donna to me. I'll deal with her another time.'

'I've got a reputation to protect, you know. You don't become a legend overnight. I don't want a load of cops digging around on my patch. You never know what they might find . . . ex-girlfriends, weed, porno mags, a used johnnie . . . you know, that kinda thing.'

'Charlie! Jack died on your patch!'

Charlie scowled silently for a minute. 'You'd better be careful where you tread, Nicco,' he said finally. 'You're walking into a dark hole, and if you're not careful, you'll never find your way out. Take my advice. Forget about Jack. Get on with your life.'

'You still don't understand, do you, Charlie?'

'OK,' Charlie grunted. 'Make me understand.'

As the waitress brought their lunch, Niccolo unfolded his napkin. 'All right, I will,' he said. 'It's a long story.'

It was almost the end of the summer. Childish pleas to stay at Okinawa 'for ever and ever' had naturally fallen on deaf ears, and in a few days Jack and Niccolo would go back to Tokyo for the start of the new school year.

'*Maybe Isabella-san and Bronwen-san will bring you here next summer,*' *Mizuno-san said comfortingly. 'I am happy for Yoshiro, that he has made such good friends. And I am happy for myself too. Instead of one boy, I now have three. You are all very dear to me. My humble dwelling is always your home.*'

The boys had taken the boat out alone many times before, so that last day Mizuno-san stayed ashore mending nets and tinkering with bits of machinery.

'Not more than one hundred yards offshore, do you hear?' he said sternly. 'And no jumping overboard! If you get into trouble, it's too far for me to come and pull you out.'

They spent a happy morning trolling, and landed plenty of fish. Then Yoshiro announced that he was hungry and wanted to go back.

'If we throw the net, we'll get lots of fish. That'll be a surprise for Mizuno-san,' said Niccolo. He stood up in the boat, and carefully held the net as he had been taught. But just as he threw it, a wave rocked the boat slightly, unbalancing him so that he sat down with a thump and his throw fell short.

'Look, you've got it all tangled round the propeller,' Jack groaned.

'We must untangle it,' said Yoshiro. 'Grandfather will be angry if the propeller makes a hole in his net.'

'Don't worry – I'll do it.' And Niccolo leaned over and started tugging at the net. After a few minutes, he sat up and said, 'It won't come. I can't get hold of it properly.' He leaned over again, squirming further and further over the gunwale until he was more out of the boat than in. Inevitably, he fell in head first, and came up laughing and spitting sea water.

'That's better, I can do it now,' he said, hanging on to the propeller with one hand while he tried to unwind the net with the other. The water wasn't cold, and the sea was calm, and it would only take a minute. Then he would clamber back into the boat.

Suddenly a shocking blow struck him. He felt no pain, only a numbing cold as he was dragged helplessly down. He was being shaken so violently he couldn't have breathed even if he'd tried. His mind stopped. Time itself stopped. And a few seconds became eternity.

Then, just as shockingly, he was thrust up again into light and air. He was floating. He had only a fleeting impression of another tremendous blow, and frantic splashing, before he let himself fade away into the welcoming dark.

*

It was early evening when he woke up. He was lying in a clean white bed, feeling muzzy and sick, and his mother was holding his hand and crying. His father was there too. At first they wouldn't tell him what had happened; they just repeated, 'It's all right, sweetheart. You're safe now.'

But he became so agitated that eventually his father sat down beside the bed, and told him. 'A shark got you by the leg,' he said. 'It bit you quite badly, but it's all been stitched up and it'll be fine.'

'Did it get Jack?' Niccolo asked urgently. 'And Yoshiro?'

Feroz looked at Isabella, who bit her lip and nodded as if giving him permission to go ahead. 'Jack's safe. He's with his parents now. But Yoshiro – well, Yoshiro was very, very brave. He stood up in the boat and hit the shark with the oar, as hard as he could. He hit it so hard he fell in. And the shark let you go. But – I'm sorry, Nicco – it took Yoshiro instead. Mizuno-san and some other people came in boats, and Mizuno-san hauled you out of the water.'

'But what about Yoshiro? Is he all right?'

'They're looking for him now,' was all Feroz said.

After that, Niccolo was given some pills to make him sleep.

The next morning, the first thing he asked was, 'Have they found Yoshiro yet?'

Isabella had sat by his bed all night. Now she shut her eyes and the tears ran down her cheeks. She nodded. 'Yes, they have. But Nicco, the shark hurt him so badly that he died.'

Young Niccolo roared with anguish. A nurse came running, and after a few seconds' hurried conversation with Isabella, gave him an injection that knocked him out for the rest of the day.

Towards evening he woke up. As he surfaced through the mist of drug-induced sleep, he heard voices talking about him as if he were not present, either in body or in spirit. Niccolo could barely hear the words – the pain in his leg was too great – but he could recognise the voices.

'Carcharias taurus,' said the first. 'We call it the sand tiger shark.

403

Some call it the grey nurse shark. The bites are unmistakable.' The voice was cold and masculine.

'Have you seen these types of wounds before?' enquired a second voice. It was his mother's voice. It was warm and comforting, close and soft. It was a beautiful voice.

'This is the first case I have seen in four years,' continued the first voice. It was Jack's father. 'Sand tiger sharks are commonly sighted around these waters, but usually they're harmless. This one seems to have been agitated.'

'What do they look like?' It was Mamma again.

'They have fang-like razor-sharp teeth and piercing yellow eyes.'

'But why did this one attack my baby?'

'It's a predator,' answered Professor Ford. 'However deeply buried, the instinct to attack is simply in its nature.'

Mizuno's fellow-fishermen had found what little remained of Yoshiro just before nightfall, and brought it ashore. The neighbours walked with Mizuno, keeping a respectful distance, as he carried his beloved grandson, wrapped in a white cloth, up the beach to his house. 'We will bury him tomorrow,' was all he said.

Niccolo was drugged and unconscious, and in any case too ill to leave hospital, but Isabella and Feroz went, and so did Jack and his parents. Jack did not utter a word from the moment the fishermen found him, alone in the boat, glassy-eyed, mute and shaking, until after Yoshiro had been laid to rest at the top of the hill.

It was from Jack that Niccolo heard later what happened next. Mizuno indicated that the mourners should go back down the hill without him. He took Jack's hand, and they stood for a while looking at the newly covered grave in silence.

'It was not your fault,' Mizuno said. 'It was not Nicco-san's fault. It was not Yoshiro's fault. It was not even the shark's fault, since it is a predator by nature. It simply happened. However, Yoshiro acted honourably and with courage, and for that I give thanks.'

'But I didn't do anything,' Jack said dully. 'I didn't try to save Nicco. Yoshiro did it all.'

'I was watching you all from the shore,' Mizuno said. 'I saw him stand up and hit the shark. Only one of you could have done that. And I saw him fall in. No one could have saved him. Even I could not have saved him. And you know I would have given my own life gladly for his.'

'I wish I was dead too,' Jack said miserably.

Mizuno-san crouched down and looked up into Jack's eyes. 'I want you to promise me two things, Jack-san,' he said earnestly. 'One is that you will never again say you wish you were dead. The other is that you will not let Yoshiro's death be wasted. He saved Nicco-san's life. Now, Nicco-san is younger than you; he is impulsive and sometimes reckless. You are older, and in some ways wiser, than he is. So will you promise to look after him, guide him, and be an elder brother to him, always? That will wipe out any fault on your part, if you do that.'

Jack sniffed back tears, and nodded.

'Good.' Mizuno-san stood up stiffly. 'I only have two boys now, and you are both leaving me. I would like you to come back here for another summer, but fate may take you both far away. You will only have each other. So you must look after each other, trust each other, and never let one another down. Promise me.'

Jack nodded again.

'Say it!' Mizuno-san commanded sternly.

'I promise.'

Niccolo sat back in his chair. 'And since then,' he said to Charlie, 'whenever I needed Jack, he was always there for me. When I had nowhere to live, Jack put a roof over my head. When I needed a job, Jack found me one. When I was short of money, Jack wrote me an open cheque. I always said I'd pay him back. But I never did.'

Charlie put his fork down. He hadn't touched his lunch. 'That's a hell of a story,' he said. 'I had no idea about any of it. But of course I see why you feel you owe Jack. And if Jack had stuck to his promise, it doesn't square with the suicide verdict, does it?'

'Jack only asked for my help once,' Niccolo went on. 'It was on the night he died – but I wasn't there.'

'Where were you?'

'I was with Lucy. But that's over now.' Niccolo still felt a tiny shred of loyalty to Lucy that prevented him telling Charlie that she had accepted money from Larry to spy on him. 'Charlie, I can't let Jack die disgraced,' he pleaded. 'I have to clear his name. I have to protect his honour.'

Charlie chuckled. 'Who do you think you are – Braveheart? There's no such thing as honour any more. It disappeared with the Knights of the Round Table. Grow up, kiddo.'

'In your world, honour may hold no value, but in Jack's world, nothing else mattered.'

'And what about *your* world, Nicco? What do *you* believe in?'

'It doesn't matter what I believe in. I'm not doing this for me. I'm doing it for my friend.' Niccolo fiddled with the cutlery in front of him. 'Jack dedicated his life to me. He made sacrifices so that I wouldn't have to. He pushed me up even if it meant keeping himself down. And he did it all for a promise – just one lousy, fucking promise. I never asked for his help, but he gave it to me anyway and I love him for it. Do you understand? I love him for it! Now he's dead and I owe him. I owe him so much it makes me want to cry. I don't know what honour means to me, Charlie, but I know it meant everything to Jack. So I'm going to make damn sure nobody takes it away from him! Do you fucking understand me now?'

Charlie swallowed the lump in his throat and nodded. 'I understand you now,' he said.

CHAPTER 47

Niccolo whipped out a soiled business card and placed it on the counter at Elm House. 'I'm looking for this man,' he said.

The receptionist reluctantly put down her book and examined the dirty, dog-eared card with visible distaste. 'You're at the wrong place, sir. This is the Serious Fraud Office. The Financial Services Authority is in Canary Wharf.' She pointed to the address on the card, as if to imply that Niccolo was illiterate.

'Mr Veyrieras has left the FSA. He now works for you guys. Could you check for me, please?'

The receptionist heaved a sigh and punched some strokes into her keyboard. 'Ah, yes,' she said brusquely. 'There is a Mr Veyrieras here. May I ask the nature of your enquiry, sir?'

'Mr Veyrieras knows a friend of mine – he was murdered. I have some information he may want to hear.'

Her eyes widened with surprise, but professionalism won. She simply said, 'I'll call him and let him know you're on the way up, sir.'

At first, the meeting felt cold, official, formal, clinical. There were no pleasantries, no small talk, no coffee or tea, just business.

'I'm certain that Jack stumbled across some kind of fraud

before he died,' Niccolo said urgently. 'I don't have the full details, and I don't know much about the substance of it, but it was big, I'm sure of that. And Jack suspected that Larry Sikorski was behind it.' Niccolo pulled out Arnaud's tattered business card. 'The police found this on Jack's body.'

Until now, Arnaud had said little. He had listened quietly and taken copious notes. He took his old card and stared at it. When he finally spoke, he said, 'We recognise the courage it takes for individuals to approach us. You have done the right thing in coming to us, Niccolo – is it OK if I call you Niccolo?'

'Yes, of course.'

'Tell me about your job, Niccolo,' asked Arnaud, preparing to scribe. 'What is your relationship with Mr Sikorski?'

'I'm a Telecoms analyst. My boss, Rupert Southgate, reports to Larry Sikorski. I've been under pressure from Mr Sikorski to change some of my calls. One of them was Globecom. I had it on a Sell, and Mr Sikorski ordered me to switch to a Buy. When I refused, lots of weird things happened. Mr Sikorski took my best stocks away from me. Now he's trying to fire me on some bogus disciplinary charge. I think my friend Jack knew exactly what Larry was up to, but he got killed before he could tell me what it was.'

Arnaud stopped scribbling. 'What I'm about to tell you is strictly off the record.'

Niccolo felt obliged to nod.

'Larry Sikorski has been on the FSA's Wanted list for some time, and I have been on his trail. He is a smart operator. He has managed to keep himself clean so far. He has friends in high places. I have noticed that few people tend to cross him in the City. Those that do often get hurt.'

'Jack got killed.'

'You have my sincerest condolences for the death of your friend. Unfortunately, we have no powers to investigate Mr Ford's murder – the police will have to deal with that. Here at the SFO, we catch fraudsters. We know that Sikorski has profited in the past from insider dealing. If we get a conviction, we can put him behind bars for ten years.'

'How close are you to a conviction?'

Arnaud laughed. 'You're asking the wrong guy, Niccolo. If it were up to me, Sikorski and his merry band of international white-collar thieves would have been locked up years ago and the key thrown away. Unfortunately, in this country it takes a judge and jury to get a conviction. We have a lot of evidence, but Crown prosecutors are rarely willing even to consider taking on a case of this magnitude without at least one star witness – someone who is willing to testify against Sikorski.'

'What if I agree to testify against him?'

'You could do that. But if you do, I must warn you that it would be your word against his. A good lawyer can make even the most seasoned banker look like an idiot in the witness box. Needless to say, Saracen Laing can afford the best legal counsel. Once they are through with you, it's unlikely that you would ever work in the City again.'

Niccolo nodded, trying his damnedest not to look intimidated.

'However, if several other analysts were to come forward and back up your version of events, then it would no longer be merely your word against his.'

'I can give you names.'

'We already have names. But it's not so easy to get people to testify in court. It's a public affair. Their livelihoods – their reputations – are put at risk.'

'Have you asked any of them?'

'Of course. But Larry Sikorski is a big cheese in the City. He is well connected, in business and in government. Many of your colleagues are scared to come forward. He seems untouchable.'

'So there's nothing you can do?'

'There's a lot we can do. But the chances of a successful conviction based on your testimony alone are very slim, and the risk for you is very high. However, if you're willing to take that risk, we may have enough to start building a case.'

'Start building a case, Mr Veyrieras.'

Ever since the coroner's suicide verdict, DS Harcourt had been looking for new evidence with which to reopen the Jack Ford case. New evidence required new contacts, and Arnaud Veyrieras had proved to be a very reliable one. The two men regularly swapped information. The arrangement was to keep their relationship off the record, at least for now. Plain-clothed WPC McKeever was happy to act as go-between.

DS Harcourt's gut had told him early on in his investigation that Larry Sikorski was in some way linked to Jack Ford's murder. DS Harcourt's head, however, told him that pinning a murder charge on Sikorski would be next to impossible without new evidence. And with the case closed, Sikorski's flat was now off-limits to the police, eliminating any chance of collecting any. Yet if he couldn't send Larry down for murder, could he get him on a lesser offence?

'What is it those Frog buggers say?' he asked WPC McKeever rhetorically. '*Cherchez la femme*. Look for the woman. And if my school French serves me well, *femme* also means wife, doesn't it? I think we'll contrive to have another word with the lovely Mrs Donna Ford.'

News of Globecom's takeover of Yamaguchi Telecom broke during after-trading hours in Tokyo, hitting Kloomberg's screens in London at 9 a.m. The Japanese regulatory authorities were in total disarray. They had not seen this coming, and appeared to be in grave danger of retreating into a long-drawn-out sulk. On

410

several earlier occasions, they had made it clear that they would have preferred a Japanese company to acquire YamTel. Globecom had acted with great cunning. Hostile takeovers are rare in Japan, and those involving foreigners carry the additional risk of almost certainly becoming a national scandal.

The *Financial Telegraph*'s website summed up the mood in corporate Japan: *Britain's Globecom springs dawn raid on unloved Japanese telecom jewel.* The article went on to say that Globecom had struck a deal with YamTel's unions and pensions trustees, who held twenty-two per cent of the company, securing their support for the takeover in return for job guarantees. Through various 'friendly investors' Kenneth Oakes had sewn up another twenty-nine per cent, giving him effective control of the Japanese telecom operator. The union deal meant that Oakes had got control of YamTel on the cheap. YamTel's management had been sidelined, betrayed by its own workers.

At Globecom's London headquarters, the champagne had been flowing since the early hours of the morning. Globecom had become the world's largest telecom company overnight. Kenneth Oakes' day of glory had arrived. City pundits were applauding his courage and foresight in snapping up a key player in a dynamic market at a bargain basement price.

Globecom's share price opened at £2.22, shot up to £3.12 within minutes and climbed steadily during the day to close at £3.31.

'Your Highness, I'm pleased to tell you there has been real progress. Your investment has increased by fifty per cent in one day.'

'About time too,' the Prince said ungraciously. 'Should we sell now, before the share price falls again?'

'No, sir. There is much, much more to be made. We would be wise to leave it for a little while longer.'

'You had better be right, my friend.'

CHAPTER 48

Exactly one month later, a convoy of black Rovers coasted in single file down King William Street towards the river, and pulled over just outside the European headquarters of Saracen Laing. A nearby traffic warden prepared to pounce, but several dark suits jumped out, flashing badges, before marching purposefully into the building. Two of the heavier suits, with shaved heads and visible earpieces, stayed behind to guard the vehicles.

Inside, the suits flashed some more badges and marched determinedly past Security, up the escalators and on to the trading floor. When they got there, they scanned the terrain, located their target and closed in fast.

Sukuhara's office door was open. Bulldog stood up as the entourage approached. The suits stormed past her into the office of the most senior Saracen banker outside New York.

'Are you Mr John Sukuhara?' asked one of the suits.

'Yes,' he answered brusquely.

'My name is Arnaud Veyrieras. I work for the Serious Fraud Office. I have here a statement of charges.' Arnaud handed Sukuhara a sealed white envelope. 'It details our intention to institute criminal proceedings against Saracen Laing. We will be searching the premises, and may sequestrate certain records. If you have any objections, please say so now.'

Sukuhara appeared stunned. He pressed the intercom to Bulldog's desk and yelled, 'Get Peterson down here. Now!'

For a few minutes Sukuhara made an unsuccessful attempt at small talk. Finally Peterson arrived, gasping for breath. Sukuhara handed him the unopened envelope. 'These guys are from the SFO,' he said tersely. 'Do they have the right to search our premises?'

Peterson ripped open the envelope and read the letter.

Dear Mr Sukuhara,

Under the powers vested in me by Her Majesty's Government, I have initiated a criminal investigation into the practices followed by Saracen Laing Bank, and in particular those followed by Mr Larry Sikorski, Head of European Equity Research.

Mr Sikorski is under investigation for four counts of securities fraud. The charges relate to insider trading, market manipulation, front-running of investment research and bribery. These charges may result in prosecution. If convicted, Mr Sikorski could face up to ten years in prison and Saracen Laing fines of up to ten per cent of turnover.

In the event that Saracen Laing Bank is held to be in breach of FSA regulations governing the provision of investment advice, your banking licence may be revoked, resulting in the forced closure of all Equity Research activities of Saracen Laing Bank in the United Kingdom. In the event that specified Saracen Laing staff have compromised the quality and integrity of the investment advice that has been provided to the bank's clients, or if, as a result of their actions, they are deemed no longer fit and proper persons for the purposes of conducting securities business, they may be prosecuted individually.

During the course of our investigation we will require full access to your records. I expect the full cooperation of all officers and staff of Saracen Laing.

Yours sincerely,

Arnaud Veyrieras

Principal Investigator

Securities Division

Serious Fraud Office

When Peterson had finished reading, he said simply, 'John, I believe we would be wise to cooperate.'

Sukuhara looked like a man who had received news of a terminal illness. An SFO investigation on his watch was an unmitigated disaster. With all the dignity he could muster, he said, 'Very well, I will endeavour to help you in full with your investigations.'

Within seconds, Arnaud's cohorts had dispersed like a SWAT team.

'Would you be so kind as to direct me to the office of your Head of Equity Research?' asked Arnaud.

'Follow me,' said Sukuhara. He barged unannounced into Larry Sikorski's office and handed him the letter. In a firm voice, that let his displeasure be known, he stated, 'I expect your full co-operation into this investigation, Sikorski.'

Larry jumped to his feet as he scanned the document. 'You're Veyrieras, right? Well, this whole thing is just ludicrous. There's no foundation to any of these charges. Someone's made a mistake, my friend. A very big mistake.'

Later that afternoon Sukuhara made some management changes. Larry was suspended on full pay pending the SFO investigation. Paddy O'Shea was appointed interim Head of European Equity Research whilst retaining his responsibilities as Head of Sales

& Trading, effectively doubling his power base overnight. Dudley Rabinowitz, as Chief Compliance Officer, was asked to conduct an internal investigation into the research department so that management could dig out any skeletons before the SFO did.

The Chancellor of the Exchequer interrupted dinner at home with his family to take a telephone call from the United States Treasury Secretary. An aide rushed him down to his office, where the call was recorded.

The American got straight down to brass tacks. 'Listen, Donald, I have a problem. We've got a full-blown global banking crisis going on here in the US – and I know you guys are hurting too. It seems to me that you and I are going to have to retrieve the situation with as little collateral damage as possible.'

'I agree.'

'The first thing we need to do is to make sure our banking systems emerge from this mess stronger and more resilient.'

'Yes, indeed.'

'Now this thing with Saracen – the Serious Fraud Office investigation – how serious is it? Are we talking a small fine, a big fine, a lengthy court case? Or worse?'

'I honestly couldn't say, Bob. But I think we should let the investigation run its course. It may do more damage if we intervene.'

'Hey, I remember the shit that got stirred over the British Aerospace saga. Of course you guys need to do a thorough investigation, play it by the book. It's just that to some people on this side of the ocean, it seems more like a witch-hunt. You sure your guys know what they're doing?'

The Chancellor feigned laughter. 'I'm sure the SFO know their stuff.'

'The uncertainty is damaging on both sides. You guys are getting a bad press here. The *Wall Street Journal*'s ripping your balls off.'

'Yes, I've read some of the articles. It goes without saying that a speedy resolution is in everybody's interests, and I will do everything in my power to ensure that this matter is laid to rest as soon as possible.'

'You know, we find that in the US, a light regulatory touch often works best.'

'I agree. So far the situation is limited to one or two of the bank's senior staff, so I'm sure we can handle it without compromising the bank itself.'

'That's great to hear, because I'm not sure the banking system can ride another scandal. You don't need me to tell you that the knock-on effects will be greater on your side of the pond.'

'We both want the same things, Bob – we just need to get there in an orderly fashion.'

'Well, Donald, I'm glad we had this little chat. See you at the Climate Change Summit. I'm sure I can muster the President's support for your proposals.'

The Chancellor put the phone down, pondering his next move. The special relationship with the USA was his ticket to better things, to a more lucrative lecture circuit, to a grander reception for his memoirs – when he eventually had time to write them.

In his head there were more questions than answers. Did the SFO know what they were doing? Did Saracen Laing have a case to answer? If it all went pear-shaped, how might the Americans retaliate?

He could not recall an occasion when the British authorities had publicly charged an American corporation with such serious criminal offences. And Saracen Laing was not just any old corporation: it was America's finest banking institution, a household name across the English-speaking world. It employed more staff than Citicorp, operated in more countries than HSBC, and was more profitable than any other bank in the world. London's reputation as a leading financial centre was at stake.

The Chancellor of the Exchequer picked up the phone and dialled the Prime Minister's private line.

Over the next few months, the SFO threw what resources they could at the Sikorski case. Arnaud kept Niccolo informed of progress. 'We're close,' he would say. 'We're so close I can smell it. But we keep coming up against brick walls. For instance, we can't get authorisation for surveillance or phone-tapping. But I can assure you we are doing everything possible.'

Meanwhile Niccolo kept himself busy. He took up writing again, contributing the odd article to the local paper, and worked some evenings at a nearby bar. Sometimes he would sit in the park and think for hours about Jack, and sometimes he would cry. Each time, however, he cried less. Niccolo's mission to clear Jack's name was almost complete. He longed to be able to write and assure Mizuno-san that he had avenged Jack's honour, and for Mizuno-san to tell him that he was proud of him.

Then, out of the blue, disaster struck. The BBC's *Newsnight* was the first to break the story. They broadcast a live interview with Larry Sikorski. The following day it was all over the papers. *SFO investigation of US bank collapses*, said the *Financial Telegraph. British authorities fail to make case against Saracen Laing*, claimed its Wall Street rival.

Niccolo called Arnaud immediately. 'What the fuck happened?'

Arnaud sighed like a man who had given up on life. 'We had insufficient evidence against Sikorski. Niccolo, I can't talk now. Do you like sushi?'

*

Prince Mubarak had called a syndicate meeting at short notice in his palace. Picton was the first to arrive. When all were present, a dark-turbaned giant announced the arrival of the Prince himself. Picton took his signal from the Prince, and stood up to address the syndicate.

'I must thank you all for your forbearance these past months,' he began. 'There have been delays and setbacks beyond my control. But you have kept faith with me. And I in turn have kept faith with you.' He paused, savouring the moment. 'At last I am able to tell you – you are all rich!'

Instead of the rapturous applause he had anticipated, his words were greeted with a chilling silence.

He went on, 'The syndicate holds a total of two hundred and eighty million Globecom shares. The average purchase price was two pounds five. As of a few minutes ago, the stock was trading a cat's whisker short of four pounds dead. It is improbable that the price will rise much further, so I thought it wise to sell the stock today. This I have done . . . and netted you all a tidy profit of five hundred and forty-six million pounds. No, no . . .' he said, as sporadic clapping broke out. 'It's not me you should be thanking. It is my good friend and yours, His Royal Highness Prince Mubarak, who deserves your praise.'

The Prince smiled thinly. Mobile phones beeped, and chatter broke out as syndicate members called their wives, their girlfriends, their fathers and their brothers, some to boast of their courage and foresight in making the greatest investment of their lives, others to curse the perfidious Dr Picton, who had failed to make them as rich as he had promised.

One man crept out unnoticed. Beneath the shade of the orange trees, with only a halfwit garden boy to hear him, he took out his mobile phone and jabbed at the single number it contained. 'The day is not yet at hand, brother,' he whispered. 'The infidel dog has broken his word and we are not yet rich. So for the time being, we can buy only some of what we need. But soon, soon the Sword of Allah will strike!'

'I trusted you, Picton,' the Prince said coolly. 'You would triple our money, you said. And I assured my syndicate that it would happen. Instead, you have shamed me in the eyes of my countrymen by failing to keep your promise. Fifty per cent is a long way short of two hundred per cent.'

'Your Highness, I was wrong to make such a promise,' Picton said cautiously. 'I truly believed that everything was under my control, that nothing could go wrong. But one man has stood in our way, and we are apparently powerless to do anything about it.'

'Why? Couldn't you just throw him into the Thames, as you did the other one? Don't worry, my friend, that was a joke. Of course I understand that even the best-made plans can go wrong. And fifty per cent, while disappointing, is not a disaster.' He looked at his Rolex watch. 'I see your flight leaves in a couple of hours. I have told Karim to drive you to the airport. I expect you will find much to talk about.'

Picton bowed slightly, and mopped his damp forehead with a silk handkerchief. 'That is very thoughtful of you, sir, thank you.'

'Ah, Karim, there you are,' said the Prince. 'You will drive Dr Picton, as I asked you. Look after him well; his life is in your hands.'

Karim bowed, and followed Picton through the marble halls, grinning wolfishly in anticipation and flexing his long, supple fingers.

CHAPTER 49

Matsuri's sushi house was packed. Arnaud was sitting at the bar, a bottle of sake on the counter beside him. He signalled to Niccolo that they would go downstairs.

A petite Japanese waitress in a bright orange kimono escorted them to a private room. It was small, with a spotless tatami floor enclosed on three sides by rice-paper doors, and a knee-high ebony table set for three. They took off their shoes outside and sat cross-legged on the tatami. They got the orders out of the way, then Niccolo leaned forward, as if he were long overdue an explanation.

'Sikorski was operating some offshore trading accounts,' Arnaud told him. 'He was trading through a complex series of SPVs – Special Purpose Vehicles – registered in nominee names. They were pretty hard to trace. Anyway, after six weeks of surveillance, we did trace them and identified a large deal that we can link directly to him. He purchased eight hundred thousand Globecom shares. Guess when?'

'The day before Saracen Laing switched its rating from Sell to Buy?'

Arnaud nodded. 'The stock went up around twenty per cent

420

the next day. It climbed another thirty per cent a few days later, after Globecom announced it was buying some Japanese company.'

'YamTel.'

'That's the one. Anyway, the whole thing netted him a nice tidy personal profit of eight point five million. And we had it all on tape.'

'So how did he get away?' asked Niccolo impatiently.

'We fucked up. We had tapes of Larry's mobile telephone conversations. We had enough to send him away for ten years. Unfortunately, the judge didn't see it that way. We acted on evidence we picked up from our surveillance operations – I have a contact in the Metropolitan police force who helped us – but the surveillance op was not properly authorised. You remember I told you we were finding it impossible to obtain authorisation? We hoped that when we confronted Sikorski with the tapes, he would confess. Instead, he and his million-dollar legal team applied to the judge to disallow the evidence. And without the tapes, we didn't have much of a case. So he got off on a technicality. I am more bitterly disappointed than I can say.'

Niccolo swore softly. 'What about your friends at the FSA?'

'I have no friends at the FSA. As far as those assholes are concerned, the case is shut. It always was.'

'I never understood why you left the FSA in the first place.'

Arnaud heaved a long sigh. 'I used to work for Interpol. For many years my team tracked a career fraudster currently known as Dr Stacey Picton. We gathered a lot of evidence for many crimes in many jurisdictions, but when we handed it over to the national authorities of the relevant states, they somehow never had the balls to prosecute.'

The waitress in the orange kimono opened the paper doors. Three similar young women followed her, carrying every permutation of sushi imaginable, placed the food on the table and disappeared. They did not remove the third place setting. Arnaud continued talking as Niccolo dug in to lunch.

'At the FSA I had a very supportive boss – Amanda Sanderson. She was tough, but she gave me a chance. My investigations led me to uncover Picton's network. Sikorski played a key part. He provided Picton with inside information – information Picton used to make millions on the stock market, illegally. Sikorski, of course, did a bit of profiteering on the side, but got a huge kickback from the Picton relationship. Most of the analysts who worked for Sikorski did as they were told. Those who did not got the boot. They stayed quiet on the outside because Sikorski paid them well. And he threatened the lives of their families – and had the where-withal to carry out his threats.' Niccolo nodded with his mouth full. 'But two years ago, just as my net was closing in on Sikorski, Sanderson gave me a direct order to stop the investigation. Of course, she was only following orders herself.'

'From whom?'

'From the Chancellor of the Exchequer. He issued a gagging order on the FSA. She ignored it. She turned a blind eye and allowed me to sniff around Sikorski for several months longer until I had enough to seal a watertight case. But the Chancellor had his spies crawling all over the place. He found out and had her fired. The case was shut down.'

'Why would the Chancellor shut down the case?'

The Frenchman spread his hands and shrugged. 'No one will say for sure. It could be something as trivial as not wanting to jeopardise Saracen Laing's very generous donations to causes dear to your government's heart. Or it could be that there is some other situation we have no idea about, and we are in danger of unwittingly treading on someone's toes.'

'I see,' Niccolo said, not at all sure that he did.

'There's more. The Bank of England is concerned that if we

422

indict a senior official in one of America's largest investment banks, then the US Securities and Exchange Commission may be tempted to implement tit-for-tat measures against a British bank in New York. Things could turn nasty if a trade war erupted. If the Yanks pulled out of London, there wouldn't be much left.'

'But the SEC is cracking down hard on securities fraud,' Niccolo pointed out. 'They don't like insider trading or market manipulation any more than we do. They've come down hard on Enron, WorldCom and Tyco for this kind of thing in the past. So why would they interfere with an FSA investigation?'

'This is a delicate matter. We have to be sensitive about pressing charges. The Americans prefer to put their own back yard in order. Sometimes it's best to let them take care of their own.'

'Is that why you moved to the SFO?'

'I didn't move. When they fired my boss, Amanda Sanderson, I had no choice. I had to leave.'

Niccolo shook his head, confused. 'So why would things be any different at the SFO?'

'The Financial Services Authority falls under the Chancellor's remit. The Serious Fraud Office reports to the Attorney General, who is appointed directly by the Prime Minister. The SFO cannot take on the Attorney General. After all, he's our boss. He can pull our budget – hell, he can shut us down. But there's another party that *is* tough enough to take him on – the press. They may give us another chance to nail Sikorski. If you go public, others may come forward. The government would be forced to back a public enquiry.'

'You want me to become a whistle-blower?'

'Niccolo, I understand how difficult this would be for you personally. I'm not advising you to accept or to decline my proposal. I'm just laying my cards on the table. This is your call.'

'Why do I need to go to the press? Isn't my testimony in court good enough?'

Arnaud shook his head. 'If we go after Sikorski, we're going to start a war. And with all due respect, you are just a sergeant major in this battle. We need a general – a four-star general.'

'You mean you need a big name – a star analyst – like Charlie Doyle?'

'That's exactly what I mean. They don't come much bigger than Doyle. If we could get him on our side, it would be all over for Sikorski.'

'I can speak to Doyle. I know him well.'

'I don't think it will do any good, Mr Lamparelli. We approached him before, once in 1999 and again in 2003. We had a lot on Sikorski, but Doyle wouldn't help us. Apparently he had too much to lose.'

'Perhaps I can still change his mind.'

'Right now, anything is worth a try.'

Suddenly the paper door slid open, and Domingo entered the room. 'I do not think this gentleman requires any introduction,' said Arnaud. 'But since you've helped us so much on this case, I thought it would be appropriate for you to meet another member of the team.'

Niccolo's jaw almost hit the floor. 'You, Domingo! A government mole! But you're Head of Security at Saracen!'

'It's very nice to see you again, Mr Lamparelli, sir,' Domingo replied.

Arnaud said expansively, 'Our good friend Domingo Duarte has been on the government payroll for quite some time. Worth every penny.'

Domingo grinned, sat down on the floor, and helped himself to some sushi.

Niccolo suddenly had an idea, not a blinding flash so much as a small sliver of light. There *was* someone else who might help. 'Excuse me a moment, would you?' he said, pulling out his mobile phone and punching a number he had thought he would never ring again. 'I don't know why I didn't think of this before. Lucy?'

'Nicco! Is that you? Oh, Nicco, I've missed you so much—'

He interrupted her effusive gushing. 'Lucy, I want you to do something. Not for me – for Jack.'

'But Jack's—'

'You don't need to remind me. Look, you can do this, or you can say no. It's not going to make any difference – I really don't want to see you again. Ever. But I would think a bit better of you if you did it. And you might think a bit better of yourself.'

'I'll do anything. Anything at all. Nicco, I've never stopped loving you, you know—'

'Like I said, it's not going to make any difference. But will you just do something for Jack – please?'

Lucy sniffled, and asked in a small voice, 'What do you want me to do?'

'You told me that Larry paid you money to get close to me, as you put it, and to try and influence my decisions—'

'But that was ages ago. And it wasn't very much money.'

'More fool you, then. But you did take money from him, didn't you? Well, I want you to write a statement detailing exactly what he asked you to do, with dates of payments and the amounts . . . Yes, of course you might lose your job over it. But you always could anyway. Larry will have records of everything, and he could dump you in it at any time; he's like that. So it would look better if you came clean without being coerced or hauled into court.'

'I'll think about it,' she promised.

'No,' he insisted, ruthlessly. 'I want you to do it. Do it today. And have it biked over to Arnaud Veyrieras at the Serious Fraud Office. Yes, of course I can spell it . . .'

As he snapped the phone shut, he said to Arnaud, 'I don't know if that will help. It might be too late.'

425

The door slid open yet again, and a steely middle-aged career civil servant bustled in. 'Domingo said you'd be here,' he said, shaking hands with all three of them. 'Clive Newton, temporary Head of Enforcement at the FSA. Now, this won't take long, but you're owed explanations and apologies, both of you—'

'Excuse me,' Niccolo butted in, 'but how are you and Domingo connected?'

'And why *temporary* Head of Enforcement?' asked Arnaud.

'I wonder if I might have a chair . . . and maybe a glass of Chablis?' Arnaud speedily arranged for both. Domingo proffered a plate of sushi, which caused Clive Newton to look slightly startled. 'I – er – don't think so, thank you.'

Once comfortably settled, he embarked on his explanation.

'Mr Veyrieras, you may have wondered why your investigation into Dr Picton and Larry Sikorski seemed to be thwarted at every turn. Please accept the apologies of Her Majesty's Government, and also our thanks. You helped us a great deal. Without your dogged persistence we would not have achieved what we have. But you were in danger of helping us too much. I mean that you might have achieved your own objective, but left us unable to achieve ours.'

'Well, I don't begin to understand,' Arnaud said, helping himself to more sake. 'Domingo, do you know what this is all about?'

'Just let Mr Newton tell you. There's more to this than you know.'

'And more than I'm really free to tell you. However, I'll do my best. There is a small but important Middle Eastern country, which shall remain nameless. The . . . let's call him the Ruler – of this country, whilst a devout Muslim, is keen to be on good terms with the West, and we with him. Moreover, he has no wish to see his country's prosperity jeopardised by religious fundamentalists, who seem to be as endemic as cockroaches. This Ruler has a highly efficient intelligence service. They became aware that a fundamentalist group was plotting to exploit the greed of his country's richer citizens to obtain funds with which to buy arms and explosives to use against investors in his country. One of this group had joined a syndicate headed by the Ruler's son, a rich playboy with no more than his fair share of brains. The syndicate had been promised impossibly huge returns on their money, returns which could of course only be achieved by outright fraud.'

'I'm beginning to see now,' said Niccolo, holding his glass out for some more sake.

'The Ruler realised that the best way to attack the problem was at the root, here in London. So his Chief of Intelligence approached our department, laid out all the information he had, and asked for our help. It was one of those happy occasions where two parties' interests dovetail neatly like a jigsaw. We had been after Picton for a long time – as, Mr Veyrieras, have you – so we were able to furnish information about the flow of funds to the Ruler's enemies. But in order to act effectively, we had to be able to identify the money trail from start to finish. If either of you gentlemen had succeeded in your own entirely laudable aims, you would have derailed a much larger investigation. We couldn't allow that to happen, could we?'

'No, of course not,' Arnaud murmured.

'The Ruler had to take the distasteful step of planting spies in his son's palace, and one of them – who looks like a halfwit but isn't – recorded a mobile phone conversation that neatly caps off that end of the investigation. In recognition of this country's co-operation, the Ruler graciously – and unprecedentedly – consented to sanction investigation of the numbered accounts in his country's national bank. That has proved more informative than we could have hoped.'

'But what about Larry Sikorski?' That was all Niccolo wanted to know.

'Ah. There I'm afraid I must disappoint you. He's a scoundrel, I grant you, and hand in glove with the man who indirectly finances the Ruler's enemies, amongst other things. But in order to safeguard our own investigation, we had almost to sabotage your efforts, Mr Veyrieras' efforts with the FSA and SFO, and even those of the Metropolitan Police. By the way, I do hope your pretty friend WPC McKeever gets a promotion out of this, Mr Veyrieras.'

Newton turned back to Niccolo, his face grave. 'You lost a good friend, I understand, Mr Lamparelli. I am very sorry, since despite the defamatory rumours, we can find nothing that indicates that Mr Ford was involved in any wrongdoing whatsoever. But we have yet to clear Mrs Ford of criminal involvement.'

'Donna?' Niccolo was horrified. 'No, Donna hasn't done anything wrong. OK, she's greedy and stupid. But she's not a criminal.'

'No, but she's inextricably linked to Larry Sikorski. And he *is* a criminal. But it's up to someone else to prove that now.' Newton glanced at his watch. 'Oh my goodness, I shall be late!' he exclaimed.

'Before you go, sir,' Arnaud said, 'will you explain about Domingo?'

'With your permission, Domingo? We knew about the FSA's arrangement with Mr Duarte from the very beginning. So we approached him and asked if he would share any useful information with us. And he was good enough to agree. We owe him our gratitude.'

Domingo merely grinned and kept stuffing his mouth with sushi.

'Before I go, there's one telephone call I must make, if you'll excuse me.' Clive Newton walked all of two yards into a corner of the room, and placed a call. 'Miss Sanderson – Amanda? This is Clive Newton. I've been caretaking your job at the FSA. Yes, I said caretaking. Yes, it was only ever a temporary arrangement. Yes . . . no . . . my dear girl . . . Look, everything will be explained fully. Yes, you're expected back at the FSA tomorrow, unless you've got something more exciting to do . . . Oh, I'm so glad. I think you'll find Her Majesty's Government will be most appreciative . . .'

He snapped his phone shut. 'Something in the New Year's Honours List,' he explained with a broad grin. 'And now I really must go . . .'

Some time later, after several more rounds of sake, Niccolo leaned back on his hands and hiccuped. 'Domingo, are you a double or a triple agent? I can't work it out. And what are you going to get in the New Year's Honours List?'

Domingo's normally serious face broke into a glorious grin. 'Why should I care, Mr Lamparelli, sir? I've been on three payrolls all this time.'

After lunch, Niccolo walked down Kingsway towards Waterloo Bridge. He gazed down at the sunlight sparkling on the river and thought about all the stories Mizuno had told them at one time or another: the porcelain vase that was broken for ever; the frog and the scorpion; the monk hanging on the edge of the cliff; the young man and the old man sitting on the beach.

'The old man looks back,' he muttered to himself. 'But the young man looks forward.'

He fished out his mobile phone, and after a few false starts, found Arnaud's number.

'Arnaud, I've had too much sake, and I may not be making sense,' he started. 'But if we could find something else against

429

Larry Sikorski, something that's not connected to this Picton–Ruler thing, could the SFO bring him to court?'

Arnaud sighed. He was no more sober than Niccolo. 'If it doesn't involve the FSA, SFO, MI5, MI6, CID, FBI, BBC, ITV – well, it may be possible. But let us talk about it tomorrow, please!'

The following day, Dudley Rabinowitz tendered his resignation. Sick to the back teeth of monitoring how fast everybody else was becoming rich, Dudley had decided to embark on a get-rich-quick scheme of his own. He left the bank to set up his own fund, his sole investment being in DBK.

Paddy O'Shea returned to his old job. Larry Sikorski was re-instated as Head of European Investment Research, and John Sukuhara publicly apologised for the 'shameful way that the bank has treated such a dedicated, distinguished and long-serving member of the management team'.

Larry visited every department in the bank's London offices, except for Compliance, said hello to every member of staff who crossed his path and called all and sundry to the Rabbit Warren to celebrate his return. Those who valued their jobs crawled out of every nook and cranny to come to the great celebration. The Rabbit Warren had not seen so much business since January 2007, when Saracen Laing announced record profits – and record bonuses. The guests overflowed on to the streets. They patted Larry on the back and congratulated him for taking on the system and winning. How dare Saracen suspend him? He was a living legend. He made them more money than any previous Head of Research could dream of. And, of course, he was a good, hard-working, decent colleague.

Larry made a modest speech. He was thankful to have such great friends, he announced. Saracen Laing was his life, and always would be. And the drinks were on him.

*

Meanwhile, a few miles north-west of the Rabbit Warren, Niccolo sat alone in his Hampstead flat, a glass of wine at his side. As he wielded the fountain pen in his hand, he felt dizzy. His mind took him back to better times. He pictured life as a boy on the island, playing on the beach, hiding in Mizuno's boat, sleeping under the clear skies with Jack and Yoshiro.

Sensei – I have failed to clear Jack's name. I know who killed him, but it is impossible to prove. As long as I live, I will never cease in my quest to vindicate Jack's honour. But for now, I know that I have let Jack down, and I have let you down, Mizuno-san. Please forgive me.
Niccolo-san

Niccolo folded the letter, placed it in an envelope and slipped quietly into bed.

CHAPTER 50

Two weeks later, Niccolo met Charlie for lunch at the Singh from Punjab. They had both missed each other's company. Lunch had been long overdue.

Throughout the meal, the subject of work remained off-limits. When dessert arrived, Charlie finally capitulated. 'So what exactly went wrong with the SFO's investigation into Larry?' he asked. 'Can't those buggers get anything right?'

'Not this time, Charlie. They didn't get their surveillance ops properly authorised. So the bastard's laughing.'

'Well, you certainly have my respect, Nicco,' continued Charlie, digging into his kulfi. 'You single-handedly got the SFO to launch an investigation. Do you think they'll come back for his hide another day?'

Niccolo, aware that there was a limit to what he could tell Charlie, said, 'The case against him is closed. It can only be reopened if new evidence comes to light.'

Charlie looked up sharply. 'What kind of evidence?'

Niccolo took Arnaud Veyrieras' business card from his wallet and placed it on the table. Charlie picked it up and read it. The telephone number had been crossed out and another one scribbled above it.

'Who is this guy?' asked Charlie.

'He's the SFO's top man on the case. He says they could reopen the investigation, but they need a big name – a senior analyst in Saracen Laing – to come forward with evidence of some other wrongdoing, and testify to it in court.'

'You mean someone like me?'

'Yeah, Charlie.' Niccolo smiled at Charlie. Dear rumpled, overweight, chaotic, foul-mouthed Charlie. Charlie, who was self-destructive to the point of insanity. Charlie, whose wiles and guile had been the stuff of legend for decades. Charlie, who underneath it all was the only person Niccolo could absolutely, unequivocally trust. 'I mean someone just like you.'

But Charlie sighed regretfully. 'No, not me,' he said sadly. 'Too many bills to pay, dear boy, too many ex-wives to support. If this year's bonus goes down the pan, old Charlie's going to be in schtook. I'm not your man.'

Charlie took care of the bill. Before they left the restaurant, he slipped the business card into his pocket. Outside in the street, his curiosity got the better of him. 'So tell me, how much did you screw them for, kiddo? Rumours are circulating, you know.'

'I got no pay-off.'

'What! Are you crazy? You could sue the hell out of those bastards for what they did to you! The way Larry treated you was a disgrace. How can you walk away with nothing, goddammit?'

'They weren't asking me to sell just my own soul; they wanted me to sell Jack's, too. His life, and his honour, are worth more to me than the two million they offered me. Thanks for lunch.'

Niccolo turned and walked away. Charlie watched him go.

*

Niccolo found himself walking past the back entrance to Saracen Laing. But the once-familiar street already felt like a foreign country, somewhere he had never been. The sight of an attractive young woman striding along in front of him, dressed in fitted corduroy jeans that accentuated her leggy slenderness, cheered him. She was carrying a cardboard box. Sensing someone behind her, she looked over her shoulder, tossing her long brown hair.

'Nicco!' she exclaimed.

'Louise! I didn't recognise you!' he stuttered. 'You . . . What . . .?'

'I've quit,' she told him happily. 'It was so awful, the way we treated you. You must have hated me, Nicco. I hated myself. I simply couldn't stand it any more. So – big wide world, here I come!'

'What are you going to do?' he asked.

'Something completely different,' she said with determination. 'I trained as a teacher, you know. Science, to GSCE. But you know what teachers get paid, or rather *don't* get paid. I was seduced by the idea of a City salary because I wanted somewhere decent to live. Well, they can stuff their bloody money – I don't want it! Not at that price.'

'Is this the moment where you finally accept that drink I've offered you a few times?'

She grinned, her face radiant. 'I feel quite light-headed and irresponsible all of a sudden,' she announced. 'In fact, I feel like ordering a bottle of champagne, and inviting you to help me drink it.'

Niccolo grinned back. He couldn't think of anything he'd rather do with his afternoon.

'Two million, Nicco. Two fucking million. And you threw it away!' Charlie mumbled.

As Niccolo faded into the distance with his head held high, Charlie caught a glimpse of the man he used to be. He took a deep breath, placed his hands in his pockets and decided to take a leisurely stroll back to the office. He no longer believed in what he did. This time the master had learned from the student.

As he approached the Saracen Laing building, a trader emerged from the revolving doors. He was wearing tortoiseshell Armani sunglasses and sported a charcoal-grey Brioni suit, a Thomas Pink shirt and a Gieves and Hawkes tie. Church's brogues and a Rolex GMT Master II completed the expensive ensemble. The young man – Charlie couldn't remember his name – took out a bunch of keys and deactivated the alarm on a metallic black Porsche 911 Carrera parked just outside the building. The licence plate indicated it was brand new. The car probably cost more than the combined annual salary of a junior doctor, a teacher and a fireman – and had probably been paid for in cash.

'Two million lousy, fucking quid,' he muttered. 'If you can turn your back on that, kiddo . . .'

Charlie knew now what he had lost, and he wanted it back. He stopped just short of the car, and pulled out his mobile. He jabbed in the handwritten number on Arnaud Veyrieras' card.

'Serious Fraud Office,' answered a controlled Parisian voice.

'My name is Charlie Doyle.'

'Ah, Mr Doyle,' said the voice. 'Your reputation precedes you. I enjoy watching you on TNBC. My name is Arnaud Veyrieras.'

'I understand that you are in charge of the Larry Sikorski investigation.'

'How can I help you, Mr Doyle?' The voice was icily non-committal.

'I believe the investigation is now closed . . .'

'I am not at liberty to disclose such information, sir.'

'. . . but I understand that the case could be reopened if you had evidence against Sikorski from a senior Saracen Laing analyst – a big name, like me.'

'It may be possible. Might I enquire what sort of evidence?'

'Do you remember the Russian debt crisis of 1998? The rouble crashed through the floor – the exchange rate went from six roubles to the dollar to fourteen in about a week. Well, it would have crashed a whole lot harder and faster if Larry Sikorski hadn't put pressure on one of his stock analysts to write positive research reports on Russian-denominated stocks. The poor girl – her name was Jennifer Colley – had three kids, no husband and no choice. Thing is, Larry was in cahoots with this rich oligarch guy, who paid him big money to keep the rouble out of free-fall just long enough for him to get his investments out of Russia. Well, I knew about it. And Larry knew I knew about it. And I had four kids and two wives, who were proving kinda expensive. So I took money to keep my mouth shut. And I have documentary evidence. Is that enough for you?'

'Mr Doyle, before you make any type of commitment to us, I have to caution you. What you have told me would almost inevitably result in criminal proceedings being brought against you. You stand to lose everything. And I mean *everything* – your job, your assets, your home. You might even go to prison. Are you really sure you want to do this?'

Charlie was sweating suddenly, and his stomach was churning. He stared blankly at Arnaud Veyrieras' card. The ink had smudged so the handwritten number was no longer legible. This really was it. He could walk away now . . . but he would probably regret it for the rest of his life. He looked around. The Carrera revved up. He felt his heart beating faster. He felt the blood pumping through his veins.

'You gave it all up . . . for your friend . . .' he muttered. 'Well, he was my friend too.' He wiped the tears from his eyes. 'Let's nail that lousy son of a bitch, kiddo – once and for all!'

'Sir?' interjected Arnaud anxiously. 'Did you hear what I said?'

Charlie tightened his grip on the phone and looked up towards the sky. For a brief moment the polluted City air smelt better than anything he had ever smelt before. 'I heard you, Mr Veyrieras. And I understand the risks perfectly.' His eye caught the Porsche as it accelerated smoothly away. 'But this is a matter of honour,' he said.

ACKNOWLEDGEMENTS

My greatest thanks go to David Marshall and David Shelley for their vision and judgement. A warm and special thanks to Mary Sandys for turning my rough manuscript into something I can be proud of. Thanks also to my copy editor Jane Selley. Thank you to the whole team at Little, Brown Books – who are a wonderful bunch and have given a first-time author all the support he needed – especially Nikola Scott, Thalia Proctor, Kirsteen Astor, Emma Williams, Nathalie Morse, Sean Garrehy, Bob Mackenzie and Darren Turpin.

I wish to thank my grandmother Amy. Honest and honourable to the core, she provided the inspiration for this story. I owe everything to my parents and am grateful to Sarosh and Shaunagh, who have always been there for me when I needed them. And my sincere thanks, also, to Keith.

Most of all, I want to thank my darling Behroz for never doubting me.